Soul Seeker

The Story of Jess & Anna

I0609777

T. BRADY

Soul Seeker
The Story of Jess & Anna
All Rights Reserved.
Copyright © 2013 T. Brady
v5.0r1.0

Cover Photo © 2013 JupiterImages Corporation. All rights reserved - used with permission.

ISBN: 978-0-6152374-6-6

Library of Congress Control Number: 2012914630

PRINTED IN THE UNITED STATES OF AMERICA

To my mother who believed in me, and to Edgar Cayce,
the two responsible for awakening my spirit.

"Who are we? What are we doing here? When will we find out?
Where will we end up? Why us? And how do we return?"

We all have a soul, and we are all seeking the way . . .

Then, bind up thine feet—My son, keep thine ways aright, knowing there is the advocate with the Father, even as thy own self had before the foundations of the earth were laid—and as the foundation of that school may be laid in the efforts of thine own hand as a material witness of the physical, the mental, and the spiritual attributes of those that gather under thine guiding hand, so keep the ways, the feet, the hands of those that direct same, and when thou art called into account of those deeds done IN the body, blessed will be those that had come under the directing of thine endeavors! Keep—keep—the faith—the promise in thine self, that WE—in THIS plane—may keep in thee the guiding light to many a soul seeking the way. Ready—Ready—Let's Go! T0137-118M [Pg.1]

Edgar Cayce

March 18, 1877 — January 3, 1945

Foreward

Recently, our planet has experienced powerful weather disasters. No country is untouched. Some hint at the Polar Shift Effect the late Edgar Cayce predicted to begin in 2000. Accordingly, it's to continue throughout the next one thousand years creating major earth changes. Considering the earth's age, a thousand years is but a twinkling of the eye.

According to the current census, there are over 300 million United States citizens. Last September 26, 2011, while attending to a transaction at my place of employment, I found myself speaking to a young man who afterward sent me an email that I found the following morning. It was signed Edgar E. Cayce. I inquired if he were any relation to the late-and-great Edgar Cayce whom I had dedicated this novel to many years ago. He informed me that he was his great grandson. I immediately experienced goose bumps, and have reacted similarly every time I have thought about it since. The odds of such a synchronicity occurring is beyond extreme.

As sole author, I take responsibility of these contents. Some locations exist, but are greatly embellished by my imagination. All characters and names are fictitious or coincidental. For reasons of my own, I cannot rule out that I may have received encouragement from the other side. Remember folks, this is strictly a fictional novel.

Acknowledgments

My thanks go to the Association of Research and Enlightenment, for giving me permission—obtained during the summer of 1990—to use an excerpt from one of Edgar Cayce's readings, Pete Ross for your computer help, Jennifer Holmes for giving me the writer's guide, Tyler Gregory for the author photograph, Rhonda McBride for my personal cover, James Ferguson for editing my work, and Edgar Evans Cayce III for permission to share our synchronistic meeting.

PART I

SEEKING

1

The Male Entity

Jess Park's creative mind toyed with his recurring dream: a violet mist, a brilliant white light and a radiant blonde. The dream had resurfaced again last night. But the thought of it did not linger. He cleared his head and waited in the dark.

The sounds of an automatic weapon interrupted the quiet, lamp-lit city street. Jess tromped on his gas pedal, attempting to outrun the whizzing bullets. The source sped after him. He deftly maneuvered his steering wheel. His passenger-side tires precariously rode the deserted sidewalk. He fearlessly ran a red light. The aggressive black car tailed him. He purposely stomped the brake, creating a rear-end collision. When the broken glass and twisted metal ceased its hellish noise, all grew silent.

"*CUT.* That's a wrap, people. It's getting late, and we all have to be back here at the crack of dawn—for the last time. See you on the set tomorrow morning," the director called out to the cast.

"Hey, Jess. Do you have a minute?"

"Sure, Carl. What's up?"

The two men's eyes locked.

"Excellent driving, man. I'm really going to miss filming the series. Any good prospects?"

"I'm expecting a call from my manager. Keep your fingers crossed for me?"

"Will do, man." Carl thumped Jess on his shoulder and headed for his ride.

❉ ❉ ❉

The early autumn breeze caressed Jess's face as he sat in his parked convertible mulling over his current agenda. The car's hood periodically popped from the cooling engine. It fell on deaf ears. A roller coaster of emotions tore through his gut with tomorrow's divorce proceedings being the low, and the current prospect of starring in a new motion picture the high.

His medley of thoughts returned to the persistent dream. Last night was the third time in a week. The beautiful yellow-haired apparition had reappeared, surrounded by the swirling violet mist. Her raiment birthed the brilliant white light that outlined her perfect form always shadowing her face.

An unconscious sigh escaped the television actor. *I've been watching way too many movies*, he concluded.

His main focus returned to his long-time friend and agent. *Come on, Al. What's the holdup?*

Jess extended his long legs and exited his ride without opening the door. Breaking into a run, he crossed the tiny green patch—referred to as a yard—fully intending to hurdle the front porch rail as usual. But one long stride landed him in something soft and slippery. He slid violently, arms flailing. A sudden putrid odor engulfed his sensitive nostrils.

"*SARGENT.*"

Scanning the neighboring front yards, the German shepherd failed to appear.

"*Son . . .*" The habitual fraction of an explicative spewed from Jess's mouth as he performed a chicken scratch without adequate results. He gave up and launched the heavily soiled loafer into the air. Slowed by disappointment, he climbed the porch steps wearing one shoe and fumbled the house key into its lock.

The landline's distant ringing triggered neurotransmitters, causing a sudden excitatory state within his alerted brain. He quickly shoved the front door open.

The caller was heard pleading through the phone's speaker. "Hey, Jess . . . pick up if you're there."

Jess quickly complied. "Yo, Al, let me catch my breath." He waited for his breathing to slow. "What's up?"

Al Kalanowski answered in his not-so-young Chicago accent. "Plenty, my good buddy. I think we're about to land the big one. *The* E. J. Moyer wants to see the both of us in his office ta'night," he intoned. "Some big movie part is my educated guess. So be there at eight sharp. And, Jess . . . wear some fancy duds, will ya? We have an impression ta make."

Skillfully memorizing the recited address, Jess hung up. "Please," he prayed, "let this be it."

Five minutes behind schedule, the excited actor was escorted through the front office of the famed casting director, E. J. Moyer. Habit made him dip his six-and-a-half feet under the door frame of the executive's private suite. Being extra tall had its ups and downs. It occasionally snagged him a part, and it occasionally didn't.

Perched behind a sizeable, finely engraved desk, the white-maned Moyer momentarily rose to accept Jess's firm handshake. The already present Al shot the stunningly handsome yet humble actor an exasperated look from his temporary seat of importance.

"Hey, Al, how's it going?" Jess nodded, casually ignoring his agent's disapproving look.

Be on your best behavior—and that means good English, Al always advised.

He began reciting a short memorized excuse for his tardiness. "No apology necessary, Mr. Parks." Moyer's face tightened. "That *damned* traffic mess out there has made me late on more than one occasion. Last night, I caught a news piece about the Los Angeles traffic menace tripling within another ten years."

The serious expression on Jess's face matched Moyer's. "Well, sir, when it comes to that, it'll be time for me to get the hell out of L.A.— career or no career."

Moyer found the futuristic threat amusing. The ensuing laughter appeared to ease Al's tension.

Jess needn't worry. His manager did it for him. He shot Al a don't-sweat-it wink.

Moyer offered his guest the lavish brown leather chair next to his personal manager. "Let's get to the point of this meeting, gentlemen. That would be why I've asked you and Mr. Kalanowski here tonight, Mr. Parks."

Sitting on the edge of his seat, the young actor reassured their host. "I promise you have our undivided attention." Al's intense expression confirmed his statement. "And if you don't mind, sir, call me Jess."

Matching brows rose in unison over wire-rimmed glasses. The white head nodded. "I've been asked to cast for Nelson/Paulson Motion Picture Productions. They're scheduled to begin shooting immediately. Well, to be honest, my first choice didn't work out—the reason for your short notice. So you now have a shot at the lead role. That is, if you're interested. Of course, you'll have to read for the part. But I don't foresee any problem there. Am I right, Mr. Parks?—excuse me, Jess?"

The actor instantly felt the blood pulsing through his veins. *Don't panic*, he told himself. His lengthy silence earned a concerned glance from Al. After mentally devising a reply, he began reciting it. "Sir, I'm extremely pleased to have you consider me, but exactly what do you mean by immediately?" Leaning back in his chair, Jess inhaled a lungful of recirculated office air. Awaiting Moyer's reply squeezed his heart with self-inflicted apprehension.

"The first part of the filming starts next week in Southern Asia. We have enough time to get you there—comfortably."

Jess winced inwardly but put on his poker face. *Stay positive,* he advised himself.

E. J. began to anticipate that the actor was about to turn him down, a possibility he hadn't considered. Custom dictated that Moyer research his prospects to ensure their availability. *Time is money.* Moyer made it his personal motto.

Impatiently shuffling through the painstakingly prepared contract awaiting an immediate signature, the executive unconsciously cleared his throat. "I'm sorry. Is there a problem? Having no family ties, I assumed you'd be an excellent choice."

Divorce is never a secret in Hollywood.

Leather creaked as Jess leaned forward. He buried his face in his hands, attempting to hide the deepening anguish beginning to take over his placid facade. Beside him, Al squirmed in his chair. His large Polish features riddled with confused concern.

Jess looked up, his eyes focusing on Moyer. "There may be a problem. Our soon-to-be-dismantled cast was informed earlier today that due to damaged film footage, the schedule for the final episode is going to run over. We have to reshoot some of the final scenes."

"How much extra time do you need?"

"Three weeks minimum, sir. The show's guest star took off for another engagement. We're all forced to await her return."

Jess hesitated. "Any way to make this work . . . sir?" the actor's expression and tone pleaded.

Moyer immediately picked up the phone. Jess nervously clasped his hands between his knees, purposely tuning out the one-sided conversation. His pounding heart annoyed him because he could not still it.

It's going to work out, he thought. *Three weeks—such a short time. It couldn't possibly make that much difference.*

Jess wanted this role even though he knew nothing about it. *Perhaps it's a war movie—considering the location. I could go with that—something different. Yes, a military drama.*

The phone's receiver clicked in its base. Jess gave Al a friendly wink and looked up. Moyer's solemn expression, and the ensuing silence, gave away the negative outcome.

The casting director reverted to formality. "I'm sorry, Mr. Parks, but it looks as though nothing can be done to right this situation. The leading actors must be present at the start. The company's filming between monsoon seasons. That amounts to the next six months. A three-week delay is simply out of the question."

Jess spoke softly. "Well. That's it then."

Maintain, he directed to himself, *and maybe there'll be something else from this man in my future.*

"Sorry, Mr. Moyer, I wish it could've worked out. I've been looking for an opportunity like this because my TV series is ending," Jess laughed halfheartedly, "and I refuse to do commercials."

The actor appeared to run out of words. Al made an attempt to comfort him.

"Gee, Jess, I'm sorry. Wish I'd known. Otherwise, I could'a spared ya."

It was a flaw in Al's nature to neglect his own advice for using proper English.

"No need blaming yourself, Al." Jess conjured up more worldly excuses. "It's . . . one of those bumps in life's road. I believe certain events occur for a reason. We may not want to accept or understand them at the time, but . . ." Jess concluded with a shrug.

The actor's positive attitude impressed Moyer.

"Well gentlemen, since we've nothing further to discuss, I must excuse myself." His grave tone matched the mood. "It appears I suddenly have a late dinner engagement——in other words, a backup plan for a backup plan that didn't work out. Not the first time, I must admit. It's all part of the business," he declared, placing what was to be Jess's private contract into his desk drawer.

Jess sighed. *Bye-bye, contract.*

"May I call on you again, Mr. Parks?"

"You bet, Mr. Moyer. I'll look forward to it." Jess extended his hand across Moyer's desk. The future prospect left a trace of glowing embers within his icy disappointment.

"It's been a privilege, sir. Thank you for considering me."

"I admit I regret that this deal didn't pan out. I don't like it when my plans get changed. But I agree that this is one of those times when circumstances worked against us."

The three men shook hands all around, wished each other happy futures and parted company at the door.

The concerned agent stepped into the elevator behind his client. He studied his companion's mood, not as a manager but as an old and dear friend.

"That's the spirit." Al wanted to believe that Jess was truly okay with the outcome. Forcing cheerfulness into his voice, he asked, "How do you manage it?"

"Manage what?"

"How do you manage to take what I know has got to be a major disappointment so well?"

"You're forgetting. I'm an actor."

"Oh." Al slipped back into his own silent depression.

The pair reached the first floor of the professional building. Al followed Jess out of the main entrance into the brisk evening where the two friends stationed themselves on the bustling city sidewalk, exchanging polite amenities. A tight red skirt strolled by, distracting Jess. Once the skirt passed from view, he turned to find Al noticing him noticing the skirt. He unconsciously raised a brow at his manager, who allowed the moment to slide without comment.

Jess found himself thinking about the next day. "Yes, Al, tomorrow, I'm a *free man*. I can't help but long for a better outcome than this *newest* disappointment." His temperament suddenly altered as he emanated a scornful laugh. "So much for, *As Long As You Both Shall Live.*"

"Hey, Jess, that's a *real* shame. Me and the missus are going on thirty-one years. 'Course, it hasn't *all* been your average bed of posies, but we've managed."

"That's *roses*, Al."

"Rosies, posies—whatever. Anyway, we're still together."

Al rocked back and forth, wearing a look of true pride. His large pudgy hands tinkered with his pocket paraphernalia.

Jess laughed inwardly at his friend's minced words, but his sparkling dark-brown eyes gave him away. Al had a knack of brightening gloomy situations. He stared at his agent, recalling how far back their friendship had begun.

Al surprised Jess by responding with similar thoughts. "I remember the first time I laid eyes on you. You bumped into me while exiting that gay bar *lickety-split*."

Jess chuckled. "I bailed as soon as I figured it out. Don't get me wrong. I'm as accepting as the next guy, but gay isn't my thing. Anyway, I was attempting to kill the pain in my aching feet. I'd beat the pavement hard that day—to no avail."

Al winked. "Yeah, well, that too. Truth is you were in sad shape—green as they come, looking for any kind of acting work—as long as it wasn't a *commercial*."

Jess reacted defensively. "I didn't get a four-year degree in theatrics to push a broom or sell products I can't condone."

"Yup. No starting out on the bottom rung for you, son."

"Fate, it was, Al . . . our meeting."

"Maybe so. But, hey, *I* was lucky to find *you*."

"Come on, Al. You know I wouldn't be here if it wasn't for you."

"It works both ways, dudn't it, Jess? You've managed to chisel out a pretty good living for the both of us."

Jess gave up. No use trying to credit the man. Al was as humble as they come.

He studied Al's rugged features, so different from his own. The prodigious Polish nose and the sparkling angelic pale blue eyes that rarely missed a detail all mounted on a shorter, stockier frame.

"Two-bits for your thoughts," Al offered.

"Huh?"

"They look like they're worth it."

"You're a lucky man, Al."

The agent spat out a curt laugh. "And here I was thinkin' that *you* were the lucky one—young, talented and good looking to boot." Al smiled warmly up at Jess's towering stature. "Look at you, Jess, elegantly tall with handsome brown eyes."

"You mean *too* tall. And I prefer blue."

Al gave Jess a testy look. "Quit interruptin' me. I didn't interrupt when *you* were talking." The agent continued his complimentary list. "Ears close to your head . . . and what it must be like not having a mouthful of dental work—not to mention suffering through it."

"A little carried away there, aren't you, Al? Looks aren't everything. You know that."

He made a throaty protest. "That's some consolation, Jess. *I* know, you always say it's what's in your soul that counts. But you have that too—a decent soul. I've seen you in action. *Everybody* likes you."

Jess retorted with a hint of bitterness. "Oh, yeah? Well apparently not my lovely wife."

Al wanted to kick himself for a second time that night. He grew silent, his heart going out to his friend. Jess's comment forced him to rethink. *You don't have it all, do ya, kid?*

As if answering Al's personal thought, Jess confessed, "I'd trade it all for a family, Al. I have no one."

"Hey, now, you have *me*, kid. I'll always be here for ya—me and Rosie. We don't have ta share blood to be a family."

Al grabbed Jess's arm. "Let's not stand here gabbin' all night. I don't like seeing your chin on the ground. Come on, kid," he began, steering Jess toward the nearest bar, "I'll buy you a beer."

Jess's West Hollywood residence was close to the studios, where real estate did *not* come cheap. Hardly larger than an over-sized load, its handy location was its best asset.

Jess again grappled with the key to the front door, his alcohol-muddled mind recalled the frustration of his earlier entry before his second life-altering disappointment. Persistence resulted in success. After enabling his security system, he switched off the outside lighting and watched his taxi's tail lights disappear into darkness.

He now experienced uneasiness at having unloaded his troubles to the driver. At the time, he'd found it soothing to unburden his frustrations. Attempting to exonerate his careless behavior, he reasoned that the man hadn't seemed to recognize him. *Strangers are less likely to pass judgment . . . but loose lips can sink ships.*

The flashing light on the voice recorder greeted him in the otherwise darkened room. He hit the play button and concentrated on making out his Latino housekeeper's words.

"Good e-van-ing, *Meester* Parks. I wan to tell jou—jour wife's at-tor-ney did call to re-mem-ber jou to be at the de-vorce heer-ing at four-ter-ty after-noon manana—no, *to-mor-row*. Okay?—*Meester* Parks? *Don forget. Ver-y im-por-tant-e. No?* Jes. See jou. Ciao."

The recorder beeped, ending the laborious message.

Jess laughed without humor. *Her English is improving.*

A sudden surge of adrenalin released itself from his midsection. The pending divorce hearing triggered more uneasiness than any past professional appearance. Would his wife's attorney honor their pre-nuptial agreement . . . or attempt to override it? He grew sharply aware that tomorrow was only a few hours away.

The distraught young man recalled himself and Ariel meeting with an estate realtor over dinner, four months after pairing up. The love and pride he'd felt for his beautiful actress wife-to-be and expectations of a long and happy life had lulled the youthful actor into believing that their future together was better than bright.

What happened? Here I am . . . alone—and hating it. Was I so neglectful that Ariel was tempted to turn to another man? Maybe it was the pre-nup. If I had it to do over, I'd ignore my attorney and nix that baby.

Dreaded emotions of hate and anger began creeping into his thoughts.

Fighting it, he headed toward the kitchen, walking past his inheritance of original pre-Civil War antiques that adorned his living room—a reminder of his family history. Collectors knew of its existence. They hounded Jess for the historic relics. Though he cared less for their material worth, he couldn't part with his only reminder of family ties.

Twelve years old and parentless. The loss had left him morose. Upon reaching an older age, he was introduced to spiritual philosophy, which helped him to accept. Jess grew to believe that one's destiny was already known, but it was crucial to make good choices, because free will and fate—intertwined—is what creates that destiny.

Early on, for Jess, death became a part of life. Throughout childhood, the remaining relatives died off. His spinster aunt, who'd raised him in Kent, Ohio, left him—along with her collectibles—old enough to venture on his own.

After attending Kent State University, he took his bachelor-of-arts-in-theater degree and moved to California. It had been a mental and physical undertaking, with only himself to rely on. Three years later, his Hollywood acting career was established. The credit belonged to him—and of course, Al.

A golden glow emitted by the kitchen night light provided enough visibility for the sole occupant to maneuver around his small-but-adequate residence. In his short marriage, the lovely home he and Ariel had shared consumed a much larger piece of real estate, but now there was a for sale sign planted in front of it.

Two chilled bottles of imported beer lured Jess to the fridge. He took them along with his heavy thoughts and retired to the couch. The cushions conformed to his lengthy spine, while his stockinged feet found comfort on the coffee table. His alcohol-affected gaze wandered about his bachelor surroundings settling on the modern day furnishing beneath his feet purchased to compliment the antiques. "Why own a coffee table when I don't even drink it?"

Jess was startled by the volume of his voice. His dulled mind began mulling over the conversation in Moyer's office. Reality hit hard like a falling piece of space junk. "Son, am I depressed. Thought I knew better. Son," he repeated to the walls as if they were listening.

Sighing heavily, he opened a bottle. The first drink wet his parched throat. Jess knew better than to consume more beer. Symptoms of dehydration put him at risk for a morning hangover. But he couldn't stop.

Don't want to stop. Thought I was prepared for disappointment. Guess I was fooling myself. Big chance to advance my career with my first lead role in a new motion picture . . . blown all to hell. I wish I could erase this day from my memory. What could possibly be worse? Are you kidding? Remember tomorrow? If only I'd nailed that role, tomorrow might seem less ominous.

Jess groaned, hitting his forehead with the heel of his hand. "Oh well . . . tough breaks," he intoned.

Got to quit thinking like this. Must keep believing there's a good reason. A lousy script, maybe. Not likely. Not with a man like Moyer in charge.

He quickly drained his bottle and opened the second. *Like to get smashed. To hell with filming—and the divorce hearing. But others count on me, and I'm too nice a guy to let them down.*

Jess rose, moving toward the bathroom with his unfinished beer. 4:30 A.M. would arrive quickly.

By ten thirty, he was sound asleep. Six hours later, he raised his head and attempted to read the clock's lighted dial with sleep-filled eyes—*a few more minutes.*

But something had awakened him. He buried his face in his pillow, but the foreseen headache kept him from dozing. *May as well get an early start.* He forced himself out of his warm bed.

Clad only in boxers, he headed toward the kitchen. Some vitamin B might help cure his slight hangover.

In midyawn, his aching sleep-dulled mind registered what day it was. A vow to stay busy wouldn't allow him time to dwell on the pending divorce—one more gut-wrenching disappointment.

Yawning again, Jess flipped on the light in his small walk-in closet. Forgetting his recent vow, he quickly grew agitated over the scheduled hearing, pulling and jerking at his selected clothing. Catching his reflection in the dressing mirror, he was mildly surprised at his angry features. *Me . . . with a case of nerves? What's wrong with me?*

A long, low sigh escaped him. *Maybe after today, I can relax.* His curt laugh rang loud in his ears. *It isn't like I have my future planned out.* Loss of the starring role still stung.

On the nightstand next to the bed lay his wristwatch. He walked over to retrieve it. His reaching hand hesitated. *A gift from my wife—correction—soon-to-be, ex-wife. Memo to self: get a new watch.* Jess reluctantly put on the time piece.

Concentrating on his work schedule, he opened the blinds. The back-yard mercury vapor lamp combined with the light in the closet allowed Jess to make out the form lying in his bed. He froze. Surprise quickly turned to annoyance. *Son. Who's that?*

He began omitting possible suspects. *Not my wife—not her style. A burglar wouldn't bother to hide in my bed. Could it be an obsessed fan? Maybe the taxi driver gave me away.*

Wait a minute. This isn't possible. I distinctly remember enabling my alarm system.

The only plausible explanation gave him goose bumps. Perhaps the uninvited guest had spent the night.

Jess directed his voice at the lump, believing he had deciphered the situation.

"Okay. I'm skipping the guessing game. So if you don't mind to reveal yourself . . ."

The form remained silent. Jess's hands moved to his hips.

"Look, even if you *do* mind, I don't have time to fool around. Uh, no pun intended," he quickly interjected without humor.

Complete silence.

"I've got to be on the set in twenty minutes, so you have to leave—*right now.* And, do me a favor. Next time, let *me* call *you.*

Jess stewed at being ignored. "Say, how'd you manage to get through my alarm system anyway?"

The bundled figure remained still.

He decided to try the "nice guy" approach. "Hey, listen. I'm truly flattered."

More stony silence; no movement, no sound.

Irritation increased the volume of his voice.

"Listen here. I've never kicked a woman out of my bed, but I'm getting there fast."

The clock's startling alarm suddenly resounded throughout the room. *Could've sworn I shut that thing off.*

Finally, there was movement. Jess watched a hand grope for the alarm button. A deep masculine groan issued from the mound beneath the covers. The mystery person rolled over and sat up, throwing aside the bedclothes. Jess's intruder slowly stood, stretching and yawning. Mimicking his more than average height, he turned in Jess's direction, shocking a response out of the dumbfounded onlooker.

"What the—" he whispered. "Son-of-a—*What's happening?*"

Jess's eyes threatened to leave their sockets as he stared in icy consternation at his own exact likeness. Cold chills rose and fell along his spine. Adrenalin burned his midsection. He neglected to breathe—all symptoms of the fight-or-flight response bred in humans since the day man first walked the earth.

Like a crazy dream, Jess watched his double approach. In passing, it lightly brushed his shoulder. The slight physical contact caused the fine hair on his neck to rise. Shocked into numbing silence, he stepped back, his wild-eyed stare transfixed upon the startling imposter.

Also aware of their brief collision, his twin turned to investigate. Jess stared across the short span into his own sleep-affected eyes, a mirror image of himself. But as the seconds ticked by, he realized that his look-alike didn't see him, adding to the eerie intensity of the moment. He then heard his own voice issue forth in the form of a sleepy yawn.

The twin resumed its trek toward the bathroom. He entered and closed the door, leaving behind a bewildered Jess Parks.

Buckling at the knees, the stunned young man sank onto the bed unmindful of his gaping jaw. His breath came hard, threatening hyperventilation. Taking notice, he labored to control it. *Think logically. I must be dreaming,* he assumed, squeezing his eyes shut.

A sudden noise behind the closed door impressed upon him the reality of his sanity-threatening situation. He deliberately worked to calm himself, taking slow, deep breaths.

This is surely a dream, he thought, totally unconvinced.

The imposter emerged from the bathroom. Jess's own eyes widened as the tight muscles in his legs shot his tense body straight up like a jack-in-the-box. He landed with a bounce. Shivering uncontrollably, his head jerked in the direction of his double that paid him no attention. *Get a grip, man.*

In fascinated horror, he watched his look-alike enter his walk-in closet and dress in his selected clothing.

His twin hadn't reacted when spoken to. *Whoever that is either doesn't see me or chooses to ignore me.* Jess made a second attempt. "What's happening here?" No response. *He really doesn't see me—or hear me.*

The imposter finished dressing and left the room. *The guy looks like me—dressed like I would have.*

Feeling like a victim, Jess sat on the bed staring at nothing, unaware of the passing of time. Adrenalin continued to circulate throughout his traumatized body. The slamming of the front door once again sent him airborne. He laughed without humor at his skittish behavior. Then silence.

Minutes passed. Renewed energy returned to his limbs. The confused young man jumped up and paced about the room like a madman looking for relief, searching his muddled mind for some inkling of an explanation. Exasperated, he allowed his body to fall back onto the bed.

"Maybe this *is* a dream." He stiffened. "Yeah. I'm probably experiencing one hell of a hangover-induced nightmare. But it seems awfully real."

Jess sat up, running a hand through his lengthy brown hair. He rose and slowly walked into the bathroom, desperate to prove his newest theory. His facial expression fell when he saw the wet shaving brush, the damp towel, and the change of underwear lying on the hamper.

Lowering his lanky, shaken frame onto the commode lid, he

contemplated his next move. Elbows resting on his knees, and chin in hand, he continued his quiet conversation. *There must be some logic in all of this weirdness. But why would someone go to the trouble and expense of duplicating my face? I'm not worth that much money. There're lots of actors worth more. No enemies to speak of—*

Without warning, Jess's volatile mind suddenly began to empty of thought like water draining from a clogged sink. A sudden loss of consciousness overwhelmed him. His body instantly relaxed into jello, sliding onto the hard floor. *I am dreaming,* was his last conscious thought.

Upon awakening, Jess experienced complete calm. He felt emotionally and physically well—better than any time in his life, as though a huge burden had lifted. No concern. No pain.

Awareness of a presence grew strong—a familiar female. Long silky golden tresses cascaded over a simple flowing white robe. Her very being consumed Jess's attention. The intense brilliance of the robe itself should have blinded him, but his eyes tolerated it. A sudden realization rushed in. The spectacle before him matched his recurring dream.

She stood on stony steps above, greatly reminding him of a heavenly angel. Her mesmerizing beauty compelled him to approach her fearlessly. He glided forward as if propelled by will alone. His movement disturbed the familiar waist-deep violet mist, causing it to swirl about.

The experienced actor soon found himself staring into the black eternity of the apparition's eyes. Graceful fingers extended to delicately caress his temple. Comforting thoughts surfaced from his deep subconscious.

Without warning, as quickly as she had appeared, the mysterious lady, along with her ethereal surroundings began to fade, leaving Jess alone once more.

To Jess, the experience took place within seconds. What light that had surrounded him again faded to black.

Regaining consciousness, he experienced the sensation of the cool, hard surface of the floor tiles against his exposed skin. His eyes opened to find his own face staring back. The unexpected image caused him to flinch. The fresh memory of the morning's bizarre events immediately returned with sharp clarity, erasing the experience of the dream. Jess's own eyes continued to stare back from the bottom of the bathroom's floor-length mirror.

Picking himself up, he checked for bodily injury. Nothing seemed out of the ordinary except for a slight lingering dizziness. *Hang-over city.* He groaned and attempted to squeeze the self-induced vertigo from his head.

A glance around the bathroom reaffirmed the morning's encounter— shaving brush, towel and change of underwear. His own five o'clock shadow proved that he himself hadn't yet shaved.

Jess shook his head as if to clear it. *It appears that my look-alike wasn't a dream. But I did dream something. What was it?* He closed his eyes, allowing his mind to recall the lady in white. *Who is this mystery lady?*

In the dream, she was as real as anything he'd ever experienced. But with all that had happened that morning, separating dreams from reality confused him. To Jess, the only *logical* explanation screamed dream. But a crazy gut feeling told him that in no earthly way was any of it a normal dream.

An immediate sense of urgency grew strong. There was somewhere that he needed to be—a specific place.

Showered, shaved and standing in the living room clad only in clean boxers, Jess turned on his TV set. He tuned in to the cable's twenty four-hour weather report. With unblinking eyes, he stared at a youthful female predicting a cold snap in the nation's South Central states.

"That's it—the area I must visit." He sounded like a madman to himself, but the desire to press on greatly overwhelmed him.

Jess quickly changed the channel to a children's show. Kids sat in a circle on a carpeted floor encouraged to sing, "Row, row, row your boat gently down the stream; merrily, merrily, merrily, life is but a . . ."

"Dream," Jess accompanied. The female apparition loomed in his thoughts as the children repeated the chorus. *Curious. That song must mean something.*

A sudden driving eagerness urged him to dress. Jess blackened the screen.

Digging through his stored winter clothing triggered past memories of ski trips to Big Bear, California, and Aspen, Colorado, with his wife. The two had met at one of the resorts. *Funny, I can't remember which. I used to enjoy those trips. Nothing like being divorced by your first wedding anniversary.*

His unpleasant thought soured his expression. Shrugging it off, he continued his search, glad to be sidetracked, but the memories had already been awakened.

Jess and Ariel had fallen hard for each other, marrying four months later—a grand, fancy movie-star wedding—with lots of attendees, well wishes and gifts.

Because Ariel's sister had lost custody of her young child in a bitter divorce, Ariel had made a personal decision not to have children. "I refuse to put myself through that," she'd stated, with a simple toss of her head. Jess, longing for a family, had been devastated by her post-wedding vow.

It's like she foresaw our divorce.

Then there arose the kind of break any actor dreams of. The newlywed, Ariel Chase-Parks, up-and-coming female screen star, stunned the Box Office with her new movie. Her sudden surge in popularity initiated her coming out.

Prior to their ski-resort honeymoon, she'd auditioned for the role. Jess later surmised that if they'd met after her instant fame, they might never have married.

The whirlwind engagement, their busy lifestyle, the constant separations made life hectic. The two quickly became estranged when his successful young actress wife began to stray. Jess hadn't realized what was occurring until it was too late. Billed as the leading lady, Ariel and the leading male actor quickly grew attached.

Spiritual acceptance of his parents' death had proved easier than spiritual acceptance of his wife's infidelity. So, even though it tormented his soul, he vowed to let Ariel go. They obviously weren't meant for each other.

Jess returned to his present task. A set of quality long johns, a flannel shirt, and a sweater had joined the growing pile. Hiking boots were chosen over sneakers. He could acquire a pair later. *They do have stores in the South Central states*, he thought, directing sarcasm at himself. Arms loaded, he straightened his lanky body to its full height. In the bathroom, he included his tooth brush, a portable razor and a bar of soap. Anything else could be purchased. Finished packing, he entered the kitchen to add non-perishable food items. In the pantry, he removed a stash of hidden cash from a fake-bottom canister and stuffed his wallet.

Hurrying out with his loaded backpack, he quickly locked the door before he could change his mind.

Maybe I should've left Mrs. Z a note. Nah, why bother? My double will probably show up later, which would only confuse her. Jess paused in his thoughts. *She's already confused enough. Look who's talking,* more self-directed sarcasm.

Hesitating on the veranda and staring into the quiet street, except for his size, Jess looked every bit like a kid leaving for his first day of school.

The would-be traveler questioned himself. *What am I doing?* He looked around for someone—or something—to supply an answer. *I'm supposed to be on the set—but my gut tells me I'm already there. My double left wearing my clothes. I assume he took a taxi to pick up my car. Where else would he have gone?*

Shifting his weight, Jess mused. *Perhaps my faith is being tested. I profess to believe in spiritualism, don't I? Consider it a spiritual adventure—without danger. It's possible to have an adventure without danger . . . isn't it?*

He shrugged his shoulders—a habit he wasn't aware of possessing—and moved one step closer to the porch rail.

"So, what've I got to lose?"

Lingering indecisively, Jess felt delicately balanced on a tightrope of insanity.

Beads of sweat tickled his sides beneath clothing too heavy for the balmy autumn morning, but less to carry in his bulging pack.

"This is ludicrous," he whispered softly. "Oh, what the hell. Try listening to your own philosophy. Nothing occurs without purpose." He quickly hurdled the porch rail and landed on the grass below, feeling emotionally lighter about his final decision.

When I return, I'll be forced to deal with this mess. But according to that vision in white, it's all somehow linked. Not much to go on, but it's all I've got.

Crossing the street proved nearly fatal. Deep in thought, Jess failed to see the car turning the corner directly into his path. His sympathetic nervous system kicked in, enabling him to somersault out of harm's way before being struck. *Son! Talk about training on the set paying off.* The episode left him trembling once again. Bringing himself to a sitting position, he instinctively noted the make and model of the departing vehicle, memorizing the license plate. "Ah, what am I doing?" He shook his head. "If I'm invisible, how can I file a report?"

His vital signs having returned to normal, Jess picked himself up and checked for injuries. Fine gravel embedded in his bared elbow bounced like rain drops onto the concrete. His right knee stung under undamaged jeans. *Probably a pavement burn*, he told himself, ignoring the annoying sensation. Satisfied that no permanent damage had been done, he stood momentarily, regaining his composure.

Two young girls wrapped in light sweaters approached with sleep still evident on their youthful faces. Like a giant, Jess towered above the petite figures hurrying through the early twilight. Taking advantage of the situation, he fell into step and eavesdropped on their conversation. By the content, he was reassured that they were unaware of his presence.

He decided to experiment. "Hey, girls, got the time?" No response. "Know any good jokes? Want to visit Disney Land?"

His slowing stride ceased along with his random questions. As the light footsteps faded, a growing realization spread a ghastly expression across Jess's sober face. *Son. I was nearly run over by that car because it truly never saw me. Wonder if I would've made a bump. Great. Adventure mixed with danger.* Jess vowed to remain more alert.

Standing in line at the ticket counter in the Burbank Municipal Airport, the solitary traveler asked himself, *why?*

It soon became clear that any space he occupied couldn't be occupied by another, but everyone wanted to occupy *his* space. The confusion of the unsuspecting culprits made the situation comical. Jess smiled, dodging an extended elbow. Surmising retrospectively, he guessed he would have made a rather large bump.

Arriving at his departure gate, Jess's attention was captured by a noisy display. A five-year-old girl stood crying hysterically, flailing her arms at a woman she addressed as Mommy.

Normally, such a display would've driven him away. But he found himself drawn toward the commotion.

Moving closer, he watched with fascination as the young child continued to pound and scream and cry. The mother continued to ignore her. Jess witnessed the child's arms passing through the woman's body, and that the child wasn't of solid form.

A man he hadn't noticed before stepped forward.

"*Daddy*," she sobbed. "I want Mommy to come *too*."

"Honey, Mommy can't come. We aren't on the same side as Mommy. She doesn't see us. Can't you see how sad Mommy is? She's missing us terribly. She doesn't know we're here."

"Why, Daddy?" the child wailed. Heavy sobs convulsed her small ethereal body as she awaited her father's answer.

"Sweetheart, we're on God's side now. Let's don't blame Mommy. It isn't her fault."

The daddy picked up the little girl. "Come with me, honey. Here's somebody I want you to meet. It's your *grandmother*," he said, in a distracting, cheerful tone. A woman too youthful to be a grandmother held out her arms to the troubled child.

The fine hair on the back of Jess's neck rose yet again. He remained motionless, optimistic that the man, his daughter, and the grandmother, who were convincingly "on the other side", wouldn't notice him. Too ignorant of his own plight, he did *not* want to become involved in another.

Hurrying away from the unsettling reunion, he headed in the direction of his assigned departure gate, his mind a whirlwind of the day's experiences.

The airport wasn't overly crowded. He ducked into a gift shop to snag some reading material. A display of books suddenly toppled in front of him. The action was startling. On the other side was the guilty party, a young boy, who looked equally surprised. A reprimanding parent grabbed the child by the hand while Jess stood stone-still. He couldn't decide what disturbed him most, the falling books, or the lack of sound they made while tumbling to the floor. The reason for his entering the shop escaped him. He turned and exited as quickly as he had arrived.

Jess decided to concentrate on reaching the terminal gate. The book incident brought on a new awareness. It suddenly became obvious that the hustle and bustle of the airport was oddly muffled. But as he recalled, the ethereal voices had carried all too well. A realization struck Jess. His double, the TV, and the two girls walking had all sounded muffled—even the moving car. *Curious. Why didn't I notice this before?*

Boarding the plane with the other passengers, Jess chose a seat to his liking. Unable to shake the eeriness of the scene he'd witnessed, he closed his eyes and momentarily played it back in his over-stimulated mind. Had the father of the little girl briefly glanced in Jess's direction as if he could see Jess, and then quickly looked away as if he hadn't *wanted* to see Jess? To find one's self on the *other side* would be an overwhelming experience no matter what the circumstances. He curiously wondered in what manner the father and daughter had made their transition.

Three-hundred pounds of female flesh suddenly threatened to occupy Jess's space. After recovering from the unpleasant experience, he walked to the rear section of the plane to await the filling of assigned seats.

First class had more open seats. *That one looks safe.* Narrow spacing forced him to brush against the knees of a well-dressed elderly gentleman nodding off. The old eyelids opened, but seeing nothing closed again. Jess sighed with relief.

He gratefully relaxed in his chosen seat, which generously accommodated his exaggerated height. A lengthy arm span allowed him to periodically snatch drinks and snacks off the hostess cart to sustain him throughout the early afternoon flight.

Departing from the St. Louis airport in the small passenger plane with a southwesterly heading, Jess draped his arm over the empty neighboring seat. He could've enjoyed the forty-minute ride except for the constant air turbulence bouncing the puddle-jumper around like a small rubber ball, but the muffled drone of the small twin engines turned out to be a blessing to his comfort.

Between wispy late-afternoon clouds, Jess looked down on fresh patterns of harvested fields and meandering water courses flowing to greet the beautiful Tri-lakes of the Ozarks. Southern Missouri and North Arkansas were dotted with brilliant fall colors making the view cheery and appealing. He breathed the plane's supplied oxygen and longed for the fresh country air.

After an hour of flight, the grounded plane turned out its handful of passengers onto the tarmac, where they were herded toward the small building that sufficed for the Harrison terminal.

Easily averting the group, Jess instead walked the airport road. 62 East and Harrison highway signs pointed right. Moving with the flow of traffic, he occasionally stumbled on tufts of fading grass growing along the shoulder.

Highway 62 bypassed the town. It was typically littered with fast food chains. Aromas of fried chicken, burgers and pizza stirred his evening appetite. He fleetingly thought of putting out his thumb to speed up his progress. *Who would stop for an invisible man?*

With a few miles behind him, Jess left the highway's edge for a service station where two vehicles were parked. The thought had occurred to steal a ride. *Who'd care? No one will know—unless they try to occupy my space. I'm willing to take that chance.*

Mountain Home quickly came up in conversation between two young ladies self-servicing an Audi TT coupé—*something a single college girl would want.* He'd definitely prefer the other option—an open truck bed. The idea of cool wind bombarding his person somehow felt less threatening than a cramped back seat. *Beggars can't be choosers.*

A quick glance at a campus parking permit and a red Razorback insignia bespoke two university students heading home for the weekend. *That cinches it. I'm really in Arkansas.*

Hesitant, Jess un-shouldered his backpack glad to be free of its burden. He moved within hearing range of the young women's private conversation.

"Jill, visit the restroom with me, will you? After drinking all that soda, I won't make it another fifty miles."

The gas pump handle noisily entered its slot.

"Sure, Beck, wait up."

The owner of Jess's second option soon exited the facility's garage. He'd noted that the truck's bumper sticker read, KOOL 96.1—KCWD, Harrison, AR. *That one won't travel far.*

He was soon alone in the station lot. The girls shortly emerged from the office with the one called Jill carrying a key dangling from a wooden board. Together they walked around the side of the building. *How quaint. I haven't seen a gas station with outside bathrooms in years. In fact, if someone had told me that I would soon be visiting the state of Arkansas, I'd have called them nuts.*

Considering the circumstances, he thanked his luck and opened the unlocked passenger door. Sliding into the narrow rear seat and achieving a tolerable position became a monumental task. He crammed his pack into the only available crevice amongst the many feminine possessions.

Wonder what's in the trunk?

Minutes later, Becky, the driver, pulled onto the highway, unaware of ferrying a stowaway. Jess quickly deduced that her driving skills were reasonably adequate.

Jill, the passenger, immediately struck up a conversation that he knew he didn't care to hear. Tuning them out, he allowed his energy-drained body to unwind.

The unbeknownst passenger glanced at his watch. *Four o'clock. Funny—sunset's already occurring. Ah, yes. There's a two hour Pacific and Central Standard Time difference.* Jess reset his watch for 6:00 P.M.

The blaring radio along with Jill's overbearing voice kept him from dozing off. *Good. I must remain alert . . . be ready to move when the time comes.*

Jill and Becky's conversation floated into his thoughts.

"Beck, how come we don't run around together?"

"Night and day, I suppose."

Jill lowered the radio's volume. She looked at the driver. "Elaborate please."

Becky's hands guided the sporty coupé over the winding road ahead. Grazing pastures and groups of conifers and deciduous trees lined the highway, catching the last rays of the waning October sun. The beautiful array of crisp fall foliage drew Jess's attention. Stately red and yellow maples reminded him of the predicted winter snow. An involuntary shiver shook him. His present mental and physical status had removed him from his comfort zone.

"I get it," Jill deduced. "You're right. We're nothing alike—Jill, the experienced, and Becky, the virgin."

Becky's eyes left the highway long enough to give her rider a startled glance.

"Well . . . aren't you? No use denying it."

"Why should I deny it?" Becky's eyes returned to the road. "Virginity is something to be proud of," she stated matter of factly.

"Huh—probably afraid of getting AIDS."

Becky shot Jill a narrow-eyed glance. "I happen to be saving myself for my future husband, and I really don't give a care *how* corny it sounds."

"What a crock, Beck." Jill sounded bored.

"Well, it *happens* to be true."

Jill sighed loudly at the driver.

Jess found himself drawn to the private conversation. His chauffeur's cool tone revealed that she was unconcerned with Becky's beliefs.

"Oh, brother," he moaned to undetecting ears. "I'm listening to this conversation—and *evaluating* it. Somebody *punch* me."

The car grew quiet. A small adrenalin rush sped through Jess's system as he awaited confirmation that his spoken words went unheard. He sighed with relief.

"Beck?" Jill ventured, after a period of stillness.

"What?" Her tone revealed annoyance at the broken silence.

"Becky . . . I want you to know something about me."

Jill hesitated, awaiting the driver's response.

"Go on," Becky encouraged, knowing that it was expected.

"Truth is . . . I'm still a virgin too."

Twice Becky's eyes left the road before Jill found her voice.

"I swear to God," she adamantly stated in answer to Becky's double-take.

The driver's second glance lingered so long that she was forced to jerk the veering vehicle back into the lane.

Jess's eyes widened as the car swerved. "Hey, watch it, will you? There're *three* lives in your graceful little hands."

Becky grew suspicious of Jill's confession. "I thought you didn't believe in God."

"A girl can change her mind, can't she?"

Becky looked doubtful.

Jill continued. "It isn't because I'm waiting for my wedding night—or anything as corny as that. It's because of—well, you know —AIDS, and all of the other nightmarish STD's out there."

"Pretty scary, huh," Becky agreed. "But if you're a virgin, how come I've seen you with so many different guys?"

"Cause no one wants a steady who won't put out."

The girls exchanged knowing smiles.

"Well, Jill, don't you worry your pretty head about it. Lots of men want to marry a virgin. Mr. Right will happen. You'll see."

"Oh, brother," Jess repeated.

Becky's sudden friendliness toward her passenger brought on a wave of conversation.

Jess sighed openly.

"When I finally do it——" Jill hesitated.

"Do what?"

"*You* know——it. When I finally do it, the man I marry must be gorgeous *and* self-assured."

"You mean *experienced*. That's risky."

"Good luck finding a male virgin. Anyway, he has to want me——in *every* way."

Jill ended her dream-partner scenario with a radiant smile as though she was the first female to think of it.

Jess felt his ears grow warm.

Becky laughed. "I wouldn't mind meeting *that* guy myself."

"Sorry. He's *all mine*."

"Okay, Becky. Honestly. Are you *really* a virgin? I told you. Now you tell me."

An affirmative nod was Becky's reply, which clearly satisfied her inquisitive passenger.

Jess breathed another sigh of relief.

"Do you really think I'm pretty?"

Becky smiled at Jill. "How else could you get all those dates?"

The awkward conversation ended as quickly as it had begun.

Heavy bass exited the car's speakers.

"Listen." Jill increased the volume. "It's my favorite oldie." She matched the words in a surprisingly pleasant soprano.

Except for the radio, much to Jess's relief, the girls drove mostly in silence.

Past Bellefonte, the car made a left turn off Highway 65 onto Highway 62. Signs identifying each small town drew the stowaway's attention. *Harmon.* A few miles later, he read Bruno-Pyatt. Then Snow. Yellville followed. Outside of Yellville was Hogskin Creek. *Interesting name for a creek.* Six miles later, while bypassing the town of Flippin, Jess saw the Flippin Pharmacy sign. *Now that's funny.* Cotter came next, *a fairly normal name.* Then Gassville. *That's different.* It was the Mountain Home sign that alerted him to the trio's mutual destination, causing a fresh adrenalin surge.

Luck—or fate—struck again when the car arrived at the main shopping mall. Approximately an hour after departing from the gas station, the coupé was guided into a parking space in front of the drugstore near the main entrance.

"Needing something sanitary?" Jill teased.

"Actually, what I need is costume make-up."

The two girls locked their doors and disappeared inside, leaving Jess to make his exit. On the floor was an Arkansas map. He put it in his pack and gratefully worked his stiff, cramped body out of the confined space into the cool night air.

Overwhelmed with physical relief, he glanced at his watch. Though it had been adjusted for Central Standard Time, it clearly didn't match the wall clock inside the lighted store window that displayed a few minutes past six PM.

"How can it be six o'clock twice?"

In addition to the two hour west coast time, Jess suddenly recalled that daylight-saving time had ended. *This is confusing.* Using the outdoor lighting, he reset his watch subtracting one of the two hours he'd added earlier.

The tired Hollywood actor surveyed the well-lit parking lot. A mother leading small costumed children attached to each hand walked toward the main doors of the mall, alerting him that this was the night chosen to celebrate Halloween.

A sharp cackle startled Jess. He spun on his heels to find a young witch headed directly for him. Quickly stepping aside, he now found himself in the path of the witch's ghostly companion. More Halloween costumes surrounded him, herding the stalwart young man toward the mall entrance. *May as well check it out*, he thought.

2

The Female Entity

❖

Anna Adell's unconscious mind began to surface from its REM state beckoned by a distant ringing that demanded immediate attention. Her fluttering eyelids opened. She reached to turn off the dream-piercing alarm, falling back into her previous supine position before the noisy interruption.

It was that same dream—him again. With eyes closed, Anna's mind attempted to recapture every precious detail. She moaned and squeezed her pillow.

Who are you? Why do you continue to haunt my dreams? I don't understand my desire for you.

Dear God, I've begged you to take him out of my mind. I don't want to waste my time thinkin' about a man I'll never meet. Please, make it stop. I'm a happily married woman, for heaven sakes.

The young mother and wife often repeated her request not meaning to lie. In truth, she enjoyed the dreams, but due to her moral upbringing, and her commitment to her marriage, she wasn't comfortable experiencing them.

Anna rose from her warm bed, putting on her pink robe and fuzzy bunny slippers—last year's Christmas present from the kids. Purposely avoiding her heart-racing thoughts, she dutifully began her morning ritual of readying her two young children for school.

The aroma of Joel's recently brewed coffee enticed her toward the kitchen. After pouring herself a cup, adding cream and sugar, she shuffled back to her room to dress.

A large lump in the bed drew her attention.

For a second time, the alarm sounded. Anna jumped, sloshing hot coffee. "*Ouch.*"

The lump in the bed moved. From under the covers, a hand reached up to silence the disturbance.

The astonished onlooker froze. Though Anna watched herself get out of bed, the same bed she'd been sleeping in moments ago, her brain refused to register what her eyes were seeing.

That isn't me. I'm me.

Her likeness put on her robe—the same pink robe. She looked down for proof.

Confusion left her at a loss for a plausible excuse, other than witnessing a dream.

The aroma of coffee permeated her thoughts. *It doesn't seem like I'm dreaming. I don't remember smelling coffee in a dream.*

"WHO *ARE* YOU?"

Anna's loud shaky voice received no response. *She acts like I'm not here.*

The reality of the situation began to soak in. Lightheadedness paired with weak knees forced her to set the rattling cup and saucer on the dresser. She watched her mirror image walk about the bedroom in her own usual manner. No attempt provoked the imposter. Anna continued to observe in utter dismay, the abandoned coffee on the dresser growing cold.

Shock worked on her nervous system. Unconsciously holding her breath deprived her red blood cells of oxygen, which quickly caused her to swoon.

The double left the room. The act brought Anna out of her present weakened state. Fear seized her. *Oh no! Peter, Rachael.* She tore out of the room on her twin's heels. "Okay, God," she cried, "I'm begging for your help."

✻ ✻ ✻

The weather channel had predicted the last day of October would be brisk, but early morning sunshine pouring through the patio doors enhanced the warmth of the kitchen.

Minutes ago, those doors had closed, leaving Anna sitting alone at the breakfast bar in heavy silence. She'd been forced to observe a woman bearing her looks and mannerisms ready her children for school. Her twin had helped them dress, cooked their breakfast, and shooed them out the back door on schedule. It left her feeling numb.

What more could I have done? I made an idiot out of myself, yet no one saw me. No one heard me. Now what? Anna stared blankly. *I have to figure this out.*

Burying her face in her hands, a deep sigh escaped her. Today began a new week. Transporting the kids to school, errands, and grocery shopping were her typical Monday agenda. She assumed the schedule would be kept. *After all, it was me.*

Long seconds ticked by. She peeked through shaky fingers. Her eyes focused on a shiny object resting on the counter top.

Rachel forgot her lunch money again.

Anna picked up one of the six coins, recognizing its cool solidity on the palm of her hand. She interrupted her turbulent thoughts to study the imprinted metal. The act itself calmed her.

Think rationally, she told herself. *If I was dead . . . or if I was dreamin', I wouldn't be experiencing this coin in my hand.* Her stomach suddenly protested its emptiness, *and I wouldn't be hungry.* Anna's deductions continued to flow. *If I was dead,* an involuntary shiver ran through her petite frame, *I wouldn't have a replacement.*

Frustration overcame curiosity. *How the heck am I supposed to figure out what's happening? I've never been dead.*

In the manner of a lost soul, she ceremoniously tucked her folded hands beneath her chin and prayed. "Dear God, I need you now. Please, Lord, give me guidance."

Room air expanded her empty lungs. She held it in, expecting a profound event to occur. The ground did not shake; the sky did not rumble. Unconsciously resuming her breathing, she stared at the copper-edged coin. Anna looked at the five quarters lying on the counter. *The one in my hand makes one too many.* "Strange."

Startled by her own voice, she glanced around the otherwise unoccupied kitchen, verifying her solitude. Satisfied that she was indeed alone, the quarters again drew her attention.

Another coin was placed next to the quarter resting in her hand. She looked down at the counter. Six quarters yet remained.

"Interesting."

Anna soon held nineteen quarters, but the one she picked up always remained. Pushing her bar stool back to place her focus on the same level as the counter top, she watched the quarter with fascination as she slowly picked it up. A slight ghostly trail followed the quarter that was lifted off of the one at rest. *Too bad this isn't possible in real life.*

The conclusion spooked Anna. Allowing the ghost quarter to fall back on the original, she recalled the identical robes. Obviously she would be forced to address what appeared to be a cruel dilemma. *Am I really dead, or might I be caught in a parallel universe?*

Her stomach protested its emptiness, reminding her of a necessity in life—nourishment. Anna removed a pitcher of juice from the refrigerator, experiencing the contact of the chilled glass handle. Swirling the contents in a circular motion, the same pitcher sitting on the refrigerator shelf caught her eye. *I wonder if this is a good thing.* She answered her hunger with a glass of juice.

Venturing into the bedroom to dress, everything otherwise appeared normal. The events of the morning could well have been a bizarre dream.

The phone suddenly rang, startling Anna. Her situation made her hesitate, but she decided to answer it. She spoke anxiously into the mouth piece. "Hello?"

Again, the phone base rang. Anna jumped. She saw the receiver sitting on the hook. It was the ghost receiver she held. "What *is* this, *The*

Twilight Zone?"

Anna hung up the ghost. It made the familiar click in spite of its ethereal existence. Her hand remained on the phone while it continued to ring, triggering a reminder.

Joel—Halloween. Tonight's trick-or-treating at the mall. Joel would call from the real estate office to find out what time.

The phone fell silent. Anna numbly let go, experiencing a pang of loneliness for her husband.

Sunlight flooding the kitchen attracted her attention. With a heavy frown upon her face, she peered out of the window. Her eyes scanned the heavily wooded area stretching beyond her vegetable garden. A furry fox squirrel worked to fill its belly on the backyard acorn supply. The colorful fall foliage created a breathtaking canopy in the Ozark countryside.

It's gonna be a snowy winter. Joel had recently cut a persimmon seed in half for the kids. Its spoon shape promised snow.

Anna turned away. *I don't know what to do. I don't want be here when she returns. It's too creepy. I reckon the kids are all right. So, what do I do? It's too far to walk anywhere.*

Their rural home was a few miles from town. A car trip was always a necessity.

Drawn again to the shiny quarters, an idea began to form.

Maybe if I return to bed, I could rejoin myself . . . like the quarter . . . and the phone. Yeah, maybe that's the answer. Maybe I'm merely a part of my soul that's somehow separated from my body. That must be it.

Carefully reconstructing the morning's details, Anna climbed back into the bed she shared with her husband. Excitement and relief welled up within her. Her only plan *had* to work.

Time crawled by. Anna lay still, waiting, thinking. Peter needed a haircut. Rachael was growing so fast that she needed new Sunday school dresses. *I'll make Peter an appointment and take them shopping this Saturday.*

She lowered the covers around her chin. Her eyes wandered about the picture-perfect room filled with beautiful oak furnishings. Not a ruffle out of place; no dust in sight.

Anna recalled the coin. She sat up. *This won't work. All of me isn't here. I bet both parts of me will have to be present.* Her thoughts continued to race. *I know. I must wait until the other part of me returns. Then I'll walk back into myself.*

One agonizing hour later, Anna heard the smooth idle of her car's engine enter the drive. Her stomach somersaulted. *It's time*, she thought, glancing at the clock.

A gentle shock visible in her facial expression took hold of Anna as she watched herself enter through the back door carrying a sack of groceries in each arm. She waited for the sacks to be placed on the kitchen counter. With the double's back turned, Anna stepped forward putting her simple plan into motion.

The unexpected impact stunned her. Sudden intense pain in her nose brought on a wave of nausea and a flood of tears. She withdrew a short distance.

Her twin pivoted. "Joel?"

Anna witnessed genuine puzzlement cross her mirrored face. "You felt that." She blinked back tears, staring into her own reflective eyes.

Alerted to a possible presence, the double left the kitchen to search the spotless open living room separated in part by a jade sectional and a rice paper room divider. Joel occasionally teased his wife that entering the living room was like walking into the Orient.

"Are you here, Joel?" An unsuccessful search of the house finally satisfied Anna's mirror image, who returned to the kitchen in a more relaxed state.

Anna remained stationary, gently massaging her throbbing nose. *So much for my theory. I think it hurt me more than you.*

An unconscious sigh escaped her. *Dear God . . . why does she appear to be of flesh-and-blood while I'm invisible?*

She again took a seat at the breakfast bar, watching her likeness put away groceries. It fascinated her as the sacks were emptied and the shelves stocked. There was hesitation with the last item—coffee filters. Originally stored in the cabinet over the range, Anna had recently moved them to a drawer. *I would have hesitated like that.* The filters were placed into the drawer. *This is me. She's doing everything I would do.*

So here I sit watching myself, but I don't know how to get back in. Perhaps this is a religious experience . . . or perhaps I'm doomed to be lookin' on forever. "Please," Anna lifted her chin, "if I figure out why . . . can I get back in? . . . God?"

Frightened and bewildered, the distraught young woman buried her face in her hands. She abruptly looked up. *Strange. I don't feel bad, just confused—very confused. As a matter of fact, I feel quite well—*her brow rose, expressing her puzzlement—*actually, too well.*

The phone rang, disturbing the quiet. She observed the other Anna pick up the receiver. From her perch on the barstool, she watched and listened to the one-sided conversation.

"Is that you, Joel?"

"Sorry. I wasn't back from town yet."

"Are you at the office? I thought you were here a minute ago."

"Never mind, I'll tell you later."

"Did your real estate deal go through?"

The Anna conversing on the phone bit into a cookie taken from a new package.

"Trick-or-treating starts at six. We'll meet you at the mall."

"I'm eatin' a cookie," she had to explain. "I'll feed the kids before we leave. Okay," she responded. "See ya then." The receiver clicked in its cradle.

The observing Anna thought, *I used to say, love ya, bye. When did I stop?*

As she watched herself get cleansers from under the kitchen sink, she called out to her disappearing counterpart, "Wish I could help, but I don't think I would do you any good."

Alone again, she sighed. "This is no doubt the *longest* morning of my life."

Flashbacks of her marriage to Joel played through her mind. Inseparable at first, they had enjoyed a few years alone. Then came baby Peter—soon to be eight years old—named after his maternal grandfather. Anna couldn't imagine life without him. Rachael was a welcomed surprise. Her birth brought joy to all three family members. Big brother had wanted to hold her as soon as she'd arrived at their home.

Anna's family occupied her world. The days passed quickly, and now her youngest was of school age. Rachael was so excited about starting this year. *Where has the time gone?*

The backyard again drew her attention. She quietly slipped out the door. Her short raven-black hair framed her small oval face, capturing glints of morning sunlight. Fair skin paled even more against her azure blue eyes. The chilly autumn air quickly blushed her cheeks. A childlike petiteness belied her thirty years. People said she was pretty, but she was too humble to believe them.

Sitting on the short brick wall that divided the neighboring lot, Anna stared without seeing, her mind having reached an overload state. Tiny black ants marched slowly in and out of the cold-weather cracks on the top layer of mortar, their physical activity dulled by the recent drop in temperature.

A squirrel with several acorns stored in each cheek suddenly leaped upon the opposite end of the wall. It bounded toward Anna, allowing her no time to move. The squirrel bounced off her thigh yet managed to stay on top of the wall. It looked at the invisible barrier blocking its path with such confusion that Anna had to laugh. The curious creature didn't leave, but instead slowly inched its way forward until its twitching whiskers touched something. Anna froze. The squirrel instinctively backed up a few inches, rose up on its hindquarters, sniffing the air. It swiftly bounded off the wall and ran up the nearest tree.

Staring down at the mysterious spot from its point of safety, the squirrel barked its discomfort. It finally settled down to cut the hoarded acorns, answering the instinct to gorge before the winter supply diminished.

The incident brought Anna out of her fog. *That squirrel didn't see me,* she deduced. *I don't think it smelled me, but it certainly felt me.* She gingerly fingered her sore nose, wanting to understand what was happening. Until now, there had been nothing to relate to her morning experiences.

Anna kicked at the wall with her heels, nervously biting an uneven nail.

What would happen if I got in my car and drove? Where would I drive to? Anna sighed. *I can't stay here like this forever. Maybe there're others out there experiencing the same predicament. I could look. What could it hurt? Maybe somebody can let me in on what's happening.*

Anna looked up. "Dear Lord, I know you have a hand in this. I promise I'll listen if only you'll talk to me," she begged, keeping her face tipped skyward. She closed her eyes, concentrating on hearing God's reply. The buzzing wings of a wasp braving the chilly air to spend its last hours in the warmth of the sun filled her ears with quiet sound. A couple of squirrels barked at each other. But no heavenly words bespoke her.

I wonder what God would sound like. Noah . . . what did you hear when God spoke to you? Listen to your instincts, her inner voice replied. *Right now, it's all you have.*

She considered getting her handbag. *What for,* she laughed sarcastically, *money and a driver's license?* Instead she reached for her keys hanging on the rack inside the back door. *A car won't start without keys—not even a ghost car.*

The ghost engine turned over. Anna backed down the drive. At a glance, she saw her vehicle remain parked in its original place as she had expected.

What happens if someone tries to drive through my car? I don't think I want to find out.

After driving down the lane, Anna turned left onto the highway. She guided the car south, staying close to the vehicle in front. *I can actually tailgate without angering the driver ahead.*

The remainder of the drive proved uneventful.

A little country church that her family attended most Sundays sat off the highway on a hillside a few miles from their home. Anna drove toward it, looking for comfort.

Covered in native stone, the church seemed preserved against time. A small cemetery with neatly kempt grounds covered part of the property. Two cars were parked on the graveled drive. Anna parked some distance away.

Finding the front door of the church slightly ajar, she pushed it open and looked inside. Two elderly female volunteers belonging to the church's congregation were busy cleaning.

On the first row of pews, Anna spotted another elderly woman seated alone. A dark head scarf and a long coat hid her identity. Entering the church, she walked up the aisle to the first pew and stood across from the occupied bench. She studied the old bowed head. A hastily drawn breath viciously stung her lungs. *It can't be.*

Arguing with herself, Anna wanted to deny the ghost. But the familiar odor of mothballs exuding from the older woman's wool coat quickly convinced her that Miss Mossie's presence was real. Racked with chills, Anna attempted to hug them away. She forced herself to stumble forward, desperately drawn to find some answers. Timidly, she addressed the frail old woman without expecting a reply from someone who had recently died.

"Miss Mossie?"

The scarf-covered head turned. The cataract-diseased eyes looked up at Anna. They focused momentarily, attempting to identify the voice's owner, then quickly averted to the floor.

"Miss Mossie, I know you can see me. What're you *doing* here? *You died.* We had your funeral two weeks ago. Can you hear me at all, Miss Mossie?"

The loud sharp voice issuing from the small kyphotic body startled Anna. "I *ain't* dead, ya know. I don't remember dyin', so I *cain't* be dead, ya *hear?*"

"Well, that tears it. I *must* be dead, too," Anna deduced.

"I *ain't dead*, I tell ya." Miss Mossie looked up at Anna.

"Do you remember dyin', Miss Adell?"

"No," Anna admitted truthfully to her fellow churchgoer.

Miss Mossie continued to defend their existence. "Well, *I don't* neither. So, I *ain't dead*, and you ain't dead *neither*. We ain't dead, I tell ya. We *ain't*."

Miss Mossie's funeral scene played in Anna's mind, the eulogy, the open casket with Miss Mossie's tiny body lying peacefully within, the graveside services.

Anna spoke in a soft yet stern voice. "Miss Mossie, I was at your funeral. How long have you been sittin' here, Miss Mossie? Have you been sittin' here since your funeral?"

"I been here since *a* funeral." the curt voice returned. "An' I tell ya that it *tweren't mine*."

Miss Mossie again lifted her head to gaze at Anna. "I'm plum *starved* fer a drink. I cain't work the *dad-gum* water fountain."

Anna sighed. "I'll get you a drink, Miss Mossie. Wait here," she said, afterward, feeling ridiculous for making the suggestion.

At the fountain, Anna relieved her own thirst with the cool natural ground water. A Styrofoam cup found in the church's kitchen cupboard carried the precious liquid back to the old woman.

Fragile bird-like fingers reached for the offering but passed through it. "*Dad-gum* it. See what I mean?" Miss Mossie's voice grew dejectedly weaker. "I'm starved fer a *drink*."

Stupefied, Anna said, "Here. Let me try." She placed the cup to Miss Mossie's waiting mouth. It passed through her lips. Water poured through the old body raining onto the wooden pew. Shocked, Anna's act of kindness confirmed that Miss Mossie's form wasn't solid. She pulled back in surprise.

The old woman's head hung in defeat. Anna's pity for the apparition took over. She attempted to use reason.

"Miss Mossie . . . maybe your thirst is all in your mind." Anna knelt, staring up at the wrinkled old face, searching for a response. "Miss Mossie? Don't you think it's time for you to move on now?"

Miss Mossie replied forlornly. "Don't know where to move on to, Miss Anna."

"Why don't you ask our Lord to help you?"

"Well," Miss Mossie humped, "guess it couldn't hurt." She placed her small frail hands in prayer form and squeezed her eyes tightly shut. "Lord . . . I reckon I'm ready now—thanks ta' this sweet young thang." The old woman unfolded her hands, attempting to pat Anna's shoulder. Physical contact wasn't made, but the ghost failed to notice. "Besides, I'm kindly tired of sittin' here, anyways. So take me, Lord, if 'n you will."

Ending what was her idea of a prayer, Miss Mossie grew silent, staring straight ahead.

Anna addressed the apparition as it immediately began to fade. "Follow the light, Miss Mossie." Tears misted her sky blue eyes. "Follow the light," she repeated, assuming that the light was what the spirit was staring into.

As Miss Mossie disappeared from her vision, Anna whispered, "You *are* there, God. I *knew* it. I'm *not* dead, am I?"

Despite no explanation for her own predicament, immense relief calmed her.

Immediately after witnessing Miss Mossie's disappearance into the light, a random yet recurring vision slowly invaded her present peaceful state. The image of the man that was introduced into her quiet, isolated world by her television set surfaced yet again.

"Oh, no," she viciously sighed. *"Now, Lord?* I spend half my days thinking about that man." Anna turned up a pleading face. "Why now? It isn't right—in this sacred place. I've prayed for You to take this stranger out of my mind—to free me from the thought of him. Please, God, I can't shake it on my own no matter how hard I try. He's a stranger to me, so why, dear Father? You helped Miss Mossie, so can You please help me?"

Talking to God was her only form of comfort. She continued her oral conversation with her creator.

"I'm *so confused.* I don't wish for this. I don't know how to stop it. Sometimes it *makes* me *so darn mad."* The overtaxed Anna shook with frustration. Tears, brought on by Miss Mossie's plight and her own emotional state, soaked her soft, rosy cheeks.

At Miss Mossie's parting, she elected to leave the church. Even the cleaning ladies' heated conversation about one of the parish members couldn't capture her focused attention. She had unconsciously tuned them out.

The car responded to Anna's touch, taking her toward Mountain Home. Near the town's city limits, a car turning out of a side road on the right suddenly cut into her vehicle, missing her body by inches. She let out a long wail. Attempting to leave the road, she nearly ditched her car. A semi rig passed closely on her left. Its wake shook her vehicle. Panic seized her, refusing to let go. The engine had died. Anna's shaking fingers fumbled with the key in the ignition. Left without a choice, she pulled onto the highway behind the next passing car and stepped hard on the gas pedal, vowing to stay alert until she reached her destination.

Anna dared to glance at the time. *Eleven-thirty. Lord, will this day ever end? Whatever's goin' on doesn't affect time. It's plain weird. I see, I feel, I hear— Dead people can't feel . . . can they? It's more like I'm invisible. Maybe I ate something—or drank something . . . or what?* The young woman pounded the steering wheel with her sweaty palm, frustrated that she had no answer.

Where, Anna wondered, could she park without other vehicles bumping into hers? She chose the wide ditch between the highway and the mall parking lot. The only negative scenario, she reasoned, would be a pedestrian crossing the street at that particular spot. *Not too likely*, she decided.

The distraught young woman maneuvered through moving and parked vehicles. Killing the engine, she attempted to relax with no concern for her next move.

I wish I could turn off my brain.

She decided to try. Sitting back, Anna closed her eyes. She thought of ways to improve her marriage, successfully chasing away her turbulent thoughts.

Eventually, clearing her mind resulted in a restful state. She awoke an hour later to loud laughter. Two high-school-aged boys on foot crossed her rearview mirror headed toward a fast-food restaurant across the street.

"That was too close."

Anna started the car, pulling forward twenty feet. After the engine died, the silence was thick enough to cut. She reclined against the headrest and stared without seeing.

Where have I been? she wondered, referring to her restful period. Closing her eyes, she attempted to return.

A vision of her birth parents, who had died nine years prior in a ghastly auto accident, loomed briefly. She'd learned to end the visions quickly, still suffering intensely from their loss. The head-on crash had resulted in two charred corpses the coroner had found difficult to identify. It was the HONK-IF-YOU-LOVE-JESUS bumper sticker she'd given to her parents that continued to haunt her thoughts. For it to remain unharmed in such a brutal, explosive accident was disturbing. *Was God trying to tell me something?* she'd often wondered.

Regaining her calm state, she again drifted off.

3

Where the Twain Shall Meet

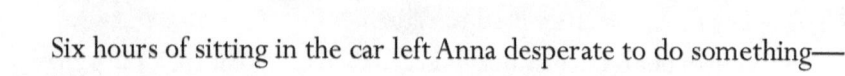

Six hours of sitting in the car left Anna desperate to do something—anything.

Navigating through the noisy throng of trick-or-treaters and parents entering and exiting the mall's main entrance proved to be taxing. The difficulty lay in steering clear of the surrounding activity without making physical contact. But someone eventually bumped her from behind. Anna wheeled around to gaze down into an upturned face.

"Excuse me." The polite young pirate—authenticated with an eye patch—quizzically shrugged upon finding no one to accept his apology. He quickly turned and disappeared into the frenzy.

Lightheadedness caused Anna to swoon from unconsciously holding her breath. It wasn't easy getting used to being invisible. She inflated her starved lungs with fresh oxygen and studied her surroundings. A snaking line of brilliant living color moved rhythmically past the shop entrances while collecting its bounty of offered treats.

She caught herself searching for familiar faces. *Stop it.* Seeing Peter and Rachael with Joel and her other self would be upsetting. *If I can't handle it,* she argued, *why did I bother to come?*

The size of the mall was such that its length could be walked at a normal gait in five minutes.

The familiar circular fountain located in its center drew her attention. A public sign, PLEASE DO NOT CLIMB ON WALL, caught her eye. *I don't think it pertains to me.*

At the four-foot-high rock barrier, Anna turned around and sat. Pulling up her legs, she moved to stand above the milling crowd and praised herself for maintaining her balance.

Glancing down at the makeshift waterfall gushing its white froth into the containment below, she saw the fountain works hidden beneath the water's surface. *Ugliness that begets beauty and receives no credit.*

The reality of her situation again captured her concentration. With arms outstretched, she slowly pivoted to face the bustling commotion below.

Please, Lord, don't let me attract another dead person.

Anna drew in a deep breath and called out.

"HEY . . . CAN ANYBODY OUT THERE HEAR ME?"

She scanned the moving faces for a response. None. She called out again, increasing the volume of her voice.

"DOES ANYONE SEE ME UP HERE?"

No one looked up.

Periodically, she took a few shaky steps along the wall's length, occasionally pausing to call out. No reaction.

Placing her hands on her hips, she released a long frustrated sigh. *What a waste of effort. One more try, and I'm calling it quits. At least I don't see any dead people.* She wrinkled her nose at the distasteful thought.

In her final attempt, few words had escaped Anna before she spotted a man on the other side of the fountain, moving in her direction. His eyes were fixed on her. As he neared, he could be heard, yet his voice was too distant for clarity.

"Me?" she mouthed, pointing at her chest as he drew closer.

Recognition slammed her as if she had taken a punch in the abdomen. Her body froze like a stone statue. She forgot to breathe. A noisy pounding within her head suddenly threatened to rupture her brain. "*Oh . . . my . . . God!*" she finally whispered.

Anna blinked hard in an attempt to erase the obviously delusional image of the man from the TV set. The man who haunted her dreams day and night was now emblazoned on the black screen inside her reeling conscience. A painful surge of adrenalin shot through her middle.

Now quite close, he called out again. She was now certain that he was addressing her. *I'm not imagining this. I know that voice!*

Reality aggressively returned. Her eyes flew open. Facial muscles involuntarily twitched. Anna's hands flew up to hide the hot blush creeping across her cheeks. Swaying precariously, she began to lose her balance.

"HEY YOU," the man continued loudly, "ON THE WALL."

Anna could now make out his words in spite of the deafening roar in her ears created by her re-circulating blood supply. He skirted the fountain's containment, closing the distance with long easy strides.

Excitement bubbled in his masculine voice. "I can hear you all over the mall," he exclaimed, now standing in front of her. "Hey, take it easy," he advised, suddenly noting her blank facial expression and unnatural color.

"You look like you're about to—"

Anna blinked hard. Forgetting where she was, she stepped back to put distance between herself and—Jess Parks.

"—fall." Jess's face expressed the horror he felt as the young woman disappeared from view. Her splash sprayed him with cold fountain water, releasing him from the mild shock created by what he'd witnessed. He leaned over the barrier to find an uninjured Anna floundering below in the frigid pool lined with wish pennies. His expression relaxed as he looked down at the soaked victim. Unable to resist adding humor to the situation, he offered, "If you needed some change, you could've asked." A genuine, handsome smile formed on his equally handsome face. He dared to tease Anna further. "So, how's the water?"

The bone-chilling experience helped Anna find her voice. "*Cold. Whadda ya think?*" Her wet, glistening skin visibly shivered. Jess broke into loud, hardy laughter. "Forgive me," he finally managed, "but you look so *pathetically funny.*"

Anna's incredible surprise was stifled by his bold yet innocent statement. "I'm glad I'm amusing you, Mr. Parks," she retorted through chattering teeth. "Are you in the habit of makin' fun of other people's mishaps?"

Jess quickly caught the acknowledgment of his surname. It happened frequently. People naturally recognized him from his TV series, but occasionally mistakenly called him by his character name. This lady didn't.

With laugher in his sparkling brown eyes, he gave Anna his reply. "I hardly think so, ma'am, but, then again, maybe I am. To tell you the truth, I've never noticed. Here—give me your hand."

Not wishing to annoy Anna further, he put on a sober face. "So . . . you know who I am. I must be honest, after what I've witnessed today, I wasn't too sure about showing myself. You're not a ghost?"

Unable to gain a steady footing on the slick rocks, Anna crawled over to the fountain wall. Grasping his underlying meaning, she answered, "No." In earnest, she returned the question. "Are you?"

The man she knew as the actor, Jess Parks, put his strong hands beneath her arms and effortlessly lifted her over the wall as if he were lifting a child. He set her down in front of him. His six-and-a-half-foot frame towered over her five feet. The eighteen-inch difference was striking, but Anna was too unsettled to notice. Jess noticed. He also noticed the odd look that passed over the petite female's face before he released her, a painful expression. *I must've really upset her.*

Despite the ice-water drenching, Anna instantly recognized the familiar sensation that the actor stirred within her, yet more potent and powerful than in her dreams. Intense emotion absorbed all of her consciousness, stealing her breath. It rocked her entire being, spreading through her chilled, numbed body like a raging wildfire, warming her in spite of her cold soggy clothing. *All he did was touch me.*

During those initial few seconds of physical contact, she had forgotten who and where she was as though her mind had turned itself off to everything but *him.* Feeling psychotically self-conscious, she lowered her gaze to her soaked shoes. Water pooled around them. *Did my expression give me away?* she wondered. A split-second glance at Jess's face satisfied her that he hadn't detected her true feelings. Her eyes returned to the puddle of water on the floor.

Son, she's beautiful, Jess thought, *tiny—but beautiful. Such perfection. It's unreal.*

Absorbing Anna's loveliness, he couldn't force his piercing brown eyes to look away. *She won't look at me. She's probably shy.*

Jess shifted his weight. The usually confident young man suddenly found himself in an unusually awkward state. *It's like I've been shot by Cupid's arrow. Shake it off,* he advised himself.

"You should get out of those wet clothes."

The moment Jess released her, Anna's full consciousness returned, leaving her drained and empty. The sensation resembled a deep loneliness—a loss of something precious. A sharp desire to reclaim that euphoria overwhelmed her. She knew how—mere physical contact.

I can't do this. I'm married. This is like a love so strong that no earthly ties could stop it. Dear Lord, this isn't normal. I've never felt like this in my life—not even with Joel. Can love be bad?

Battling her own emotions, Anna failed to notice the actor's similar reaction.

Maybe she isn't shy. Maybe she's angry with me. Stupid! I shouldn't have teased her. I should've reacted more quickly. No wonder she's angry. Now she doesn't like me. Great, Jess flinched inwardly. *The only soul that I can communicate with hates me—and she's so . . . beautiful.*

Anna surfaced from her intense state long enough to clarify that the man from her dreams was indeed standing before her—addressing her.

She responded listlessly. "What?"

"I *said* you should get out of those wet clothes. Are you okay? Look, I didn't mean to shake you up. It's my fault."

Suffering from the adrenalin rush, Anna quickly replied. "It *is* your fault. I mean, it's not every day that a person comes face to face with someone they watch on *TV*." The puddle forming under her grew larger. She softened her tone. "I can't believe you're here, is all. Where did you come from? What're you doing here —of all places?" Her weak smile faded. Shivering uncontrollably, she awaited his answer.

Jess chose honesty, risking his integrity. "What am I doing here? I actually believe that I was purposely led here by a recurring dream . . . maybe to find you. Now, if you wouldn't mind answering my question, are you really okay?"

The explanation he'd presented took a moment to compute in Anna's spent mind. To his immediate question, she replied, "Yes, of course, I'm okay—a little chilled," she sniffed, "but okay."

Momentarily forgetting her insecurity, she looked up. "But I'm not sure what you mean. You think you were led here—to Arkansas—to this mall—to find me? *Why?*"

Anna accepted her failure to decipher their circumstances. She certainly didn't expect Jess to figure it out alone. Instinctively, she sensed that she could trust and believe anything that the man standing in front of her might have to say

"I can only tell you what I know, but it isn't much. Anyway, I'm not convinced that you'll believe me."

Confusion decorated Anna's delicate features. "Very strange happenings have occurred since I woke up this morning, so at this point, I reckon I'll believe about anything. Besides, what could you possibly have to say that'd surprise me more than I presently am?"

Jess stuck his hands in his pockets and rocked back on his heels. "You too, huh?" He couldn't stop himself from gazing into Anna's sky-blue eyes.

The intensity of his stare reignited her self-consciousness. She didn't guess the real reason behind it.

Shaking her wet black hair, she turned away. Her teeth chattered as she spoke. "I must look a mess."

"Hardly. You look . . ." Jess searched for a descriptive adjective, "terrific." His hands sunk deeply into his pockets. He shrugged his shoulders. An honest smile shaped his lips. "I see beauty every day. If you've got it . . ."

Jess's candor caught Anna off guard. Painful shyness silenced her, but her physical discomfort began to override her awkwardness. "Follow me," she said. "I have an idea." Jess followed Anna as she retraced her steps toward the mall's co-ed denim shop.

Trick-or-treaters continued to file past storefronts. Entertained salesclerks obliged the seemingly endless human chain of decorated bodies and painted faces with the treats they were after. The festive young voices kept the atmosphere light.

The invisible pair entered the shop and passed by the checkout register, ignoring the salesclerk. Anna led Jess to a rack of jeans after realizing he too was wearing some of the fountain water. "These should fit. Take a pair. Get yourself a shirt too—something warm. No one will notice—if you get my drift."

Jess looked puzzled. He gestured at his full backpack. "So supplies weren't necessary?"

"Under the circumstances, Mr. Parks, it takes a while to make sense of anything." Jess shrugged and watched Anna walk to another part of the store.

Perhaps Mr. Parks hasn't discovered the ghost effect.

In the female department, she located a rack for herself. *One pair won't hurt.* Anna soothed her sensitive conscience. *After all, it isn't the same as stealing, is it?*

Out of habit, she selected three sizes—all brands being cut differently. A bright blue sweater caught her attention.

In the dressing room, she gladly gave up her wet clothes. The smallest size fit. *Now I'm sure something isn't right. I haven't worn this size since before Peter was born.*

Darn. No mirror. Anna abandoned her discarded clothing to search for a looking glass. Finding one, she surveyed her reflection and caught her breath. *That can't be me.*

She immediately scanned for the absent actor. Staring at herself in quiet fascination, Anna failed to see him emerge from the men's dressing room, moving toward her wearing a fresh change of clothes. Her hair—beginning to dry—took on its normal raven-black sheen. Her jaw grew slack as she continued to gaze upon her perfection. Her exposed skin was smooth and flawless. Long thick lashes swept her cheeks when she blinked. The blue sweater complemented her eyes. A natural rosy hue adorned her ivory complexion. *That isn't a powder blush.*

Grateful, Anna looked up. "Dear Father, do I get to keep this?"

Exposing her elbow, Anna drew in a sharp breath. *My scar's gone. Something strange is going on.* Anna pulled up her sweater and unfastened her jeans to examine her abdomen. An amazed smile lit her face when she found the ugly appendectomy scar missing. "God has gone made me perfect," she whispered.

Jess cleared his throat to make his presence known. "Yes, he has," he agreed. "Striking, isn't it—your reflection, I mean."

His unexpected masculine voice startled Anna. From the chest down, he appeared in the mirror on her right. "Are you satisfied with what you see—or is this going to get X-rated?"

Jess discovered a teasing nature he didn't know he had. *What's with me? You'd think I was a girl-struck fifteen-year-old.*

Anna tugged at the bottom of her sweater. "You're about an ornery cuss with that teasin' of yours. How long have you been standin' there anyways?" Her tone suggested that her privacy had been violated.

"I sincerely beg your pardon, ma'am, but I meant it as a compliment." *Son—I love her Southern accent.*

She fastened the new jeans under the blue sweater. "Well, you're no different, Mr. Parks."

"What does *that* mean?" Jess mentally kicked himself. *You did it again. She isn't used to this kind of teasing.*

"Men! You all have this raging desire to be funny."

Relief spread over his face at Anna's general complaint toward the other gender. "I guess it's part of our masculine make-up." He feigned honor to hide his amusement. "On behalf of all men, we beg your forgiveness." Bending at the waist to make eye contact in the mirror suggested an apologetic bow.

"It appears you don't like being teased."

Anna purposely looked away, afraid of revealing her true emotions.

After composing herself, she quickly changed the subject. "You know, I truly didn't believe I was dead. But now I'm curious. Where else can you be physically perfect except heaven?" She took a turn to stare. "I mean, look at yourself, Mr. Parks. I know you've always looked good, but—" she blushed and averted her eyes, "—have you looked at yourself lately—I mean *really* looked at yourself? You're just about *too* perfect . . . or did it occur to you to notice?"

"Contrary to what you might think, I'm not in the habit of tooting my own horn." Jess sounded hurt, but suspected that Anna hadn't meant to hint at narcissism. He bent his knees to view himself in the mirror. Mild surprise lit his overly handsome face. She was right. He hadn't noticed.

Anna spun around. "Sorry. I didn't mean to imply anything." She curtsied apologetically, turning back to the mirror to resume studying her flawless reflection.

"Do you think we could be between life and death—like in a parallel universe?" Her whispered thought was meant to relieve the awkward moment.

Jess's expression softened. Gently shaking his head, he answered, "I've heard of parallel dimensions, but at this point I can't say for sure because I have no reference."

In a comforting manner, he started to touch the troubled young woman's shoulder. She caught the gesture in the mirror and dodged his hand, tormented by guilt and shame for how her mind and body reacted to his touch. This time, however, she read the disappointment reflected in his eyes. More shame darkened her already rosy cheeks.

He thinks I don't like him. Anna turned to Jess with an apologetic smile. "Can we leave now?"

"Gonna be chilly tonight," she commented, as they passed the clerk waiting on a paying customer. They both grabbed lined denim coats off display racks before exiting the shop.

"Now what?" Anna inquired of her new acquaintance once they had exited the store, joining the throng of mall trick-or-treaters continuing on their bountiful rounds.

Jess exhibited a lack of concern for their predicament. *No sense panicking.* "First, we need a safe place where we can talk."

The Halloween crowd was beginning to thin. He spotted a vacant bench away from the entrance.

"Let's sit over there."

Unconsciously, he took Anna's small hand in his large one to lead her along. Liquid fire rocketed through her veins at his touch. The lightheadedness returned. She reacted by pulling her hand away. Jess took her action and her pale breathless expression as another sign of rejection. "Sorry," he said, pocketing his hands. He turned to hide his disappointment and continued walking toward the bench. Anna followed closely behind, fighting to gain her composure.

As they approached the bench, the mall's solitary liquor store drew Jess's attention. "Excuse me one moment, please." Anna gave him a blank look. Jess walked toward The House of Spirits.

"Great. He drinks."

Anna took a seat. She leaned back, gazing up at the suspended ceiling above. "Dear God," she sighed, "how can I look at this man without stars in my eyes?"

More tumultuous thoughts began forming in her overstressed mind. *I didn't tell him I'm married. Surely he saw my ring. It wasn't on purpose. I suppose I should mention it. How much should I tell him—and why do I believe that I could trust him with my life?*

There's no other way to color it—I just plain love this man, Lord. I can't help myself. It's a fact. I know it's a sin, because I'm a married woman.

She nervously tossed her head. *Dear Father in heaven, I beg of you to please reveal your purpose in this madness before I go utterly insane.*

Trick-or-treating had greatly tapered off. Jess entered the liquor store easily. Once inside, he took advantage of his invisibility and pocketed a pint of Crown Royal. He took another off the shelf and opened it, downing a swallow. The golden liquid warmed him internally. Glancing at the shelf where he'd removed the two bottles, he discovered that nothing was missing. The shelf remained fully stocked. His jaw fell. *Son. No wonder*

I didn't need a travel bag. Strange I hadn't realized this before. Jess recalled the clothing store. Anna had. Suddenly guiltless, he pocketed a third bottle.

The House of Spirits remained empty of customers. Its ghostly patron turned toward the lone shopkeeper behind the register who gazed out at the thinning Halloween crowd with an amused smile planted on his lips.

Looking through the glass storefront, Jess spied Anna sitting alone on the bench. He took another sip and drew in his breath, relishing the stoutness of the golden liquid. Curiosity made him stare. *She's sitting there waiting for me. That beautiful little thing is waiting for me. She's obviously more comfortable when I'm not around. What a shame.* It suddenly occurred to him that he'd forgotten to ask her name.

Emboldened by the liquor, Jess walked out of the store with an open bottle in his hand from which he'd just taken a drink. He neatly capped it, sliding it into the pocket of his new coat where it clinked against the other unopened bottles.

To Jess, the young lady appeared guarded, possibly suspicious that someone might attempt to sit on her. He smiled knowingly.

The Hollywood actor walked toward the occupied bench with a more confident gait. *I must find out her name.*

His movement caught Anna's attention. *He's coming back.* Her heart began to race. *I must settle down. I'll give myself a heart attack if I keep this up. Guide me, Lord.* She leaned back on the bench, closed her eyes and took some deep breaths. When her eyes reopened, she found Jess standing before her.

I want to create memories with you, he dared himself to say. Instead, he said, "I forgot to ask your name."

"Oh." A nervous laugh escaped her. "It's Anna, Anna Adell—*Mrs.* Anna Adell." *There. I said it. Now he knows.*

Jess's heart quickly sank like a gravely wounded battleship. *That partially explains her behavior. I failed to look for a wedding band.* He bitterly swallowed his newest disappointment.

"Anna it is. Do I make you nervous, Anna?" Bending slightly at the waist, Jess awaited her reply.

Smiling shyly, Anna confessed. "Yes . . . yes, you do." She averted her eyes, unconsciously batting her long black lashes.

"I'm sorry. I certainly don't mean to."

"It's okay." Anna kept her eyes on the floor. "It's just that . . . well, I'm a bit shy by nature—and not exactly used to being around a famous actor." Another nervous giggle somewhat soothed Jess's brutal disappointment.

"I wouldn't call myself famous," he returned. "Cary Grant is famous." Jess grimaced, suddenly reminded of the lost contract. "So you can quit being nervous. I'm a person—like you. And it would suit me better if you didn't call me Mr. Parks. *Mister* is a bit formal in our . . . unusual situation."

"Okay, so sorry. I don't mean to be rude, I'm just . . . shy," Anna reiterated. "And yes, we *are* in a bit of a situation, aren't we, Mr.—excuse me—Jess."

His relief was evident. "I was assuming you didn't like me."

"*Heavens, no.*" She reacted with sparkling laughter, which raised his spirits further.

Jess sat next to Anna at a communicative angle, leaving a comfortable space between them. A tired sigh escaped him. "It's been a long trip—all the way from Los Angeles."

"*Wow.*" Anna turned sympathetic. "I bet you're exhausted."

Jess's tone grew serious. "You spoke earlier of strange things happening to you. Would you mind trading stories?" Jess rubbed his tired eyes.

"Look out!" Anna cried, quickly jumping up.

Jess peeked through his fingers. "*Not again.*" He lurched sideways off of the bench. "That's the second time today I was nearly squashed by a lard ass."

Anna hid a vicious smile. "*Jess Parks*, you shouldn't use such ugly names."

A mischievous grin shaped his lips. "Typically, I don't, but having heard you do so earlier may have encouraged me."

The accused quickly defended herself. "What? I didn't call anyone a name."

"I believe you referred to me as an "ornery cuss"."

"I'm *so embarrassed*," Anna giggled. "I reckon I did. I was upset at the time, so I truly apologize. I'm sorry that I called you an ornery cuss." She looked away, an amused smile shaping her soft, red lips.

Swinging his arms back and forth in a relaxed manner, Jess snapped his fingers, popping each fist with an open hand.

"Then we're even."

Anna suddenly stiffened. Looking down her line of sight, Jess saw a man of average height with two kids in tow, a boy around seven in a vampire costume—the exact likeness of Anna, down to the jet-black hair—and a girl of about five years in a princess costume with long blonde Shirley Temple curls. Moving up behind them was . . . another Anna. She looked slightly different— heavier—but there was no mistaking the identity.

Recovering, Jess's gaze returned to the Anna beside him. It was her unusual beauty that registered first.

Shaking his head to clear his confused thoughts, he witnessed a physical shiver pass over her as she stood transfixed. Jess took her arm to steady her. The expected rebuff no longer stressed him. His sympathetic gesture yet again encouraged fiery blood to course through Anna's veins. It was his physical touch that broke her horror-stricken spell. She forced herself to look away. By the time she recovered, the foursome had exited the mall.

Jess elected to break the silence for her sake. "So it happened to you too." No response. "You all right?" Jess attempted sympathy. "The same thing happened to me this morning. I admit that I didn't take it well. It must be harder—having a family."

He left her to sit on the vacated bench where he patiently waited. Anna regained her composure, eventually moving to join him.

"Pretty weird, huh?"

For Jess, Anna's effort to excuse her behavior was unnecessary. He decided that now was a good time to relate his experiences of the day, speaking openly of his misty vision and how it had led him to this area.

They talked while the last of the Halloween crowd vacated the indoor mall.

Anna kept her eyes on Jess, avoiding a second possible glimpse of her family. *They're probably long gone. But she's finally looking at me, and I can't stop staring.* He was glad for the excuse.

The familiarity of Jess's voice calmed her. *He's more gorgeous than I ever dreamed. But the perfection isn't real—or is it?*

The man's incessant gaze interrupted her thoughts. *I must be staring too.* Anna lowered her eyes, her long sweeping lashes showing up strikingly against her fair skin.

Offering to share her day's experiences helped her to relax in the TV actor's presence. Anna recounted her attempt to rejoin her body.

"At least you thought of it."

Upon confession of Jess's recurring dream, she found it difficult to accept that their plight stemmed from a mere vision of purple mist and a lady in white. Yet she openly trusted the man before her along with any information he could provide.

A sudden movement caught their eye. Across the floor, a small elderly female dressed in bright pink sweats stood looking back over one shoulder. She turned and shuffled toward an unoccupied bench, halting occasionally to glance over her shoulder. Jess and Anna observed her odd behavior. It was obvious that she was speaking to herself though the distance made her words inaudible. A few more steps toward the bench, and the apparent reason became clear—a deserted brown wallet.

Anna's eyes brightened. "I bet she's here to watch the trick-or-treaters—most likely because she has nothing better to do."

The invisible on-lookers continued to watch the event unfold. When the old woman reached the bench, she leaned over to pick up the wallet, pinching the corner and lifting it as though it were a dead mouse. Jess and Anna laughed at the comical gesture.

"It's obviously not hers," Jess surmised.

The woman shuffled toward the main office, holding her find at arm's length, mumbling as she walked.

Jess spoke again. "Good for you, lady. You've moved a bit farther down the road toward enlightenment."

"What does *that* mean?"

"I believe that every time we return a lost item, we gain enlightenment." Anna looked confused. "You know: 'Do unto others as you would have them do undo you'."

Anna's features softened into a smile. "I believe that too."

I'm sure you do, pretty lady. "You'd be surprised at how many people would keep the wallet. What they don't consider is that it'll eventually be held against them."

The lights in the mall suddenly dimmed. "Cue time. We'd better leave before we get locked in." Jess rose from his seat.

"Maybe getting locked in isn't such a bad idea. We can still sense the cold."

"Just the same, I think I'd rather take my chances outside. We have somewhere we need to be, remember?"

"You mean somewhere *you* need to be. It was *your* dream."

"Yes. It was my vision, but you're in it now. Besides, where else can you go? Do you really want to go home and sit on the sidelines—watching?" Jess hadn't intended harshness, but Anna needed to accept their reality.

Stepping outside the safety of the brightly lit mall, the new partners moved away from the building.

"You wouldn't happen to have a car?" Jess inquired.

The question stopped Anna in her tracks. She looked up at Jess's face framed by tiny points of starlight in the velvety black background.

Responding to her expression, he innocently asked, "What?"

Anna's hand sliced the air for emphasis. *"Please. No cars."*

"Would you mind explaining?" he requested as they walked into the chilly autumn night.

4

The Beckoning Path

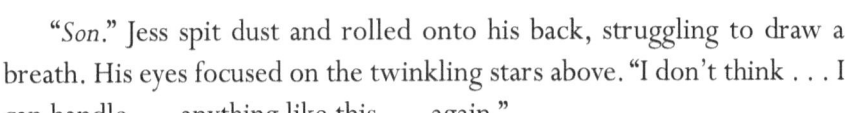

"*Son.*" Jess spit dust and rolled onto his back, struggling to draw a breath. His eyes focused on the twinkling stars above. "I don't think . . . I can handle . . . anything like this . . . again."

Deafening silence filled his padded ears. He lifted his head to pull off his helmet.

"Anna?"

No answer.

Panic set in. He rose to his knees and scanned the immediate area. A nearby streetlamp aided him in locating her still form. Anna lay sprawled on the leaf-strewn ground a few yards away.

"*Anna.*" Jess crawled on all fours. He crunched through dead leaves, quickly covering the distance between them.

The stunned young woman lay flat on her back. In an attempt to improve her ability to breathe, she'd managed to draw up her legs. Her eyes were open when Jess reached her side. He immediately deduced that she was having difficulty expanding her lungs.

"*Anna. Thank God you're okay.*"

Jess spoke soothingly. "Listen to me, Anna. Calm down and take small breaths." He patted her wrists in turn. She nodded, mostly to relieve his anxiety. Air rushed in. "That's it," he coached.

The dry leaves rustled under her body as she moved her arms and legs to check for broken bones.

"I think . . . I had . . . the wind knocked out of me."

She attempted to rise.

"Sure you can stand?"

She nodded.

Jess helped her up and gently removed her helmet. "Anna, you could've been *killed*."

"*We* could've been killed," Anna corrected.

"Yeah, well, I'm sorry that I didn't learn from your experience with the car."

Jess stood stiffly with his hands on his hips. "That's it. We hoof it from here."

His exasperated stance stemmed from his apparently unwise choice. "Was that dumb motorbike idea really mine?"

He tossed the helmet near the downed bike and began brushing debris from his clothing, then Anna's.

"Don't blame yourself." She wished he'd allow her to brush off her own clothes. "I agreed to the motorbike. *Brrr* . . . my feet are freezing anyways," she admitted, sticking her ice-cold hands in her pockets. She dared not reveal how warm her body coupled with his had remained during the ride.

Jess reflected. "Obviously *nothing's* safe for us. I certainly didn't expect someone to come around that curve in our lane."

"But you handled it—skillfully, and we appear to be unharmed."

"Sometimes I'm allowed to perform my own stunts, and it's paying off in our current situation."

"Yes, back to our situation—it isn't much further," Anna offered. "Maybe twelve mile or so—as the crow flies. But the road makes for faster traveling, so we have to stick with it a ways. There's a river to cross—hills to go 'round. Later, we can detour from the highway through some pasture and woods." She paused briefly, looking up at Jess. "With some luck, we can make it in a day."

Her hurried words distracted her from the physical stirrings that his touch had created.

At least she's reasoning well. His concern for accidental injury began to subside.

He noticed Anna shivering in the chilly night air. "It's getting colder." The temptation to warm her in his arms was strong, but he knowingly predicted that she would only pull away.

"Temperature drops fast in these hills on a clear night." The words were somewhat muffled through her chattering teeth.

"No cloud cover. The day's heat is radiating into space. It happens in California too. Most evenings tend to be cool.

"We need shelter. It's too risky walking in the dark." Jess spied the few generously spaced streetlamps as he surveyed their surroundings. "Is this the outskirts of a town?"

"Salesville?" Anna laughed the name. "More like a wide spot."

"Ahead is a Y in the road. There's a small store in its straddle. A right turn will take us toward Birdman's Cave and Calico Rock."

"Calico Rock?"

"That's a town."

"There are some old cabins to the right of this curve. They kinda serve as a motel—if you can call it that. Oak Park Resort's the name. Don't know how good they'd be—haven't ever stayed there. The road to the left passes a fish hatchery and crosses Lake Norfork, and travels on to Pineville. But it's out of our way."

"Okay then. Let's check out those cabins. But first, I need to ditch the bike."

Anna giggled without humor. "It's already ditched."

Jess looked thoughtful. "So it is."

Finding a bike with two helmets attached hadn't been an easy task. He regretted leaving it. Being on foot was time consuming.

The black night began to weigh on Anna's mind. "Sure is dark. I always thought Halloween night should have a full moon, but I hear that doesn't happen often. The last one was nearly fifty year ago."

"It's definitely fitting—makes it a little *spookier*."

"Terrific." Anna glared at Jess but moved a little closer. He smiled inwardly pretending not to notice.

Oak Park Resort was well lit with mercury-vapor lamps. Half of the huts were painted white with mint green trim; the other half, mint green with white trim. *Quaint,* Jess thought, walking up to a parked car sitting in the courtyard with Iowa tags. The engine-heated hood still popped. There was no one in sight. "Looks like good timing."

"Or fate is with us," Anna offered, her face lacking expression.

The two cold, wary travelers stood facing each other in front of the motel office.

"Jess, I just considered something. Think they'll see us opening the door?"

Jess thought back on the day. "I can't answer that."

"Me neither. No one's been around to watch me—except at the church. But I was too upset about Miss Mossie to pay much mind."

"It's probably best we don't take any chances until we know for sure. We certainly don't want to scare anyone to death. We'll have to wait until someone else opens the door."

"We need a cabin key. This job's on you. You're small enough to slip through. Are you with me, Anna?"

"Is there a choice?"

"No."

The door abruptly opened. Sounds of civilization burst forth. Women's voices competed with an old *I Love Lucy* rerun. An occasional male baritone chimed in.

"*Will you look at that?*" Jess's mood bore frustration. "It's way too crowded. Even *you* couldn't make it through that door."

After the door closed behind the Iowa couple, they crossed the courtyard and entered cabin number six.

Anna grew despondent.

"Now what?"

Jess stared blankly. Harshness laced his words. "*Who knows?*"

Anna stepped back.

He realized that his tone had upset her. "Sorry. I didn't mean to snap. It's not you. It's me. I'm losing my patience." He rubbed his brow. "It's been a long day."

The door to cabin number six opened, and the stout Iowa lady cautiously emerged. She waddled back to the brightly lit office.

The two frustrated onlookers impatiently watched her sluggish movements as she slowly made her way up the steps.

"We'll take you up on that offer for a bag of ice," she informed the female office manager through the open door.

"Be right with ya."

She returned with a key. "We keep the ice box locked, ya know. Young hoodlums like takin' advantage—iffin' we'd let 'um."

The two women descended the creaking wooden staircase, their bulky forms bouncing off the safety rails.

"Now's our chance." Jess darted forward after the trailing lady descended the last step. The plighted young couple succeeded in entering the office unnoticed.

"*Son*. It's like a sauna in here," Jess exclaimed, locating the source. An overloaded potbellied stove radiated its hellish heat about the small room. Summery blue gingham curtains hanging in the window gently swayed from a cold draft of outside air somewhat justifying the over-adequate temperature.

Anna cased the room, wrinkling her nose at the dusty corners. The older male manager occupied a sagging brown couch adorned with loud flowery double-knit cushions. A blaring TV resting in the corner on two plastic milk crates captured his immediate attention.

"Someone must be hard of hearing."

Jess spied the individual sets of cabin keys hanging on the wall behind what served for a registration desk. "Let's grab a key before the lady manager returns." He reached his long arm across, hesitating. He looked back at his cohort. "One cabin . . . or two?"

Anna's pulse rate quickly climbed. *Be honest. Tell him the truth. He'll believe you.* "I'm afraid to stay alone." A facial muscle twitched revealing the young wife and mother's mental dilemma.

Jess turned away to hide his pleased smile. "Pick a number between one and eight. Remember, six is taken."

"One," Anna responded, overzealously.

He grabbed the first key. "Cabin number one it is."

Moments later, they were inside the cracker-box hut located closest to the highway.

The window curtains hung still. "This room's better insulated than the office." Jess located the heat source, a propane gas-fed radiator, and increased its output. The room soon reached a comfortable temperature.

Anna sat on the edge of the bed that consumed most of their living quarters. "I'm going across the street to the gas-mart to get us something to eat. We have a kitchen—tiny as it is." She tensely rambled on. "Who'd a-thought one could get so much furniture into such a small space." She giggled nervously, and immediately felt awkward for doing so.

"At least we have a full-size bed." Jess avoided looking at his roommate. He busied himself removing his coat.

Another nervous giggle escaped her. "Well, I don't know about you, but *I'm starved*. Want anything in particular?"

The word "particular" came out *pa-tic-a-ler*. It amused Jess. He stifled a smile, turning it into a yawn.

"Bring something along the lines of healthy—no junk, *please*."

"You want something healthy—from a gas-mart. I'll do my best. Be back directly."

She swiftly exited, gently closing the door of the hut behind her. To Anna, braving the dark night was more appealing than trying to make idle chatter with a stranger. But was Jess Parks really a stranger? She had spent so much time thinking of him . . . and now . . . here he was . . . in the flesh. Anna pinched herself to see if she would wake up. She did not. Instead, she quickly changed her thoughts. Thinking about his physical presence made her feel insane.

The wait was short. A customized pickup built well above the ground pulled into the parking lot, ablaze with flashy yellow running lights. A young male driver emerged. Anna read *cowboy* from his attire. She followed him closely through the squeaky screened door.

The warmth of the heated room welcomed her. She vigorously rubbed her hands together while surveying the interior of the small country establishment.

Reminding herself that she wasn't stealing, Anna began gathering the much needed groceries. Strolling up and down the aisles, she plucked name-brand items off the shelves, watching them come away in her hands with the originals remaining in place. She studied the can she held. *I wonder which one's real.*

Anna's chosen items were hotdog buns, a loaf of whole wheat bread, packaged crackers, and a large can of vegetarian stew along with sacks of raw sunflower seeds. At the refrigerator section, she selected a large bottle of orange juice, a small carton of milk and hot dogs. From the produce aisle, she gathered the last of the fresh fruit.

I need a sack.

She quietly placed her arm load of groceries on the counter well away from the clerk who was taking the cowboy's money for a bottle of soda and a pack of cigarettes.

Eyeing the two men, she stepped back accidentally brushing the top of the orange juice bottle with her arm. It crashed to the floor splashing her jeans with its chilled contents. Anna sucked air into her lungs and froze—waiting.

The clerk paused in his transaction and looked in her direction. He addressed his solitary patron in a slow country drawl. "You hear somethin' . . . like glass breakin'?"

His cowboy costumer answered through a puff of smoke. "Guess I didn't. Prob'ly somebody broke a bottle outside."

"Yeah, prob'ly . . . or it was one of those crazy sounds you hear ever' once in a while and cain't account for."

The cowboy grunted through another puff of smoke and turned to leave, contemplating as he made his exit that the store clerk might be a bit peculiar.

A slight breeze generated by the passing customer thawed Anna's frozen stance. A delicate sigh of relief flowed from her. She boldly addressed the clerk, knowing that all would go unnoticed. "There may not be anything on *your* side fella, but there's a huge mess on mine."

With a wary eye, she picked up the broken glass and dumped it into a waste receptacle.

After replacing the juice, Anna quickly packed her sack.

"Put that on my tab," she addressed, to ears that didn't hear her, and out the door she went.

A bathroom, thank God. Lack of water pressure made the noise of the flushing commode linger. Jess prayed that the sound would subside before Anna returned.

The cabin's only electronic device worked. "Great—cable." He switched to the local twenty-four-hour weather channel and sat on the bed. Judging the distance to the pillow behind him, he lay back tucking his finger-laced hands beneath his head. A pleasurable groan escaped him.

Jess read the printed scroll crossing the bottom of the screen. "Low tonight . . . mid fifties. Not bad. High tomorrow in the low sixties . . . with a small cold front moving through the area in the afternoon. Low tomorrow night, fifty degrees—could be worse."

A sudden shiver coursed through his exhausted body in spite of the room's warmth. The memory of the little girl at the airport kept replaying in his mind.

They were on this side—the side Anna and I are on. I'm sure the father saw me—yet he ignored me. Why? Maybe he was spooked too. Could he have known I wasn't dead?

The incident coincided with Anna's story about the old woman at the church.

Nothing makes sense, because we aren't dead—I don't think. Jess reviewed the events leading up to the discovery of his twin. *The taxi brought me home, so I couldn't have died in a car wreck, and I didn't drink enough alcohol to kill me. I could've suffered a brain aneurysm while I slept. What about Anna? She was at home too, a mere coincidence—or not?*

He attempted to shake his uneasiness by shifting his thoughts. *Tomorrow we should reach our destination given by the lady in my dream—Birdman's Cave. Possibly then, this whole thing will end itself. There's another synchronicity, that Anna knows the way to Birdman's Cave. How weird is that? I'm now convinced that she definitely plays a part in this . . . bizarre odyssey.*

Anna's lengthy absence began to nag at Jess. A sense of isolation descended upon him. He jumped up and lunged for the door leading outside. It flew open at his insistence. Anna was crossing the highway and coming toward him.

"*Anna*," Jess called. She looked so small and helpless. He ran out to meet her, relieving her of her burden. "You okay?"

"Fine and dandy. Why?"

"Oh, nothing," Jess trailed. "I was merely concerned, the conditions being what they are. You took longer than I anticipated."

"Well, really, I'm fine."

"Good to know."

The two walked toward hut number one.

"Something strange occurred while I was in the store, though." Anna paused in her step. "I knocked over a bottle of orange juice, and the glass shattered on the floor. Look at my *jeans*. It made a *terrible* commotion. Then the clerk asked this cowboy customer if he'd heard the sound of breaking glass. When the cowboy said, no—here comes the weird part—the clerk told him that he thought it might be one of those odd sounds you sometimes hear that can't be explained. It makes you wonder. I mean, even I have had similar experiences . . . hearing noises that I couldn't explain—like someone calling my name, and there's no one there. Haven't you?"

"I'd have to say yes. It could be that some of us are more attuned to our sixth sense, or maybe the division between parallel dimensions isn't so thick for us."

Jess shifted the grocery sack in his arms and scanned the surrounding darkness.

"That means there're others like us."

His obvious discomfort toward the darkness encouraged Anna to drop her voice to a whisper.

"Apparently, they've always been there—but now, *we're them*."

Anna's profound statement sunk in. She felt awkward speaking of unfamiliar variations in her belief, yet Jess listened intently as though her conjectures were within his principles.

"You're saying you believe in parallel universes?"

"The real question may be *do I have a choice?*" she answered.

An eerie suspicion suddenly invaded Jess's occupied mind, causing the hair on the nape of his neck to stiffen, one of unworldly forms hiding amongst the trees in the darkened woods. He hid his uneasiness from Anna. "I'm hungry. Let's go in." He scrutinized the darkness from the relative safety of the hut's entrance, then closed and bolted the door behind them.

"At least we don't have to worry about scarin' people." Eager to share her discovery, Anna removed her jacket and plopped onto the bed, releasing a loud tired groan.

"Because . . . ?" Jess unloaded the grocery sack onto the table, silently grimacing at the package of hot dogs in his hand.

"After the broken bottle incident, I decided to see what would happen when I walked out alone. I looked back, and the clerk didn't act like he saw me leaving."

"Good to know." Jess held up the fruit. "Ah, breakfast."

Anna reflected as she watched Jess putting away groceries. "This morning when I answered my phone, I picked up the receiver, but the phone kept ringing. That's when I realized that the receiver was still in its cradle. It was like I was holding its ghost. I call it the ghost effect."

"I didn't pick up on your *ghost* effect until I was in the liquor store. That's when I realized that the bottles I took off the shelf still remained." Looking confused, he shook his head. "That really makes no sense."

"So you thought we were stealing?"

"Of *course,* I didn't look at it as stealing. It wasn't as if we had a choice. We were merely dealing with the circumstances."

Anna's eyes narrowed. "*Anyways*, my point is that I should've known that nobody could see us coming or going."

Jess looked directly at her. "Then I should have known too. Give yourself a break. This is all pretty new to both of us. I haven't figured it all out either."

"Something else I've noticed." Anna rose from the bed. "When you and I are alone, there aren't any ghost trails."

"Mind if I shower first?" Anna crossed the small span of floor leading to the bathroom. She turned, awaiting his reply.

"Go ahead. My stomach is more interested in getting fed. I'll get some of this food ready."

Jess halted his task to study Anna standing in the door frame. A leaf fragment clung to her hair. *Son. She's so tiny.*

"You're sure?"

"Yeah, I'm sure. Bachelors *do* know how to open cans and boil water. Oops." Jess grinned apologetically for his sarcasm. "You're right. We men *are* bad."

This time, Anna chose to let the comment slide. "Okay. I won't be long."

Her partner's reference to bachelors brought a smile to her lips. *He isn't married.*

Jess breathed a silent sigh of relief and returned to his kitchen duties, his mind working on a hypothesis for Anna's observation of the absence of the ghostly trails.

Anna closed the door and stared down at the lock. *If I lock it, he'll hear me, and then he'll think I don't trust him. But I really do trust him ... don't I? Yes. I do.* She didn't lock the door.

An about-face in the tiny bathroom put her at the sink. She quickly moved to turn on the shower as high as it would go jerking and pulling at the fastenings on her jeans. Her stream hit the water before she finished sitting. She shivered with relief.

The flush reverberated throughout the guest cabin. Jess knowingly glanced toward the noise and smiled. He returned to the task of opening a can of vegetarian stew, wearing a house dish towel draped across his shoulder.

Buck naked for the first time since her transition, Anna again found herself mesmerized by her perfect body. Her inspection lasted long enough for the hot water to regulate after the toilet flush.

Another dilemma nagged her. *Do I wear dirty jeans, or do I wash them and go out wrapped in a towel?* Hanging onto her trust, she decided to go out with the towel around her waist.

Five minutes after her shower, Anna exited the steamy little bathroom refreshed—sweater on and towel in place.

Jess sat casually at the dining table, his size dwarfing the tiny two-seater. He spoke when she glanced his way.

"Deja vu."

Anna's expression remained blank.

"Your hair is wet again."

The cook rose from the table and stirred something on the stove.

"Thanks for the meatless stew," he said, and took a taste from the spoon. "You really want me to cook those hot dogs?" His disapproving brow nodded at the unopened pack on the counter.

Giggling nervously, she shook her damp hair, loosening the soaked strands. "*No.* Stew sounds fine. The kids . . . they like hot dogs. I, uh, don't know what I was thinking."

She draped her wet jeans across the warm radiator and sat on the bed grateful that Jess hadn't commented on her towel skirt.

Jess studied Anna's mood. A forlorn look passed over her delicate features. Gaining her trust weighed heavily on his mind. She had no one else to turn to. He wiped his hands on the dish towel hanging from his shoulder and voiced his concern. "Are you okay . . . I mean . . . are you worried about your kids?"

"Uh, no—not really *worried.* Joel's a good father. I'm sure they're okay. And it isn't like they're being cared for by a stranger . . . I mean, it *was me* back there," Anna gestured toward herself, "maybe with a part missing—my part—whatever that means."

"I hadn't thought of that either. There must be a part of me missing back in L.A." Jess shook his head as if to clear it.

"It's that my kids are my life. My whole world revolves around them. I miss them terribly. It's the hardest part about this." One corner of her mouth pulled into a half smile.

She's a good mom, Jess surmised, remaining silent.

Shortly, he approached Anna and bowed deeply at the waist, carefully balancing a steaming bowl of stew in each hand. "Ma'am, shall we dine?"

They ate in silence until their hunger subsided.

"If you don't mind, I'll share something with you. But you must promise you won't be offended." She awaited his response.

"Since you're gracious enough to warn me in advance, I most certainly won't take offense."

Jess was grateful for the opportunity to study her.

"Continue."

"The definition for *Deja vu* . . . it means you have experienced a new event. People misuse the word, as you just did. The fact that you saw me with wet hair earlier clearly makes it not true *Deja vu*. However, if you see me at this moment with wet hair and you believe you have in the past, but actually haven't, then that would be true *Deja vu*."

Anna appeared guarded. Her body language alerted him that she lacked confidence. Jess pretended not to notice. The sparkle in his eyes proved he'd taken no offence.

"Your scope of knowledge is impressive."

Mild surprise for not being chastised for her boldness turned into a smile. It touched his heart. He returned it.

"Honestly . . . since meeting you, I've learned a lot.

"Hey, I thought about what you said about the ghost effect being missing when we're together. Maybe it's proof of our situation while we're apart, but when we're together, we have each other to remind us of what's happening. What do you think?"

"I think that makes as much sense as anything."

Hating to spoil the moment, but knowing it was necessary, Jess gestured toward the bed with the end of his spoon.

"There's something we need to discuss." Scraping his bowl clean, he calmly took his last bite. "Let's try and be adult about this. It's not like we have a choice . . . since there's no couch. Remember, you agreed to the one room. Anyway, the office is probably closed."

Jess avoided eye contact until he finished speaking.

The idea of sleeping together created the same effect as if he had physically touched her. Her face grew pale and her lip twitched.

"Anna, what's going on with you? You're stuck with me whether you like it or *not*."

Jess pulled the towel from his shoulder and threw it on the table. His chair threatened to tip over as he rose too quickly.

Having contemplated Anna's reaction, he took quick command of the situation. He picked her up in his arms and carried her to the right side of the bed.

"I think you're making this a bit too hard—*and* . . . if I weren't a gentleman, I'd give you a toss."

He gently laid Anna down and covered her. The tingling sensation from their physical contact stayed with him as he tidied the tiny kitchenette.

Recovered from Jess's abruptness, Anna spoke apologetically.

"We haven't brushed our teeth."

A soft edge of sarcasm entered his tone as he continued to polish the clean stove top.

"Do you have a tooth brush?"

"No."

"Somehow, I don't think it matters. Forget it and go to sleep."

Jess finished the cleanup, knowing he needn't bother. Their mess wouldn't affect the next occupants, but Anna had fallen into a deep restful state, so his plan had worked. After a quick shower, he gratefully climbed into the other side of the bed fully dressed, instantly joining her.

In a clear dream, he visualized the lady-in-white they now sought. She spoke soothingly. "*Your presence is felt. Keep a steady course. Learn to know thyself and your companion. Continue to seek the truth and the Way.*"

"... *the truth and the Way*," Jess mumbled in his sleep.

The following morning, his eyes opened first. Morning sunlight framed the curtained windows. He silently welcomed the new day.

Anna lay facing him. She still slept. He saw a few fresh tears dampening her cheek and nose. It reminded him of a child saddened by a dream. He reached out to touch a tiny salty droplet. Complete contentedness enveloped him. But the moment didn't last. His wary bed partner's eyes fluttered. He quickly shut his, feigning sleep.

At discovering her cheeks wet with tears, Anna sat up.

Jess stirred, his voice truly groggy. "What is it?"

"Nothing." Anna rubbed her wet, sleep-swollen eyes. How did she dare admit that her dreams were of him, that the tears were for the familiar ache she experienced for wanting to have a part in his life. "I forgot where I was. That's all. Sorry I woke you."

He allowed her to believe that she had. "It's okay." His curiosity burned to know what had caused her tears, but he wouldn't invade her privacy.

Jess rolled onto his back and stretched his long stiff body, his feet extending well past the foot of the bed. He looked at Anna. "Better get going. Judging from the strength of the sunlight, it's long past time to be on our way."

Together the two rested travelers left the hut, taking in the Ozark's cool morning air.

"It's another three mile or so on to Norfork."

Jess again noticed that Anna habitually left the *s* off of mile— more country idiom.

They walked the three miles mostly in silence. A short rest at the bridge where the Norfork River joined the White River gave Jess time to enjoy the fantastic view. His body relaxed, but his eyes continuously roamed the scenic panorama, soaking up the magnificent Arkansas landscape.

"Time to go," Anna announced.

Resuming their trek, the highway began to decline past the Norfork

Bridge through the main part of the small town until it reached a bend in the road.

Beyond that point, the road climbed ever upward. Jess caught sight of the ninety-degree angle midway. Past the angle, the road veered to the right. "*Son.* Would you look at that? I thought we were *already* climbing. How far up does Norfork Hill go?"

"A ways," Anna confessed.

Jess released a loud sigh.

Anna chuckled softly. "It's only a hill."

"Then I'd hate to see your mountains."

"Once we round that upper curve, the road will gradually turn back the other way and soon level out. You're looking at the most drastic instance, but I must warn you, all of Highway 5 South is *pretty* hilly."

"Maybe we could hitch a ride."

"*Oh, no.*" Anna never broke her stride. "Come along. It'll be around noon when we reach the top."

Jess sighed with frustration. "—or later."

The exhausting climb coupled with the added heat of the midday sun left them needing rest.

"We made it." Jess dropped to the ground to catch his breath. He loosened his boots but didn't remove them. It would be difficult to put them on swollen, blistered feet. He unbuttoned his outer shirt, allowing the sun-warmed breeze to penetrate his inner clothing.

Anna sat nearby and removed her high-tops, alternately massaging her tired feet. Jess picked up one tiny shoe. It looked miniature in his large hand. He compared the little shoe to his own. She continued rubbing each foot but knew what he was thinking.

"I look at it as having less flesh to ache."

Jess grinned. "Touché."

Anna smiled back.

"Right now, I'd like to be wearing sneakers. I should've visited that shoe store in the mall. I'm paying for it now. Any shoe stores in the vicinity?"

"Sorry, Jess. You're out of luck."

Upon hearing his name, he smiled. He dismissed his discomfort and turned to view and judge the remaining uphill distance.

Anna surveyed the road ahead. "We aren't at the top yet, but we're close. After a rest, what's left won't seem so bad."

"You're holding up well, Anna."

"I'm used to family hikes. I *am* tired, though."

She leaned back, supporting her head with finger-laced hands and gazed at the crisp blue sky. Wispy cirrus clouds hung high above, warning of a weather front moving through. "Weather's changing—air's drier. Temperature's gonna drop soon."

"The front's moving through early. Last night, the weather channel said it wasn't supposed to arrive until late afternoon."

"Typical Arkansas weather, *believe me*."

The pleasant sixty-six degree breeze quickly dried their sweat. Occasional traffic noise bit into their conversation.

Jess rubbed at the beginnings of a blister inside his unlaced boot. He glanced at the midday sun. "Are we there yet?"

Anna smiled at his childish question. "More than half way—from Mountain Home, that is. It's another twelve mile or so."

"Think we can make it by dark, Annie?"

The play on her name didn't displease her. It sounded—friendly. Best friends and her deceased father and mother had called her Annie.

She shrugged. "It's not impossible. Up ahead, we'll leave the highway—long as nobody minds us cuttin' across their property." Anna thought about her comment. "Guess that ain't a problem."

Charged with heightened sensitivity, the resulting soft masculine chuckle created a pleasant tingling within her.

Their lunch was stored in Anna's coat pockets. She removed the items and laid them out on an unfolded napkin.

Pouring raw sunflower seeds directly from the package into his upturned mouth, Jess suddenly remembered the map he'd acquired from his ride to Mountain Home. He dug it out of his pack and spread it on the ground.

Anna spoke before he could comment. "Notice where the road veers left past the Izard County line . . . and makes a little hump."

Jess located the county line. His eyes followed her directions.

"When we reach that point, we can cut right and save a few mile—if you like. It'll put us right close to Birdman's Cave. Best-case scenario, we'd be there before nightfall. Dark comes early."

"Can't we get there faster by sticking to the highway?"

Jess finished the seeds and tucked the empty bag into his pocket.

"Not on foot." Anna pulled on a shoe. "Since there's no danger of snakes . . . or tiggers and chicks, I don't see why we can't take the shortcut. It'll save us time."

Jess wrinkled his nose. "Tiggers and chicks?"

She rolled her eyes. "Did I say that? I meant chicks and tiggers."

At her second slip-of-the-tongue, Anna broke into gales of hearty laughter. Falling back on a bed of dry leaves, she rolled on the ground laughing until tears streamed down her cheeks. Jess found it impossible not to laugh with her. She finally managed some control and sat up wiping her wet eyes.

"*What I meant to say* was ticks and chiggers."

"Ticks, I know. What exactly is a chigger?"

"It's a tiny red mite—barely visible to the naked eye. There's a dense population of them in the Ozarks." Anna put on her other shoe. "Chiggers attach themselves to the skin and deposit an enzyme to dissolve tissue. Chigger bites start out as white whelps, which eventually turn red. The itch is worse than a mosquito bite. Roll-on deodorant relieves mine. Some say that once you experience the itch, the chigger's long gone."

"There you go again . . . educating me."

Anna picked up an apple and started to bite into it.

Jess stopped her. "Now, I have some information for *you* . . . if you promise you won't take offense."

Anna grinned. "I promise."

"Eating fruit on top of other food isn't really good for humans. Fruit digests much faster creating a purification factor. It greatly slows the whole digestion process. The repercussions might be a sudden case of indigestion or a headache."

It was her turn to look surprised.

"Apples should be eaten by themselves. Save it for later. You can eat it for a snack—only a suggestion—for your benefit. Of course, suit yourself." Jess stood and brushed the seat of his jeans.

Anna tucked the apple away. "I had no idea. Thank you for your helpful hint." That Jess had shown concern for her well-being mildly elated her.

"Yes, well, most people don't know—or don't care."

"Best be going. Dark comes early," she reminded.

Turning eastward, she mentally calculated their remaining travel distance. "We've come twelve mile, I'd say, with about ten to go. The county line is another four." She studied the angle of the sun. "It's near noon. We'll be cutting it close for sure."

Jess witnessed Anna's scrutinizing behavior. Though she spoke aloud, she was obviously addressing herself.

"Only ten hours of daylight, according to the almanac," she continued. "Weather's supposed to be mostly clear and warm today—till that front arrives."

Anna whistled softly. "Look at those mares' tails," she whispered. She stared at the afternoon sky in quiet wonder. Jess copied her.

Remembering last night's weather report, he commented, "There could be something to that almanac."

"I do my plantin' by it."

"Planting?"

"Just a garden. Can't *live* without a garden—always had one, always will."

The two hikers started off in silence saving their body energy for the remainder of the climb.

A fallen branch slapped Anna smartly across the shin. "*Ouch*. One thing's for sure," she said, reaching down to rub the fresh sore spot without breaking her stride, "we haven't been spared from physical pain."

Cars continued to pass by as the two wanderers walked the highway's shoulder.

"I'm surprised by the amount of traffic."

"A lot of folk live a country life—don't care for the larger towns. Area's filling up—like everywhere else. This big old world's getting mighty crowded."

"You're right about that."

"I wonder when it's all gonna come to a bursting point." Anna fell silent.

Jess pondered the unanswerable. "Those problems we can't trouble ourselves over. They tend to work themselves out—part of having faith, you know?"

He finished his sentence with a smile. Anna returned it, winning his heart yet again. The emotions her presence stirred within continued to surprise him.

They eventually reached the foot of a large hill that Jess had spotted from a distance. He was relieved to see that the road circled to the left as his partner had described.

"Don't worry. The road declines on the other side. That's when we'll come into Old Joe."

"I wonder if there really was some fellow named Old Joe."

"Most likely."

Old Joe's combination grocery and gas station had welcomed its customers for at least fifty years. Few other buildings and homes littered the roadside. Minutes later, the tiny Arkansas community lay at their backs.

"Is that it?"

"That's it for Old Joe."

"We must be slowing our pace." Jess noted the angle of the sun and looked at his watch. He stopped walking. "Can you believe it? My *watch* has stopped. I've only had it a year." He slammed his fist through the air. "What *lousy timing*."

He looked at Anna with a pained expression. "Sorry. I've been cursed with bad puns lately."

Her ensuing laughter helped lighten the situation.

"Hold on, now. Don't go flyin' off the handle yet. It so happens that I'm pretty good at guessing time, and *I* don't need a bat-tree." Anna continued her study of the sun's angle. "Don't ever miss by much. You said noon last time you looked? Shadows have lengthened . . . so my guess is . . . two o'clock."

Jess's new favorite thing to do was to study his partner's mannerisms. *She's certainly in touch with her circadian rhythm.*

"We've come about three mile since lunch. There's another mile-and-a-half to the county line. The hills slow our progress."

Jess performed his own mental calculation. "We have about three hours of daylight. Still think we're going to make it by dark?"

"Best-case scenario, remember."

His forlorn expression melted Anna's heart. She smiled shyly and looked away.

With her hands on her hips, she unconsciously traced the dirt with the toe of her shoe. "What difference does it make *when* we get there? What're you so all-fired in a hurry about, anyways?"

Jess looked blank. "I don't know. I feel an *urgency* to stay on track—to get this *ordeal* over with." He tapped his temple. "I keep sensing a directional flow. I don't know, Anna. I can't find words to explain it. It's all so *crazy.*" Jess spun in a full circle. "Like, what the hell am I doing here?" He threw up his hands. As gravity pulled them down, the slapping sound they made on his thighs rang out. He looked at his companion questioningly.

The smile on Anna's lips relaxed him. "Come on, then," she intoned. "Let's keep moving."

An additional mile and a half brought them around a curve to find a sharp decline in the road. At the bottom, a low-water bridge spanned Moccasin Creek, which divided the county line. The view consisted of a beautiful grass-green valley surrounded by rolling hills. Past the bridge, the road gradually sloped upward and to the left. It crested another knob and disappeared on the other side. Near the top of the hill and to the right of the highway sat an old two-story white farm house. The surrounding grounds were well kempt. The structure stood in good repair, creating an eye-appealing vision of hominess in the Ozarks.

"Somebody lives here," Jess remarked.

"That house is where we cut right. Calico Rock's eight more mile up the road, but the cave's closer—five mile as the crow flies."

"—if we don't veer off course." Jess's tone warned.

"Shouldn't . . . with the sun to our backs."

"I guess that helps—plus the fact that you grew up in this area."

"I grew up at Dolph—near Pineville and Calico Rock."

Jess glanced at the late afternoon sun. "About three-thirty?" He looked at Anna for confirmation.

"Close enough." She shook her head. "We're definitely not gonna make it by dark. Sun sets around five-fifteen."

"Farmer's Almanac?"

"Yep. It'll take pure luck to find that cave after dark. I doubt *I* can, and *I* know the area—somewhat. We've got less than two hours to travel what's left. We'll really have to push it."

Jess held out his arms. "Okay, Annie, lead on."

They started up the hill toward the house. "It's gonna take a week for me to get over this," Anna announced, encouraged by her aching lower anatomy.

A bluetick coon hound suddenly appeared. Running toward them full speed, it showed no sign of slowing. Its steady gallop veered toward Jess who expertly jumped straight into the air to avoid being struck. Seconds later, he landed solidly on his feet.

"Son, that was close!" The shaken victim watched the dog disappear into the woods barking at its mysterious prey.

Again, Anna was attacked by hysterical laughter. She fell to the ground and rolled on the dry autumn grass. *"You should have seen your face."* Her laughter rippled through the country air. The gales eventually subsided. She managed to rise, stumbling in the process.

Jess walked up to Anna. Grabbing her shoulders, he shook her gently, failing to hide his own grin.

"*What's so funny?* Had you been in my place, you and that dog would be lying here in a pile."

But Jess's words couldn't be taken seriously.

Envisioning the experience set her off again. "Yeah," she managed, "it was your long legs that saved you."

The familiar flush crept into her awareness. *He's touching me.* She quickly sobered and stepped back gently breaking his hold. She wiped the jovial tears using the back of her hand.

"We're wasting valuable daylight. My fault. We'd best go."

Anna turned and walked quickly up the hill, leaving the bewildered young man alone in the middle of the grassy field.

That young lady changes character faster than anyone I've ever seen. She should've been an actress.

Jess surfaced from his thoughts and followed. His long stride soon caught him up.

Walking in silence, the Row Your Boat song persistently occupied Jess's mind. Again, he chased the tune away using a meditation technique.

A sudden pain shot through Anna's right lower abdomen as they passed through the stand of woods behind the house. Recognizing its familiarity, she ignored it until it intensified.

Darn, does it have to be now?

The microscopic Graafian vesicle had begun to push its way to the surface of Anna's right ovary and would burst forth to be caught up by the fimbriate extremity of the fallopian tube— Mittelschmerz—a side effect of ovulation. Her family doctor had informed her that Mittelschmertz was neither common nor rare; however, some women suffer more than others.

The discomfort increased sharply. Anna gradually dropped behind. *Great timing. All this walking must be making it worse.* She began breathing with the pain, but dropped to her knees when the intensity peaked.

Anna called out in a weak voice. "*Jess.*" Out of normal hearing range, Jess trekked onward. "*JESS.*"

Disturbed from his thoughts, he ceased walking and turned. "What's up?"

Jess started back toward Anna eventually detecting her strained expression. He broke into a trot.

Reaching her side, he dropped to his knees. "Are you okay?"

A full blush covered her cheeks. "Yeah, but I'd like to rest a minute— if you don't mind. I don't feel much like goin' on."

The long afternoon shadows worried Jess, but he carefully chose his words to ease Anna's mind.

"Okay, sure. We're due for one anyhow. I see two trees with our names on them."

Silently offering his hand, Anna accepted.

Her intense pain blocked the searing fire normally brought on by his touch. But for Jess, a deepening awareness of his attraction for Anna heightened when their hands locked. He easily levered her body weight.

His hold again lingered too long so that she was forced to break it. Jess's eyes stayed on hers. Anna looked away.

Wincing inwardly from her physical pain, Anna eased over to one of the targeted trees. Taking her seat, she sighed loudly. Jess sat across from her stretching out his long legs. Anna drew hers up for added comfort.

"This pain usually lasts an hour or so."

Anna quickly closed her eyes. *That was stupid.* She guessed what was forthcoming.

The actor prided himself at reading body language. He quickly deduced Anna's added emotional discomfort. Without a word, he reached inside his jacket pocket and pulled out a small bottle of Crown Royal, offering her the honey-colored liquor.

Anna rolled her eyes. "No, thanks."

"This is all I have."

"The smell of whiskey turns my stomach."

"So pinch your nose. *Come on*, Annie. Do it for me—for you—for our mission—for whatever." Jess placed the bottle at her feet.

Anna hesitated. "Since you mentioned it, just what do you think our *mission* is?"

Jess looked thoughtful.

"You must have *some* idea, something in your past, maybe?"

"Seriously, I don't see how my past involves you, but somehow you fit into all this, or else you wouldn't be here. I must admit—if I may—it's like I know you . . . like I've always known you." Jess searched Anna's cool blue eyes. "That's not a line. It's the truth."

Anna picked up the tiny proffered bottle. "Yeah, me too."

Jess's eyes brightened at her confession. "Odd . . . isn't it."

Emboldened, he decided to share more. "Anna, I'm strongly attracted to you. I can't help myself."

Anna looked at Jess and then looked away. "I'm married to Joel, thirteen years now—no affairs, Joel, or me."

He picked up on Anna's placement of the s after the word "years". *She's uncomfortable talking about it*, he deduced.

"I was married—until yesterday." Jess picked up some twigs and tossed them one at a time. "I missed my divorce hearing. Anyway, this part of me did. Guess that's *one* good thing."

Anna experienced a sudden twinge at the thought of Jess being married. "I didn't know you were married. Want to share?" She halfway expected Jess to refuse.

"Oh. We had a large wedding, but Ariel wasn't a screen star at the time, so the media basically ignored us, which is fine by me. I happen to relish my privacy. As for the marriage breaking up . . . well, not too many days ago I came home from a long grueling day on the set to find my car keys in the toilet." Jess turned sad eyes toward Anna. "The water was yellow."

"*Oh, my,*" she returned, truly surprised by his story.

Jess grunted. "Ariel 'Dear John'ed' me. She found someone she preferred more. I made the mistake of arguing with her."

After a short pause, he continued to unburden himself. "I can now look back and see that I let myself get caught up in a typical Hollywood relationship . . . married for the wrong reasons—looks, popularity. And, now . . ." Jess threw his last twig, ". . . I'm paying for it." He glared at the ground. "Doesn't say much for my character, does it?"

Anna felt the urge to protest Jess's personal judgment.

"I didn't believe it could happen to me."

"No one ever does," she offered.

Jess lifted his eyes and gazed into the distance. "I had planned to be married for the rest of my life—have kids. Then Ariel refused to consider a child . . . claimed her sister had lost one in a nasty custody battle. But it's kind of funny . . . as though I'm now realizing that we didn't really belong together." He fell silent.

"Perhaps that was best for her niece or nephew. The mother's always awarded custody, unless she's deemed unfit.

"Anyways, I'm sorry your divorce was tough on you, but I doubt it was your fault—a victim of circumstances, I expect."

"Thank you. I appreciate your defense, but everyone has their side. Lessons learned . . . some necessary karma, maybe."

"Karma—a Buddhist term. You aren't Buddhist, are you?"

Another stabbing pain encouraged Anna to accept the intended elixir. The lid twisted off easily. She pinched her nose and brought the bottle to her lips. Her body convulsed violently as she swallowed some of the distilled liquid. But she held her nose and drank more.

"*Quick*." Anna fanned her face with her hand. "Give me something to chase this with so I can keep it down."

Beside himself with inner laughter, Jess handed Anna a bottle of water. He drew upon his acting ability for self-control, while Anna attempted to wash away the foul aftertaste.

"*Ugh*. That's nasty. How can you *like* it?"

Again her body convulsed.

"And why is someone who's so worried about what they eat drinking alcohol anyways?"

"A fair question—one vice I've yet to give up. The day will come when I can let it go. Addiction is a form of underdevelopment of the soul. It's a matter of self-discipline to rid ourselves of vices. Everything unnecessary in life that a person can let go of puts him closer to complete enlightenment, hence, absorption with the supreme spirit. Once we

achieve a state of nirvana—the extinction of all desires and passions—
we'll no longer return to earthly lives. *That's* Buddhism."

"Ah, but only Christ was completely enlightened."

"—and Buddha, and Mohammed, and Mother Teresa— Don't you
understand? They *all* dedicated their lives to the Supreme Being. But take
Christ in the Christian religion, for instance. We're supposed to live what
He taught."

"Yes . . . your point?"

". . . and the truth will make you free. Learn to live the truth and
nothing will ever bother you."

"Have *you* learned to live the truth, Jess Parks?"

Jess paused. *If I had, I wouldn't be sitting here desiring you.* "I confess that
I haven't yet learned it all."

"What's the definition of *karma* anyways?"

"I'm surprised you ask, as educated as you seem. *Karma* means our
actions as a whole. How we treat life is how life treats us. For every action,
there is a *reaction*, good or bad, short-term or long-term. Understand?"

"Yes. You're saying, an eye for an eye."

"Correct, but in a spiritual sense—not a human-judgment sense."

"I can relate, but I don't believe in any reincarnation nonsense."

"Well . . . to each his own."

"You do?"

Anna handed the Crown Royal back to Jess. He opened it and took
a long drink.

"You didn't wipe my germs off—"

Jess choked, coughing and laughing simultaneously. The aspirated
liquor burned his lungs. Tears streamed from his eyes. He ceased his
laughter and portrayed a look of pure wretchedness.

The display shocked Anna. She drew in a sharp breath. "Stop it!"

Jess wrinkled his brow and then relaxed. "Sorry. I can't resist an
opportunity to practice. Crying at will has always been tough for me."
He smiled and wiped away his crocodile tears.

"Well, you can go practice somewhere *else*."

His vulnerable expression had frightened Anna. She relied heavily on Jess for strength and protection.

He closed his eyes and exhaled. *Curb your carelessness. You'll lose her trust again,* he told himself.

"I said I'm sorry. I didn't expect you to react."

"Then what *did* you expect?"

"I didn't expect *anything.*"

Surprisingly, Anna rose and came to sit next to him, resting her back against his tree. No effort was made to rekindle their conversation. Jess let it go.

Desperate to continue their trek, Anna comfortably took the bottle from his hand and wiped the top with her sleeve. The effects of the first drink helped prepare her for another.

Jess sat quietly, enjoying his physical response to her closeness. His immediate happiness seemed to greatly depend on these few special moments.

As the alcohol relaxed her body, her localized pain subsided. She wiped the top of the bottle again and handed it back.

"I don't believe germs matter here. Besides, alcohol's a natural sterilant, okay?"

"Guess we don't have to worry about catching a cold off each other then."

The last of the afternoon sunlight filtered through the autumn foliage, highlighting the blue sheen in Anna's hair.

She slowly shook her head. "Ain't gonna make it now. Gets chilly after dark, you know."

Jess worked his brows Groucho Marx style and smiled.

Anna read his amusement and guessed the reason. "No comment on my improper use of a contraction?"

"*Ain't* happens to be a conventional word in this part of the country. I don't use it myself—didn't grow up with it."

Jess sensed he had avoided hurt pride. Again, his spirits soared.

"Anna . . ."

"Yes?"

"Mind if I ask a personal question?" he began, not waiting for a reply. "Have you ever met someone that you took an instant liking to? What I'm getting at is . . . do you believe in . . . love at first sight?" Jess sucked in a breath and froze. He immediately assumed his mistake.

Flustered by his abruptness, Anna made a show of brushing off imaginary dirt from her clothes. Jess braved a glance her way. She eventually lifted her face to look directly into his dark brown eyes. Her tone held a serious note. "Honestly, I'd have to say, yes. But it was a little different for me." She spoke with an edge of hesitancy. "You see, years ago, shortly after Joel and I married . . ." Anna carefully chose her words, ". . . I became aware of the existence of a certain individual—"

Jess encouraged her to continue. "Another man?"

She answered sarcastically. "No . . . a woman. *Yes . . . another man.*" She giggled, easing her curtness, and brushed away more invisible dirt. "Anyways, I found myself falling for . . . this man."

Her cheeks were heavily blushed. The alcohol had transformed her. Jess enjoyed the change.

"It reached the point where he was constantly on my mind. I mean . . . I was always thinkin' about him. I could be washin' dishes or drivin' the car, and *poof* . . . there he was," she intoned. Drama crept into her voice. "I started thinking I was obsessed. But please understand. I didn't *want* to be obsessed. Then somewhere I read that a person obsessed with an individual acted compulsively— like making anonymous phone calls, writing letters and hanging pictures on their walls. Well, I never did any of those things."

Anna hushed. She averted her eyes. *I'm talking too much. Darn this alcohol. What if he figures out I'm talking about him?*

Jess ventured, "Do you . . . still have these feelings?"

"Truthfully, yes. I *still* have these feelings."

A jealous twinge shot through Jess's gut. *Two rivals. Wish I hadn't asked.*

"Don't beat yourself up over it." He deeply desired to comfort her physically but feared more rejection.

Anna stealthily changed the subject. "We've got a major problem to consider."

The abrupt change obviously confused Jess. "What?"

"We *happen* to be in our last hour of daylight. We *happen* to be a few mile short of the cave entrance. Maybe we can find an old barn or a hunting cabin."

She quickly stood. "Sorry I slowed us down. I really couldn't help it."

"*Whoops* . . . I'm a little dizzy." She tested her balance. "Must be the booze," she said, and giggled into her hand. "I don't care much for alcohol."

"Hey, don't worry about it." He smiled behind his words. "We both needed the rest. We've come a long way on foot."

"Pain gone?"

Anna nodded.

"Female problems?"

Jess knew he was pushing it. He took the last drink and slid the empty bottle into his pocket.

The alcohol encouraged her.

"You really wanna know?"

Jess nodded.

"You're sure?"

Jess gave a second nod.

"Well, I get this pain nearly every month—when I ovulate."

Again, Jess surprised Anna. "Mittelschmerz—middle-of-the-month pain. I knew someone who had it. I can teach you a meditation technique that will decrease your discomfort."

"Medication technique?"

"Meditation," Jess corrected.

"Well, sir, I might take you up on that—later."

Anna comfortably walked in the direction that she believed would lead them toward their desired destination. The analgesic nature of the Crown Royal greatly impressed her.

The two wary travelers hurried through another mile before coming upon the answer to their prayers, a tiny abandoned cabin. The barn-like gray hues of the structure hinted at its true age.

"Looks like a summer house. Before air conditioning, folks used to build them next to their homes. They were slept in during the hottest days. The large screened windows are situated East and West to catch the best breeze. The main house must have burned down some time ago. There might be an old chimney standing nearby," Anna offered, scanning the brush in the settling twilight.

"Well, maybe this summer house still has a bed." Jess peered through one dingy window.

Anna loudly directed her voice at Jess from the other side of the cabin. "THERE'S FRESH GARBAGE BACK HERE."

He tried the front door. "IT'S NOT LOCKED."

The summer house was standing on a stacked limestone foundation. There were no access steps, long since rotted away. Jess used his long legs to gain entrance.

Anna rounded the corner of the cabin.

"Wait while I test the strength of the floor. If it holds—"

He disappeared inside. She stood quietly, listening to his creaking footsteps amplified by the hollow foundation.

Jess soon reappeared. "Good news." He offered her a hand up. "A little messy," he noted, kicking through debris on the floor. "Take a look at this." Jess proudly exhibited a full-size fully made bed complete with a tarnished brass headboard. "There's food and water too." A bookcase occupying one corner held a variety of canned goods and a sterno kit. A full five-gallon water bucket sat in a corner. "It's good. I tried it."

"Somebody's recently been here. I'm thinking they left in a hurry. Stay put while I take a look. I want to make sure nobody's in the immediate vicinity. We don't need any surprises."

"Good idea. There're drugs in these hills. We're next door to one of the most methamphetamine-infested states in the country."

"Great," Jess commented, before jumping to the ground.

After her eyes adjusted, Anna surveyed the mess. A broom leaned precariously in a cobweb-filled corner. Unwilling to find out if the web was occupied, she raked it out with a soiled dinner fork.

Beginning at the far wall, she swept everything in her path out of the door. What lay on top of the book shelf was raked into an empty cardboard box and pitched outside. It landed in the heap below. She jumped down and kicked the debris under the foundation. Satisfied, she regained entry and continued her clean-up. Within minutes, she was smiling at her progress.

Another smile shaped her lips when she lifted the cover off the full water bucket and found it potable as Jess had promised. She soon had an area clean enough to prepare food.

Darkness forced her to stop and search for an artificial light source. She quickly found a kerosene lantern. *Not if I can help it.* The fumes would be unwelcome. Sterno was bad enough.

A couple of large candles turned up in a box under the bed. After lighting the candles, Anna resumed her meal preparation. Canned brown beans, butter beans and a surviving box of unopened crackers made up the menu.

At Jess's return, he discovered her sitting on the bed with folded legs—eating.

"Did you make that mess outside?"

"Yes, sir."

"I see you can handle Sterno."

"Mmm, camping," she reminded. "Sorry I didn't wait." She cheerfully gestured toward the warmed food. "There's plenty though. You've been gone awhile. See anything out there? I'll *die* if somebody shows up while we're here. Go ahead and wash up. Water's good—like you said."

She pointed her spoon at the bed. "I shook out the blankets—in case of spiders."

Leaning against the door jamb, Jess remained silent. He wore a gentle smile as he listened to Anna's lengthy update.

She looks like a teenager sitting there.

"Missed me, huh?" he teased, following her windy greeting.

Anna stopped chewing and stared at Jess. *Dear God, he's handsome*, she thought.

"Well? You gonna stand there starving when you could be sitting and eating? Grab a plate and take a load off."

Slow to get to know, Jess enjoyed this bolder Anna. His charming laughter rang off the walls, but he heartily followed her welcomed advice.

The foot of the bed was shared for their evening meal.

"No brown beans?"

"They're seasoned with pork. Crackers and butter beans will do."

"So you're a true vegetarian."

"Nah—I just try to avoid meat."

Having finished her plate, Anna slipped off the bed and walked to the door. Though the alcohol sedative had worn off, the short rest had relieved the ache in her legs. "At least we had an indoor bathroom last night." She carefully stepped down into the darkness.

Jess finished the food on his plate. He helped Anna back inside and jumped to the ground to scout around once more.

The dead spirits they had in turn encountered occupied his thoughts. *They can't harm us. Only our fear can harm us.*

Anna had fallen asleep upon his return. After blowing out the candles, he lay down beside her fully dressed. But with no source of heat, he quickly slipped under the piled blankets.

Again, it wasn't a large bed. His feet hung substantially off the end. *Doesn't anyone around here own a queen or king-size mattress?* Turning on his side, he drew up his long legs. In minutes, he was fast asleep.

Jess grew aware of Anna lying close. The tingling within his body generated intense passion. He reached for her. Anna's eyes opened. She had sensed his touch even in her sleep. He feared her rejection but kept his gaze steadfast. She stared back. He rose on one arm and leaned forward, his mouth coming down on hers. Anna accepted his steamy kiss. Jess sensed his own physical reaction. They both groaned in their fervor.

Something awakened him from his dream. He remained motionless, straining to hear any sound. Anna's even breathing told him she still slept.

Aware of his increased pulse rate, he looked longingly at Anna, grateful that the darkness hid his emotions. The dream—he longed to return to it, but his mind remained alert.

There it was again. He rose slowly on one elbow. No mistaking the noise. Distracted from his immediate desire, he listened intently. Minutes passed. His propped arm grew numb. *Nothing. Probably a deer or a raccoon.*

Quietly, Jess rose from the bed. He needed to be convinced of their solitude. Otherwise, he couldn't rest.

To avoid awakening or alarming Anna, he stealthily moved through the pitch-dark room, directing his footsteps around squeaky floorboards. He peered out into the black night through the ratty window curtains. Heavy panic seized him. The tiny shack was surrounded by human-like figures clad in gray cloaks. Hand-held lanterns lit their features, expressionless and pale as death itself. The far window revealed more figures. Jess stole over to the door, grasping the cold knob in his hand—hesitating. *They know we're here. We're completely surrounded. There's no escape.*

The adrenalin in his body loosed itself in waves. His breath came hard. His hands shook. *You're causing your own fear. Come on, man. You're smarter than this, so stop.*

He took a deep breath. *May as well find out what they want.*

Looking back at Anna, he made the decision not to awaken her. *Let her sleep—if possible.*

Jess opened the door. Deathly quiet permeated his senses. He looked down at the closest figure.

"*You must come,*" the figure said, in a masculine voice.

Jess momentarily shut his eyes, hoping the uninvited guests would disappear into dreamland. Upon opening them, they hadn't.

"Looks like there's not gonna be a cavalry," he quietly intoned.

Taking a deep breath, Jess nodded that he understood.

Borrowing Anna's tactic of prayerful requests, he silently pleaded. *Please get us out of this one, God.*

Jess attempted to awaken Anna. He tried everything. Nothing made her respond. *No way am I leaving her alone.*

After putting on her shoes and wrapping her coat around her, he picked her up in his arms.

The one step down was quite hazardous in spite of his generous height, but he managed his burden without incident.

Peering into the eerie lantern-lit night, Jess addressed the nearest gray-clad figure. "Now what?"

"*You must come*," the one repeated, turning and walking toward the dark woods.

"Okay . . ." Jess spoke under his breath, ". . . we'll play your game— for now."

Carrying his charge, he followed, surrounded by the others.

So, this is what it's like to be forced against your will. Not a pleasant experience. Maybe this property belongs to them. Maybe they want us to leave.

The strange party marched forward, entering a dense swirling white mist.

They must be ghosts, or else they couldn't see us. If they're ghosts, they can't harm us.

Jess failed to comfort himself. Like a draining pool, his thoughts began to fade. He quickly recognized the sensation of losing consciousness, while holding the sleeping Anna in his arms.

PART II

CATHARSIS

5

Suffering Souls

———◆———

Jess's waking mind began to register what his fluttering eyes endeavored to focus upon—vertical lines. He raised his head. *I'm lying on a floor . . . and . . . are these bars?*

His muddled thoughts continued to clear. A quick visual survey revealed his predicament. Ingrained caution silenced him.

This looks like a cage.

Jess remembered Anna and instantly dropped his guard.

"*Anna?*"

Her body lay twisted in a far corner. His harsh whisper did not stir her. Panic turned on his adrenalin. He rolled over on all fours and silently crossed the flat surface supporting them.

Straightening Anna's legs, he checked her breathing. She was. A sigh of relief escaped him as he watched her begin to stir. Her delicate moan was a welcomed sound.

"Where are we?" Anna unknowingly smiled at Jess as her eyes focused on his face. "I'm so *sleepy*." She batted her thick black lashes, fighting the urge to return to her deep state of rest. Her arms stretched as her body underwent its waking process. Anna froze in midyawn, slowly absorbing their immediate environment.

"Where are we?" She abruptly sat up pivoting her head. "Jess . . . are we in a cage?" Her surprise stifled her fear.

"Not so loud," Jess whispered, placing a finger before his lips. "I don't know. I woke up before you. The last thing I remember was carrying you through the woods——"

"Carrying me through the woods!"

Jess shushed her again.

"*Well.* You wouldn't wake up when the gray people came."

Anna voluntarily lowered her voice.

"Who are the *gray people?*"

The whites of her eyes grew large as she awaited his reply.

The two unwilling prisoners, while studying each other, spontaneously acknowledged through eerie intuition the intruding stares from beyond the bars of their confinement. The gray-clad human-like figures stood with their gaze transfixed upon the occupied circus-type animal cage.

With their backs together, Jess and Anna immediately rose to their feet, surveying the breathtaking 360-degree panoramic view. The downward slope of the land placed the cage at the apex.

Encircling them were hordes and hordes of the cloaked gray forms as far as their eyes could see. A quick study of their silent audience revealed them to be slow and dull. The grayish garb purposely lacked color or style.

Most onlookers gazed at the barred enclosure perched on the summit as if possessing knowledge of some drama about to unfold.

An early morning haze hung in the air, smelling of extinguished campfires, suggesting the hordes had spent the night.

While Jess and Anna remained caged, they watched as the familiar timepiece—the sun—sluggishly crossed the unnatural sky. Everything was dull, the people, the burnt, trampled grass. Even the sun looked dull compared to its usual bright self.

Neither of the two captives felt brave enough to attempt communication with the Grays, who eventually grew tired of staring and wandered away to their separate little groups.

The entire day passed with the two jailbirds finding their only comfort in huddling close together. Later, as the sun began to dip beyond the distant horizon, the individual units began to reestablish evening fires, refusing to stray from their invisible boundaries.

No one had offered them food or drink.

Jess questioned Anna. "Are you hungry?"

"Not really."

"Thirsty?"

"No . . . are you?"

"*No*—" Jess sounded surprised. "—and I find that very strange. We should at least be tired from sitting here all day."

"Wonder how long they plan to leave us in here?"

The darkening sky discomforted Jess. His wariness of the Grays had diminished from lack of confrontation. He rose and began pacing the length of the cage.

"I can't *stand* being this helpless. It's like watching a drama where the actor willingly accepts his fate."

"Jess, you're making me nervous."

The pacing man faced his cellmate sitting on the floor.

"This cage is locked. I've never been locked up before. Have you?" He expected a negative reply and received one.

"Maybe I have a suppressed fear of . . . claustrophobia."

Anna spoke calmly, pulling Jess's focus back to the present. "Our imprisonment doesn't appear to be our choice."

"Yes. *No*. I'm not sure. But perhaps we can find out."

Jess ceased his nervous pacing. He grabbed the bars and studied the gray masses gathered below. Through the dusk, he scanned the lower hills and dales covered with sunburnt grass flowing down to meet the distant horizon.

"I bet it wouldn't faze these folks if we exited this cage and walked away."

Anna gazed beyond the bars. "You tried the door. It's locked. Besides, where would we go?"

Jess looked at her with narrowed eyes. "Good point."

"Suppose we try talking to one of the Grays?" she proposed.

He contemplated her suggestion while continuing to scan the darkening horizon. A line of lit torches suddenly crested a distant hill far below. He remained silent until he was sure that the mysterious flames were steadily marching toward them.

"Anna, company's coming."

She rose and stared through the bars at Jess's discovery.

"Who do you suppose it could be?" she asked, watching the advancing party.

"I have no earthly idea. My guess is someone with authority."

The masses parted in waves, allowing the torchbearers to pass. "At this rate, it'll be pitch dark before they reach us. That is, I assume they're headed for us."

Jess winced inwardly. *Too late.* Seeing Anna's stricken expression, he cursed his mistake. Unconsciously rubbing the stubble on his chin, he turned his face away. His left hand gripped the bar above. *Time to practice self-control.*

The actor searched through his mental bag of theatrical emotions. Resisting all thought in a meditative manner, he allowed his facial muscles to relax. Using an actor's trick, he continued to deep breathe until complete calmness overcame him. His pulse rate naturally slowed. It was good that Anna didn't interrupt.

As the marching party drew near, it was easy to spot the abnormally tall man in the lead. His tremendous height towered well above the others. Baggy white pantaloons and a billowy white blouse made up his attire. A dark blue waist sash and matching head turban mimicked the genie from *Aladdin's Lamp.* With soldier-like strides, the giant man glided forward in spite of his tremendous size. Studying the procession, it became obvious that he was lord and master and all of the masses were his subjects.

Son. He must be all of nine feet tall. Jess prayed that his jailmate wouldn't notice.

The occupants of the cage continued to watch the silent party marching ever upward, winding its way through the campfires dotting the sloped, colorless land.

Thunderous footsteps began to reach their ears and rattle the cage bars as the giant approached. As the deep, dark night settled in, the marchers finally arrived.

The earth tremors ceased when the giant halted in front of Anna and Jess's containment. He crossed his massive arms and tipped his head, examining the two captives with inquisitive eyes. His feet were positioned slightly apart to balance his huge frame. The large man looked bored and not at all winded from his lengthy trek.

With a pounding heart, Jess labored to present an air of calm against both the giant man's presence and Anna's petite, quivering body pressed against his. For her sake, he managed to exude an offhanded manner.

Leaning toward her so that only she could hear, Jess lightly commented on the giant's genie-like appearance. Anna's open-mouthed, wide-eyed response remained frozen upon her face.

Jess's six-and-a-half feet, added to the distance of the cage floor from the ground, placed him at eye level with their assumed captor. Silent summations passed between the two men of above-average stature aided by the torches borne by the Grays.

The deep bass voice belonging to the man of colossal size issued forth from his parted lips, intensifying Anna's uncontrollable quiver. Jess draped his arm across her shoulder for reassurance. Adrenalin flowed heavily through his solar plexus, but his outer appearance remained unmoved.

"I, AHRIMAN, HAVE TRAVELED HERE TO PERSONALLY INFORM YOU THAT AN ERROR HAS BEEN MADE." Anna recoiled at the decibel level of his delivered words. "MY *IMBECILE SERVANTS* . . . AH, SO IT SEEMS, HAVE MISJUDGED YOUR JOURNEY'S END." Ahriman rolled his eyes in disgust. "YOU ARE FREE TO LEAVE."

The captives stood in shocked silence.

It wasn't what Jess had expected to hear. His mind raced with the good news. *Thank God, it's over.*

He quickly deduced by Anna's continued trembling that she hadn't yet comprehended. He firmly squeezed her shoulder in an attempt to help her focus.

Jess quickly regained his composure. "That's it?" His voice sounded small.

The giant replied. "THAT IS ALL."

Jess raised his brow. "No explanation . . . no apology?"

"EXPLANATION? APOLOGY?"

The ground quaked as the gargantuan quivered with merriment, expelling his humorous laughter upon them. The giant quickly sobered. "I, AHRIMAN, HAVE SPOKEN." He drew in an audible breath and continued. "HEAR ME NOW. THIS IS A RARE OCCURRENCE. YOU MAY CONSIDER YOURSELVES . . . UH . . . I BELIEVE THE TERM IS *LUCKY*." His bellowing laugher again issued forth rattling the metal bars of the cage.

Jess took advantage of the next silent pause and boldly asked, "If you don't mind, sir, at what time will our so-called *lucky* release take place?"

"TIME . . . TIME?"

"Yes, sir. When?"

In a giant-sized brain, Jess could understand the misplacement of a few definitions. But the delay and the increasing darkness was beginning to make him edgy.

"AH, YES . . . *TIME*."

Jess's quick mind guessed the giant's forthcoming reaction. He gripped the bars for support and was met with roaring laughter. Minutes passed before the deafening sound subsided.

Wiping at the huge tears created by his own mirth, Ahriman replied, "IT MUST BE SOON, OR PERHAPS I SHALL KEEP YOU BOTH FOR MY OWN PERSONAL ENTERTAINMENT. I HAVE NOT MET ANYONE WITH SUCH EMOTION IN A *LONG . . . LONG . . . TIME*."

Emotion! I'll show you emotion. Jess checked his impatience, refusing to allow it to shadow his countenance. *What a dull life you must lead, Ahriman.* He addressed his guffawing captor with one casual word. "Well?"

More minutes passed before the master regained his composure. Without further conversation, the entire party turned and retraced its steps in the direction from which they'd come with Ahriman mumbling something to himself about time. His torchbearers followed, leaving Jess and Anna in pitch darkness. Now and again, they detected the rumble of the unusually large man's bellowing laughter across the increasing distance.

Recovering her voice, Anna spoke. "What a strange man . . . and so *huge* . . . and what's so funny about time anyways?"

The rough sound of sandpaper filled her ears as Jess again rubbed his unshaven jaw while contemplating his response.

"My guess is time is non-existent in his world."

The door of the cage opened easily even though no one had touched the lock. Jess didn't ponder how or why.

"Let's go, Anna, before someone changes his mind and he wants to keep us because he finds us amusing."

Before exiting the cage, she turned to Jess and wrapped her arms around his chest in the form of a hug.

Pleasure lit his face. "What's that for?"

"For taking care of me so bravely, and because . . . I honestly care about you."

Anna deprived her cellmate of an opportunity to reply. She quickly turned and jumped to the ground. Jess floated after.

Faced with the Grays beyond the cage, Anna clung to her partner. "These guys give me the willies. They look so . . . lifeless."

"I believe you have something there, Anna. This place reminds me of Purgatory."

Anna grew excited. *"Wow,* Jess. That's it. Purgatory—a place to cleanse their souls."

Together, the two descended the hillocks, weaving through the expressionless hordes. But the suffering souls paid no heed to the pair of fleeing travelers with their own heated purpose—to continue their unknown quest that had so abruptly been interrupted. As they skirted the well-spaced campfires, they were grateful that the darkness helped hide the senseless, staring faces.

Sudden fear attacked Jess, making his skin crawl. Forcing himself to not look back lest someone had taken their place, he quickly pulled Anna along, trying not to make her stumble.

They walked for approximately one mile, but the hordes showed no sign of thinning. The inky darkness of the moonless night had settled around them.

Jess looked up. "Something's different."

"What?"

"No stars."

Anna followed his gaze. It was true. The campfires provided the only light.

At last, the crowd began to thin. Another mile put the silent, suffering souls behind them.

"Jess, where's that light coming from?"

Studying the darkened land ahead, he noted a ground-level glow. They walked a bit farther before he attempted an explanation.

"It's these rocks. They're emitting some sort of luminescent light. Funny. I was wishing for some way to see. Glow-in-the-dark rocks. Wouldn't these be a hot item to market?"

Jess attempted to pick one up, but it was solidly planted. *How odd.*

Grateful for the unexpected light-source, he started forward.

"Watch your step. I hear a small stream ahead."

"I can't see it."

"I can't either."

Anna listened intently. "Now I hear it."

Jess recalled how long it'd been since they had drunk or eaten. "Does the sound of running water tempt your thirst?"

"Nope. I'm fine. Really."

"Me too. I wouldn't drink from an unknown source anyway."

They managed to cross the narrow, shallow stream and entered into more craggy terrain. The rocks continued to cast their eerie glow, allowing the two companions to study what lay at their feet.

"I'm glad to be out of there. That walk will haunt me forever."

Jess's confidence had risen at Anna's confession of affection. He boldly hugged her. "Me too." He ended his affectionate gesture before she could. But it seemed that she hadn't minded.

"To possess nothin' but the robe on your back . . ."

"You can't take it with you," Jess reminded. "Besides, material possessions don't matter."

"So where do you think we are?"

"No clue. Doesn't look much like Arkansas. This is definitely *one strange place*."

"It's as though I'm dreamin'—that I'll wake up any minute."

"If you are, we're sharing the same dream. Maybe we're experiencing some sort of mind link."

Jess had given them more to ponder as they continued their trek, each in silent thought.

Anna stumbled again.

"The rocks are spacing out and leaving us with less light. It's too dark to travel on foot."

Jess scouted the surrounding area. "This place looks as good as any. Let's camp here for the night. I'll try to get a fire going. I still have matches." He reached into his shirt pocket for confirmation.

"You've got *my* vote," Anna gratefully replied.

"Since we don't have any food, I guess we don't have to worry about dinner. I'm not hungry, anyways." Anna looked questioningly at Jess. "No food or water in how long? It *does* seem like a dream."

"It's very perplexing." Jess shook his head. "Maybe it's only been minutes instead of hours. I think I'm beginning to understand the giant's humor about time."

Anna scrounged up dried pieces of thick dead roots she found lying between the dwindling rocks. Jess used them to build a recessed fire.

When the fire burned steady, they chose the least uncomfortable rock to rest against for the night.

Anna allowed Jess to cradle her for the sake of comfort. She was becoming accustomed to the warm energy flowing between them.

Time dragged. Neither could sleep. Lying still in their makeshift bed seemed to invite misery.

Anna's eyes suddenly opened, having sensed something. Jess's face loomed directly above.

"Jess, you startled me."

The young man didn't move. His blank expression puzzled her. He continued to stare.

"What is it?"

Anna stifled a yawn and attempted to rise. Her movement brought them closer. She gazed into Jess's dark brown eyes, and caught her breath when she realized he was about to kiss her. Jess's mouth came down on hers, hot and demanding. Anna desperately wanted to respond. She felt her own smoldering passion burst into fiery flames, but her moral conscience spoke to her, and she listened. Denying her burning physical desire, she fell back on their stony bed.

Guilt and shame attacked her, sparking her defensive nature. She slapped Jess's face with an open hand. The contact stunned them both, Jess, not so much by force as by action.

"WHAT IN GOD'S NAME DO YOU THINK YOU'RE DOING?" she cried.

Anna jumped up, stumbling in the process. Her confusion and clumsiness increased her anger. Jess had proved trustworthy—until now. What had happened? How could he betray her trust? She repeated her question.

In his seated position, Jess lowered his eyes. He labored to speak. "Anna . . . I'm *sorry*. I didn't mean to make you angry. I—I love you." Taking advantage of her silence, he continued. "I have all these strange mixed feelings . . . and they're causing me to act like—like a different person. I'm *sorry*. Please understand."

Anna's shoulders stiffened.

"*WHAT?*" she shrieked. "*How dare you, Jess Parks.* You aren't the only one with—*feelings.*"

Jess straightened. "Anna," he attempted to interrupt. But she wouldn't allow it.

"I've spent the last years of my *life* thinking about you and hardly anything else . . . whether I wanted to or not. *You* have possessed my thoughts—day and night—and it's driving me *stark-raving mad*. And what gives you the right to force yourself on me? I have a husband and two children, and I *won't* go back with guilt on my conscience. Can *you* understand *that?*"

"*Oh*," she moaned, shaking with rage and flailing her arms. "I can't *stand* it another minute. Hot angry tears coursed down her cheeks. "Right now, I *hate* you, Jess Parks! *Stay away* from me, you hear?" Anna's shoulders heaved with her sobs.

Jess lifted his chin, his face contorted with the shock and misery of Anna's condemnation *and* her secret confession. He wisely remained silent.

In her fit of anger, she turned and stomped to the other side of the fire where she attempted to settle herself.

Her troubled mind wouldn't allow her to experience sleep—if sleep were possible. Their confrontation had been too intense.

If not for darkness, Anna would have seen that Jess was hurting too. She immediately chastised her behavior. Jess didn't deserve her heated defense. He had only followed his instincts, to show his love for her by doing something unlike himself, and yet, apologizing for it. True, his actions had frightened her. But what had frightened her more—Jess's unexpected kiss—or her passionate reaction? The manner in which Jess was drawn to her would in any other circumstance be welcomed.

She wanted to run to him, to put her arms around him and never let go. Joel and the kids felt so distant—like a dying memory. And Jess was here—warm and real. What would she do without him when their experience together ended? She cried to herself, racked with guilt about wanting to be with him.

Throughout the night, she remained in a daze, occasionally stealing glances to determine if Jess was where she'd last left him. The separation tore at her heart.

Jess, too, glanced in her direction. Her movement told him that she was awake. His chaotic thoughts spun with great speed. Yes, she'd chastised him for the kiss, but for her to acknowledge that she'd spent part of her life longing for him was emotionally elating. *I can't ignore this. We're out in the middle of God knows where.* He again reached into his theatrical bag of emotions, searching for relief from the awkwardness.

Tossing a few more sticks into the dwindling fire, he stood and walked over to where Anna lay. "Look, Anna, I won't try to defend my behavior, but I don't mind telling you that I've never wanted anyone so badly as—as I want you now." Hand gestures enhanced his heartfelt confession. "Honestly, I'm overwhelmed with this . . . unnatural *desire*. I know it's none of my business what you do with your life, Anna, but there isn't a damn thing that anyone—and I mean *anyone*—can do or say to make me change how I feel about you. Look—I *do* respect you . . . but if something doesn't give pretty soon . . . *I'm* the one who's going to go stark-raving mad."

Anna looked up. The confessor's breath was labored from the bearing of his heart. She remained silent. Tear-stained cheeks burned at the fresh memory of his passionate kiss.

Her emotions mirrored his. Jess knew that now. But Anna's sense of family stood between them. He had to admire her for it. *If Ariel had shared Anna's morals, I'd still be married.*

There was nothing more to say. Jess helplessly shook his head. The palms of his hands turned skyward. He shrugged his shoulders. "I need to be alone with my thoughts." He glanced back as he walked away. "I won't go far."

Jess believed that Anna's safety wouldn't be jeopardized. Once the suffering souls were behind them, they'd seen no wildlife or any other living thing in this nameless godforsaken place except for the scraggly shrubs that made up their firewood.

The sullen young man strode past the edge of the campfire light and perched upon one of the larger glowing rocks. There he silently prayed. *Dear God, please help me to realize that this situation will work itself out because I can't see it happening.*

The pale sun in the strange land began to lighten the horizon. A short distance away, his female companion lay with her back to the fire wrestling with her own turbulent thoughts.

Jess stood and stretched out of habit. Though he'd sat on the rock for a long while, stiffness did not plague him. He strolled to the opposite side of his abandoned seat.

A cave, hidden from view, now exposed its yawning entrance to his alert retinas. Discovering it surprised him. The subterranean hole grabbed his curiosity. He walked up to the opening to investigate. The ceiling would easily accommodate a man of his height. The dirt floor lay undisturbed. *Could this be Birdman's Cave . . . the cave we've been searching for?*

Ahead, deep within its bowels, Jess spied what looked like a tiny five-point star. *What's a star doing in a cave?*

To ignore the source of light and return to camp crossed his mind. Instead, he dismissed his thought. Stepping past the entrance, he walked toward the beckoning cave star.

Time dragged since they had left the tiny cabin deep in the Arkansas Ozarks. *When was it . . . two days ago? Maybe it's true that time is merely a concept for the living.*

Again, Jess caught himself singing the Row-Your-Boat song. The lyrics gave him an odd sense of comfort. Try as he might, he couldn't get the tune to leave him, so he sang out heartily. The closeness of the cave walls made his voice carry. If nothing else, he would make his arrival known.

Jess's thoughts interrupted his song. Reality convinced him that the cave wasn't a natural occurrence. He continued his lone trek, contemplating its creation. *Who would dig such a long straight tunnel . . . and why?*

The walk was long. Halfway, he turned and marveled at the distance traveled, realizing that the five points of light had been an illusion. Looking back reversed the effect. The entrance was now the tiny glowing star.

The passageway suddenly widened into an immense cavern.

"*Son, that's huge.*" Jess stood gaping at a simple bowl-shaped architectural design. The natural composition of its surface illuminated itself—much like the glowing rocks. *It's a—* The puzzling discovery left his unfinished thought hanging.

Jess sensed that the structure was deserted and took it as an open invitation to look around. *If nobody's home, then I shouldn't be intruding.* He shoved his hands into his pockets and cleared his throat. "I've made it this far. Hang it all . . . I'm going in." His soft-spoken words were absorbed by the enclosed space.

The structure itself enticingly bid his entry. His clad feet made no sound mounting the spotless white steps. Their spongy texture gave slightly as if foot comfort were a priority. He applauded the anonymous inventor.

With great relief, he scanned the large open room, finding it empty except for a circular dais. The interior floor remained cushiony, and the walls oddly emitted their own mysterious light.

It appears there's no one to greet me.

Jess cautiously approached the dais measuring six feet in diameter and six inches deep. Its surface was a shade of black that reminded him of empty space. In contrast, everything else was brilliant white—like the outer structure.

The visitor stepped up onto the platform with no regard for consequence. The walls in the room dimmed and began to shimmer with tiny prismatic colors. A dense, white column of light shot up from the dais' circumference, encapsulating Jess. He looked up. The encircling light fed into a counterpart above.

A sudden flash of memory forced itself into his mind, the same thoughts he'd entertained while occupying his stony perch, berating himself for his lustful behavior toward Anna.

Anna. I want her. I want you, Anna.

The column of light suddenly ceased, freeing Jess's captured mind and body. The physical release brought his head down from its upward gaze with a jerk. His brow furrowed.

Why was I——? Seeing his reflected image halted his thought.

Initially, Jess believed he was peering into a mirror until the supposed reflection moved.

Oh, no. Not again.

An identical twin glared menacingly at Jess, obviously bearing great hostility.

He sees me. Jess recalled the undetecting stare of his first exact likeness, which felt like an eternity ago.

His frightful-looking double leaned forward expelling its foul, hot breath in his face.

It spoke. "Why, you look . . . *surprised.* Have I caught you . . . off guard?"

The unwanted menace produced deep, throaty laughter behind a closed mouth.

"I'm the part of your personality you tend to suppress. What's the matter? Don't you care for my . . . presence?"

As an actor, Jess had viewed his own performances many times. There was no mistaking his voice—with a hint of sinister.

"We haven't met face to face," it commented, remaining expressionless except for a twitch at the corner of its mouth. "Can you feel my contempt? I intend to kick your soft, little *ass.*"

A wicked laugh attached itself to the end of its sentence, leaving Jess speechless.

Mortified at witnessing this evil self, Jess asked, "What's your problem with me?"

A sudden concern for Anna's safety flashed through his tumultuous thoughts.

"Worried about *her* . . . yes?" A devious smile played upon the snarling upper lip. "Maybe you've noticed, and maybe you haven't. *Your* thoughts are *my* thoughts. So, lover boy, when you gonna score with her . . . or am I going to have to do it . . . *myself?*"

Jess's double repeated its sinister laugh. The verbal intimidation had suggested more than a personal threat.

Angered into a response, Jess clinched both fists. His watchful eyes narrowed.

The evil twin acknowledged the defensive reaction. "*Ah,* that's better.

You have life in you yet."

Placing its open hands on Jess's shoulders, the double shoved him off the dais. The startled victim landed in a sprawled position on the chamber room's cushioned surface. The fall stunned and surprised Jess, but no physical harm occurred.

Face devoid of expression, the Mister Hyde character leapt from the platform. It landed a hard kick at the bottom of Jess's right shoe. The force drove his femoral head into its acetabulum. Stunned by the physical attack, his hip joint immediately began to throb.

Since their arrival in Purgatory, Anna and Jess had experienced no discomfort, but the facility he now occupied offered lifelike repercussions. Pain was again a reality.

"Hey, *wimp* . . . *Mama's boy*," Jess's dark side taunted.

The victim responded. "Listen man, your ignorance is showing. We're not kids here. Why don't you knock it off?"

The retort alerted Jess's menacing aggressor that his victim's stress level had greatly increased. The evil twin laughed. "'Knock it off', he says. *Wimp*. Why don't you get up and fight me like a—" the suppressed side of Jess checked his words, "—like a *she-lion*. Yes. I bet you bite and scratch like a *she-lion*. Come on, she-lion. Show me what you've got. Get up and *fight* me. What *say* you?"

The six-foot-four doppelganger kicked at Jess, attempting to evoke more anger. Alert to danger, Jess skillfully dodged his aggressor's accurate blows.

Negativity is increasing his strength. He's purposely trying to make me mad. Jess studied his attacker, knowing that any further contact would result in more personal injury. *I'm definitely no match for him. He's every bit as big as I am—and stronger. I'm not a fighter. Son. How do I get out of this?*

"You can't," his doppelganger sneered, proving possession of Jess's thoughts.

"Jess?" Anna's soft distant voice echoed about the chamber. Startled by her unexpected arrival, Jess twisted around to identify Anna standing at the opening.

"*Anna!* What are you *doing* here?" he wailed, finding himself faced with her immediate safety.

"Well, well, well, looky here." Laughter bubbled deep within Jess's twin. "Iffin' it ain't the pretty little lady herself. Now ain't this nice and cozy."

The perversive counterpart stood with his hands resting on his hips studying the faces of his victims.

Anna immediately recognized the Jess she knew and trusted.

"I uh . . . I uh . . . was looking for you, Jess. I saw this cave . . . and the light . . . and I . . ." Anna's words trailed weakly.

"Lookin' fer me, *darlin'*?" the vile twin directed at her.

Anna quickly deduced that her native accent was being violated by the shocking mockery of her beloved companion.

She studied Jess's double. Only the two men's mannerisms differed. Her confused eyes flitted from one face to the other. Ignoring the look-alike's words, she tore her eyes away from the threatening twin to look at her partner questioningly.

"What's going on, Jess?"

Disallowing his eyes to leave his aggressor, Jess quickly explained. "When I arrived, the place was deserted. I stepped on that dais and *he* appeared." Jess nodded at the latest bit of trouble.

Anna's gaze returned to the subject of their conversation.

Fear welled up in Jess when the twin took a sudden step toward her. Adrenalin surged from its seemingly endless reservoir.

With Jess's attention diverted toward Anna, the twin delivered another deft kick. Jess's peripheral vision caught the act. He dodged and rolled out of his attacker's reach. Evil, mocking laugher burst forth from his tormenter as he again turned his attention to Anna.

Utilizing the training required for his acting stunts, Jess lunged at its legs, locking his arms tightly around them. Both bodies crashed to the floor. Jess's double attempted to roll. Thrashing like a gator wrestling its prey, it managed to work one leg free.

Anna watched in horror. Squeezing her laced hands, she pressed her thumbs against her mouth to silence her screams. But one managed to escape when the room resounded with the cracking sound of human bone.

The attacker had smashed its freed foot into Jess's mandible. In a half lying, half sitting position, consumed with pain, Jess couldn't move. His mouth hung open unnaturally. The guttural sound from his throat was meant to be a cry of agony.

The evil counterpart that had inflicted the indescribable pain upon Jess laughed triumphantly.

"*Jess*," Anna pleaded as it came at her. "*JESS!*"

Her terrified screams pierced Jess's thoughts. He managed to sit upright. Through overflowing tear ducts, he saw Anna back away. He saw her look toward him for help.

Jess mentally formed a plan. The severe pain that occupied his entire being might be enough to cloud his thoughts from his mad twin. Using a mind-clearing technique, he blanked his thoughts further, reinforcing the loss of projection to his evil self.

Jess's wild gesturing at Anna behind his assailant's back caught her attention. Through stolen glances, she watched Jess remove his belt. She watched him rise and limp silently across the padded floor. She watched him wrap the ends of his belt tightly around each hand.

"You can quit lookin' at him darlin'. The wimp ain't any good to you now. You see, he's weak . . . probably passed out . . . couldn't take the pain."

The cessation of thoughts from his good side hadn't gone unnoticed by the doppelganger, who'd mistakenly assumed.

Reaching for Anna, he relished in her fear. "I'm gonna finish what *he* started, ya know."

Anna's unnatural scream froze in her throat. The madman was so close that she felt the blast of his putrid breath. Seeing Jess's features so wrought with evil greatly dismayed her.

Relying on his own hypothesis, the true Jess made his move. Suddenly appearing in her aft vision, he stealthly slid his belt over the unsuspecting head past the face to the neck, silently, deadly. Jess jerked back with all of the strength he could muster. The grisly noise filled their ears.

The skull's freshly fractured pivot point lacerated the spinal cord causing instant death. The tables thus turned, the newest victim crashed to the floor.

Jess and Anna's eyes met, both staring without seeing, their facial features distorted with the horror of it all.

"*Jess.*" Distress weakened Anna's voice. "Look what you've done! You *killed* him. She stared incredulously at the lifeless body lying in a crumpled heap.

Jess attempted speech with his mangled jaw. "Maybe not. Help me get him onto the dais," he mumbled, failing to be understood.

"*What?*" Anna managed to tear her gaze away from the lifeless body. "*Oh, Jess.* You're hurt *badly.*"

Jess bent down. With both hands he gripped his twin and began dragging him toward the elevated platform.

Anna interpreted his actions. Shaking herself, she rejoined the moment and aided him in dragging the lifeless body.

With his jaw hanging, Jess mustered his strength to pull one limp arm of the cadaver over his shoulder and singly hoist it to a standing position beside him on the dais.

"Stand back," he warned.

Anna remained panic-stricken. "*What?*"

Violently gesturing with one free arm, he staggered under the weight of his victim. Anna gasped. She reacted by stepping forward, but Jess managed to regain his balance.

Obeying his request, she stepped back. Again, she pressed her thumbs against her lips, and then moved her thumbs to speak. "Jess, I'm *afraid* for you."

Too late—her words fell on deaf ears.

Anna saw Jess look up as he and his burden were quickly engulfed in a column of pure white light. She staggered back, silently mesmerized by the scene before her. Seconds later, the light fell away. Jess stood on the dais alone—unmoving.

Anna rushed forward. "*Jess.*" He dropped his head from its upward fixed position to look at Anna and smiled. "*Jess.*" Anna laughed. "Your jaw. It's healed!"

Jess jumped off the dais landing directly in front of her. "*Oh, Jess.*" Anna wrapped her arms around the tall man. He returned her embrace.

Relief brought a cascade of tears. She spoke through sobs. "What happened?"

"Aw, Annie. *It's okay.*" Jess soothed her with a rocking motion as he brushed her hair gently away from her tear-soaked face. He waited for her sobs to subside. "Everything's fine now. Let's get the heck out of here."

His calm words helped to ease her frayed nerves. Jess reached for her hand and directed her toward the cave's faraway entrance that would now serve as their exit.

"I'll attempt to explain what I think's happening. It suddenly came to me on the dais."

Nearing the cave entrance, Anna sensed the lightness in Jess's voice and gait.

"So you see, if you can believe that thoughts are deeds, then it's been *my* thoughts all along that have been creating this turmoil surrounding us. Somehow, this place generates my thoughts into action—like when I was wishing for light and the glowing rocks appeared. Our thoughts are everything, Anna." Jess reasoned further. "They structure our entire lives. Now I understand the importance of controlling them—especially till we're out of here."

"I think I understand, Jess. But what about *my* thoughts?"

"That, I can't answer. Maybe it's just my turn. Maybe your time's coming—and, who knows when?" He squeezed her hand. "I'm just sorry I didn't catch on sooner."

Anna began reviewing her most recent thoughts. A small shiver traversed her. She felt great relief knowing they were safely tucked away in her brain's recesses—for the moment.

"But Jess, how could you have known?"

"Ah, the purpose of this lesson is to learn by experience. That's it—in a nutshell."

The intelligent display of reasoning through their predicament impressed Anna. It showed in her countenance.

Jess stopped and faced her. "I'm feeling somewhat confident about understanding our situation, Anna. Not the *who or what,* but the *when.* I think it all has to do with the beginning—not the evening we met, and not when each of us first noticed the crazy events happening around us . . . but the true beginning, when the Supreme Being created us—when our souls were born—when our minds turned on, so to speak—like all is meant to be. You follow me?"

Anna smiled and nodded at Jess's rambling, which he took for a yes and continued.

"Since the other morning, I've expected weird events to unfold, but I never in a million years expected my thoughts to be carried out." Jess's eyes briefly focused in the distance.

"Seems like a long time ago, dudn't it, Jess?"

"Anyway—" Jess sorted through his thoughts, "—it began with that sense of isolation—the cage. Then I assumed someone of authority would show up—Ahriman." Jess's tone softened. "And the unplanned kiss—my incessant desire for you."

Anna felt her face flush. "Jess . . ."

"Let me finish."

She began walking to hide the physical reaction of her emotions. Caught up in his personal synopsis, Jess failed to detect her emotional discomfort. He hurried after, fueled by realization.

"I—I was battling with my feelings for you—thinking that they were . . . well . . . *bad.* And even though that jerk back there was an ASPD case, he was still a part of me that I apparently can't live without. I trust that the good in me keeps him subdued."

"It does," Anna encouraged. "What's ASPD?"

"Antisocial personality disorder. Science thinks it's due to a faulty brain. Most victims begin showing symptoms in their youth. They may lack remorse and responsibility. They tend to be aggressive and deceitful. You've probably heard the term *failure to conform to the norm*."

"I'd say we all have the potential for ASPD."

"I'd have to agree. I've been mad enough to do the unspeakable. But something stops me. It's called a conscience. A few are born without one, for reasons unknown, but it happens."

Jess faced Anna. "Look. I said I haven't figured out why this is happening to us—not yet, anyway . . ." He took her hands in his, ". . . that is, *why* you and I are here . . . together . . . now." A smile played on his lips. Anna reacted with a shiver. "But I *do* know we *are* here together . . . now." Jess pulled Anna close. "And all that matters is *right* now. At this moment, you're all that exists in my world, Anna. I'm not ashamed or embarrassed to say I love you."

She knew he meant it.

"We're no longer in the past. We've been brought together for who knows what reason. Maybe it's as simple as being in each other's company. And who knows what lies ahead for us? But for now our immediate futures obviously lie together. It's the only explanation that makes sense. So why fight it?"

Ignoring her instinct to doubt, Anna clung to Jess's words.

"Our situation has changed," Jess rationalized. "*We've* changed. We can't take what we've learned on this journey and blow it off. Anyway, *I* can't."

Anna remained silent. Her contented smile was answer enough. This new enlightenment Jess spouted was foreign, but she would accept it as she accepted him. Once again, she felt comfortable with their relationship.

They continued walking toward the shining-star entrance. Jess began to softly hum, "Merrily, merrily, merrily, life is but a dream."

Spurred by sudden insight, he interrupted his song. "I think I know how to get us out of here."

"You do?"

"I have only to wish it, my dear."

"Then, whadda ya waitin' for? Wish it—*please*."

The cave opening was finally reached.

"Ah, blessed sunlight—even if it *is* dull. You know, it's possible this sun really provides no warmth at all, that our minds assume—like a phantom sensation hardwired into our brains."

Whether a phantom sensation or not, the two travelers managed to enjoy the familiar rays. Exiting the cave lent them both a surge of good expectations.

Surveying the immediate area, Jess hesitated. "Because my thoughts turn to deeds, I want to approach this cautiously. I must think carefully. There's so much to consider—like where to wish us to." Jess turned to Anna. "Any suggestions?"

Anna gave his question thought. The wrong decision could be disastrous. Consequences could result in separation. She shook her head. "No. You decide."

Jess returned to the same stony perch he'd previously occupied. So many changes had occurred since he'd last sat there. He was grateful they were inadvertently happy ones.

Anna wandered about silently while Jess thought out a plan. She seated herself at the southern base of a little sandy knoll to soak up the unnatural sunlight. If her brain was capable of receiving phantom sensations, she would willingly enjoy them.

At some point in his pondering, Jess turned to search for her. Spying her position, his eyes focused on the mound of sand looming behind her.

"Anna, don't sit there. I don't want us taking any chances. That sand pile behind you looks unstable."

The hill began to quake.

"Get up and come to me. *Anna*—get up *now*."

She started to obey, but the loose sand began to slide violently as the last word left his lips. She was buried in seconds.

"*ANNA!*" Jess jumped from his seated position and dove at the freshly formed pile. His hands dug like shovels, but more sand kept filling his efforts. He mindlessly dug, eventually gaining ground.

Three minutes without air at most, he recalled. *How long's it been . . . one or two?*

Jess dug frantically, whipping sand behind him.

There . . . one precious arm. He grabbed and pulled. *No good. Dig more. Another arm . . . Anna's face.*

Thank God. Am I in time?

He pulled Anna free. Her eyes were shut, dark lashes covered in fine granules. Limp and unconscious, he picked her up.

"Oh, God, no!"

Jess ran the short distance to the entrance of the cave. Anna's neck hung limply like the body of his counterpart. "Please, God. Don't take her from me now."

Bearing his burden, Jess ran the length of the tunnel. Hot tears threatened to impede his vision. Driven by his goal to save Anna, he blinked them back, concentrating on reaching the white star.

The frenzied young man ran up the white stairs, mounting them two at a time. Maintaining a dead run, he leapt upon the dais. He stood Anna on her feet to insure physical contact with the base. Encircling his arms beneath hers, he held her close, bearing her weight. His winded breaths blew her raven hair in wisps.

The dais had proved it could heal. But could it bring Anna back? Earlier, Jess had experienced an inner peace at his own reuniting. Confident that the part of himself—hate and resentment—wouldn't overpower him again, he proceeded with his only plan.

Glancing down, his unchecked tears fell upon Anna's precious face. The fear of discovering no breath kept his gaze from lingering.

He squeezed both eyes shut and found himself yearning for the tiny faraway cabin, and the soft feather mattress. He opened his eyes and looked up to find the white light surrounding them.

"Dear God, *please,*" he prayed, as hot tears coursed down his beard-stubbled face.

6

In Between

Jess awoke to darkness. His nose inhaled the musty odor of the old feather-stuffed mattress beneath his tense body. *We're back in the summer house,* was his first conscious thought. Sensing Anna's sleeping form beside him, he lay still, allowing his eyes to adjust. *Thank you, God.* His hand gently caressed her raven-black hair, but his movements did not disturb her.

How do I know what happened wasn't a crazy dream? His suspiciously stiff body racked with exhaustion was answer enough. *Will Anna remember when she wakes? What if she doesn't——or what if she also suspects the experience was a dream? Should I bring it up——or should I keep it to myself?* Jess yawned hard. *Guess I'll keep it to myself——if she doesn't mention it. Our experience did seem more for me than for her. In the morning I'll look for some tangible evidence. Then I'll base my decision.*

A sudden cramp in his right foot brought him out of his semi-conscious state. He reactively flexed it. *Ow. Welcome back to the real world.* The disoriented young man allowed himself to drift into exhausted sleep.

Early morning sun kisses warmed the faces of the two companions as they left the tiny one-room cabin.

Anna had awakened refreshed and in high spirits. Jess sensed an obvious difference in her attitude toward him but couldn't pin it on the events of the past night. She chattered amiably but didn't mention the supposed dream.

He kept his vow to remain silent. The lack of any trace of sand on himself or Anna led him to believe that the experience was meant only for him. *Some dream.*

Strong, golden rays continued to greet them through the surrounding stately oaks standing at attention indefinitely. After strolling a short distance through the trees, Jess abruptly halted.

Busy chattering and concentrating on the ground in front of her, Anna ran into him. "Jess, why'd you stop?"

Silence.

She walked around him. Shading her eyes with her hand, she looked up at his furrowed brow. He was staring ahead, mouth agape. "What is it?" Anna spun on her heels expecting the worst.

Isolated in the middle of the woods, a well-tended clearing yielded neat tidy rows of fully grown cannabis plants. Having gone to seed, they now stood on dry stalks.

Jess whistled softly. *"Would you look at that?* I've never seen a marijuana patch before. Wow. It's *huge.*"

Anna stood in awe. "Me neither. It looks ready for harvest."

Great care had gone into the cultivation of the money-making crop. The wet weather spring flowing along one side of the previously pastured field guaranteed each plant would be well endowed with leafy branches, bringing more to the bargaining table.

Jess envisioned night pickers taking advantage of the harvest moon since past. *Perhaps the privy party had wound up in the pokey, hence the unpicked pot patch.* He laughed inwardly at his newly created tongue-twister.

"*That's* the reason for the deserted cabin. It must've been home to the pot growers. Something, or *someone*—perhaps you and I— may have spooked them. Whatever the reason, they haven't come back—yet."

"Lucky us. Just the same, we'd better start watching for booby traps. We *are* susceptible, ya know."

Her partner nodded, his eyes still glued to the illegal crop.

Anna buried her hands under her arm pits to warm them from the chill that hung in the morning air. The promised cool front now occupied the region.

"You ever smoke the stuff?" she bluntly inquired.

Jess looked down at Anna with raised brows. Slightly embarrassed, he replied truthfully. "Well, yeah—in the ignorance of my youth. Strictly for entertainment, though."

Anna waited to see if he would share more. He didn't.

"I tried it once," she offered in her petite, shy voice, "under peer pressure, of course. Didn't much care for it—I mean, the loss of thought control and all."

The confession surprised Jess. His own embarrassment faded. "Yeah, well, negative experiences can teach us strong lessons."

Anna watched Jess study the crop. "Well? Are we gonna stand here lookin' at it all day?"

"N-o-o. But stay close—and keep your eyes peeled."

"*Yes, sir.* I don't have a problem with that. *No, sir.*"

"I'd bet money that the safest path is right down the middle."

"Why not backtrack—steer wide of the whole darn thing?"

"*Because* . . . we could run into more trouble. Let's try it my way. It's just a hunch."

Jess started forward. "Wait here. When I signal, follow *exactly* in my footsteps. So pay attention. Okay?" He turned without awaiting an answer.

"Huh," Jess murmured, moments later.

"What?" Anna demanded, believing he'd found something.

He looked back with a teasing smile on his lips. "I *can't begin* to picture you—"

"*Believe it,*" Anna returned smartly, cutting him off.

He wisely chose to end the conversation. Cautiously moving forward, he gestured for Anna to follow. She quickly caught up. "Wait here," he told her again and continued alone.

Anna heard Jess snicker.

"What's so *darn funny?*"

"You!" He looked back at her with a big grin. "I'm sorry, but I can't even—"

"Can you just drop it?" she asked, wishing she'd not been so quick to confess.

Jess squatted. Using a dry branch, he investigated the entrance of the tilled row covered with dried leaves directly in front of him. A loud snap startled them both. "*Whoa.* Ouch! A small animal trap—large enough to bite some toes. It's capable of damage—but not deadly. So much for my "safer-down-the-middle" theory." He further inspected the trap and slung it aside.

Undaunted by the discovery, Anna passed him with her own tree branch in hand.

"Hold up at the other end," he warned.

Jess stood and followed. He paused midway to examine some of the dry cannabis leaves still clinging to their stalks. The leaves crunched under pressure and drifted to the ground leaving a strong pungent odor on his fingers. *Probably good weed.* He attempted to wipe away the familiar odor on his jeans.

Past memories rushed in. *My old college buddy ought to be about due for parole. One missed party. It could have just as easily been me.* Jess shivered at his private thought. He saw Anna waiting for him.

She guessed that Jess was reflecting on his past and waited patiently. He eventually moved forward.

"Whacha thinking about back there?"

"Oh . . . past events that I probably shouldn't waste good brain power on." Anna chose to respect his privacy.

No more booby traps were found. The two left the clearing and the marijuana patch behind. Jess elected to leave his past as well.

The sullenness of his silence drew an inquiry from Anna.

"Now whacha thinking about?"

"If only we could see up ahead."

"You want to see up ahead? Climb a tree. That one looks good." She pointed at an ageless giant on the upper side of the clearing.

"Sure—if I were twelve."

"What? I can't believe I'm hearing that coming from you, Jess Parks. The day I can't climb a tree is the day I'll admit I'm *old*."

In the warmth of the midmorning sunshine, the majestic elm beckoned. Without another glance at her male companion, Anna ran toward it.

Slipping off her shoes, she set them neatly at the tree's base. Using her arms and legs, she shimmied up the trunk. A twelve-year-old couldn't have done better. She quickly gained access to the lowest lying branches, pausing only when the topmost limb capable of bearing her weight was reached. Seating herself in the fork of a branch, Anna looked down, grateful that she hadn't faltered under Jess's watchful gaze.

"You've obviously done this before. So how's the view?"

"Great." Anna scouted the surrounding area to gain a perspective of their location. Her chosen tree overlooked a pasture where several head of cattle grazed, taking for granted their clean, quiet country existence.

Jess stewed below. Anna's childlike behavior hadn't surprised him. "Mind if I join you?" he finally braved.

Anna giggled with pleasure. "Why, sir, I'd be delighted."

Jess warily approached the tree. *Piece of cake*, he thought, attempting to convince himself.

The observer remained silent not wanting to spoil the mood. Without being obvious, her eyes followed Jess's clumsy ascent, boots and all.

His excessive height aided him in gaining access to the lower limbs. Weaving his long, slender body through the upper close-knit branches made the rest of his climb slow and awkward.

Anna enjoyed every grunt and groan.

The climber arrived at a branch capable of supporting his weight below and across from Anna's perch. Swinging over one long leg, he hoisted himself into a sitting position and leaned his back against the upper main trunk. Slightly winded, he took a moment to recuperate. His breathing soon stabilized.

"So you do this often?"

Leaning forward to clear her view, Anna replied, "Only in cooler weather, when the critters hibernate—especially snakes."

Having witnessed his awkward ascent, Anna openly expressed her conclusion. "Being extra tall doesn't always seem convenient."

"True. On occasion, it is."

With the intention of witnessing her reaction, which always entertained him, he addressed her slightly negative observation. "I could say the same about being short."

Anna sat back, resting her head against the tree's trunk. She smiled inwardly. "Isn't it nice that we're both comfortable with our own size? So many people aren't."

Touché, he thought, but responded with, "Yes. It's nice."

Both grew silent while taking in the peaceful view. Too much distance yet remained between them and their desired destination.

"What makes you want to live in Arkansas, Anna? I know you grew up around here, but it isn't as though you don't have a choice."

"That's an odd question. Not only was I born here, but I happen to believe I live in one of the most beautiful places in the world." She felt compelled to explain further. "I've seen pictures of far away countries and very few rival the beauty and cleanliness of the Ozarks. What's so *all-fired* wrong with Arkansas, anyways?"

"Well . . . this state is known for being . . . a bit underdeveloped. I mean, what does it have to offer?"

"Plenty—if you like to breathe cleaner air, drink cleaner water, and eat fruits that grow in the wild without scrubbing them first. You can even eat the snow. Can you claim that where you live?"

Although his question referred to jobs and opportunities, an agreeable expression spread over his face. To Anna, his silence was answer enough.

Jess's roaming eyes searched the field below. A few blades of fescue that had escaped the last mowing waved softly, caressed by a gentle breeze, reminding him of Anna's shiny, black hair that now blew gently about her face. His lips formed a soft smile.

Lingering shades of yellow, red and orange belonging to the deciduous woods did their part in creating what was left of the spectacular fall scenery.

"It *is* beautiful, as you say—and noticeably so after living in a polluted city where the air is mostly smog, and drinking water is continuously recycled."

"You ever get tired of it?"

"I leave every chance I get."

"I see."

The actor cringed. *Nailed again.* "Touché," he whispered.

With sudden clarity, his mind flashed back to the forced kiss that had occurred in last night's dream. He recalled how Anna had wanted to respond, that split second of shared passion—the fire that had raged through his body. The memory warmed him now, and he blushed with it. He relished her confessed torment of his presence. *How had she put it . . . possessed by the thought of me day and night?* He shivered, despite the warm afternoon air.

A long silence passed between them. Anna broke it.

"Whacha thinkin' about?"

Her childish question startled him. "You ask that a lot. I'm actually taking advantage of the silence. I'm transcending."

"Sorry. I don't mean to be irritating. Did you say, transcending?"

"Yes, a form of meditation. I'm attempting to clear my mind."

"I see. What for?"

"You shouldn't interrupt someone's meditation."

"Oh. Sorry. I didn't realize."

"Of course you didn't. I'm the one who should apologize."

Jess's loud sigh stemmed mainly from frustration. *My desire for you is so strong, but I'll control it, Anna dear, for your sake.*

"So do you meditate a lot?"

"Yes, when I get the chance. Everyone should." Jess strained to peer at his audience of one through the branches. "It helps to create a closer relationship to the Supreme Being. It also helps to physically heal the body and relieve stress—which happens to be the number one killer of us humans. I think you'd enjoy it."

"Mmm, maybe."

Anna idly swung one foot. *I would gladly do anything you suggest, Mr. Parks.* Frightened that her thought could be construed as lustful, she immediately recalled her vow for purity. *What had Jess said about his own thoughts coming true? It could be my turn next. And who knows when?*

"Ever watch the Grammys?" Jess asked out of the blue.

Anna's defensive instinct kicked in. She answered cautiously. "Of course. We *have* television in Arkansas, as you've discovered."

He ignored the sarcasm. His goal was to quiz her for knowledge of last night's dream. Why the sudden closeness between them? Had she too experienced it? Her confession of being hounded by his existence had begun to eat at him.

"I only accept the invitation if I can't get out of it. Mostly, I use filming as my excuse. I'm not big on fancy galas. That's about all it means to me—a chance to strut your stuff."

The silence was suddenly loud. Birds chirped and a dog barked in the distance.

"When I was six," he continued, "Mom made me attend a dress-up birthday party. Most kids like parties. I hated it. Like I said, fancy affairs don't interest me."

"Mmm, me neither," Anna nodded, smiling enticingly.

A plucked dry leaf lying on her palm crunched as she closed her hand. She opened it and directed a breath at the bits and pieces which slowly scattered in the gentle afternoon breeze.

"Why?" Jess asked, confusing Anna.

"Why what?"

"Why do you watch them?"

He's baiting me, she perceived. *Does he suspect something? How could he know? Should I lie?*

"Uh, well . . ."

Anna took a deep breath. *I can't lie.* Her stomach fluttered. She took another breath, readying herself to speak, and then released the breath saying nothing. *How can I talk around this? Think, Anna, think.* She decided to answer with a question, tossing the ball back into his court.

"Why do you ask?"

"Just curious. You don't ask me about my career."

Anna returned the volley. "What *should* I ask?"

"Oh, you know," Jess intoned, "typical questions. How'd you get into acting? Do you like what you do? How much time do you spend on the set? Where do the episodes get filmed? What are your outside interests? Are you waited on hand and foot?"

Anna giggled upon hearing the latter.

Son, I love her laugh. "Believe me, that last one's a favorite."

The smile remained on her face. "Well?"

"Well, what?"

"Are you waited on hand and foot?"

"*I* don't think so. I have a maid in once a week."

"A maid . . . once a week," Anna repeated.

"Yes. She's Latino—a recent immigrant, I think—but she has a green card."

Anna giggled again.

"Very little English, mind you—mostly Latino."

"Can you communicate?"

"I've had a conversational course in Spanish, and she's tackling our language. We manage."

Reaching for another dry leaf, Anna tore it away from its lifelong hold. After staring at the palmate pattern, she closed her hand over its lifelessness changing its shape forever. The noisy crunch filled her ears. She blew at the debris.

How could she admit to Jess that she'd made it a personal ritual to sit through all televised award shows hoping to catch a live glimpse of his face—the face that haunted her innermost thoughts? How could she admit to this man that she didn't care about questioning his life, when she felt so complete having him near?

"It's funny how I've always felt like I know you." Anna made her comment without thinking her words through. She immediately realized her mistake.

His guard up, Jess immediately caught it. "Always . . . always? What do you mean, *always* felt like you know me?" The vivid dream-confession loomed largely in his head.

Too late. Anna cringed at Jess's demand for an answer. "What I *meant* was . . ." Anna stammered, ". . . that it's like I've always known you, Jess. That's what I *meant* to say."

"That's *not* what you said, Annie. You said, and I quote, "I've *always* felt like I know you. That's past tense."

Jess leaned away from the tree. Through the branches, Anna definitely looked alarmed.

"Were you thinking about me before I came to Arkansas?"

Anna watched the words leave his mouth and then defensively turned away.

"Out with it, Annie. What's going on? Do you know why I was sent here to find you?" Jess guessed by her reaction to his question that she didn't.

"No. No, *of course,* I don't know." Anna threw up her hands. "I don't know *what* to say, Jess. It's . . . it's as if . . . somehow . . . I know you . . . the inner you . . . as if I recognize your soul. I know it doesn't make much sense."

Jess knew Anna felt cornered. He backed off. "Nothing makes much sense these days. But it's up to us to *make* sense of it. At least you're trying."

"Jess, I don't *give a darn* about your career *or* your looks. It's what's inside you—what's in your soul that I care about."

Momentarily forgetting his precarious position, Jess attempted to stand. He wanted to be closer to Anna, to see her face, read her expression. He managed to steady himself.

"Jess, I don't know what to do . . . because I don't understand."

Sudden tears flooded her eyes.

Contemplating her words, Jess allowed his body to relax. "Me too," he replied.

The events of the past night, whether a dream or reality, had aided Jess in curbing his intense passion for the young woman. Now he was witnessing Anna's own passionate battle for him. He felt for her. But deep down, he was elated. This time when he reached out to touch her, he knew without doubt it wasn't rejection he felt rippling across her body, but a passion much like his own, so intense that it pained her.

The shiver that now convulsed her body from his hand caressing hers, he pretended not to notice. The barely audible moan that escaped through her parted lips, he pretended not to hear.

He didn't make his companion suffer long. "Let's be on our way, shall we? Tree sitting makes my bones stiff." Gentleness in his tone gave away the prodigious young man's lightheartedness.

More graceful in his descent, he quickly lowered himself through the thick branches. Anna followed suit, grateful for the end of their awkward conversation.

Relieved by the physical distance between them, she joined her partner in walking their unknown path.

By early afternoon, the morning ground fog had risen birthing huge popcorn clouds now scurrying across the crisp autumn sky. Cloud shadows came and went.

Anna shielded her eyes and studied the heavy white cumulus hanging directly above. Bits of its billowy composition protruded, forming a large puffed-cheek caricature with ferocious eyes. It spewed forth its quarrelsome breath as if clearing a path ahead.

Darker clouds to the south concerned her. "It could rain on us."

"Is that a definite maybe?"

Anna's breathing had grown laborious as she struggled to match Jess's long strides.

"Do you realize how hard it is for me to keep up?"

Jess halted. "Sorry. I keep forgetting. Sometimes my mind wanders.

You were saying?"

"Rain clouds mostly follow the water courses," she explained, looking southward. "I'm sure we're in the cave's vicinity because it's close to the river."

Staring up at her partner, Anna shielded her eyes from the sun. "Tell me, sir. Have you ever had to look up at anyone?"

Jess smiled. "Oh, a few basketball players maybe."

Anna didn't notice his smile fade. The violent physical battle with his sinister twin had suddenly entered his thoughts.

His partner's sudden excitement quickly brought him back. Twirling in circles, she cried, "This is it, Jess. We're *finally* here."

Familiar landmarks had begun to appear for the last thirty minutes, but she'd elected to remain silent and surprise him with the end of their trip staring them in the face.

"Look," she pointed ahead.

"I don't see anything."

"Your eyes deceive you." Anna kept her pace. "Come closer," she said, motioning with her head.

The two companions approached the cave's entrance. The mouth lay back in the shadows, dipping below ground level under chunks of glade rock hanging like camouflage drapes. Accumulated dead leaves blended in creating a perfect cover.

"That's it? I guess I was expecting something more. It isn't much to look at."

"Well?"

"Well?" Jess returned. "I don't think I'm ready to go in yet."

Anna's eyes narrowed. His words surprised her.

"Well, maybe we don't have to go inside. Maybe whoever directed us here will . . . show up."

Jess unconsciously rubbed his heavy five o'clock shadow while standing in the warmth of the true sun. He tipped his face to absorb its soothing rays.

"It's probably past noon," Anna deduced.

Jess avoided eye contact. Now that they had arrived, he was hesitant about their next move. He surprised her again by suddenly seating himself on the bare ground. Removing an orange from his coat pocket, he said, "Last one. Share it with you."

Anna sat, watching Jess dig into the skin of the orange with short, manicured, slightly soiled nails. She was puzzled by his mild reaction at finding the cave, the one thing they'd both so desperately sought. She decided not to push the matter.

"I don't see you in commercials. How come?"

Jess paused and looked at Anna. "That's because I choose not to," he offered, continuing to peel the orange.

"The reason being . . .?"

"For one thing," Jess stole glances at Anna while he proceeded with his task. "I believe in eating foods that nourish the body. That excludes currently popular fast food. And," he tossed the naked orange into the air and quickly caught it, "I don't use household chemicals, and I'm not much on material possessions these days. So why should I promote anything that I wouldn't use myself? That would be hypocritical."

"Are you implying that you don't care about money and prestige? Then why choose acting? I thought actors desired luxury."

"Lots do. Some don't. Not *this* one—at present.

"I actually became hooked on stage acting in college. I took a risk and changed my major from business to theatrics simply because I liked acting. It's all I wanted to do. You might say, it suits me."

"Yes, it does—suit you, I mean."

Jess nodded. "You finally did it."

"Did what?"

"You asked me a question about my career."

"Yes. I did."

Anna kept him talking.

"What kind of diet do you follow?"

"Oh, no processed foods—if I can help it. I eat fruit in the morning, and I watch my combinations—a basic natural hygiene diet, really. It's necessary to keep a balanced pH level. More alkaline is better. But in any diet, moderation is the true key.

"It's funny how a mother will go to great lengths to protect her children, but she doesn't give it a second thought to offer them candy or a hot dog or some other junk food on a regular basis." Jess finished peeling the orange and divided it, handing half to Anna. "All she sees is the pleasure on the child's face at that instant. A few hours later, when the child is reacting from the ingredients and giving her a hard time, she doesn't correlate the two. She doesn't picture her child lying on an operating table at the age of fifty—heart laid bare while doctors work to clear clogged arteries."

Anna detected a sudden bitterness in his words.

"My dad didn't make it to the operating table. He died young, in a matter of minutes—massive coronary. He had a lean build and mistakenly thought he could eat what he wanted. Mom couldn't bear life without him. She followed shortly after." Jess's jaw visibly tightened. "I watched her die of a broken heart."

He glanced at his traveling mate and thought, *Because of you, I now understand her behavior.*

The story saddened Anna. *No wonder he eats healthy.* She knew of death from her own parents. "Mine are gone too," she explained, "killed in a car accident shortly after Joel and I married. They never had the opportunity to enjoy their grandchildren."

Jess remained silent, wondering how the accident had occurred. Anna didn't offer further explanation. He let it go. *She'll tell me when she's comfortable.*

"At least they crossed over together," he offered.

Anna nodded.

The invisible clock ticked as the two ate their orange in the outdoor silence.

"Guilty," Anna suddenly admitted.

"Guilty for what?"

"All right, I *promise* to give my kids a better diet. That is, if I get the chance."

"It wasn't my intention to implicate you."

"*Oh, yes it was . . . and, well you should,*" she said, picturing Jess holding up the hot dogs on their first night together. "I'm not trying to be defensive, Jess. Anybody with common sense knows you're right. We don't live in the Dark Ages. These are modern times. Plenty of knowledge on proper diet and physical health exists. It's up to the individual to be smart about it. Heart disease is another major killer these days."

Stealing another glance, he made no further comment. Drawn even closer to Anna by her sudden burst of enlightenment, he felt that he'd intuited her wisdom correctly.

Anna rose and began to pace. Once, he caught her staring.

"All right, Anna, out with it."

His partner feigned ignorance.

"Silence won't work. I know you have something on your mind, so out with it."

"Well . . . there *is something*." She turned to face him, jamming her hands deeply into her pockets. She spoke softly. "Could we talk—specifically, I mean?"

Jess studied Anna, mentally noting her youthful appearance. *Maybe she wants to talk about us.* "Okay. Shoot."

"Not here." Anna's eyes suspiciously panned the immediate area. "Let's walk." With Jess at her side, she wouldn't have to look directly into his eyes while she further confessed to him. She waited for him to rise.

Tossing aside a piece of coiled rope he'd brought from the summer house, Jess followed Anna's lead, wishing she'd talk about something he wanted to hear. Butterflies tickled his stomach as they walked a short distance before her words finally came.

"I've decided not to keep this to myself any longer. What would you think if someone," Anna hesitated, searching for the right words, "loved you *so much* that they couldn't describe it? The truth is . . ." she took a deep breath, ". . . there's no explanation for these strong emotions I'm experiencing. Jess, I—"

"Annie—" he interrupted, wanting to sooth her awkwardness.

"No, Jess, let me finish before I lose my nerve. It's all so *strange* . . . watching you on the TV . . . and now, here you are—and we're developing a relationship I couldn't ever imagine possible."

Anna abandoned her shyness and looked up at Jess with eyes that matched the sky. Her earnest expression tugged at his heartstrings.

"At times, I honestly believed I'd see you—somehow, someday. Believe me. I've had some heated arguments with myself over that. Now, tell me that I'm not a crazy person?"

Jess moved to stop Anna's forward progress. He grasped her shoulders and shook her gently. "*Anna*. What're you telling me?"

She quickly looked away. "Can't you understand? What *I* want doesn't take priority. There're other people involved in my life. I have obligations. I *must* be fair to my family."

Her heavy emphasis kept him silent. Loosening herself from his grasp, she turned away.

The scene she'd made at the campfire flashed through his mind. *I can't argue with her. She has to come to her own terms.*

He took a deep breath. "What about being fair to yourself?"

"Honestly, I need to think."

At least she's beginning to share. "O—kay."

A fallen oak lay across their path. Anna straddled its trunk and sat. Jess eased himself to the ground, allowing the aged wood to support his tired back. He exhaled loudly.

Grass laden with chlorophyll struggled to live in spite of the cooler nights. Jess picked one of the few fresh blades and stuck it between his teeth, savoring the sweet juice. He turned toward Anna. A grassy blade stuck out of her mouth as well. They both grinned hugely at their similitude.

Leaning back on her hands, she exclaimed, "Ahh, for one night in my own bed." Jess murmured his accord.

Their silence grew lengthy, each deep in personal thought.

Anna spoke first. "Jess, what if—" She paused in her awkwardness. "—our developing relationship turns physical? What if all this soon ends, and we wind up returning to our normal lives? You know me well enough by now to realize that I can't live with that kind of guilt, and that I couldn't do such a selfish thing as leave my husband—not for anyone. I don't mean to imply that you'd ask me," she quickly interjected, "but where else can all this lead?"

"You told me that you love me."

"Yes, but I married Joel—before I knew you existed."

"Do you love him?"

Anna silently prepared her answer. "Of course. How can you live with someone for thirteen years and not love them? We have our own relationship—live in the same house—share the same kids."

"Let me rephrase my question. Are you *in* love with him?"

Anna stared without seeing. "We were kids when we first met," she began. "Joel wore this courtin' look. I haven't seen that look in a long time. Like most married couples, we've taken each other for granted." Anna defended Joel. "But he's a good man, a good father, and a good husband."

"Annie."

She sighed heavily. "*No*. Does that satisfy you? How could I be," she confessed, undermined by her need to be honest, "when I have such *intense* feelings for you?"

Drawing in a sharp breath, Anna studied Jess's profile. "I refuse to give in to my love for you, Jess. This is gonna end sooner or later. You'll go your way, and I'll go mine." A wicked sadness filled her, spilling over into her words. "I'll die a thousand deaths when we part," she said, assuming the inevitable.

"Then what's the point of your confession?"

"What can be gained by keeping it to myself? Besides, who better has reason to know than you?"

Jess attempted to sort through his own feelings. The rhythm of his heart had greatly increased. He reached for Anna who reared back in alarm.

"*Please* . . . don't. Your touch is too much for me." Her body shuddered outwardly. "Spare me the agony of refusing you."

He lowered his hand. The small spark he'd felt suddenly extinguished. His troubled eyes locked on hers.

"We'll always be together, Anna, no matter what." He touched his pounding heart. "I won't give up."

The restriction growing in his throat urged him into silence. He rose from his seated position. Gathering strength from his conviction, he walked away, leaving Anna alone with her morals.

His distraught partner watched him go. Hugging her knees, she silently prayed he was right.

The flashlight in Jess's hand investigated the dark recesses of the cave's empty chamber room. Anna lay on her stomach beside him. Jess spotted a black opening that might lead into the cave's depths.

He rolled over and sat up. "I don't get it. There doesn't appear to be anything here. I don't know what to think. If this turns out to be a wild goose chase—"

"Hey, you're doubting yourself. Quit it."

Jess groaned. "This is *so hard.*" He ran his long slender fingers through his lengthy locks.

"What's hard? The hard part's over. Now we sit and wait."

"No. That *isn't* what I mean. What's hard is remaining detached from my emotions."

"Then let's talk—to pass the time." She copied Jess rolling over and sitting up Indian style.

He looked at her, mildly surprised. After considering her suggestion, he said, "All right, we'll talk."

Scratching at his scruffy beard, he noticed Anna's smile. "It's itching," he confessed.

"So what do we talk about?" he inquired, not wanting to get started on an uncomfortable subject.

"Want to talk about yourself?"

"Nope. Do you want to talk about *yourself?*"

"No . . ." Anna trailed.

More silence.

After a period of contemplation, Anna finally began. "That first morning when I saw my own image, I thought my soul had somehow slipped out of my body, like those life-after-death stories. And remember when I told you I tried to get back into my body, only it didn't work? I came to realize that *I* occupied space, and my double occupied space," Anna studied a fingernail, "but we couldn't occupy the *same* space. My twin couldn't see me. It's like I was a ghost. But when I bumped into her, she felt it happen."

She waited for Jess's response.

He recalled the airport passengers running into him. "But oddly, we aren't ghosts to each other.

"I've read about near-death experiences," he continued. "It's surprising how many have been recorded, and those who'd described their stories pretty much concurred. But I personally believe when we die, the veil of protection is lifted. When we review our lives, the blinders come off. We recognize our wrongs even though we may deny them to our last breath."

Jess grew quiet. He gingerly moved his hand over Anna's, watching her shiver. This time she didn't pull away. Instead, her eyes remained fixed on his. He saw in them what a man might fantasize seeing in the depths of his lover's eyes: adoration, respect and desire.

Again Anna broke the spell. She rose to her feet. Her delicate features grew thoughtful.

"Maybe we're getting a glimpse of heaven."

Jess was disappointed and sorry that the moment had ended so abruptly. But he accepted it.

"I'm leaning toward ruling out a parallel universe. Because if that were the case, there should be more people on this side. We would've made an even switch with our counterparts, possibly never noticing the difference. No, it's something else."

"Point taken. Maybe we *are* on the side of the dead. However, we don't run into many ghosts. But I truly believe we aren't dead. Maybe we're stuck—in between."

"I can't debate that. But for what purpose?" Jess mostly asked himself, staring at nothing.

Moments later, he rose and busied himself, clearing ground and building a campfire. The sun had traveled most of the sky, leaving them in the deep shade of the surrounding trees. The air had cooled. A fire was needed for warmth while they waited.

Once the fire was going to his satisfaction, he seated himself near Anna, anticipating the comfort of her closeness. Her presence helped break the monotony of having little to do—totally opposite of his accustomed lifestyle.

"Do you really believe in God?" she abruptly asked.

It felt like a trick question. *Now what does she have in mind?* Jess answered cautiously. "Last time I checked—a Supreme Being, anyway. Don't most people?"

"Don't humor me."

"Ouch!" Jess's face lost expression. He blinked innocently.

"I'm serious, Jess. Do you believe Jesus was the son of God?"

"*Is* a son of God," Jess corrected. "We're all sons *and* daughters. You, me—"

"Well . . . yes, but *you* know what I mean. Do you believe that he carried a message for God?"

"Jesus *was* God—manifested in human form, Anna. 'I and the Father are One' . . . remember?"

Anna rolled her eyes. "That's not how I learned it."

"I haven't continued to attend church and bible studies like you have. I prefer the spiritual path. It's more comforting to me."

"What about Satan? Do you believe he exists?"

Jess tipped his head to one side and studied Anna through squinted eyes. This question he knew would require a thoughtful answer. She patiently awaited his reply.

He picked up a few pebbles and tossed them at nothing. "I believe in evil. I hear of it in the news every day—reports of individuals insanely killing or abusing their own family members for irrational reasons, terrorist factions bombing innocent bystanders to force their beliefs on others. War, child abuse— Shall I go on?"

Anna's hand encircled Jess's bicep. His muscles were tight with tension. He looked at her quizzically. The tension began to flow from him as he studied her intent expression.

He released a sigh. "So what's your point?"

"Those evils you named are the obvious wiles Satan conducts. What about the not-so-obvious wiles?"

"Okay, Annie. What're you getting at? You think we're dealing with Satan?"

"I think we should consider the possibility." Anna's eyes reflected the small campfire beautifying her countenance.

"You're dead serious!" Jess concluded.

"What if we're being duped—being led by the dark side?"

Her own words frightened her.

"Annie, I want to encourage you to stop thinking of Satan as having red skin, horns, and an arrow-tipped tail. Remember, Satan's an angel—a fallen one, I'll give you that, but an angel nonetheless." Jess sighed. "I believe we create our own evil and our own good."

He waited for his advice to sink in. "You're a victim of mindless conformity, Anna. You're allowing religion to tell you how to think— how to live."

Anna was shocked by Jess's admonishment. "Your opinion doesn't matter," she snapped. "*I'm* comfortable with it."

"How can you not question what is being taught to you?"

"What do *you* know? You *said* you no longer attend church."

"Anna, I go to church every day . . . in here." He pointed to his heart. "God isn't in a building or in a song book. He's right here . . . within us. Attending church isn't going to get you into the Kingdom of Heaven. You have to get yourself there. For the Kingdom lies within . . . remember?"

Anna looked abashed.

"You've read your Bible, haven't you?"

"Of course. I'm sure I've read it all by now. My Sunday school class studies all the books individually."

Jess continued. "I'm concentrating on the words Jesus spoke. He never told anyone that they would die and burn in hell forever. Spirituality teaches that Jesus meant his words to be symbolic. Most people misunderstand."

"And how did you come to determine this?" Anna suddenly felt less inclined to be defensive.

"I've studied spiritualism. We're all spiritual beings. You do agree, don't you?"

She contemplated her answer, ready to defend her beliefs. "I suppose."

"It appears to me," Jess continued, "that the basic problem is most people aren't taught spirituality. Many haven't learned how to think for themselves. Their thoughts get dictated to them all their young lives by others with narrowed vision. Well, I for one, refuse to be dictated to. My spiritual studies have taught me to think for myself. And that's how the Supreme Being intended it. His gift to us is free will, is it not?"

Anna stewed on his words. "But why would a church teach its members incorrectly?"

"They don't purposely do it. It gets passed on like a bad habit. Do you realize how many times the Christian Bible has been revised? Books have been purposely left out; congregations split due to disagreements, over and over—all in the name of God. It's funny how He gets the credit for religious divisions, when humans should be crediting themselves. Look, you *must* know that your religion's Bible isn't the same as the Catholics'. It isn't the same Bible that Muslims follow, or Jews, or any of the other western Christian religions. Do you think you can convince any of those organizations that their religion is wrong . . . and only yours is right? And do you think that they'll *believe* you? I say *good luck with that*."

"Why do you believe God would allow such misunderstandings to occur?" she asked.

"Perhaps it's the Supreme Being's way of allowing us to be different. By all means, stick with your religion if it gives you comfort. I don't mean to imply church is bad or religions are wrong. What I'm implying is . . . there's more.

"It's my opinion that the best part about organized religion is it gives folks a sense of connectedness. It keeps them from fearing the unknown. People need to know they have a future even after death. Without that sense of security, I strongly believe that there'd be great anarchy.

"The fault lies in materialism. It's hard to conceive that you can't take it with you. God—or Allah—or Yahweh—or Krishna—or whatever you choose to call the Supreme Being—isn't in a material place. Heaven isn't material. If it were, our bodies wouldn't die.

"If Satan existed now in physical form, then it'd mean he's incredibly old—or living, dying, and reincarnating repeatedly. Neither possibility makes sense according to your Christian doctrines because agelessness defies the laws of nature. And— right or wrong—reincarnation is not a Christian belief. Yet, the idea of his presence is taken for granted." Jess hesitated. "Satan *is* our evil deeds—our wrong thoughts, Anna. That's all he is to me."

Anna no longer felt that Jess was attacking her beliefs. Rather, just the opposite. Did he not tell her to believe what she felt comfortable with?

"Interesting point of view you have there. So why do you refer to God as the Supreme Being?"

"Two reasons. The first one being that I do it out of respect for those who choose to believe that God is either female or of no sex. And second, because the Supreme God shouldn't be confused with other gods."

"What other gods? There aren't any other gods," Anna insisted.

"Did I not mention a Catholic God, a Muslim God, and a Mormon God, etcetera, etcetera? There's also those gods mentioned in the Book of Genesis."

Speaking calmly, Jess looked directly into Anna's eyes. "I believe I heard you say you've read the Bible? How could you miss the mention of the other gods?"

"You're awfully knowledgeable about religion," she remarked.

"Does that surprise you? It's part of knowing thyself. Actually, I've read more than the Holy Bible."

Anna's brow rose. "You've read the Bible?"

"Cover to cover," Jess admitted. "This is how I see it. People can spend their entire lives refusing to waste time on religion and take a chance that when they die, there's nothing else. They merely cease to exist. The opposite scenario is that there's actually an afterlife unbelievers haven't prepared for. My gut tells me those who pass believing in the Supreme Being will pass easier than those who don't. Personally, I truly believe."

The lovely Anna listened intently. Jess briefly wondered how much of his philosophy she might accept, her beliefs being so different from his own.

He continued. "It's true we humans are our own worst enemy because we fear unnecessarily. For example, think of how much fear we possessed as children, believing in the proverbial monster under the bed. As adults, we realize there *was no monster*. That was unnecessary fear. It's what we constantly do throughout our lives—fear what never comes about. *This* is what we need to learn to control. In hindsight, our personal problems have a natural way of working out, and if we can remember that, then we can let go of fear. Having come this far in your life, you do agree, don't you?"

The expression on her face told him she did.

"You're a ball of fire, Annie. You have great potential. I sense it. I could help you learn *so much*. Won't you let me teach you what I know? The truth will make you free." His gentle smile was meant to tempt her. "Think about it. I promise I won't lead you astray. Knowledge leads to wisdom. It's our greatest gift. Ignorance is the enemy." Jess shrugged. "Decide for yourself."

Silent in thought, Anna kept her seat on the ground, arms wrapped about her legs and chin resting on her knees. Jess certainly surprised her with his beliefs and knowledge. She'd never experienced the presence of an advanced spiritual follower. It was all new. Despite his revelation, her opinion of him did not change. Instead, it grew even stronger.

Jess rose and checked the campfire. He approached the cave's mouth and turned to Anna. "I want to have a look. I won't go far." As he worked his body into the chamber room's small yawning hole, he carefully examined the narrow tunnel ahead with his artificial light source. A musty odor permeated the air, reminding him of wild animals. *I neglected to inquire about the possibility of bears.*

7

Transmutation

Anna peered into the inky blackness of the cave. No sign of Jess's flashlight. *He must have gone further in.* She softly called his name, assuming that the sound of her voice would carry.

"Right here, Anna. There's a bend in the tunnel ahead of you. I found another room. Want to take a look?"

"I'd have to feel my way. It's pitch black."

"Wait a second— *Son*. Where's that *light* coming from?"

"What, Jess?"

Peering ahead, his cramped body froze. The abrupt change from the purest of black to the purest of white overwhelmed his shrinking pupils. He struggled to focus, shielding his eyes with his arm.

The recurring dream suddenly materialized before him. Gone was the violet mist. In its place, a shining blue aura radiated outwardly, highlighting the familiar tall, slender form that gently shadowed a perfect face. Her brilliant snow-white gown shimmered as though it were a living thing.

"Greetings, Jess. My name is Merry." A pleasant tinkling resonance that Jess took for laughter filled the confined volume of the naturally formed cave.

Jess regarded the sublime personage. He feared speaking lest the apparition should fade.

"I know you have many questions, Jess Parks. All are warranted, and all will soon be answered."

Merry's brief address was meant to ease her abrupt appearance, but Jess remained frozen.

"You may lose your caution. There is no evil here . . . unless you bring it with you." Again, the tinkling laughter intended to lighten the moment.

Her name matches her demeanor. Jess found his voice. "No Ma'am, no evil here." He sought to verify his recent experience. "When I passed out in my bathroom . . . *you* were in my dream."

"Correct. I simply appeared within your subconscious."

The female apparition's long, golden tresses glistened and moved with her.

Transfixed by the living image before him, Jess managed to break the spell and brave a simple question.

"*Why?*"

"*Why?*" Merry returned in a soft soprano, her warm smile hinting at amusement.

"*Why everything?*"

"Dear Jess, remember your spiritual studies. Do not allow yourself to be overwhelmed. Flow with your experiences and learn from them— even the difficult ones, for *they* teach the most. Absorb each lesson. Always expect the best. If you follow these guidelines, your soul's journey will be joyful and simple."

The excessively tall man squeezed himself out of the tunnel's perpendicular shaft and stood before his hostess on the cave's earthen floor.

"I'm sure that's good advice, Merry, but I've come a long way, and I haven't a clue about what's going on. Would you please enlighten me?" he politely asked.

The lady in white hesitated as if pondering his request. She peered over his shoulder into the darkness beyond. "Pardon me, but your companion approaches."

Jess reversed the flashlight. Rounding the corner on hands and knees, the unexpected vision of Merry halted his female partner's forward progress.

"No time to be bashful." He reached in and pulled Anna out, grunting through the effort of maneuvering in the confined space.

Fatigue caused him to exhale heavily before beginning a proper introduction. "Anna, this is Merry. And from what I gather, she's been expecting us."

"Greetings, Anna Adell." Merry's tinkling laughter created a pleasant echo.

Anna gawked. The vision of her partner's detailed dream stood before her. "Ow!—greetings," she returned after Jess's elbow connected with her upper arm.

Both noted that their hostess had addressed them by name.

"Come." The simple command caressed their waiting ears. Merry turned and moved into the blue-hued light that consumed her shimmering spirit before their watchful eyes.

Desperate for answers, they stared at each other questioningly.

Too tired to protest, Jess shrugged. "Like she said, let's go with the flow." Taking Anna's small hand, he moved to follow Merry.

The brilliant light they entered had no visible source. On the other side, the trio stepped out into a large spacious room. More multi-hued lights danced on white walls.

Anna registered surprise. "This looks a lot like that other place."

Jess's emotional reaction could not at first be defined. Suddenly, his dark brown eyes seemed capable of piercing steel.

"*And what other place would you be referring to?*"

Anna exhaled through pursed lips. Closing her eyes, she remained silent.

"*Anna?*" Jess waited.

"*Well!* I was too embarrassed to talk about it. Besides, I thought I dreamed the whole thing."

A forced countenance controlled his response. "So our journey to Gray Land really happened. And you allowed me to go on believing it was a dream."

"*Jess,* I'm *sorry.*" Anna averted her eyes in the manner of a naughty child.

Jess's chaotic thoughts reeled with activity. Tight-lipped, he said, "Never mind. Let's just concentrate on the present, shall we?"

Merry addressed Jess, reminding them both of her presence. "Why fuss with your true mate so?"

Stunned by Merry's words, the companions eyed each other. "True mate?" they chorused.

Merry knew of their conflicting emotions.

"Two deeply attracted souls—spiritually drawn together in past lives experiencing a combination of relationships, mother and daughter, father and son—or lovers. Many combinations come about for the purpose of gaining enlightenment. Do you not sense a mysteriously strong bond?"

Jess easily comprehended the concepts Merry spoke of. A light suddenly turned on. He faced Anna. His mood swiftly altered, indicative of his tone. "*Now* I understand. *And . . .* I might add that I'm *not displeased.*"

"So, Merry, would I be correct in assuming that Anna and I had karmic lessons to complete in our present lives before we could again be together?"

Balanced precariously on the edge of the desired reply, Jess felt as though the profundity of her answer might save or destroy him.

Anna digested Jess's question. Before their spirit guide could respond, she asked one of her own.

"What about my family?"

Jess fidgeted at the reminder of Anna's family obligations. The brown eyes-of-steel returned. Why would his true mate so carelessly dash his spirits?

"Do not stress over Anna's morals, Jess. It's a highly regarded quality of her character—an honor to the One."

"Anna, dear . . ."

Uh oh. She cringed against any personal exposure, and her partner's glaring eyes.

Merry read her fear. She spoke soothingly. "Dear Anna, Jess is correct. You must learn to accept change—a difficult lesson for many earth-bound souls."

Merry attempted a more general concept. "When a loved one chooses to make the transition from life to the spirit, is it not for the living to find the strength to let them go? We are nothing but a sea of souls—God's companions—entangled in our woven webs of experiences crossing paths hither and yon."

"Anna, you are needed for another purpose. Do not fight it. Flow *with* it."

Merry's voice and mannerism reminded her of Glenda, Oz's good witch of the North. She suspected that this fair lady addressing them was simply playing a part.

Anna spoke openly. "Honestly? . . . I've occasionally felt helpless about controlling the outcome of my life. But how do we know what our true path is?"

"Destiny is not controlled. *You* create your destiny with the gift of the Omnipotence—free will. Each soul comes into its new life with self-chosen lessons. God has nothing to do with your experiences. However, the One will guide you—if asked—through the voice within. Listen to and heed the inner voice, the voice of your God, Anna, and your Supreme Being, Jess. The Omnipotence will not steer you wrong. Each individual's past, present, and future are known by the One because the past, present and future *are* one."

"If I've lived other lives, why can't I remember them?"

"The veil of protection is a blessing. For you, Anna, it was lifted when you caught your first glimpse of Jess. Your subconscious recognized your true mate, not by his appearance, but by his mannerisms due to the many lives you have consecutively shared.

"In life, the veil is necessary. Imagine if everyone experienced the same, recognizing past friends and relatives and finding it impossible to be with them."

"It's *awful*." Anna looked at her mate. A slight shiver traversed her small form.

Jess's shoulders suddenly relaxed. He was deeply moved by the years of emotional torment reflected in her eyes.

"The veil also shrouds what we've chosen to learn in this life, for we choose our lessons before we enter the body. And that is how fate comes into play."

Merry dipped her frame and bid her charges to follow. She led them down a simple hall. "My solid form that you see before you is for your benefit. It grows weary."

"Yes, we are still in the cave."

Jess was startled. Merry had read his thought—and answered it.

"In this plane, thoughts are one." Merry glanced back at her charges. "It takes time to become reaccustomed to the practice."

Jess burned with curiosity. "Exactly what do you mean when you say *this plane?*"

"This particular plane is the threshold between life and spirit. It's been given many names."

"Why this threshold?"

"Your flesh-and-blood bodies can not pass through permanently. The spiritual plane is purely ethereal."

"You mentioned that in this plane, thoughts are one. So why can't Anna and I read each others thoughts?"

"In your case, it was deemed unproductive. Think about it."

Jess acknowledged her comment with a simple nod.

"But what about the other night . . . that place with the cage?"

"Ah, yes, a purgatory created by the Grays themselves. An in-between plane entered after death meant to purge the soul of its earthly sins so that it may enter heaven and avoid hell. They sensed your presence and came for you believing that you were meant to join them."

"I'm familiar with Purgatory. Then the Grays put themselves there." The idea repulsed Anna. "Will they ever get out?"

"Yes, they placed themselves there because they choose to believe in Purgatory, but they may leave at any time to seek more pleasant places."

Merry hesitated and turned to face her guests.

"You see, our thoughts are everything. We create with our thoughts no matter in which plane we find ourselves. Those souls will remain there until they believe otherwise."

Jess was sharply reminded of his own good and evil thoughts becoming actions.

Anna voiced her concern. "Can't they be reasoned with?"

"Can you be reasoned with, dear Anna?" Merry returned, smiling sweetly.

Touché, she thought, borrowing her partner's preferred cliché, momentarily forgetting the others could hear.

Jess and Merry made eye contact, smiling knowingly.

"The living are childlike. They must experience before they are convinced, hence life's lessons—the hard way," Merry explained, as her company trailed after.

Instinctively, Anna sensed that it was intended for her to ponder her own questions. The memory of an earlier conversation with Jess about religion outside of the cave surfaced. *Maybe he's right. Perhaps the most profound spiritual knowledge has been made less of—and I've truly allowed others who're also victims of lost knowledge to direct me through my life—the blind leading the blind . . . That or—*

Anna felt Jess watching her. She grew aware of their linked hands and felt his sudden squeeze. Looking into understanding eyes, she chose to suppress her doubt—for the moment.

"Where do the lights come from?" Anna asked, watching their hypnotizing dance across the intensely white walls as if they possessed a mind of their own.

Merry answered with her mind instead of her voice. *They would be our thoughts*, she conveyed.

"What generates their colors?"

Explain to her, Jess, the hostess conveyed to her male guest.

The thought transference felt awkward. Jess chose to verbalize his theory.

"It's said that all of the colors of the light spectrum, when brought together, form pure white—hence, perfect thought."

The radiantly flowing attire worn by their guide impressed upon them her own innocent purity.

"So the colors imply impure thought," Anna deduced.

Again, Merry signaled Jess to respond.

"Well, not so much impure—more like random thought which boils down to a matter of free choice. Realistically, humans aren't capable of thinking in a pure and orderly fashion."

"Let us experiment." Merry searched their puzzled faces. "Hum the word "one" in your mind."

Anna and Jess joined her telepathically. The three maintained the musical note creating one long syllable. The colors disappeared. The wall was now a brilliant white. The joy of it put smiles on their faces. The spiritual guide ceased to hum. The wall remained white without her accompaniment. But as soon as Anna and Jess broke the chant and resumed their thoughts, the colors began to return. As more time passed, more colors appeared.

"*Son*. This is *great*. We can now monitor our thoughts, Annie."

Anna glared at Jess. "Should you be using that *word* in here?"

Jess felt his face redden.

Merry's laughter tickled their ears. "I take no offense at words, Anna. Jess merely uses it as an expression of surprise."

Merry moved forward. "Let us continue."

The scenery before them opened yet into another white room. Plush white carpet lay beneath their feet. A comfortable white sofa sat in front of a lit fireplace built into a white wall. The orange and red flames greatly contrasted.

"*So much white*," Anna voiced.

Merry's graceful hands hovered like two peacefully coexisting doves. "This symbol of spiritual purity allows the mind to use its creative imagination more effectively. Fire is also a form of purity."

"Please, be seated." Their advisor sat opposite the two.

"So we aren't dead." The realization relieved Jess.

"Your permitted spirit forms allow your presence here. However, you continue to witness your material bodies to cause you less confusion. This also follows death to provide a less traumatic transition to the afterlife."

"So any physical pain we experience in this plane isn't real."

"Correct. It's carried over from your physical existence—a trick of the mind—ghost pain, as Anna calls it. Your brain sees it and convinces you to experience it."

"And I assume that our physical perfection is also temporary." Jess awaited her response.

Anna impatiently interrupted. "When will we go home, Merry? We *are* going home, aren't we?"

The stunning spirit's smiling blue eyes matched her pleasant demeanor. She perceived that of the two, Jess was most patient and therefore elected to address Anna first.

"Be patient with your journey home, Anna dear. There are yet more lessons to absorb."

Anna's sharp pause cued Jess to direct another question at his extraordinarily beautiful hostess. "And your present composition is only temporary?"

"It is for your benefit—until our communication is complete. Except for brief moments, I've always existed in spirit form. My material appearance is tolerable for short intervals—even somewhat pleasant— though existing in free spirit is much less cumbersome. I have not experienced life on Earth."

Merry in turn studied the earnest expressions of her guests. There again came the tinkling laughter. "But we are not here to discuss *me*."

"Exactly what *are* we here to discuss?" Jess asked.

"Why you have journeyed here, of course."

"Great! This is what I've been waiting for—to find out what this is about." Jess's facial expression revealed his relief. "Forgive me, but it's been difficult to accept. *Okay*. So first, why Arkansas?"

Merry's eyes traveled from Jess to Anna. Jess followed her gaze and understood the answer.

"Why this cave—and why us?"

Again Merry laughed, gesturing with outstretched arms. "It is all for the Way. Few know to seek the true Way. It has been all but forgotten in your bustling world. I am simply here to remind you that the Way is God's spiritual communication with the living."

"Oh, *I* get it. Jesus *is* God's communication line—to us." Anna looked pleased with herself. "It must have to do with him saying, 'I am the way, the truth, and the life—'"

"*One* of God's communication lines . . ." Jess interjected.

Anna glared at her true mate and finished quoting her scripture. "—no man cometh unto the Father, but by *me*."

Caught up in the revelation, Merry overlooked her guest's discord. Her eyes danced with excitement.

"Many have neglected the spiritual aspect. They need to be reminded that God is all. From God we stem and to God we shall return, taking with us our collective knowledge. There is nothing more and nothing less."

Jess gave Merry a look of understanding.

"Humans are too material-minded. They no longer remember that they are spiritual beings who should be striving for wisdom and knowledge, not possessions. To gain through devotion, diligence and aiding your fellow man is what they should be concerned with."

"There is a loss of communication with the Creator. Because the One is within us, we must be still and listen. The Omnipotence will guide us through our lives perfectly—if we listen. It is the promise."

Merry's audience remained attentive.

"The chosen are messengers sent by God to remind us of our true origin. It was told by them—Christ, Buddha, Mohammad, and others—that the Kingdom is in the midst of the people. The Kingdom is within each of us. "Seek first the Kingdom within." The more we attune ourselves with the One, the more perfect our thoughts will be—like the chosen."

"Wow," Jess said. "It's beginning to make sense."

"Advocacy without understanding is a lost cause. So it is with utmost importance that the chosen revitalize the true Way."

"And so we come to the question of *why* you two are here. We seek those souls who are content to serve others. To be in service to others is the true purpose of the living."

Anna spoke. "I *knew* this had something to do with God."

It was Jess's turn to sting. "You at first thought that it had something to do with Satan."

Anna now found herself the embarrassed one.

Merry attempted to sooth her guest's freshly bruised ego. "Do not fret, Anna. Jess was correct when he said that good and evil are products of the mind. You can choose not to have anything to do with your Satan. Those people who become involved with evil do so willingly out of desire for gains—power and wealth, for instance. Needless to say, gains based on greed do not transition well."

"For what is a man profited, if he shall gain the whole world, and lose his own soul?" Anna quoted.

Jess nodded his agreement. *She does know her scriptures.*

"What occurs in an individual's life is to be learned from. The most is gained from long-suffering. Strong lessons in life advance the spirit— if the soul is willing, of course. Not every soul possessing a human body advances. Some souls regress—fall back, thus long-suffering may inadvertently aid in enlightenment. Souls will progress much faster when they learn to be still and listen to the still, small voice within."

"So why do good people have to suffer?"

"Suffering creates compassion, Anna dear. Can a man who has not suffered truly offer compassion?"

Merry continued, blue eyes on blue. "It is best to pay debts before leaving the earth plane—else they greatly increase in the form of Karma—an eye for an eye, so to speak. Those who commit wrong acts in ignorance are considered innocent, whilst those who purposely commit wrong acts are not. It is that simple."

"But many that are first shall be last; and the last shall be first," Anna again quoted from the Holy Bible.

The enlightened apparition addressed her guests. "This refers to the outcome of human haughtiness and arrogance. A defensive attitude is costly. Those who place themselves before others may find that the repercussions are not worth a so-called *moment-in-front* once their transition comes about. The problem being it is then too late. And so you have the wailing and gnashing of teeth."

"But how can *any* church—" Anna paused in her question, studying Jess's reaction, "—fail to teach God's word correctly?"

"Church is not negative, Anna, but it must be kept in perspective. Some denominations have become too dogmatic, too material-minded, forgetting the true Way. Branching off occurs from disagreement. This is the fault of the human ego."

Once again, Anna quoted, "Beware of false prophets which come to you in sheep's clothing . . ."

The male presence rolled his eyes. *Here comes her negativity again.* Jess marveled at their spirit guide's patience.

"The chosen have always proven easy to recognize," Merry quickly retorted. She silently addressed Jess, and then awaited his reaction. He closed his eyes and bowed his head. Mission accomplished. She had given him a different perspective toward Anna's impressive knowledge of the New Testament. He lifted his chin and conveyed his understanding with a simple nod.

"How come Jess is always right?"

"I'm not always right, Anna."

"Jess studies the Way and the truth," Merry offered.

"And I reckon I haven't." Anna's tone reflected resignation.

Merry addressed them both. "Know this. Everything learned is a form of enlightenment. It does not have to be religion-based. Each soul advances at its own pace. Take what has befallen you and use it as a guide. You are seeking the truth—which is what we all seek. Look within and determine for yourself. You are now reminded of the knowledge you possess and therefore are no longer ignorant."

The spirit guide paused, allowing her words to soak in. "The mind is everything. It houses our conscience, our soul. We sculpt it with our knowledge. The Way aids our progress."

"I'm still not understanding *why us?*"

"Again, Jess, the two of you have existed under the veil of protection given to all souls seeking to inhabit this planet. Due to the veil, you have been unaware of your part to help spread the true Way. I'm simply here to remind you. This you will soon come to fully understand. Your role is to help those souls in need. Believe it. You and Anna chose this role as I chose mine.

"Now, back to Jess's assumption. As I mentioned previously, you are spirits taken leave of your human bodies. Once removed from the physical plane, you left behind human imperfections. When you reenter, you will find yourselves exactly as before."

Anna wore her disappointment. Merry sensed the reason.

"If you are unhappy with your physical self, Anna, work to change it. Perfecting your mind and spirit will allow your body to respond in a like manner—for the body, mind, and spirit are one. However, when you follow the Way, you will experience such inner peace that vanity will no longer be a part of your makeup."

"What about my family . . . Joel, and the children?"

"Situations change. Variations are a large part of the Way. That's how God experiences—through us. Know that your children and your husband are also individual souls, and that they too have their own purpose to fulfill. We are *all* enfolded in God's love. Think not of tomorrow, for tomorrow will care for itself."

"So, in effect," Jess interpreted, "what you're saying is . . . love the one you're with."

"Always," Merry acknowledged with a gentle smile.

Her angelic eyes studied the two seekers. "This cave was chosen as a portal. It is close to Anna's home, and even though it is secluded, Anna knew of its existence. And as for you, Jess, we felt it best to distance you from your make-believe world of the performing arts, and your more luxurious lifestyle, and to place you in a more common setting—somewhat like your childhood."

"You're speaking for others," Jess noted. "Who are *we?*"

"*We* are a collective group of souls gathered in the higher spirit realm to do service to the living. We do not wish to experience another Lemuria or Atlantis on Earth."

Anna failed to recognize the latter name. "Lemuria?"

"It was an ancient human civilization—before Atlantis—that also failed to survive, signifying the loss of the true Way. For one reason or another, both were destroyed. But that's another story.

"It is time to prepare for the Way," their hostess announced. "It is to be a spiritual event that begins within the human soul, and the more who are made to understand, the sooner its arrival."

"Merry . . . would you be you referring to the Second Coming?" Anna asked excitedly.

Merry laughed lightly. "Titles are mere words. It is the meaning that counts. Besides, this endeavor encompasses more than the Christian community."

Jess waited for Anna to burst into another Bible quote. When she didn't, he added, "People disagree on what the Second Coming actually means—when it will occur. Many Christian denominations believe they're the only ones invited to participate, and everyone else will be, shall we say, *out of luck*."

Pausing, Jess continued. "So what's to become of those turned off to God *and* religion due to the dogma you mentioned?"

"They will be the ones who will find spiritual truths most attractive. Those with formal religious beliefs of all types," she stated, pausing to study Anna, "will also recognize the true Way."

Jess's expression quickly turned to one of puzzlement.

"Formal religion practiced all one's life provides secure comfort, which is fine as long as no wrong thoughts come of it. For instance, every man and woman calling themself a child of God must allow other individuals to practice the religion of their choice without exception or demand. Belittle no other; ridicule no other; judge no other. The authority to do so is denied to any soul.

"Historically, religious differences breed war. There can be no peace until each is willing to accept the other. God does not play favorites. *Everyone* is equal in the Supreme Being's eyes. To think differently is to allow ego to overcome rationality. We all experience for God."

"That's it? So what exactly can *we* do?" Jess asked, gesturing toward Anna and himself.

"Revitalize God's existence. In the history of souls, the One has always worked through us. Why should that ever change?"

Jess laughed nervously. "And how do you suggest we achieve that monumental task?"

"Always remember that you two alone do not bear the weight of the world's outcome. There are others besides yourselves who are a part of this endeavor. Your two souls have been placed in the midst of the apathy and discontent on this planet to use your God-given talents to achieve your part. Go within self and talk to the One. He will guide you in your monumental task."

Merry paused briefly. "I trust that I have answered all of your questions . . . yes?" She looked to each grave face. Neither Jess nor Anna disagreed.

Their guide rose. "You may rest before you depart. Come."

Merry led her charges down a lengthy white hall, pausing before a pair of closed doors. "Here are two adjoining rooms."

Anna assumed that this was intended for her moral comfort.

"We will speak again after you have rested." Their hostess turned and departed.

The two companions hesitated in their privacy. Jess sensed Anna's tenseness.

"Can we talk, Jess?"

He happily complied, "Of course," not wishing to part from his true mate.

"Let's go inside."

They quietly entered their accommodations through the nearest door and were met with generous furnishings. Jess mentally appreciated the supplied comforts of their unfamiliar surroundings. Lodgings up until now had been quite taxing.

Anna quickly shut the door and turned to Jess. "*We must be careful,*" she whispered, her eyes suspiciously scanning the room. "It's prophesied that a false Christ will suddenly appear, and that the multitudes will turn and worship him."

Jess couldn't believe what he was hearing. A disconcerting look replaced his startled expression.

Anna spoke hurriedly. "Many will be fooled. It's to occur at the end of times. But those who see with God's eyes will recognize the real truth. And they'll rebel against this false Christ and be persecuted." Anna's words stopped flowing. She studied Jess.

"Anna—you think—that this—that Merry— Anna, my darling, *not again.*"

"*Well,*" she whispered dramatically, "*it's certainly possible.*"

"Will you *ever* feel safe?" Jess sighed helplessly. He took the distraught young woman in his arms. "Anna, I'm afraid that Merry heard your thoughts. She knew what was going on in your mind, and I didn't." He sighed again holding her at arm's length.

"Anna . . . have you sensed any evil since we arrived?" She shook her head. "Did you sense that Merry was evil?"

"No," she had to admit.

"*Anna, Anna.*" Jess lifted her chin and stared into her eyes. "It isn't your fault." He felt only the need to comfort her. "These ideas in your head only harm *you.* Can't you *see* that, sweetheart?"

Jess pulled her closer, stroking her rigid body.

"Please, do yourself a favor. Relax and go with it, like Merry advised. Nothing terrible is going to happen. Nothing evil is going on—only that you and I will learn how to access what we've been capable of all along."

Anna hid her doubtful expression.

"Listen. I'll be right next door. So why don't you get into that luxurious looking tub over there and relax those tense muscles." He gently massaged her knotted shoulders. "Then lie down and rest on a *real* bed. I'll look in on you shortly. Okay?"

His kind words were meant to soothe his agitated partner. He let go of her and moved toward the room's inner adjoining door. Upon opening it, he was pleased to find a similar room.

Turning back, he hesitated, "All right, Anna?"

Anna sulked, but agreed. "*Okay.*"

"You *know* I wouldn't leave you if I didn't think you were safe, don't you?"

"I guess so," she responded weakly.

Jess returned to her. He again raised her chin and lightly kissed her pouting lips. A most incredibly delicious sensation flowed through them.

Still hesitant to leave his troubled partner, he again looked over his shoulder. *One more reassurance before I'm out of her sight.* "I'm here if you need me, Anna."

The door closed behind Jess. He leaned against it, glad to be alone. *God knows I love her, but she sure tries my patience.*

The male guest quickly located what was needed for his bath and ran a tub of hot water. His whole body relaxed as he sank into the treasured wetness. A shiver of pure pleasure swept over him. He quietly prepared his mind for meditation, asking for guidance to help him understand and accept.

Anna thought the knock on her door came from Jess until she realized it originated from the door leading into the hall. She slowly tiptoed across the floor. Her heart raced. She forced herself to ask, "Who is it, please?"

"It is I, Merry. May I see you?"

It was embarrassing to think that Merry knew of her suspicions. Anna hesitated.

"Dear Anna, will you please allow me to enter?"

"Is Jess—"

"Jess is in his room. It is with you alone I wish to speak."

Anna opened the door to Merry. "Shouldn't he be here too?"

Merry shook her long golden tresses and laughed. "Dear Anna, you are safe with me. You create your own fear—like a child afraid of the dark. You have only to change your attitude and your fears will vanish."

The warmth in Merry's deep, dark-blue eyes evaporated Anna's discomfort. She allowed her hostess to lead her toward the lavish four-poster bed.

In the midst of her inner turmoil, Anna's mind had blocked her immediate surroundings. She began to take notice. To the right of the door adjoining the two rooms was her bath. Opposite was the bed. A generous full-length mirror was stationed on the wall next to the bed. Anna caught her breath as they passed. Her own reflection stared back. There was no reflection of Merry.

The breathtaking apparition sensed Anna's confusion. Not wanting to lose what little confidence she'd gained in the young woman, she quickly clapped her hands together and spoke with childlike exuberance.

"Now, Anna, I wish to take you on a journey."

Anna looked startled.

"It is to be a journey of the mind."

Merry allowed her voice to flow quickly and evenly.

"Our spirits will be leaving our bodies temporarily, so we must be stabilized. Lying down is best." She helped herself onto the bed. Straightening her attire, she lay in a supine position, releasing a long feminine sigh.

Anna stood watching with wide eyes. Her serious expression made her spirit guide giggle.

"Come, my dear," she encouraged. "Remember that fear is nothing more than a negative thought."

An out-of-the-body experience. It does sound appealing. Good Christians claim to have experienced it. Jess said to go with the flow. Okay. Here goes.

Any further thoughts of refusing vanished. She climbed onto the bed and lay quietly beside Merry and said, "If you think it'll help."

Reaching across the space between them, Merry instructed Anna to join hands so that their spirits would remain together. Anna complied.

"Ready, ready, let's go!" Merry smiled as she looked into her guest's beautiful, sparkling twin blue orbs full of anticipation.

"Close your eyes, Anna. Breathe in deeply through your nose while counting to six. Hold to the count of three, and breathe out through your mouth, counting to six. Again, inhale and count to six, hold your breath for three, and exhale for six. Keep repeating until you reach a relaxed state."

Anna obeyed the simple instructions. The last material thing she witnessed was the pulsating, colorful activity diminishing from the white ceiling above.

A sudden upward rush—like being strapped to the front of a rocket ship—overwhelmed her senses.

Accustoming herself to the sensation, she witnessed a stirring of new emotions, as well as those long forgotten. She felt Merry's comforting presence.

The two universal travelers left their temporary bodies behind and moved forward in the form of sparkling galaxy dust. Their essence swirled about one another—like children playing.

The discovery of being in open outer space shocked and surprised the ethereal spirit of Anna. A glance behind revealed the earth growing smaller as the distance increased. Vertigo hit hard. She faced forward. The presence of the essence of Merry again calmed her. She soon became engrossed with their trek across the earth's solar system.

The space traveler's direction reversed with astounding suddenness. They were drawn back from the outermost planets: Neptune, Uranus, Saturn, Jupiter, Mars, Earth, Venus and Mercury. The huge sun grew in the foreground. It felt warm but did not burn.

Water splashed about the tub as Jess jerked awake. His body and mind had succumbed to exhaustion. Seconds passed while his disoriented thoughts cleared.

Experiencing a sudden uneasiness concerning Anna, he rose. The sound of water dripping from him filled the room. A generous white towel sufficiently dried him. A lent white robe fit perfectly.

Gingerly opening the adjoining door, he peered inside. Seeing no one, he walked further into the room. His scouting eyes settled on Anna and Merry lying together on the more-than-adequate sized bed. With a puzzled brow, he took one hesitant step, then another and another. He eventually arrived at the foot, staring first at Anna.

Are they sleeping? They're so still.

Again, Jess checked Anna's breathing. She was.

Though his curiosity burned, he chose not to disturb them. Having made that decision somewhat relaxed him.

Straightening, Jess locked his hands behind his back. Uncertainty made him decide to wait.

What if they sleep all day—or is it night? Jess searched for a clue to tell him the time and found none. Habit made him shrug.

Wham. Sudden optical stimulation received by the two drifting spirits hit hard like bright lights in an interrogation room.

Anna's mind convinced her that she was standing in a nineteenth century one-room log cabin. She detected Merry's presence. Examination of the room revealed basic furniture. A handmade rocking chair drew her attention. Its back was to her. She willed herself to view its occupants—a young father, naked from the waist up, holding a young infant clothed only in a crude diaper. The baby lay across the father's shoulder above his beating heart. Except for the rocker's motion, there was no other movement in the room.

The baby appeared to be sleeping until Anna changed her position, revealing its open eyes. The vision itself touched her heart. Love sensed between father and child was not unlike what she now shared with Jess. Sensations experienced by the two true mates weren't so much like human sexual desire, but like pure immeasurable, unconditional love. She had experienced a similar connection with Merry when their essence had entwined.

Anna comprehended that she was looking into the past—hers and Jess's. *This is us . . . in another life . . . another time.* The infant was herself. The young father was Jess.

Another's mind may have disbelieved, but Anna's could not. Profound incite resulted in the lifting of the remaining veil of protection. Her fear of the unknown simply ceased.

God is all—all is God, and all shall be as it should.

She now understood the difference between spiritual thought and material thought.

Merry sensed that Anna was ready to return.

Batting heavy eyelids, Anna's soft moans stirred newly surfaced emotions within her waiting partner. Her awakening ended Jess's mental dilemma—to remain and wait, or to wait in the comfort of his room.

Letting go of Merry's hand, Anna immediately attempted to sit up. Merry yet lay still. Noticing Jess through her peripheral vision, a sudden burst of excitement flooded her overstimulated mind.

"Jess! *Oh, Jess.*" After excitedly whispering his name, she swung her feet off the massive bed and stood before him, her eyes glued to his. On tiptoes, Anna threw her arms around him, pressing her face against his chest.

"I love you *so much*, Jess. I promise I won't deny it again."

Exceedingly surprised, Jess returned the warm embrace, bending slightly at the waist to accommodate the difference in their height. "*Whoa*, here. What's happening?"

"Something *wonderful,* Jess." Anna's great enthusiasm bubbled forth. She lifted knowing eyes, eyes that had discovered something truly wonderful, eyes that wanted to share her discovery.

Merry's arousal disturbed them. Their attention turned toward the occupied bed. "Forgive me. I had an extra errand."

Jess was puzzled by her choice of words. Anna wasn't.

Merry slowly rose, burdened by her physical form. She quickly composed herself and moved toward the door. Before exiting, she turned to speak, making a sweeping motion with her arm.

"Anna, why not take Jess on a journey?"

"You mean . . . by myself?"

"Go in the same manner." Merry again entertained them with her tinkling laughter before her departure.

"What happened, Anna? You are absolutely *radiating*. My curiosity is really peaked. What journey?"

Anna eagerly tugged at Jess's arm. She led him to the bed and gave him a surprising shove. Jess was forced to sit back. "Go on, now . . . get comfortable." She climbed up and over her gawking partner, lying supine with a pillow tucked beneath her head.

From his seated position, her surprised partner watched with amusement until Anna was completely settled. Using his arms and hands, he maneuvered himself into a similar position, tucking his robe in all the right places.

"I'm not properly attired for this."

"*Nonsense*. It won't matter at all."

Jess stared up at the ceiling. "Now what?"

"Take my hand," Anna intoned.

Anna had believed that Merry was responsible for their astral flight. She had no clue as to how the trip they were about to experience would come about.

"Now, close your eyes."

It happened immediately. Together Jess and Anna's essence left their bodies. Anna willed their spirits to entwine. The heightened sensation threatened to dominate their experience.

In no earthly way could they discern time passing as their souls flowed in, around and through each other in a continuous caressing manner. Human sex paled in comparison.

Anna took Jess soaring—outward, away. Faster than light they sped, traversing the galaxy known to them as the Milky Way. Stars streaked across their heavenly vision.

Eons may well have passed before the combined essence again

became two separate entities. The essence of Jess was astounded, Anna's, exhilarated.

Jess had read about such experiences but believed it happened only within the imagination. What was happening now was unlike anything he'd ever imagined. It felt so *real*.

Suddenly drawn back in the direction from which they'd come, Anna noticed a silver trail extending before each of them, serving to attach the two astro-travelers to their origin, directing their safe return. Anna pointed out the silver cords to Jess.

Their motion now reversed, the essence of Jess and Anna retrospectively passed by the familiar planets of their solar system, heading toward the blue orb called Earth.

Slammed into an abrupt, startling change, Jess and Anna peer into the cramped cockpit of a World War II bomber. In movie-like sequence, they view the two men who occupy its space knowing they are watching themselves. Comradery is easily sensed. One man's face, hysterically contorted, the other showing resignation. The latter grips a microphone.

"*Mayday, Mayday!*" he calls into the mike. "*Mayday, Mayday!*" he repeats. "*We're going down.*"

The telltale whine in the aircraft's defective engine allows Jess to decipher the situation. Anna senses it too.

Those men are us.

Not to witness the crash itself, the scenes change. Anna is again ecstatic that Jess will view the same baby and father. He watches the quiet replay. Strong emotions flow between the two spectators. The same unconditional love they now realize carries from lifetime to lifetime— the same two souls repeatedly drawn together.

The next scene Anna hasn't yet witnessed. The blinding white briefly confuses them. They will themselves forward and discover a white world of frozen ice and snow. An igloo looms near like a ghost in the distance. They move toward it. A lone figure bundled in heavy animal skins stands outside the entrance, holding a string of fresh caught fish. The figure ducks and enters. Jess and Anna's spirits draw near to view the inside activities. Fish is stored, and furs fly. A man slides under the coverings of the family's single bed to warm himself next to his woman who busily suckles their infant son.

The same unconditional love flows between the onlookers.

Anna's thoughts became one with Jess.

I am the mother, she conveys.

I am the father, he returns.

A fourth scene takes place. A young Italian mother-to-be, lovely of face, stands with her young and handsome, well-to-do Italian husband aboard an immigrant's ship moored in the harbor. Bound for America, they wave to the crowds of relatives and well-wishers on the docks below. Two months would the journey take. The woman gives birth at sea, dying of complications along with the newborn infant. The young man, overwhelmed with grief, finds relief when his spirit also escapes from its flesh-and-blood body as the ship that he sails on founders, plunging to the seafloor never to reach its destination—Anna, the young mother, Jess, the young husband.

Unconditional love is felt flowing between the characters in the scenes. The two true mates are detached from the tragedies that had befallen them many times and many years ago.

Their minds remained linked.

This journey we're on is all about love, our shared love. It is enough for now.

The extraordinary journey ends. They find themselves back on the accommodating bed.

Jess attempted to rise, but fell back, giving himself more time to recover. "I understand Merry's reference. Flesh *is* burdensome."

Neither spoke, both absorbed in their coexperience.

At length, Anna spoke her thoughts. "Wouldn't it be wonderful to be mind-linked forever?"

"How quickly you forget, my dear. Random thoughts aren't always pleasant. Some of yours wouldn't set well with me, and some of mine wouldn't set well with you. In the spirit, it's fine. But I doubt it would work in the flesh until we can learn to control our human way of thinking.

Our experience in Purgatory proved that."

Watching the moving colored lights that represented their chaotic human thoughts on the white ceiling above further strengthened Jess's insight.

"I know you're right, but I shall wish for it anyway."

"You know what they say . . . be careful what you wish for."

"There's no way that my mind linked with yours could result in any negative experience," Anna professed.

She smiled at Jess with narrowed eyes and moved to another subject. "I think I can now express myself in words."

Jess focused on her closeness, mentally noting her blue-black hair contrasting sharply against the snowy whiteness of the pillow beneath her lovely head. The vision it created would forever remain emblazoned in his memory.

Anna rolled on to her side facing Jess. "As I've said before, your soul is what impresses me. Nothing else matters."

"How intuitive of you," Jess responded. "I concur."

Anna broke the mood. "I haven't had a chance to bathe yet. Do you mind?"

Gentle laughter escaped him. "No, I don't mind. I will return to my own bath, thank you."

He rose, attempting to shake off the heaviness of his physical mass without results. "*Son,*" he replied, moving sluggishly forward.

"Jess . . ."

He paused without turning.

"I don't mind if you leave me now, because I know when you close the door behind you, I *will* see you again."

With one hand wrapped around the door frame, he looked back. "Let's take it from moment to moment. Agreed?"

His words greatly relieved Anna.

"Agreed."

Merry again sat with her guests on the plush white sofa. "My best advice has been given. It bears repeating as many times as necessary until it is retained. All the spiritual literature of worth says same. "Ask, and it shall be given to you." It is only when interpreted that it becomes flawed. Do not interpret. Merely accept.

"Much study is required. Go now and use your God-given talents to do your part to bring forth the truth and the Way to the world of the living. It will come to you."

"You've left us with nothing more to ask," Jess stated. "I understand what's expected of me. I must go back to L.A. What better way to reach out than through the visual arts? I can write a book—*we* can write a book." Jess winked at Anna. "And who knows," he encircled her with his arm, drawing them physically closer together, "maybe a movie will follow."

Merry's laugher played out like the music of a sweet melody. "Anna, dear, you appear surprised."

"Well, I knew Jess would go back to L. A., but I didn't believe it possible for me to go with him."

"I still have questions, Merry." Anna glanced at Jess while she spoke. "How do we return to our bodies? What about the closeness revealed to us—the bond that Jess and I share? How can we be together when I have a family?"

Jess's eyes noticeably sparkled. "Too many details, Anna. Remember agreeing to *live in the moment?*" He knew in his heart that the questions asked would direct his mate toward acceptance.

The inner cave looked blacker after the contrast of their white haven from which they'd departed. Jess's small flashlight sent out its puny glow.

Maneuvering their way toward the exit required complete concentration. Neither spoke.

At the first glimpse of sunlight, Anna resumed conversation. Her mind had obviously been busy construing their situation.

"Write a book, Jess? I don't know the first thing about writing a book. Do you?"

"Anyone can write a book. Blind people write books. Poverty-stricken people write books. *We* can write a book. Think positively, Annie. All we have to do is put words on paper."

"What if it doesn't sell?"

"Hold up." Jess closed the space between them. "Anna . . . you're reverting. Before we walk out of this cave, you must promise me—and yourself—that you'll attempt to stop thinking negatively. We carry the truth with us now. It's what Christ is still trying to teach all these years after his death. I know it's going to be difficult at first, but once we form the habit—"

"Jess . . . again, you're right." *I thank God for you*, she silently declared. "Please, help me, Jess. Keep reminding me."

"It goes both ways. I'm sure we'll have to remind each other."

"Oh, Jess. I'm so happy! It's as though everything is perfect. I want it to last."

"*You* are in control of that, my sweet."

"Oops. I did it again, didn't I? I may be a lost cause."

"No, just human. Consider that we have an entire lifetime of negativity to unlearn."

Anna wanted to pinch herself. "Can this happiness last?" She instantly reviewed her question and reasoned that by answering it herself, she could undo its negativity. "Yes, it can."

Jess didn't allow her positive words to go unnoticed. "That's the spirit, Annie—and I mean that in more ways than one." His mate had obviously accepted their spiritual experiences in spite of their abrupt unveiling.

Excitement welled up in Jess as they stepped out into a warm spring day. "Do you *believe* this? It appears we've been holed up for quite some time. In fact, it looks as though winter has come and gone. Fitting, isn't it?"

The spring-like temperature reminded them that time had no bearing in the plane between human life and spirit. Being out in the open welcomed human emotions of joy and freedom. Jess's toothy grin was catching. Dancing and laughter defined their relief.

"Say there."

The sudden, strange voice startled their celebration. Their laughter quickly ceased.

"Whadda ya doin' trespassin' on posted land? This here's private property, ya know."

The voice belonged to an elderly gentleman dressed in denim overalls and a plaid flannel shirt with rolled-up sleeves. From beneath a shady elm, he slowly strolled toward the surprised couple.

"Uh, sorry, sir. We came through the woods and didn't notice any posted signs—an honest mistake."

Jess smiled at the short little man approaching them. "You can see us?" he added, not considering how odd his words sounded.

"O' course I can see ya. Are ya admittin' to hidin' on me? Well, this here's private property," he offered again. "Say, do I know you? You look *awful* familiar."

Anna caught his question and played on it. "Hello, sir. This is Jess Parks, the T.V. actor."

Jess rolled his eyes and rocked back on his heels in quiet reserve, slightly embarrassed at being identified.

The property owner failed to acknowledge the female equal to his own height. He continued to ponder over Jess's familiarity. "Oh, say, now I recognize you. I seen you on the TV. Well, sir, I'm proud ta meet ya." He stuck out his rough farmer's hand for Jess to shake.

"Tom Birdman's the name. This here's Birdman Cave—named after me—on account it's on my property." The trespassers simultaneously nodded. "I wouldn't recommend you a goin' in that there cave, see. You might meet up with a bear or some other kinda wild varmint."

"Meeting up with a bear sounds rather tame at this point, but we'll be happy to take your advice, sir."

"Huh, Mr. Birdman, this is Anna, my . . . fiancée." Jess prepared to silence the astonished young woman glaring at him. He leaned forward and whispered rather loudly. "Well, we were about to get engaged." He gave the old man a sly wink. "I haven't asked her yet."

Mr. Birdman studied Jess long and hard. Concluding that his hearing was off, he finally ventured, "Well, I reckon I wouldn't mind a' meetin' her iffin' she was to show up directly." The seasoned farmer broke into a toothless grin. "I'll say!" He said, continuing to study the actor. "Well— I'll say!" he repeated, embarrassing himself. "Didn't realize you were so tall, Mr. Parks."

"Please, sir. Call me Jess." The smile on Jess's face quickly faded, turning into a look of awkward surprise.

A startled noise escaped Anna's throat. "The man obviously doesn't see me."

Jess replied, "Uh huh." He wanted the friendly old gentleman to believe the comment was directed at him. *That's all I need is for this farmer to think I'm talking to an invisible person. Add that to a trespassing violation.*

Tom cleared his throat. "Say, I'm makin' a trip to Harrison to pick up a part for my ol' tractor. Need a lift anywheres?"

Anna and Jess exchanged glances.

"How's that for fate?" Anna exclaimed.

Quickly conjuring an excuse for being caught alone on the man's personal property, Jess stated, "As a matter of fact, sir, it's looking like my entourage may have abandoned me—as a practical joke."

He winced inwardly. *Couldn't I have done better?*

"Been sent on a snipe hunt, eh?"

It worked. "Something like that, sir."

"Looks like I could be yer opportunity to kindly turn it around." The land owner expressed his delight at playing a part in the presumed joke.

"It looks that way, sir, and I'd be much obliged," Jess intoned.

❋ ❋ ❋

Luck was with them. The small plane contained empty seats. On-board passengers were caught up in their own worlds.

Anna jabbered incessantly on the plane ride to L.A. "Why do you think I'm still invisible, and you're not?"

Jess lost count of the times she'd asked that question. "Anna, be still," his soft, stern voice demanded when his mind had grown tired of it. Anna looked hurt. He purposely changed the subject.

"You *know* I meant what I said . . . about us being engaged."

"I know," Anna whispered, forgetting her recently injured feelings. She nervously tapped her finger on the armrest. *How can I be here with Jess, when I'm married to Joel?* The idea nagged her. *Live for today,* Merry had said. She attempted to refrain from negative thinking by concentrating on her present environment.

At length, she suddenly burst into tears. *"I just can't believe it."*

Surprised by the sudden outburst of emotion, Jess abandoned his own restless thoughts to comfort her in his arms. "I'm sorry, Anna. What can't you believe?"

"I can't believe I'm so *happy* and so scared half-to-death at the same time."

Jess laughed his relief and hugged Anna tight. He felt a shiver run through her petite body. He felt his own blood warm to her closeness. Their immediate desires quickly won over. Anna lifted her face, and Jess tenderly kissed her waiting lips.

8

The Truth Shall Set You Free

"No, no, no, Al." Jess paced his dining room floor emphasizing his words with arm movements. "No white robes, no headquarters and *no organization.*"

"Well then, what're ya talking about, Jess? It *does* have something ta do with God and religion, didn't it?"

Jess looked at Al's puzzled face and broke into giddy laughter.

"What's so funny?"

"You need to relax a little, Al. You're all tensed up!"

Jess deserted the subject. "How's your health been lately?"

"Oh, okey-dokey, I guess. Rosie's been after me to go see a doctor on account of a few pains around my heart lately. But I tell her as soon as business lets up a bit, I'll make me an appointment, and she's happy."

Jess squatted by Al's chair, his body weight resting on one leg. He peered into cool blue eyes that reminded him of Anna.

"Better follow good advice. I'd like you to be around for a long while—witness the good things to come, you know?"

Jess resumed the previous subject.

"What we're trying to accomplish with our book, Al, is to get people to start thinking about God as being within us—within everything. We're trying, Al, to show people who aren't comfortable in a conventional church that it's okay to believe that way, that there is another way to be comfortable with their creator—through spiritualism. We want to remind people that God is a spirit rather than a material being sitting

above us on a fluffy, white cloud, waiting to pass out harsh judgment—
which, of course, is another subject." Jess pointed a finger toward his own
chest. "God is within—always. We can hear God's advice—if we listen to
the voice within. It's the voice that warns us when we should or shouldn't
follow through with an action or an idea. What I'm saying is, we should
trust and believe all of the time, not when it's satisfying or convenient."

"Yeah, yeah, yeah," Al intoned. "God is within," he echoed, obviously
uncomfortable with the subject.

Jess rose from his kneeling position and resumed pacing. "Al," the
manager cringed upon hearing his name, "when I create something—say
a work of art—it's God who creates that work of art through me. His
creation provided me with talent. And we in turn use our God-given
talents to make our way through life— whether it's a building contractor,
a doctor, or a railroad engineer. And . . . when I give you a gift, it's really
God giving you a gift through me. Understand? We . . . are his channels.
He manages his creation through us—his children. And . . . God is only
good. God is only pure love."

Jess returned to Al's chair.

"Oh, I get it." Al attempted an analogy. "If you and Anna had a baby, it
would be a gift from God."

"Strange way to put it, Al, but it works."

"But I know that. Everybody knows that. It's an old adage, that a baby
is a gift from heaven."

"Exactly, my man, and it should be applied to everything in our lives.
Even negative situations usually have positive outcomes."

Al shook his head. "If only you could hear yourself. You sound like a
religious fanatic. What's happened to you? How come you're so different?"
There was pleading in the older man's tone. "For the last couple of
months, it's like a part of your personality's been missing—and now this.
Jess, what's going on with you?"

Jess voiced his thought. "Maybe I should come at this from a different
angle." He spun to face his manager. "Listen, Al. It's every soul's destiny
to return to its source. So why put off learning what we need to know

to get there? We're only here for a short time compared to all eternity."

He patted Al on the shoulder. "I'm not concerned, Al. It'll all come to you. You'll see."

Al sighed heavily. "Yeah, yeah, yeah," he intoned. "I'll see."

Jess changed the beaten subject. "Will we make the appointment on time?"

"Yeah, we'll be on time. Quit worrying, will ya? I'm more concerned with how Moyer's going to react."

Jess ignored his agent's doubt.

"Great. Isn't it funny how everything works out? Having sat in that chair with Moyer before will help. See what I've been saying, Al? Everything always falls into place."

"Yeah, yeah, divine order."

"So, when do I get ta' meet this *girl-of-your-dreams*? I can't believe you've kept her from me. Why haven't you produced her yet? I'm beginning to wonder if she really exists. You sure you're not makin' her up?"

Wearing a rose-tinted blouse and a short cream-colored skirt that swirled about her shapely legs, Anna walked into the room as if Al's questions had cued her. Jess's eyes were instantly drawn to his eternal love. He smiled at her loveliness.

"Of course she exists, Al." *You just can't see her.*

"Your description of her sounds like the girl of *my* dreams."

Anna beamed.

"So, when's the two of ya getting hitched?"

Al's question startled both visible and invisible parties. Anna's smile disappeared, replaced by a concerned frown. Jess's previous insight bore merit. Being a fly on the wall didn't always turn out to be a positive experience.

Jess shot Anna an apologetic smile.

Al again surprised them. "Say. What if *your* Anna comes to live with me and Rosie until you two finalize your plans?"

Jess cleared his throat.

"Oh, *come on*. Why not? And hey, I have an even *greater* idea." Al squirmed in his chair like an excited child. "You two get married, and you move in too, Jess."

The actor had to laugh at his manager's enthusiasm.

"Aw, why not? We have plenty o' room, me and Rosie. Besides, your place is *way* too small, and you know how hard it is to find another one around here. The more, the merrier, I always say. It'll be a blast!"

Anna started to giggle, much to Jess's relief. "I know you mean it, and I'm deeply touched by your offer. Tell you what, Al. I'll present the idea to Anna, and we'll consider it."

Jess sneaked a wink at his invisible guest.

"Honest? Great."

Al's eyes lit up like Jess had never witnessed.

"Great." Al repeated.

"Is it time?" Jess asked.

Al glanced at his wrist watch. "Yeah, it's time." He slowly rose, mumbling something about his arthritis acting up again.

Jess approached Anna and gently leaned against her. The thrill of her touch sent familiar waves of pleasure through his body.

He whispered in her ear. "Remember, Anna, my house is yours. Make yourself comfortable. I have no secrets to keep from you."

Anna smiled her appreciation at Jess's considerateness and gave a shy nod. "Don't forget to pick up more printer paper. And *be careful*. Remember, you're visible, hence vulnerable."

"Wherever I go and whatever happens, I'll be okay. We know that we'll always be together." He bent down to kiss her rosy cheek.

"You *know* what I mean. Watch it, Jess Parks. Here he comes. We don't want him thinking you're crazier than he already does."

"Time ta' go, Jess."

"Let me drive, Al."

He tossed Jess the keys.

"You may be a decent driver," Jess lied, "but sometimes you scare me to *death*."

"Well," Al laughed good-naturedly, "I have to admit, sometimes I scare myself."

The engine's hum unconsciously lulled the two men's thoughts.

"Hey, Jess, I been meaning to ask—"

"Yeah?"

"I know this ain't none of my business, but you guys *are* doin' it—having sex, I mean."

"Al!" Jess cringed. His face reddened. "*No.* We aren't *doing it*. Not yet, anyway."

"You're kidding." Al sat quietly shaking his head. "There's definitely something about you that's very different."

"Maybe it's not so important."

"*You've changed.*" Al envisioned the red bombshell sauntering by the professional building a few months earlier.

"Yeah," Jess laughed without humor. "Maybe so. Look, Al." Jess wanted to tell his friend the truth, that his desire for Anna had been his biggest trial. But it was *his* trial. Instead, he said, "As a seeker of knowledge, it was a shortcoming I was able to overcome, that's all."

"Now you're *really* scaring me."

"It's not meant to be scary, Al. When a soul seeks to understand, that soul realizes what matters—like you, Al. *You* matter."

"*Me?* I matter?"

"*You* are one of God's souls searching for knowledge."

"I'm a soul seeking knowledge," Al repeated. "I guess that does sound important."

"Hmm, soul seeking," Jess thought aloud. "That's rather catchy. Yeah, I like it—Soul Seeker." He mentally noted to run possible titles past Anna.

He returned to the main topic of their conversation. "Tell me, Al, why do we convince ourselves we don't make a difference? Each of us is a link in the chain of universal consciousness. Do you realize what happens when a link breaks?"

Al guessed, "Death?"

"More like the universe gets out of whack. Maybe that's when *really* bad things happen, and why it's imperative we stay on track."

A moment of silence passed between the two men. Jess resumed voicing his thoughts.

"We should constantly remind each other of our importance. Believing we're important stabilizes a person's mentality and gives life meaning. If we all felt special the world would be better off."

Al looked bewildered. "What could possibly make everyone in the world believe they're special?"

Jess gave his manager a knowledgeable glance. "Why, participating in achieving world peace, of course."

"Huh?" Al squeaked. *"You're not serious."*

"I'm *dead* serious." Jess stole another glance from his driving seat. "I'm telling you, Al. It's big. As a participant, you'd *have* to feel special."

"Either you're *really* on some mission for God, or you've gone *totally wacko*."

"World peace will arrive—"

Al cut in. "But nobody knows *when*."

"True, but what's wrong with letting God know we're ready by treating each other with dignity, love, and respect."

Jess began again. "World peace will arrive—," he glared at Al as if daring him to interrupt a second time, "—when everyone finally understands that the Kingdom of God is within us."

"Oh. So you *don't* have a specific date in mind. *What a relief.* Does it mean the end of the world and all that—ya think?"

Jess ignored Al's sarcasm.

"It's probably safe to say, the end of the world as it is today."

"Aw, do we have ta? Can't things stay the same? I'm not too fond of change, you know."

"Come on, Al. Don't you want a better world? Think of it," Jess intoned. "No more crime; no more suffering."

"That would be nice, I suppose. But it's too late for me, Jess. My soul's already damned. I haven't attended church like I should've—Easter Sunday and Christmas at best. You know, *God will smite you and cast you into the fiery pits of hell.* I mean, that's what I've always heard."

"Al, it took me a long time to figure out why I felt uncomfortable in church. It's that fear factor you just mentioned. More people might attend church if the fear factor were dropped. I can't accept it, and I think lots of folks agree. *I* believe that heaven and hell are within our minds as well as God and his kingdom. If we don't have God within, then all the churchgoing in a lifetime won't protect us from the hell we create for ourselves. We'll all be lost souls."

"With so many different beliefs these days, how do we assume which one's right?"

"I think it's a matter of which one is right for *you*. Of course, everyone has the right to practice a religion of choice, but they don't have the right to force it on others. That goes for *every* religion including those that accept reincarnation. If it's uncomfortable, don't wear it—simple as that."

"*Come on*, Jess. There's no such thing as reincarnation."

"Al, do you honestly think you were born without having previously existed? What makes you think that you all of a sudden came into being when you were pulled out of the womb? The theory behind the scientific Law of Conservation of Energy states that energy changes form but can be neither created nor destroyed." Therefore, everything was something to begin with. Spiritualism applies the same principle to living souls. The earth is one big classroom, and we're its spiritual students.

"What about the human genetic code that researchers have unfolded? Perhaps we actually choose our genome structure before birth so that we'll have a certain color of eyes, skin, hair—and intended diseases or afflictions to direct us toward enlightenment. This could occur simply by carefully choosing our parents. How's that for controlling your own destiny?

"Defensive behavior also controls destiny. It stems from guilt and is easily read: a raised voice, avoidance of eye contact, adamant denial. A soul's better off making amends and paying for wrongdoings before leaving the earth plane. It will ensure enlightenment of the soul. In other words, *we're* the masters of our own destiny."

Al appeared to follow Jess's meaning. "You're saying, go out with a clean slate. That's reasonable."

"Anyway, the consensus is that we'll either experience happiness and self-respect or shame and remorse over our earthly deeds. *We will judge ourselves.*"

"I guess you're making *some* sense."

"There you go, Al. It does make sense. I'm not making this up. I have sources. Relax . . . and stop resisting. Try flowing with it. It'll all work out. You'll see."

"Hey, looky here. We talked so much, I don't remember the trip." Al's tone revealed relief. He realized his friend's open spiritual philosophy wasn't going away. An adjustment period was needed.

The actor and his manager strolled through the professional building side by side, both contemplating different futures.

Jess ducked and entered Moyer's office. Everything looked the same, triggering a popup memory of Anna explaining *deja'vu* their first night together, which resulted in a smile.

Fluorescent light reflected off familiar metal rimmed glasses. Moyer rose, circling his desk to greet the two familiar faces. "Good day, gentlemen." He shook their hands in turn. "What's all the excitement about?"

Jess took his cue. "We're looking for help in getting a movie into production, sir. The script is nearly finished."

"Go on," Moyer encouraged.

"Mr. Moyer, I wouldn't be here if it weren't important."

"Have a seat." Moyer returned to his chair.

Jess sat back in a relaxed manner.

"I sense something different about you, Jess. More confidence."

Eyes lowered, Jess collected his thoughts and looked up.

"Mr. Moyer, I'm expecting a box-office hit."

Moyer leaned over his desk.

"What makes you so sure?"

"I know it, sir. I just know," the author stated with conviction. "It's a feel-good story," he continued. "The content covers what an audience might anticipate—and more. It's fast-paced, intense, and packed with adventure." The descriptive adjectives quickly stacked up as Jess pitched their work. "Of course, it's a love story. What great book isn't?"

"True," Moyer agreed.

Approaching from a different angle, he continued. "E.J, since I last sat in this office, I've been to places and seen things that I can't begin to explain. As a result, my outlook on life has tremendously changed—the reason for my boost in confidence. I've added some of my experiences to the script—with flair, of course."

"Of course," Moyer repeated. He shook a forefinger at Jess. "I like that—real experiences—and I like your confidence. I don't figure you for a wild goose."

The manager and actor exchanged a quick glance. Al signaled Jess to ease up, not wishing to sway Moyer the wrong way.

The casting director's curiosity peaked. "And just where *have* you been, Jess?"

An answer was previously prepared. "On a grand adventure, sir. Take me hours to tell it. But I wouldn't trade it for the world."

"Uh huh," Moyer paused. "What's the plot?"

Neither was surprised by the question. Though the plot had been considered, the main genre remained undecided.

"World acceptance—not nation-to-nation, but man-to-man."

"Hmm." Moyer sat quietly behind his glasses. The turning wheels and meshing gears were nearly audible. "I'm interested—because it's you. But I don't believe anyone has ever tackled man-to-man peace before. It's considered impossible." He braved the next question. "The genre?"

Jess looked like a trapped rat. "Uh—" He looked at Al, his shoulders beginning to shrug. His manager's expression read, *you're on your own, son.*

Stick with the confidence, Jess's inner voice suggested. Any tension in his shoulders quickly faded. He continued to exude self-assurance. "Let's call it a medley of genre."

Moyer cleared his throat. "A medley of genre," he repeated. "That's the most difficult to achieve."

Al fidgeted, but Jess held fast, convinced it would help him meet their goal.

"Honestly, I'm going with my gut. All right, I'll bite. Your timing couldn't have been better. I need a new project. Can you maintain a tight schedule?"

"You bet, sir."

"So when can I expect a rough draft?"

Jess smiled his pleasure. "Soon, Mr. Moyer. Very soon."

"All right then, gentlemen. Keep in touch."

The three men rose and shook hands.

Back in the car, Jess worked his way through the maze of the underground parking lot and up to the traffic's edge. His passenger warily eyed the oncoming congestion.

"We don't have to do this, you know. Let's make it easier on ourselves and get us a driver. Huh, Jess?"

"Now, Al. You know my thoughts on that."

"I know. You want your independence. I just want to *live*."

"Get your own driver, then."

Al shook his head at Jess and attempted a laugh. "Guess I already got one."

After a period of silence, Al spoke. "Hey. How about that Solidarity, huh? April 17, 1989. I can't forget that date. I honest-to-God cried real tears." The older gentleman shook his head. "If only my folks had lived to see it."

Jess responded with silent surprise. What had possessed Al to suddenly bring up an event that occurred years ago?

He spoke cautiously. "I was moved too, Al."

"Yeah, Jess?"

"Sure, Al."

Jess's brow furrowed. Lately, his friend's thoughts tended to ramble. *I better see to his doctor appointment myself*, he vowed.

"So what brought *that* on?"

"Well, even though I wasn't born in Poland, it's the homeland of my ancestors—my brothers."

All this talk must be affecting him emotionally.

"Everyone on this planet shares a brotherhood. Maybe the key is learning to get along in youth—start out young."

"Tell me, Al, what's the point in ignoring our destiny? God is all— plain and simple—the beginning and the end. There's no place to go except back to Him. Eventually, we all will. Some may take longer than others, depending on each individual's level of enlightenment. Every progressive life is meant to improve our way of thinking bringing us closer to God. Humans have been around a long time, so it isn't like we haven't had time to work on it.

"World peace is within us. It's up to the living to welcome it, and some of us are meant to help prepare for its arrival."

"Whoa, Jess. Maybe *you* have to."

"Now, Al. I'll venture to say that you're a part of it."

"But I don't *want* to be in that kind of limelight."

"I wasn't sure I wanted it either. But it's only right to do what's asked of us."

"You mean what's asked of *you*." Al directed a guilt-ridden glance at the driver. "Oh, boy," he sighed, "I guess you're right."

"Things will work themselves out, Al. They have a tendency to do that, you know. So quit worrying about troubles that don't exist. It creates more stress. We could all do without added stress."

"You think I can learn to stop worrying at my age?"

"I think we could *both* learn—as long as we're willing."

"Good luck with that. But the first thing I'm gonna work on is getting you two *hitched*."

Jess chuckled.

"You know, I don't get it. Your behavior makes me think Anna is already married." Al laughed at his silly suspicion.

A nerve twitched near the corner of Jess's mouth. His eyes remained glued to the road ahead.

I'm prepared for this. Now, I'm going to find out how well, unless he decides to drop—

"Jess, you didn't laugh. How come you didn't laugh, Jess? How come you're not saying anything, Jess? *Oh, Jess.* Don't tell me that dear sweet girl of yours is married? But—nah, she *can't* be. She doesn't sound like the type. And, hey, what was it you once told me—and I quote, '*I don't go for married women?*' Help me out here, Jess. Am I on ta something?"

Jess glanced at his friend. His face burned red.

Al sucked in his breath. His voice rose above a whisper. "It's true, huh. No *wonder* you guys aren't doing it."

Jess remained calm. "You can stop jumping to conclusions, Al. There happens to be a lot involved with our situation. In reality, she's still at home with her family. Only a part of her is here."

"*A part of her?* You're speaking metaphorically?"

"No, Al. You don't understand. I mean a part of her is separated from her living body."

Al looked at Jess. The whites of his eyes doubled in size.

Jess quickly decided to go for honesty. "You keep mentioning a change in my personality some months back. Well, you're right. It was because a part of me left my body. Then, I found myself on a quest that led me to Anna. We wound up on the quest together." Jess's voice rose in volume. "I'm trying to tell you, Al. Unexplainable things happened to us. We were even both invisible all the while."

Jess stole a glance at his passenger while maintaining a safe distance from the car in front. "*Please,* stop looking at me like that."

He resumed his confession. "The two of us eventually wound up in a cave near a small town called Calico Rock—in Arkansas. That's where Anna's from. Well, not Calico Rock, but in the vicinity. Then there was a white room where we spoke with the lady that haunted my dreams—"

"Spare me the details, will ya?" Al wailed. "Save it for your book." His voice suddenly weakened. "Oh . . . my heart's acting a little funny—kinda fluttery."

"Listen, Al. I don't expect you to believe what I'm saying."

"Good!"

"But God as my witness," Jess turned pleading eyes toward his longtime friend, "it's all true."

"You sure somebody didn't drug you . . . that you didn't hallucinate all this? Because, that's what it sounds like."

"For six months? Come on, Al. That isn't realistic either. Tell you what. If it'll help, I'll prove it to you. We'll go back to Arkansas—you, me and Anna."

"What're you saying—that Anna's *here?*" Al visually surveyed the car. "She's here now—and I can't *see* her?"

Jess spoke calmly to his distraught friend. "No, Al. But she *is* at my house."

"Jess, we've been friends a long time—through thick and thin. But you're asking too much of me. Why must you tell me this? I wish you'd kept it to yourself."

Jess looked hurt. "You're my family, Al. If I can't tell you, who *can* I tell? I don't have anyone else—except Anna. My true mate's been revealed to me, and I wanted to share it with the one person I'm closest to. Besides, I don't know *how* to keep secrets from you. You're too good at figuring things out."

"Oh, brother." Al managed to look guilty after receiving such a direct, heartfelt complement.

"I know! We'll go to Arkansas," Jess spewed definitively, "and the cave. *That* ought to convince you. That's what we'll do—the three of us. Okay, Al?"

"Ah, Jess. You don't have to go to all that trouble. If it makes you happy, I'll believe you." Al cringed. "Sorry. That didn't come out like I meant it." He made another attempt. "If *you* believe it happened, then it must have happened. Okay? I'll believe you, Jess. But I don't wanna. Why, it's *crazy* talk. And this invisible Anna of yours? What sort of plans do you have for *her?*"

"Somehow I was able to reenter my body while inside that cave. Anna will have to do the same."

"You're not afraid of losing her?"

"Don't you get it, Al? I *won't* lose her. She's a part of me . . . forever." Jess gripped the steering wheel. "I'd prefer to keep her in this lifetime though."

Al ignored the wish. "What made you bring her here?"

"I couldn't abandon her. She's still invisible—and helpless. Together, we've been given a job to do—to write this book."

"Oh, is *that* all? I was thinking that you couldn't stand the thought of being apart from her."

Al had struck a cord. Jess knew he was right. *Anna needs me and I need her.*

9

Keepers of the Way

———◆———

"That's it for me. I'm drawing a blank." Jess stared at the monitor, his fingers poised over the keyboard.

"End edit," Anna encouraged, standing behind his chair. Jess punched a few keys, shutting down the drive.

"The usual?"

"Yeah . . . let's go." Jess hesitated in his chair.

"Still thinking about Al?"

"I can't keep from it."

Anna kneaded his shoulders to relieve his tension.

"It couldn't be helped. You know I don't expect you to lie."

"I know. But you saw the look on his face when he left here. We must go back, Anna . . . if only for Al's sake."

"Don't you think that Al would've been with us the first time if it had been meant for him to share our experience?"

"I thought about that," he admitted. "It's difficult to judge who else is involved. That part wasn't explained."

Jess faced Anna.

She addressed his concern further. "We're doing okay, Jess. Come on. Let's get to our lucid dreaming. Otherwise, this book isn't gonna get finished."

"Okay. You take the couch. I'll take the floor."

Jess lay down beside the couch. Anna gave him a pillow to tuck beneath his head. She reached for his hand, and he took it.

He rose up to gaze into her clear blue eyes.

"You know that distracts me."

Jess resumed his position and began the regimen of relaxing his entire body. A vision of Anna loomed before his closed lids. He couldn't think her away, so he stopped trying. Reaching an arm up and wrapping it around her tiny waist, he gently pulled her down on top of him. They kissed passionately. He experienced suppressed urges spilling forth into a flood of burning desire. Making his intentions known, Anna rolled over for him. His body moved over hers. Out of his mind with desire, he—

"Whacha thinkin' about?" Anna asked.

Jess's eyes flew open. His breathing sounded disturbed.

"Huh? Oh." He sat up turning his back to the couch. A deep flush masked his face.

"This isn't working."

"Give it time. It'll come," Anna encouraged.

"No, Anna. I don't mean the lucid dreaming. I mean me—us."

Jess sighed heavily. "Do you really want to know what I was thinking? I was about to mentally make love to you. Anna . . . I'm losing confidence. I'm not sure why, but our experience seems less real. I *know* it happened." Jess looked to Anna for confirmation. "I have you as proof—unless . . . I'm imagining you.

"I want to go back, Anna. Not only for Al's sake . . . but for yours and mine as well. Something isn't right yet."

"What isn't right?"

"You're invisible, and we're too . . . doubtful."

"Jess, don't beat yourself up for wanting me. It's only natural to desire a physical relationship with someone you deeply love. You're *human*. Maybe someday—"

"The key word: *someday*." Jess's face relaxed. Anna's words managed to spark the expectation of a future together in their current life.

"Anna," Jess took her hand, ignoring the electric sensation that their combined touch created. "Will you go back to the cave with Al and me? I know it's asking a lot, but will you . . . *can* you?"

Anna concealed her unsettledness. "Of course. When?"

"Great. Tomorrow—in the morning. I'll go call Al."

Jess searched for the cordless phone. He came back and sat on the couch next to his invisible house guest. The number he dialed gave way to a ring. He looked at Anna for reassurance and received it in the form of a weak smile. He returned it.

"Hello. Is that you, Rose? No? Tell her it's Jess." He muffled the phone speaker. "Rose's sister. She's gone after Rose," he told Anna while he waited. "Rose . . . what is it? I can't understand you." Jess's posture stiffened. "Do what now? Al's *what*? Are you telling me . . . *Al's dead?*"

Anna quickly slid to the edge of the couch, her pulse rate kick-started by the one-sided conversation.

Jess's silent pause grew lengthy. His eyes stared straight ahead. "We'll be right there." He hung up. "Anna, we have to meet Rose at the hospital. An ambulance took Al's body there."

"What *happened?*" She grabbed Jess's arm, threatening to leave a bruise. "How is it possible? Al *can't* be gone."

"Heart attack, Rose said. *Dear God*, why didn't I heed the warning signs. He told me his heart felt funny. I should've taken him to get that checkup right then and there. My God, Anna, it's *my fault*. I told him about us, and his weak heart couldn't take it. I'm numb. My friend . . . my manager . . . my father figure is . . . *gone*—just like that."

Jess's mood unnerved Anna. She spoke cautiously. "Now Jess, let's rationalize this." She looked into his panic-stricken eyes. "Al's not gone. We have everlasting life, remember? We both know this. Al merely changed from the material to the spiritual." Anna's tone peaked. "*Please,* don't go getting too upset."

Jess suddenly came to and hugged Anna tightly. "It's okay, Anna. I remember. It's . . . a shock, that's all. He was here only hours ago. I'm having a hard time digesting it." He looked at Anna blankly. "What do you suppose all of this means?"

He rose, not waiting for a reply. "Let's go."

Standing next to each other, Jess studied his and Anna's mirrored reflection in the double glass doors of the hospital's emergency entrance. Darkness lay beyond. He cleared his throat and slowly shook his head. "Look at us, Anna. I'm twice your size. I'd understand if you—"

"Not another word, Jess Parks, or you and I will have our first argument—as a future engaged couple."

Anna's protest penetrated Jess's depression. "Sorry. Negative thinking on my part. Love hath no conditions."

He sadly smiled down at her sweet face. They held each other's gaze, brown eyes on blue.

A young man Jess hadn't noticed said, "Excuse me. Would you be speaking to me, sir?"

The unexpected interruption startled Jess. He shrugged. "Sorry. I'm talking to myself," he replied, wondering if the stranger had witnessed the two shadows when only one could be explained.

"Oh." The stranger cautiously moved away.

Jess detected no alarm. He looked around before speaking again. "What do you say to us taking off now—instead of waiting until morning? Rosie has plenty of family around her. She's too numb to notice me anyway. There's nothing left to do here, and I can't even *think* about sleeping. We can catch the midnight flight out. It shouldn't be heavily booked. Care to be on it?"

"That's fine." Anna nodded without looking up. "It's just that leaving the hospital seems so . . . final."

"I know," Jess agreed.

The plane turned out to be unusually crowded. "I guessed wrong. The flight was delayed in order to fill the seats," Jess whispered to Anna at his side as they walked past the ticket counter. "You ride in my lap—again."

"For four hours?"

"Want to wait till morning?" Jess smiled. "Don't worry. I'm looking forward to it."

An elderly female shuffled by. Her odd expression was directed at the tall man wearing dark shades and a hat in the middle of the night, and who appeared to be talking to himself.

Jess ignored her. Walking past the boarding gate, the odd couple entered the plane and found their seat. Jess placed a loose carry-on bag overhead. He sat and motioned Anna to take her place in his lap. A middle-aged woman was sitting in the window seat.

"I reckon I'll talk and you'll listen," Anna mused. It earned a huge smile from Jess who tried to look like someone who didn't have a person sitting on his lap.

Cradled and still, Anna took advantage. "Wish I had a feather."

Muffling his voice, Jess warned, "Let's not get carried away."

"Were you speaking to me, young man?"

"Pardon? I *said* it's kind of crowded tonight."

She glared up at the actor still wearing his disguise. Jess decided to attempt an excuse for his out-of-place eye wear. "The air-conditioning system dries out my contacts."

The woman, staring boldly at Jess, found her voice. "Those dark glasses aren't fooling *me*. You look *awfully* familiar."

Anna burst out laughing.

Jess directed an unsuccessfully stern look at Anna, but her laughter was catching.

"I beg your pardon. Was something funny? "

He quickly sobered. "Huh . . . no fair, ma'am, that you know me, and *I* don't know *you*."

Anna had heard *that* line before.

"Dan Parker's the name." He offered his hand.

She ignored Jess's friendly gesture. "Oh. I guess you *look* like someone else."

The awkwardness relieved, Jess nodded. The woman began to show an exaggerated interest with a magazine, putting an end to their conversation. Jess pulled his hat low. A gentle pinch warned Anna to cool it.

"*Ow!* We could've driven, you know." Jess cleared his throat loudly as a second warning. Anna resigned herself.

Sleep finally came to them. A few hours later, discomfort woke Jess. He needed to shift Anna's weight to restore circulation to one side of his body. His movements gave away his discomfort. Awakened, she repositioned herself without being asked. Sleep did not return.

"Jess," Anna finally said, "I'm gonna say this now because you can't argue with me." She attempted lightheartedness. "I've gotta go home. You know it; I know it. That's all there is to it. You gotta accept it. I can't stay invisible forever."

Jess felt his heart sink. It was the topic he dreaded most. Would their parting in this life come to pass? *I won't think about it*, he told himself. *Believe in the Way. Concentrate on the Way. We haven't come this far to lose each other now.*

Their direct flight from Burbank, California, had put them in Springfield, Missouri, at 5:30 a.m. After a short delay, they had boarded the small prop plane that transported them to Arkansas.

A set of keys dangled from Jess's extended hand. He jingled them at Anna, who was waiting for him outside the Harrison terminal. "It's the only rent-a-car available." He pointed to a white Mercury Sable sitting by itself at the end of the paved parking lot. "Let's get going."

Together, they walked toward the car. The dutiful sun created a pink rise in the eastern sky. Dew drops sparkled like a sprinkling of diamonds decorating the ground.

Before the next lap of their journey began, Jess drew in an appreciated lungful of fresh Ozark mountain air. Anna copied. No comment was necessary.

"It's close to seven o'clock. You tired?" Jess opened the passenger door for Anna. "We have a seventy-five mile drive ahead of us. Sleep—if you like."

"I *am* tired, but I couldn't possibly sleep a *wink*."

Driving past the familiar fast-food joints and the self-service gas station where he'd stolen his previous ride, Jess recalled it all with crisp clarity.

Breakfast smells riding the breeze entered through the lowered windows, reminding them of their empty stomachs. Jess pulled into a grocery store parking lot. "Be back in a minute." He returned with a bag of fresh fruit that would satisfy their hunger and thirst.

Anna had grown used to his usual breakfasts and relished them herself. She handed Jess pieces of fruit while he drove.

The Sable turned off Highway 65 South and onto Highway 62 East toward Mountain Home. A future right turn on Highway 5 South would lead them to their final destination.

The two drove in silence.

Anna suddenly reached over and lightly pinched Jess.

He reacted dramatically. *"Ow. What?"*

Anna wore a devilish smile. On a whim, he slowed the car and pulled off the highway.

Growing excited, Anna said, "Now, wait a darn minute! I was only paying you *back*."

She giggled as Jess reached for her. He began tickling her. Anna laughed delightedly.

"I don't even know if you're ticklish. Are you ticklish?" Anna continued to laugh. "You *are* ticklish." Jess laughed too.

Eventually, he sobered. His brown eyes gazed into her blue ones. A sudden, ugly thought of Anna's leaving him increased his heart rate. He tried to still it. The emotions building within him made him reach for her and hold her tight. His hot tears threatened to rain on her shiny black hair. He swallowed a sob before it could escape.

"Remember this, Jess. If we become separated, I'm forever yours. And when we pass from these lives, our souls will be together again. Know in your heart we belong together for all eternity. Next to God, I love you most."

Jess drew comfort from Anna's words. "I know," he whispered.

Cupping her small face in his large hands, he lightly kissed her lips. A soft moan escaped her.

Jess suddenly broke away. "We'd better get going."

The remainder of the drive proved uneventful. They parked the car one quarter mile short of their destination.

"Mind walking?"

Anna shook her head.

If they met up with their friend, Mr. Birdman, it was certain he would welcome Jess back.

"What if you can't get in?"

Anna's sudden question startled Jess.

"What if your material form won't allow you to pass through the barrier in the cave?"

"Then you'll have to go in alone. Can you do it, Anna?"

Anna studied the landscape beyond the car window. "You know I'll do anything for us."

After an awkward silence, she said, "Let's go with the flow."

Jess smiled. "It'll work out for us, Anna. You'll see."

More silence.

"Listen. If you *do* go home—" Jess concentrated to keep his voice from cracking. "Maybe we can figure out a way to stay in touch . . . a secret post office box . . . or we could call each other when no one's around . . ." His voice trailed.

Jess opened his door and stepped out.

Anna followed, directing a question over the top of the car. "What if my return triggers our minds into erasing all thoughts and memories of our time together?"

Jess panicked. "*Son.* I haven't thought of that." His mind whirled. He suddenly shook his head. "Hold on, Anna. *Please* don't be negative. Not now."

"Jess, it *happens* to be a possibility, and I *want* to discuss it."

"The Way, Anna, think of the Way."

"Tell me again?" Her tone hinted panic.

"God's way, Annie. We must believe all of the time, not only when it's easy."

"Think about it. What's the purpose of us going through all of this only to have our memories erased? For some reason, our veil has been lifted, and we now seek that reason."

Jess backed away from the car with outstretched arms. In a theatrical voice, he called out, "*There is nothing to fear but fear itself.*" He watched Anna's reaction. "We worry for nothing, you know. Have faith, Annie. It'll all work out. If I have to, I'll keep repeating it," he said, tapping his head with his forefinger, "until it becomes permanently ingrained."

Jess suddenly halted. He quickly closed the distance between them and hooked Anna's arm in his, leading her forward. "Isn't it funny how we have to keep reminding each other? We have the right idea, but we lack the discipline, my raven-haired beauty."

Jess began singing. "Row, row, row your boat, gently down the stream, merrily, merrily, merrily, life is but a dream." Anna smiled hugely. Jess nodded his approval. She joined him in chorus, their cheerful song interrupting the quiet surroundings.

The late spring air felt warm. Inside, the cool contrast of Birdman's Cave greeted them. They entered the tunnel without hesitation—Anna first.

"Look, Jess. See it?"

"No. I don't see anything."

"It's right in front of us."

Jess detected Anna's disappointment. Astutely absorbing the situation, he hid his uneasiness.

"Anna, *go on.*" She looked back at Jess visible in the glow of his flashlight. "Go *on*," he firmly repeated.

Anna moved forward. Alone, she witnessed the familiar brilliant, ethereal light. Jess watched her disappear into darkness.

Sitting back allowed him more physical comfort. He rubbed his fresh beard stubble. An eerie shiver suddenly ran through his body. *What if Anna doesn't come back for days . . . or months . . . or—— Stop thinking negatively. Remember the Way. Remember the Way.*

Turning off the flashlight to save the batteries, Jess closed his eyes against the consuming blackness. He proceeded to engage in soothing meditation.

The room was as Anna remembered. A cool fire burned in spite of the warmer weather outside. The snow-white sofa was again occupied, but by someone other than Merry. Anna discerned that the individual was male. Facing the back of the sofa shielded his identity. Anna's position suddenly shifted without having taken a step. She found herself in front of the sofa facing its occupant. The shock forced air into her lungs.

"*Al.*"

"Please, Anna. Don't be alarmed."

Al's presence quickly calmed her. He was not the first ghost she'd witnessed.

"It's okay." He smiled warmly.

"*Al.* You——I——you startled me! That's all. How *are* you? You look so . . . *well.*"

"I'm so happy, Anna. I'm *free.*"

"I wish Jess could see you now."

"Ah, Jess. Jess is good—so *very* good. We've been blessed to know him. He is destined to keep the Way. If only I had been blessed with the knowledge while I was among the living. No matter. We know only what we're supposed to know while in the physical realm. Now that I've passed, it's all coming back. Anna, it's *your* time to transition back to the living, and we are here to help."

"We?"

"Anna." A familiar male voice called from behind. The air Anna breathed singed her lungs. She swung around.

"*JOEL?*"

"I'm here, Anna. There now, don't go looking like a mouse caught stealing the cheese. You've nothing to feel guilty about. Anna, your behavior as usual has been exemplary. You continue to impress with your high morals. No one could have acted better."

"But—"

"But what? Do you think I expect you to ignore your bond to eternal love? Hasn't it occurred to you that I too might have an eternal bond with a soul other than yourself? One earthly marriage doesn't necessarily an eternal love make. Lessons were learned through our companionship. And now, it's time for each of us to move on to *greener pastures,* as they say." Joel smiled tenderly at Anna. "Remember the wedding vow, 'till-death-do-us part'?"

Anna's voice was no more than a whisper. "You mean—" She looked to Al for confirmation. Al merely smiled.

"It's okay to say it, Anna," Joel encouraged.

"—you *died?*" Anna suddenly felt dizzy.

"How do you think I came to be here?"

"I reckon I just didn't *think.* When?"

"It's been three earthly months ago. Do not mourn me, for you see I am well."

To Anna, Joel looked more than well.

"You're free, Anna—free to go back to Jess, to our children. They don't understand the change in their mother's disposition. Till now, my death has been your excuse. You must merge with your material form. Important duties lie ahead. Goodbye, Anna. We'll meet again."

The image of Anna's husband faded to nothingness. She stood transfixed until Al interrupted her racing thoughts.

"Huh? Oh. Sorry, Al. I'm completely overwhelmed."

"Ah, but the wondrous human mind is able to cope. Tell me you can't accept sharing a life with Jess—with your children."

Al's words warmed Anna's heart. "Oh, but I think I *can*." Her hands framed her face. "You speak of dreams I didn't dare imagine."

"This I know. Because of your wonderful virtue, it will be easy for you to keep the Way."

"Jess says the Way is a clear path to God."

"Jess is correct. The Master is a Keeper of the Way."

"You mean Jesus?"

"Yes. That's who I mean."

Anna began to pace. Excitement poured through her. "I can hardly think straight, Al. It's almost too much." She stopped pacing and faced him. Her eyes flashed fire. "Now what?"

Al laughed heartily. "That, I cannot say. You must go find out for yourself. Be *off* with you, Anna. There is nothing more to accomplish here. Jess is waiting."

Anna's laughter bordered on hysteria. She moved toward Al, intending to wrap her arms around his neck, but hesitated.

"Is it okay?"

Al laughed at Anna's seriousness. "It's okay."

She hugged him hard, halfway surprised at his solidity. "This is for Jess too."

Al's eyes twinkled. "I think I'm going to like this spirit life." Hand in hand, the two exchanged long looks.

Anna found herself drawn to the glowing white portal that would lead her to a new beginning.

Al began to sing. "Row, row, row your boat, gently down the stream, merrily, merrily, merrily—"

Anna looked back, joining him in verse. "—life is but a dream."

Enveloped in darkness, she called out to Jess.

He jerked awake. "I'm here, Anna. What's going on?"

Groping for the flashlight resting in his lap, he pointed its overwhelming brilliance in the direction of her voice. She dodged the harshness, signaling Jess to focus above her head.

"How long have I been gone?"

"I'm not sure. Probably minutes. I fell asleep."

Relief flooded him at her return. "Are you okay? What happened in there?"

"Jess! *Oh, Jess.*"

Something within Anna snapped. A tremendous release of built-up tension burst forth in a flood of tears. Her loud sobs stunned him. He leaned forward to take her arm and pull her to him. She fell against his chest, quickly soaking his shirt.

Why was Anna so hysterical? Jess feared the worst.

"*Anna.* Are you hurt?"

Anna found her voice. "No."

"Then what is it?" he tenderly demanded. Though another moment passed, he did not pressure her.

"I'm sorry, Jess. Can we get out of here? I don't like the dark."

"Neither do I. Can you manage?" Anna responded with a nod, wiping her wet face.

They worked their way toward the entrance. Jess led. Light streamed into the cave's yawning mouth, welcoming their exit. The ground grew warm beneath them.

Jess sat cradling Anna to his already soaked chest. He soothingly brushed her hair. "Now, tell me what happened?"

"Jess . . . you won't believe it. I saw *Joel* in there."

"*What?* Did he *hurt* you?"

"No." Anna looked up into Jess's eyes. "He wouldn't ever hurt me, Jess. He's *dead.* Joel's *dead.* He's *been* dead for *three months.*"

Jess sat numbly, struggling to absorb the unbelievable turn of events. "So *that's* what has you so upset."

"No, you don't understand."

"Apparently not."

"Joel's fine," Anna said, between sobs. "He's *happy.* He told me not to mourn him. And somehow, Jess, I don't feel like I should." Anna drew her brows together in puzzlement. "Don't you see?"

"No. But that's okay. Go on."

"You won't believe who else I saw. Al. He was in there too. He was sitting on the white sofa. Remember it?"

Jess nodded dramatically.

Anna's tears began to dry through the recounting of her experience. "*Oh, Jess*. Al was *so happy*. He *told* me so."

Again the distraught young woman burst into fresh tears. She continued relating her emotional experience. The words eventually stopped coming.

"You mean it's over . . . it's *actually over?*"

Anna rose to her knees. "It's over, Jess. Yes. It's over." Her sudden laughter filled the air. Jess laughed too. They caught each other up in a long hard hug.

"What time is it? I'd like to be home when the kids arrive on the school bus."

"*Okay*—the kids. Yes. I'll *gladly* take you home. It's probably best I'm not present when they arrive. I'll wait close by and come to the door after you've had some time alone. Keep in mind, Anna. You've missed them, but they haven't missed you."

"There's so much to *consider*." Jess palmed his head with both hands. "My mind's about to *explode*."

"I know," Anna giggled, losing herself in Jess's eyes. "I haven't allowed myself to—"

"Me neither." Jess held his true mate tight, and for the first time since they'd met felt secure in their future.

"*Son*. I'm a little nervous. Do you think Peter and Rachael will like me?"

10

Anna's Kids

The familiar surroundings of her home comforted Anna. She traveled from one room to another, ending up in her own bedroom. Nothing was changed.

The closet—proof. She opened Joel's. *Yes.* All of his belongings were gone. A few of Anna's own things now occupied the empty space. *It's true then. I don't even know what killed him.*

Having spoken with Joel in the other plane alleviated any heavy sadness that she might ordinarily have experienced. Anna viewed it as a personal blessing. A loud sigh escaped her. She closed the door, leaning her back against it. Her recent past felt like a lifetime ago.

Taking clean clothing out of her dresser, she headed for the bathroom, thinking a warm shower might help to soothe her physical exhaustion and clear her overloaded mind.

A floor-length mirror hung on the back of the door. It caught her eye as she stepped out of the shower stall.

Anna critically examined herself. All of her lifelong flaws had returned. *Were they ever gone?* In the past, they might have bothered her. But due to recent events, she could no longer take them to heart. She studied the appendectomy scar. *Nothing I can do about that. I'll consider it a causality-of-life wound.* Jess's diet had shaved off a few unwanted pounds. She studied her wrinkle-free face. *After all, I'm only thirty. I could use a haircut.*

She quickly dressed.

Today, the children rode the school bus home. Excited, she walked to the highway's edge and patiently waited, deep in thought.

Anna didn't want events to appear out of the ordinary. She intuited that some things had changed since the passing of her husband, but routine was crucial. She felt badly for the children losing their father at such a young age. She would concentrate on them now.

Arriving early, the wait for the school bus was long. Though Anna studied the immediate area, her eyes couldn't focus. The bus arrived promptly. The children disembarked and ran to their mother. Forcing self-control, Anna attempted a normal greeting. Peter and Rachael hadn't noticed the extra hugs. Any opposition to the norm Anna painstakingly avoided. Simple chores were performed before the usual snacks were handed out.

"Well? Whacha think?" Anna smiled. A deep and utter calm beautified her countenance.

Jess rested casually against a door frame, one leg crossing the other. He quickly surveyed his surroundings, showing more interest in Anna.

They stood close. Jess's breath tickled her sensitive ear.

"Nice. Modest—yet attractive. Very neat; very clean. I can appreciate it."

Anna wondered if Jess were critiquing her instead.

"Thank you."

"I see a fondness of the Orient—perhaps a past life?"

She shrugged off his comment, but her smile remained. He warmly returned it.

Anna felt Jess's examining eyes. She lowered hers to the floor. "I'm glad you think I look okay."

Jess sensed her insecurity. "Hey, you've accepted *my* flaws."

Relying on his charm, he quickly borrowed Anna's phrase. "Next to

God, I love you most."

Anna's eyes revealed her seriousness. "I don't know . . . maybe I'm assuming—"

"Hey. I'm assuming too," he interrupted. "Do you recall Merry's words—that our physical faults seem more noticeable in our own eyes? So know this. To me, Anna, you're perfect."

"You're perfect, too, Jess."

He rolled his eyes and tossed his head in the direction of Peter and Rachael. "I think they like me." His happy grin relieved the awkward moment.

"*Love* is a better word." Anna flipped the dishtowel in her hand. "They haven't seen a man cook before. Meal preparation wasn't exactly a family affair." The dishtowel snapped again more sharply. "Supper was wonderful. Thanks."

"Yeah, well, expect some griping and complaining for the next few weeks. Because that's about how long it takes to get used to being weaned from processed food. The older, the harder. You're sure you want to start this with them, Anna?"

She batted her long lashes. "But they *loved* the meal."

"It's something new, which will wear off quickly."

"Then we'll use the Way to make it easier."

"Now you're talking. You have two wonderful children, Anna. But like all kids, they're going to need discipline."

Anna read his mind. "Sweetheart, you have my permission."

"There's a lot to consider."

"Jess, I don't know what it's like to have others doing for you. I've always taken care of myself. I don't have any money to speak of. Most of my clothes were given to me. I rarely buy new ones." Anna blushed at her confession. "It isn't that we're poor. It's that it isn't important to me."

"Let me share something with you. I'm more impressed with people who can take care of themselves than with perfectly normal people who expect to be cared for. I suspect on that issue we agree. Why else would you have asked me if I had hired help?"

Anna relaxed. She shook a finger at him. "You opened yourself up to that, Jess Parks."

"Did I?"

"Maybe we're a lot alike," he pointed out.

"So what've you thought about doing with your life, Anna?"

"Well. I always wanted to teach. I help with a Sunday school class, and I *do* enjoy it."

"A teacher—it suits you. Can you get training around here?"

"I can start at the branch college in town. But . . . teaching isn't a glamorous job, Jess."

"You aren't a glamorous person. Liz Taylor was glamorous. I happen to appreciate you as you are."

He abruptly changed the subject. "I've been thinking hard and heavy. I know you have too. Here's a plan I've come up with. Tell me what you think. You said Peter and Rachael will be out of school in a couple of weeks. Why don't you see the kids through, and I'll go back to L. A. to get things ready for the three of you."

"Oh, I don't know," Anna cautiously replied. "I haven't ever considered moving. This has always been my home, Jess."

"Then let's make it for the summer. Three months. By then, you and the kids will know if you're contented there. If not, you'll come back and start the school term here. Deal?"

"Besides, the book must be finished."

"The *book*. I nearly forgot. Yes. You have a point. We can't ignore it. Yes, it *must* be finished."

"Okay. Then it's settled. We'll come. Oh, my! The kids will be *thrilled*. They've never been past the state of Missouri."

"What about you, Jess? What's in your future?"

Jess held Anna's hands. "You are my future, Anna. Other than that, the book, I guess. It'll be successful. We both know it. Folks will believe the book is fiction. That's best. Our goal is to create something appealing that'll help prepare for the Way to become a part of everyone's existence. Think of it as a means to an end. The Way, in itself, will generate acceptance for all." Excitement grew in Jess. "Then there's a movie to make. I can't think beyond that."

His expression grew thoughtful. "Behold, I will send my messenger, and he shall prepare the way before me," he quoted, from the book of "Malachi". Maybe the word "messenger" was meant to be plural."

Anna's eyes danced.

"Have you given any thought to playing your own part?"

"*No.* So forget it, Jess Parks."

The actor rolled his eyes. *Her shyness is surfacing.* He reminded himself to bring it up later.

"So. You have the kids and California to consider. And *I* must return for Al's funeral. Rose would want me there."

Jess anxiously clapped his hands. "Shall we go tell the kids? Maybe we can help them with their homework."

"I can already tell you're gonna make a fine father figure."

Anna spun on her heels. "Race ya."

Jess emerged from Peter's room when Anna called his name.

"Guess what? Rachael has a fever."

"Kind of sudden, isn't it?"

"That's how kids are—fine one minute, and not so fine the next. I'll give her some children's—"

Jess interrupted. "Fever's actually a good thing. It's meant to burn off an invading virus. If you give her something to suppress it, the fever will probably return. How high is it?"

"A hundred and one."

"That's below alarming. Let's bundle her up and give it two hours. If it hasn't broken, give her what you think is best. Deal?"

Anna gave him a trusting smile. "Deal."

"I don't suppose you have any herbal tea?"

"Sorry. No."

"I'm going to take a look in the kitchen. Remember. Keep her covered. We want her to sweat."

Jess returned shortly. "I made a vinegar poultice. It's smelly, but it's effective in reducing fever. My Aunt used it on me."

He approached Rachael. "Is she sleeping?"

Anna looked up from her chair by the bed. "Not yet. I think the fever's made her chatty." She smiled at her daughter.

"Mind if I wrap you in vinegar-soaked towels, Rachael?"

"No. It smells like pickles."

"Do you like pickles?"

"Yeah."

"Then think of it as pickle juice."

"Pickle juice, yum."

"Can you drink a little pickle juice for me?" he asked, handing her a small concoction of apple-cider vinegar, honey, and water.

"Sure," Rachael replied, taking the cup and sipping from it. "Tastes like *sweet* pickle juice."

The young child allowed Jess to apply the home remedy.

Anna watched, pleased with his gentle touch. "Having a health nut in the family will be handy."

"I've been called worse," he teased.

"Jess," Anna bit her lower lip, "this is an easy one." She nodded toward Rachael. "Sure you want to get involved?"

Jess gazed intently into Anna's questioning eyes. "I'm sure—and don't ask me again. I know it's awkward, but practice assuming that it's all playing out as it should. Okay?"

"Okay," she returned softly.

"How'd it go with Peter?"

"We did great. Homework's finished."

She smiled her thanks.

An hour later, the fever broke.

Anna quizzed her daughter.

"I feel fine, Mommy. Can I go to school tomorrow?"

"If there's no fever in the morning—and no other symptoms, you may go to school."

"Yippee!" Rachael cried, above a whisper.

"Now good night, young lady. Your brother is already asleep."

"Good night, Mommy. Good night, Dylan," Rachael said, reverting to using the actor's television series name. She instantly realized her mistake and corrected herself. "I mean, *Jess*."

"That's okay, Rachael. It happens all the time. Good night, little one," he called softly from the doorway. A blossoming love for Anna's daughter warmed his heart.

Jess and Anna stood in the hall exchanging eye contact. He bent to kiss her mouth. She shivered from the caress of his soft lips. Her legs became rubber. She slid to the floor.

"First time I've had *this* effect on anyone." Jess allowed her to rest momentarily before offering his hand. Anna took it. He pulled her up lightly and gently pushed her against the wall. "I have ways of showing my love." He leaned against her to prove his words. She understood his message.

"Jess—" Anna broke away with what strength she possessed.

"I know, sweetheart. Part of being a good parent is being responsible, but I want you to know my thoughts."

"Guess I should go. The neighbors probably know there's a strange man here. I wouldn't want to spoil your *shining* reputation."

Jess grew serious. "I'm going to have to leave you— for now. If you don't show up when I send for you . . . I'll be back. So please, show up."

"I will. I promise."

Anna felt her throat tighten. "I don't want you to go. I don't want to be separated for *any* length of time."

"If it's any consolation, I feel the same. Do you realize how long we've been together? Two weeks apart sounds too long. Remember that we have eternity. Remember the Way. It'll all work out. Absorb yourself in the kids. We'll survive."

"Remember the Way," she repeated. "We no longer have to be so concerned. Everything always works out."

Jess nodded his agreement. "Always keep that at the front of your mind."

The couple sat briefly on the couch. Their lips locked in a warm, tender kiss for several moments. Together they rose and walked to the door. No other words passed between them. Jess slipped out and was gone.

Anna pulled the hide-a-bed out of the living-room sofa. She wouldn't allow her mind to become troubled with conflicting emotions. Her marriage to Joel—and the bed they'd shared—was now in the past.

Tight muscles protested as Anna maximized the leg-stretching pose—a trade off, one week of yoga and basic natural hygiene diet for five more lost pounds.

Sitting in full lotus, she closed her eyes and began her breathing technique, allowing her thoughts to form and play out in her mind as she focused within.

Thank you for Jess, she silently prayed. *Thank you for showing me that You are within me. Thank you for blessing me with the wisdom to know my body is a temple, and I should care for it as much as I care for my spiritual development. Thank you, God, for the Way.*

Releasing herself from her pose, Anna picked up her mat. *The kids are due. Better get supper early.*

Peter and Rachael noisily entered the house. The aroma of fresh baked bread and steamed vegetables hung in the air.

Anna peeked around the corner. "Looky what came today," she exclaimed, waving three first-class airline tickets and a charge card.

"Whoa!" Peter remarked. "Those *real?*"

"Yes." Anna waltzed around the kitchen, her eyes sparkling at the thought of seeing Jess.

"Tomorrow, we go shopping for traveling clothes. Jess suggested we get good luggage. We'll need it in the future."

"You didn't mention our trip to California . . . ? I know it wasn't easy. But let's see if we like it before we make any permanent announcements. Okay?"

Rachael sensed her mother's relief. "It's okay, Mom. The waiting part's over."

"And now, it's time for the *fun* part, kids. Tomorrow morning, we'll go to Springfield—"

"—buy what we need—" Peter interjected.

"—and spend the night?" Rachael finished with a question.

Anna nodded. "Two nights. We'll leave on our first airplane ride Monday. Isn't it *exciting?*"

Rachael clapped her hands and squealed her delight.

Peter grew serious. "What about the car?"

"It's sold. The buyer agreed to pick it up in Springfield. See how things work out?"

"Now, let's have supper."

"Can we eat out tomorrow, Mom? I'm tired of boiled 'tatos'."

"I don't see a problem with that, Rach. Okay with you, Pete?" Anna thought that she might go deaf.

Peter stared solemnly out of the back door from his chair. "Things sure are different since Dad's been gone."

Rachael picked up on his mood. Her small arms crossed her little chest. "I'm still mad at him for leavin' us."

Anna felt stunned. She slowly took a seat, forming in her mind carefully thought-out words. "Kids . . . your dad didn't leave us to be cruel. It's that his time in this life was complete. He was ready to move on. We all will—eventually. So don't begrudge him. Try to be happy that he's now closer to God."

"Happy?" Peter's anger came through. "That he's *dead?*"

"Think of it this way, Pete. If you died, and Rachael and I were mad at you for leaving us, how would you feel about that?"

"Well . . . I suppose I wouldn't like it. But it wouldn't matter, 'cuz I'd be dead."

"Oh, but you're wrong, Pete. It would matter a lot. What if you could see Rachael and me from the other side and you knew we were mad at you for leaving us. I think it would make you very sad."

"So my anger is making Dad sad."

"I believe so." Anna folded her hands and placed them on the table. "Peter . . . try to let him go. Dad wants us to pick up and go on with our lives."

"How do you know, Mommy?" Rachael asked.

Anna decided to take a chance. "Because, I saw him in a dream a couple of months after—" She paused. "Kids . . . your father looked happy, and he told me not to mourn him, and that he knew about my friend, Jess."

"Your *friend*, Mom?" Peter curtly interjected. "What kind of relationship do you and Jess have?"

Kids are so smart. Anna cleared her throat. "We have a respectable one, son."

"Anyway, Dad said he understood why Jess and I had special feelings for each other, and that it was okay with him if we were together. I know Jess was a surprise. He was a surprise to me too."

Peter looked confused. "You mean Dad *encouraged* it?" Anna nodded, "Honest. As a matter of fact, your father's death allowed the two of us—excuse me—the four of us to get together."

"Come on, Pete. Think about it. Has Mom ever lied to us?"

Rachael's wise insight impressed Anna. She keenly awaited her son's response.

"No," he grudgingly admitted.

"And I promise you both . . . I never will."

Peter accepted his mom's promise. "*Okay*. Mom, did Dad say anything about us?"

"Yes." Anna smiled at them both. "He told me to take good care of our children because you need me. So is he right?"

Peter and Rachael rose from their chairs and hugged their mother in turn.

"Yeah. He's right," Peter agreed.

"Mommy?"

"Yes, Rachael?"

"Did Dad tell you to *marry* Jess?"

Jess watched the shimmering heat rise from the hot tarmac. He played with the idea of having a ready-made family, and maybe someday, he and Anna would create a new addition.

The plane finally landed and taxied toward the parked vehicle. A portable staircase was rolled up to the door. Anna and her children emerged, escorted by a flight attendant who walked them down the steps. Spotting the vehicle described to her, the attendant directed them toward Jess. The staircase was rolled away, and the plane resumed its taxi to the terminal.

"*Wow*, Mom. *Look at that.*" Peter whistled. "A brand-spankin-new *rig*. *Wow*. It's a thooster!" he declared.

Jess climbed out of the shiny new vehicle, beaming. "What exactly is a "thooster"?"

"It's *big*," Peter loudly explained.

"I thought we might need the extra room."

Jess squatted and grabbed one kid per arm. His affectionate action moved Anna.

Hugging her last, he said, "You look good enough to eat."

Holding her at arms length, he admired her summer dress that enhanced her eyes and revealed more of her recent weight loss.

"Yoga," she explained.

"Ahh, *yoga*."

"The library had some books on yoga. I checked them out and started doing it on my own. *I love it.*"

"Wonderful. It suits you. If you're interested, we'll get you enrolled in a class. That way you can get professional guidance."

Anna smiled hugely. "I'll have you know that I can execute some of the poses *perfectly*."

"Execute?" Jess repeated.

Anna's smile faded. "I'm from Arkansas, but I'm *not* ignorant."

"Whoa! No offense intended," Jess shot back. He quickly made a mental note to avoid prodding Anna's defensive nature. *She must be tired. Understandable.*

"Good. Then none taken."

Anna changed the subject. "Why did we disembark here?"

"It's a perk."

Peter interrupted. "What's a perk?"

"It's a fringe benefit," his mother offered.

"Oh." The contented Peter quickly disappeared from sight.

"You do realize what would've happened had I entered the airport terminal."

"I understand."

"Don't worry. You'll be okay—if we can keep the newshounds from picking up your scent."

Rachael latched onto the odd title. "What's a newshound?"

Jess chuckled at her innocent curiosity. He folded himself down to her size. "Well, Rachael, it's a news reporter who wants to impress his boss." Rachael nodded once and ran around the vehicle to look for Peter.

Jess rose and pulled Anna to him and boldly admitted, "I've missed you so much. I was just enjoying a lucid dream—us consummating our relationship. It's okay, Anna. You aren't married; I'm not married."

Peter's face popped out from behind the vehicle. "What does "consummating" mean?"

Like trapped rats, the open-mouthed adults stared at each other. Neither spoke. Peter quickly shrugged it off and continued his inspection of the new sport-utility vehicle. Jess looked relieved.

"Get used to the awkward questions," Anna informed.

She returned to the previous subject. "You already know my opinion, Jess."

"Yes . . . I *do* know—and so the reason for our first stop. Come on, gang. Pile in."

Their luggage loaded, Jess skillfully drove them out of the bustling airport parking lot.

"You can ask, but I won't tell," Jess directed at Anna about their destination. "It's a surprise."

"Say, guys. Did I mention that tomorrow is Disney Day? Each year the studio rents a day at Disney Land for the children of the stars. It's a way for us to play without being bothered by reporters."

"I know, I know!" Rachael cried out in her little-girl voice. "Autographer hounds who want to impress their bosses."

The vehicle's occupants roared with laughter. Jess was the first to compose himself. "Something like that, Rachael."

"So, does anyone want to go to Disney Land tomorrow?"

The affirmative coming from the back seat made Jess duck his head. "*Son.* I wouldn't have imagined that two little kids—"

"Watch who you're calling little," Peter warned.

"Pardon me—one little kid—mind if I call you little, Rachael?"

Rachael giggled. "No, I *am* little."

"*Okay.* I wouldn't have imagined that one little kid and one *big* kid could make so much noise. Anyway, we're on then, right?"

"Right," Peter and Rachael chorused at a more reasonable decibel level.

Peter elbowed Rachael. "*Told* ya we'd go to Disney Land."

Jess overheard and smiled. He had achieved his simple goal; give them something to look forward to.

They rode in silence. The children were content to peer through the windows at sunny California and think about a day at Disney Land. Anna continuously stole glances at the man who made her heart soar.

Jess stopped the vehicle in front of a corner jewelry store. He turned around in his seat and blurted out his proposal. "Say, kids . . . what's your opinion about me marrying your Mom?" Anna's face turned into a royal flush. Jess smiled hugely at her.

Peter broke the deafening silence. The sharpness in his reply stood out. "It's a little soon, isn't it?"

Jess decided to respond to Peter's judgment. "Listen, Pete. Okay if I call you Pete?"

Peter sighed uncomfortably. "Yeah, I guess."

"Listen, Pete. Your mother and I believe that we should get the most out of every day of life." Jess looked to Anna for approval. "We'd like to teach you kids to feel the same way. For example, if it's a quiet day, then live a quiet day. If it's an exciting day, then live an exciting day. A simpler way of putting it is, go with the flow. You understand what I'm saying, Pete?"

"Yes, sir."

"Rachael?"

"I think so, sir."

"We're all partners here—in everything we do. I don't want to rock the boat. So, *may* I have your permission to ask your mother to marry me?" Jess repeated.

Peter thought about their conversation at the dinner table the night before they left their home. "If it's okay with Dad," he sighed, "I reckon it's okay with me."

Jess looked at Anna quizzically. She formed the words silently. "I'll explain later."

"Rachael—honey—what's your opinion?"

Rachael replied sweetly, "You have *my permission*."

Jess revealed his relief with laughter. He looked at Anna and whispered, "I don't know what you said to them, but I didn't expect it to be this easy."

"Let's go in," he addressed them all. "I want your mom to pick out her ring."

Inside the store, Jess hinted to the jeweler to conceal price tags. He knew Anna would base her selection accordingly.

"Choose the one that pleases you most," he informed her.

Anna settled on a modest half-carat diamond engagement ring with a blue sapphire wrap-around. Not the largest; not the smallest.

"Comes in a set," the jeweler offered. The set consisted of an additional gold wedding band with a dozen small recessed diamonds. They took the set.

Jess selected a matching band. "Now, all we need is a date."

"Come here, Mom." Peter stood peering into a glass case. "Look at these Mickey Mouse watches. Aren't they *great?*"

Anna cleverly settled Peter down. "Remember, you have a birthday coming up."

With Anna distracted, Jess turned to pay for his purchase. "While you're at it," he quietly addressed the jeweler, "throw in one of those Mickey Mouse watches." Jess winked. "The boy has a birthday coming up."

The jeweler smiled. "Handsome family."

Because the sale was already made, Jess believed he meant it.

The four-wheel-drive moved smoothly through traffic as if driven by a pro. Anna was again impressed with Jess's multiple capabilities. She had no clue where they were going, contented to let him guide them through the next moments of their lives. Bliss kept a smile on her face.

Jess popped the steering wheel with the heel of his hand after another stolen glance at Anna. Once again, he guided the vehicle to a halt. He twisted slightly and grabbed his startled front-seat passenger for a quick kiss. Peter and Rachael watched in surprised silence. Jess released Anna and turned to beam at them, his brown eyes sparkling like glitter.

"*My family,*" he said, like little else mattered.

It suddenly occurred to Anna why Jess was reacting in this manner. *I've been so worried about us being a burden that I've failed to comprehend his happiness. He's had no one to love him—no living family for quite some time. And now he has us.* Anna fully relaxed for the first time since their arrival.

The bold smiles Anna's children wore encouraged Jess. He faced forward and started the engine, stealing one more loving glance at his future wife.

Peter turned to Rachael. In a whisper meant for her alone, he said, "I think Jess needs us." Rachael nodded hugely.

Soon Anna recognized familiar store fronts and streets. *I really was here.* Jess glanced her way as if he'd read her mind. A short time later, he pulled into an unfamiliar drive leading to a spacious two-story home. "What's this?" Anna inquired.

Jess replied enthusiastically. "This is where we're all going to live." He leaned toward Anna. "You might say fate selected it for us. This is Al and Rose's home. She chose to live with her sister and wants us to have it."

"*Oh, my.*" Anna fought tears. "*No, I don't mind. I'm speechless.*"

"Then come on, Speechless. Let's go take a look."

"Kids, I want to explain why we won't have our own in-ground swimming pool. They're a lot of work, and they can take up the whole backyard. Pools can be dangerous if not respected. However, we *do* have a membership at a nearby club. So . . . you kids can swim any time it's convenient. Okay?" Jess ended as they reached the front door to the house.

"*Okay*," they chorused.

The house proved spacious on the inside. Bedrooms with adjoining baths occupied the second level. A formal living room, dining room, and den along with a large open kitchen and sunroom full of live plants made up the first floor. Jess led them through a set of French doors opening onto a lengthy, wide-terraced deck, bordered by flowering bushes. Native California fruit trees spread their shady branches across the generous backyard.

"*Oh, Jess.* This is better than any old swimmin' pool," Anna exclaimed. Her darting eyes caught sight of the garden spot ready and awaiting planting, strategically placed in the sunniest corner. She drew in her breath. "Our own garden? How *thoughtful.* I couldn't *live* without a garden." Anna beamed.

"I know gardens are already up, but it isn't too late to plant entirely, and you can decorate with flowers to your heart's content."

Descending the steps, Anna entered the freshly furrowed rows. "I must be *dreaming*. This dirt's been hauled in—and fertilized too. I can hardly *wait*." She restrained herself from running her hands through the rich sun-warmed earth. There'd be plenty of time to stain her freshly manicured nails.

She sat on the bottom step, soaking it all in. Jess sat beside her. They watched the children explore their new world.

"Remember, I share mine—you share yours. It's a fair arrangement, Anna."

"It's fair," she agreed.

He took her hand. "Now that the kids are busy exploring, we can set our wedding date. And let's make it soon. *Real* soon."

"Look. I think Pete's spotted a tree house setting."

Jess's request, though highly anticipated, created uneasiness in Anna. "It's all moving along faster than I expected." She studied Jess's sparkling eyes. The sunlight brought out tiny flecks of gold she hadn't noticed.

He gave her hand a gentle squeeze. *All she has to do is look at me and my heart melts.*

"What happened to us spending the summer, huh?"

"Can you think of any reason why we can't have a home here . . . *and* in Arkansas?" he asked. "We can keep your house—or better yet—build a new house . . . whatever you like. Say yes. *Please*. Love the one you're with, remember?" Anna found his endearing proposal irresistible.

"What about the book?" she reminded.

"With the wedding out of the way, we can concentrate on our writing all the more. Annie, you saw the computer room. It used to be a spare bedroom." He laughed curtly. "*I'm* not expecting company. Are you?"

Pleased with Jess's forethought, Anna answered with her twinkling, azure-blue eyes.

She rose abruptly. "Shall we go unpack?"

Jess stopped Anna on the second stair, their height difference made more even. Both leaned forward, their lips touching. Passion flowed hot like erupting lava. Emotional control hung precariously by a burning thread. It was Jess who broke the fiery kiss. They supported each other, drained of physical strength.

"Care to spend a little time on the book this evening?"

"It's okay with me—if the kids don't need us."

"I imagine they'll find *something* to occupy their time."

"What kind of a wedding would you like?"

Anna was unprepared. "Well . . ."

"Name it."

"We—Joel and I—"Anna amended, "—didn't have a formal wedding." She lowered her eyes. "We married young. I was barely eighteen. He was nineteen." Anna looked up. "A courthouse wedding isn't so glamorous. I later regretted not having a church wedding. You know how *un-smart* kids can be."

Jess couldn't place blame for Joel's impatience. "Ariel and I had a monstrous wedding. It was more like an entertainer's gala, all quite grand—but kind of . . . cold. I asked myself why I put myself through it." Shaking off the memory, he said, "But now, I realize it was meant for me to have that experience because our personal experiences are what shape us—make us wiser."

"But never mind all that. This is *our* wedding. It has nothing to do with Joel or Ariel. It'll be a fresh start. We can do what we want. If we want a small wedding, we'll have a small wedding."

Anna laughed again, which she presently did more often.

"What?" Jess smiled at her laughter.

"I was thinking. Who will we invite?"

"Good point." Jess studied hard. "Rosie would want to come— to represent Al. I *do* have friends—and *you* have friends." He suddenly appeared doubtful. "We could invite the homeless—or we could have it on the beach and invite whoever's there."

Anna felt giddy. "I'm sure we'll come up with *something*."

"Seriously. What about having it at the club? We must set a date. How about two weeks?"

"*Two weeks*," Anna shot back.

"You're putting me off, Anna, darling." He pulled her close. "I'd rather we didn't wait at all. Two weeks. That's long enough to get a reply from any invitations we decide to send."

She sighed in his arms. "Let's send them immediately."

"So it's decided." The happy groom-to-be tenderly caressed his one true mate.

"It makes me weak when you do that." She released herself and momentarily stood alone, allowing her emotions to stabilize. Jess rarely spoke of his ex. Anna felt closer for sharing. She turned and locked her arm in his. "Time's a-wasting." Together they walked up the steps and into their new life.

"Whoa!" Anna stared straight up at the gigantic roller coaster looming largely before them. "You expect me to ride on *that*?"

Peter pulled her arm. "*Come on, Mom. We gotta ride it*. It's a *thooster*," he exclaimed.

"Rachael?"

She grabbed her mother's free arm. "We gotta, Mom, 'cuz it's a *thooster*," she mimicked.

"I'm game," Jess offered in a calm, cheery voice. His provided T-shirt read, "Just Your Average Joe".

Anna glared at him. "You're a big help . . . *Joe*." To her son, she said, "Tell you what. I'll force myself to go on that *thing* if you'll force yourself to try broccoli next time we have it for dinner. Deal?"

Anna's son recognized he'd been had. "Oh, *Mom. Deal*."

The foursome walked up to the ride's entrance gate.

"Love these short lines."

"I know," Anna agreed. "It's wonderful."

Their small group squeezed into the first car. Anna sat on the inside. The two children followed, leaving Jess to sit on the outside. Anna already felt like screaming. Everyone was quiet with anticipation while the other cars loaded. The coaster finally jerked into movement.

"Hang on, everybody," Anna yelled. "Here we go!" Her heart pounded. She wanted to cover her eyes. The coaster gained speed and then began to climb. It slowly crested the first hill of track and roared down the other side, creating strange sensations in their stomachs. Anna let loose with a scream to deafen any ear with Rachael following suit. Peter and Jess controlled themselves with loud laughter.

Embarrassed by her behavior, Anna apologized profusely when the ride ended.

"Hold up a minute."

Jess made them pause at the exit while the cars loaded up a fresh batch of riders. Minutes later, the train took off and crested the top track. Anna heard the screams of its riders as they roared down the other side.

"Hear that? Everyone does it. Ease up, okay? It's all in fun."

"Thank you." Anna stood on tiptoe. Jess knew that she wanted to be kissed. He obliged.

Peter protested their public display of romance. "*Mom.* There's people looking."

Anna and Jess broke their kiss and laughed. They glanced over at the sulking Peter. Rachael giggled into her hand.

Jess elected to divert the awkward moment. "Let's be off to the pirate ship, me hearties."

Anna joined in. "Which way?"

"I don't know? Which way, Pete?"

"How do you expect a little kid—oops—a *big* kid to know?" Peter smiled at his slip. The awkward moment melted. "I remember," Peter shouted. "There's a map back this way. *Come on.*"

They found umbrella-covered seats at the Main Street Cone Shop and sat down to enjoy frozen concoctions. Rachael had chosen a Mickey Mouse ice-cream bar. The others ordered sundaes.

"*You're gonna eat that?*" Anna questioned her health-nut fiancé.

"Sure. There's nothing wrong with occasional cheating. As a matter of fact," he faced all three of them and boldly stated," I, Jess Parks, declare this entire day to be, cheating day. But realize you probably won't feel so great, for a couple of days. That's the consequence. Your bodies aren't used to this kind of food. Peter . . . Rachael . . . Anna?"

"We understand," the three said in unison.

Jess convincingly added, "I guarantee that you won't want to do it often."

Peter squirmed with delight. "*Son*. This is the best sundae I ever *tasted*," he stated through a mouthful.

Jess guessed what was forthcoming. He quickly fended off Anna's retribution.

"Uh, Pete, let's leave that one for me. How about *wow* instead."

"Okay," Peter happily agreed, not taking his eyes off his gooey feast. "*Wow*. This is the best sundae I ever *tasted*."

"My Mickey Mouse is good too," Rachael added, with chocolate smeared from one side of her face to the other.

Contented with Jess's quick reaction, Mom chimed in with a gooey grin. "Mine too."

"Here, here," Jess agreed, his spoon raised.

"Hey. There goes someone I need to speak with." The actor rose from his seat. "Do you mind?" he addressed Anna. "I'll be right back." He threw down his napkin without awaiting her answer and quickly headed for a woman leading a young boy by the hand. She had a more-than-perfect figure Anna had to admire.

The reaction was genuine pleasure at Jess's unexpected greeting. Anna looked away, not wanting to eavesdrop. Minutes passed and Jess returned. One quick glance informed Anna that the woman was accompanying him.

"Anna, I'd like you to meet the wife of one of my fellow actors. This is Bella Shea. She's a yoga instructor."

"How do you do, Anna?" Bella spoke with a deep, feminine voice of foreign origin. Anna noticed her and the child's olive skin and dark hair. "Jess tells me you and your daughter are interested in my yoga class." She politely awaited Anna's affirmation.

Anna immediately responded. "Oh, yes."

"I happen to have a few openings in my mother-and-daughter beginner class. Can you come to my studio on Monday?"

Her English was flawless. Anna looked to Jess before replying. Go for it, his expression told her.

"Name the time." Anna's demeanor remained calm. Only the shine in her eyes gave away her excitement.

"I prefer having school-aged children in the late afternoon."

Anna glanced at Jess with a grateful smile. "Perfect."

"Say, four o'clock? See you then," Bella replied as she gracefully backed away and departed with her anxious charge.

"My, how things work out for this family."

Jess beamed. "Call it fate. Enjoy your good. You deserve it."

"Thanks," Anna replied, looking deeply into his eyes. "Now eat your sundae. It's melting."

"Yes, *Mom*," Jess kidded.

They located and toured Pirates of the Caribbean. The children grew considerably quiet while riding the bateau through Dead Man's Grotto and sat up straight as they experienced the pirate-ship battle with the Spanish. The ride from beginning to end successfully captivated and thrilled its audience.

The warm afternoon sun walked its familiar westward path unnoticed, while the family foursome geared up for another Disneyland attraction.

"What's next on our list?" Jess inquired of the trio facing him.

"Small World," Rachael cried first.

"Space Mountain," Peter demanded.

"Okay, okay. We'll do both, but one at a time."

"Map reader," Jess called to Peter, in an animated voice. "*Which way do we go . . . which way do we go?*"

Laugher rewarded him.

❀ ❀ ❀

Jess eventually glanced at his watch. "Dinner time," he called. "And I know *just* the place. *I* can have a healthy dinner and *you* can have pizza—"

"Yummy, pizza," Rachael cried.

"—or sea food."

"Yummy, lobster," Rachael cried again.

The host shrugged his shoulder in Rachael's direction. "This kid knows what's good."

"You want lobster, Rachael? Consider it yours."

Peter sized up the proffered menu. "I'll go with pizza."

Jess led them to Tomorrowland Terrace Restaurant, an outdoor café. The four diners placed their orders.

"Anyone save room for dessert?"

The family group then moved to a designated area for the Tomorrowland Terrace Fireworks Dessert Party, where a buffet of sweets satisfied their palates.

Mickey himself greeted them at their table. Rachael shyly dipped her head when he spoke to her, but her joy was apparent. Peter tried to look mature while talking with the giant mouse. Their parents exchanged winks across the table.

After the spectacular nighttime display, Jess suggested they enter the Tomorrowland Terrace Dance Club. They joined with other celebrities to rest their weary legs and enjoy the day's end. Anna was mildly surprised to see such famous faces surrounding her family. All of the guests were genuinely enjoying themselves. No one made a show of recognizing Jess, and he showed no interest in leaving their table to mingle with others. His attention remained devoted to Anna and the children, for which she was grateful. *If only your T-shirt slogan worked as well in public.*

Some of the stars and their dates took to the small dance floor to enjoy a slow song presented by the superb live entertainment. Jess rose and stood beside Anna's chair. In a gentlemanly manner, he addressed his future wife. "Care to dance, Ma'am?"

Anna sat up straight as his words sunk in. *Dancing? I hadn't considered dancing.* "Uh . . . I uh—the children. I have to stay with the children." Her forced excuse and excited tone threatened to expose her insecurity.

"No one is going to bother these children. Now come, my darling." He gently pulled her hand, refusing to take no for an answer. "It'll be our first time in public."

Anna unwillingly rose to her feet. She again resisted. "Oh, Jess . . . *please.* I—*can't,*" she whispered.

He detected her reluctance. "What do you mean, dear sweet woman of mine, you can't?" he whispered back. "I know your feet are tired. But Anna, darling, don't you know that when you're dancing with the one you love, all of your pain disappears?" He handsomely batted his lashes.

"It's not *that.*"

A crease grew between Jess's brow line. "Anna, didn't you and Joel ever—"

"*No.* I haven't danced since I was a young teenager." The shy Anna lowered her eyes.

"Then I'm asking you to place your trust in me." Allowing no further protest, he gently led her onto the dance floor.

The flustered young woman was suddenly being whirled about and extended to the length of her fingertips. For a brief moment, she held her breath. Jess then drew her to him, rocking her gently in his lead. Anna surprised herself and kept up.

"See? It's not so hard."

She flashed a bashful smile. "You're doing all the work."

Jess cooed. "It isn't work, sweet Anna. It's *pure pleasure.*"

No one stared. Even the two dancers paid no attention to the difference in their heights.

When the music ended, Jess led Anna back to their table.

"Gosh, Mom, I didn't know you could do that."

"That makes two of us, son." Anna felt relieved to be seated.

"Would dance lessons boost your confidence?" Jess inquired from his seated position.

"Yes. It'd be fun. But only if you're the teacher."

Jess adoringly noted her South Central accent and was pleased with her condition. "Deal."

"Shall we wind up this evening?"

"Yeah, I'm beat." Peter's statement surprised both adults. "There's always next year," the seven-year-old projected. Rachael was too tired to comment.

Pleasant relief passed between Anna and Jess.

"Okay, one last trek to the car. Piggyback ride, Rachael?" Jess hoisted the child onto his shoulders and led his charges toward the theme park's gate. "Home again, home again, jiggity, jig."

11

"...Any Other Name..."

The California sun was beginning to sink, coloring their world in orange and pink hues.

Jess addressed his future wife. "I would venture to say that Disney Day was a huge success."

"I'd say," she echoed.

The driver turned the key in the ignition.

Anna checked her weary children.

Each buried in personal thought, the family rode in silence.

Anna occasionally studied the engagement ring on her finger. Jess noticed but didn't comment. In the rearview mirror, he witnessed Rachael's sleepy head rise and fall. Peter appeared morose. *He's tired.* Jess let it go.

He glanced at his bride-to-be. "If it's okay with you, I'd like to talk about our wedding."

Anna abruptly returned to the present. She tipped her head and studied the driver. "Okay. What?"

"Now that we have drawn up a guest list, we need to get the invitations out right away—like tomorrow. I'll make a trip to the post office in the morning."

"Tomorrow's Sunday," Anna reminded.

Fanning his fingers above the steering wheel, Jess said, "Monday, then. I'll mail them Monday."

"Don't fret, my darling. Time's passing quickly. Think what we have to look forward to." She allowed her future husband to use his vivid imagination.

Jess gave Anna a knowing look. "Remember, I'm driving." He looked at Peter to see if he was paying attention to their conversation. He wasn't.

"What do you think about me adopting the kids?"

"I think we should discuss it in private," Anna replied in a whispered tone. She glanced back at Peter to determine if he'd overheard. He had.

"You mean change our last name to *Parks*?" Peter's sour tone bounced off the car's interior.

Jess looked apologetic. "Uh oh, bad timing. Sorry."

"It's okay. He's tired." Anna's weak smile lacked reassurance.

"What about Dad? You *said* he could still see us. Wouldn't his feelings be hurt?"

"Uh . . . can we talk about this later?" Jess ventured.

"*NO WAY*," Peter shouted.

"Pete, you'll scare your sister," Anna warned her son.

Believing it might help, Jess lowered his voice. "It's okay, guys. Let's drop it for now."

The remainder of the ride passed in silence.

Back at home, Peter hurried straight to his room.

"Let's give him some time alone," Jess suggested. "Then we can take turns talking to him."

At a loss, Anna shrugged in agreement. "Help me put Rachael to bed?" Jess brushed her teeth and washed her face. Anna put her in pajamas. Together, they left her room.

"I'll go first." Anna arrived at Peter's door and knocked lightly. "Peter? May I come in?"

She interpreted Peter's mumble as an affirmative answer and peeked around the door.

"Pete?"

Peter lay on his bed fully dressed. His arms rested under his head. "What, Mom?"

"Everything okay?"

"I *guess* so." Peter rose up on his elbows. "We don't have to change our last name if we don't want to, do we?"

"No, of course not. Jess wouldn't want that."

"Are you here to talk me into it?"

"Not really. I want you to understand why Jess suggested it. I want you to be able to view the idea from different angles. Do you understand, son?"

"I reckon."

"Peter . . . the best thing a person can learn for the betterment of himself," Anna began, sitting on the corner of his bed, "is to think with an open mind. This is something we have to train ourselves to do. It's easy to be narrow-minded, but much more difficult to be open-minded."

Anna waited for her words to sink in. She continued. "Let's try and figure out why Jess so generously offered—I might add—to give you his name."

Anna hesitated, allowing Peter to start.

"'Cuz he doesn't have kids of his own?"

Anna nodded. "That's one idea. What else?" she encouraged. "Think hard."

"He wants us to avoid having to explain different last names for the rest of our lives?"

"Any more, Pete?"

"'Cuz maybe . . . he loves us?" Peter attempted to hide a smile, but a small one escaped.

"*Bingo.*"

"But *Mom*." Peter sat up. "How can he love us so *fast*? We hardly even *know* each other."

"Love doesn't always have to grow, son. Sometimes it's just . . . there. We don't always have an explanation. But we do have to accept . . . and go on . . . and do the best we can. *I* believe the time will come when we'll understand the bigger picture."

"After we die?"

"I don't think the word "die" is appropriate here. "Die" means cease to exist, which really isn't what happens to us. We merely transform back into spiritual form. That's why death is referred to as 'going home'."

"So, son, when we *do* make the transition, we may discover that Jess has loved us before—and that's why he loves us so much now."

"You and Dad and Rachael and I have loved each other before?"

"It's quite possible. We all came from God, and to God we will return, because we're a part of Him."

"Is any of this making you feel better?"

"Maybe. It's a lot to study on. Sorry I've been so rebellious."

Anna smiled at her almost eight-year-old's big word.

"I want to remind you that your happiness is something *you* control. I can only supply you with knowledge from my own experience. It's up to you to apply it in your life. It would certainly save you a lot of unpleasantness."

Anna looked lovingly at her son. "Is it okay if Jess comes in? I think he's mighty unhappy about upsetting you."

"Yeah, it's okay. Mom? I'm a little embarrassed. Jess really *is* a cool guy."

"Yes. He is." Anna hesitated at the door. "Peter . . . one more thing. Remember that God loves you through Jess. By loving Jess, you love God. And that goes for all people."

Anna slipped out. She found Jess waiting. Her encouraging smile allowed him to relax. "He wants to see you now."

Without a word to Anna, Jess knocked lightly and entered. "Pete. What's up?"

In his prone position, Peter awkwardly waited for Jess to speak.

Having armed himself with words, Jess began. "There was once a famous playwright . . . and poet . . . who lived long before you and me. He was considered to be quite intelligent. Those who study acting in college study his works."

"Shakespeare," Peter spouted.

Smart kid. "Yes. Shakespeare. He once wrote, "That which we call a rose, by any other name, would smell as sweet". Do you understand what that means?" Jess slowly repeated the sentence breaking it into parts. "That which we call a rose . . . by any other name . . . would smell as sweet."

"It's saying . . ." Peter deciphered, ". . . that if a rose was called broccoli . . . it would still be the flower that it is, and it would still smell like one. What you're trying to tell me is that if my last name was changed to Parks, I would still be me."

Jess's expression showed his pleasure. "Listen, Peter, I don't expect you to change your name if you aren't comfortable with it, okay? I wasn't thinking. I guess I'm moving too fast. I promise to slow down. It's just that I'm a little excited. It's so wonderful to suddenly have a family. Can you possibly forgive me?"

Peter smiled. "Sure, and I'll try to curb my short fuse. Is it okay if I just call you Jess? I don't know if I can ever call you Dad. I may be too old to start. But Rachael can. She's still young."

Greatly relieved, Jess laughed inwardly. *Out of the mouths of babes.* "*Jess is fine, Pete.*"

"I still don't know if I'll change my last name. But I'll think about it. Hmm . . . Peter Parks. It does kinda have a good ring to it—in case I decide to be an actor like you."

"That it does, Pete. But whatever you decide is okay with me."

"And Jess? Thanks for making Mom so happy."

Am I conversing with a child or an adult?

Before Jess could close the door, Peter spoke again. "Jess . . . you make it real easy for me to care about you."

A gentle smile touched the tall man's lips. He left exhilarated.

Peter burst through the front door with his new friend in pursuit. "MOM, I'M HOME. GOTTA A BUDDY WITH ME. WE'RE GOIN' TO MY ROOM."

Peter and his friend raced up the stairs, flung open the door to Peter's room and flopped down on the bed to catch their breath.

"Whoa!" Peter panted. "Good race. Definitely a tie, huh, Patch?"

Patch sat up, eyeing his new buddy. "You sure do talk different, Pete. I like it."

Patch's disposition suddenly changed. He shook his head sadly. "My parents were divorced last year. My dad works in Washington, D.C. He's into money markets and stocks. I wish *he* was an actor instead. We hardly see him. He's so busy with his job and all . . ." Patch's words trailed as his eyes scanned the room. "You *lucky duck*. All this, and Jess Parks for a *dad*."

Peter glared at Patch. "My real dad died. You call that lucky?"

"I guess not. But at least you have a mom that hangs around. And Jess Parks is going to be your *dad*. Can I meet him, huh? Is he a great guy or what?"

Peter giggled. "He's a pretty great guy, I have to admit."

"Are you changing your last name to Parks?" Patch tried out the new name. "Peter Parks. Sounds good—better than Peter Adell."

Peter froze. His mind tumbled. *It does sound good. Dad . . . is it really okay with you? Mom says that changes are usually for the better. Sometimes it takes awhile to see it.*

"Yeah. Jess mentioned adopting us. He's letting me think about it. I guess I've decided I will. Can you stay for dinner? Mom won't mind. Maybe I'll announce my decision then."

"You mean you had to *think* about it? *Why?*"

"I wanted to consider my real father's feelings."

"But you said he was dead, didn't you?"

"Yeah, but I still think he knows what's going on."

"You mean you think he can see us?" Patch began examining the room for Peter's father's ghost. "Right *now? Creepy.*"

Peter shoved Patch playfully. Both boys rolled on the bed laughing and poking each other, the possibility of a ghost's presence completely forgotten.

Patch paused. "*Your mom cooks?*" he asked, incredulously.

❄ ❄ ❄

"Eww, Broccoli." Pete looked down at the steamed dark green stalk on his dinner plate.

"Remember our deal," Anna firmly reminded.

"Yes, Mom." Peter poked at the vegetable without enthusiasm. He speared the stalk and gingerly took a bite, chewing dramatically.

"Well?" Anna inquired.

"I *guess* I could get used to it, but it doesn't *taste* very good."

Patch enthusiastically said, "I'll have some more, please."

Peter looked at Patch's plate. He had eaten the broccoli and was asking for more. *He's trying to impress Mom and Jess.*

Anna beamed. "Certainly Patch."

Not to be outdone by his friend, Peter ventured to make his announcement. He looked at Jess. "Mom . . . Jess, I've decided that you can adopt us."

Anna choked on a bite of food. Jess's fork stopped short of his mouth. The adults gaped at each other across the table.

Anna spoke first. "That's wonderful, Pete. Isn't that wonderful, Jess?" She looked from one face to the other.

"That was quick." Jess commented. "Sure you don't need more time to think about it?"

"No. I'm sure."

Peter quickly changed the subject. "Patch and I tried out for the track team. Our school in Arkansas doesn't have a track team for kids our age. California's *great*."

Still in shock, Jess commented, "They like to start them young to mold good runners."

Peter ate the broccoli on his plate till it was gone.

Anna sat quietly. "Want seconds, Pete?"

Peter smiled grimly. "Mom, don't push your luck."

Anna laughed and winked at Jess.

"Well, Pete, I think this calls for a toast. I'll get the glasses, but only a little," he advised.

"We know. Too much water dilutes the digestive juices," the diners chorused.

In preparation of the toast, the dinner party grew thoughtful. Jess raised his glass. "To our new beginning—and to Peter's new friend, Patch." All of the glasses clinked together, ringing out the merriment of the lighthearted occasion.

"Speaking of names," Jess ventured, "how did you come by yours, Patch? It's a little unusual."

"When I was little, Mom said I wore out the knees in my jeans. She had to patch my patches, 'cuz I wore those out too. So Patch just kind of stuck."

Peter and Jess exchanged knowing looks. "Any other name," Peter said, winking at Jess.

PART III

REVELATION

12

The Advocate

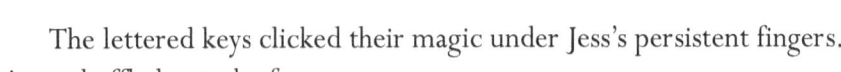

The lettered keys clicked their magic under Jess's persistent fingers. Anna shuffled a stack of papers.

"Why don't you take a break and check my notes for the next chapter? You've been at it for hours. I've done my best to write them like we discussed. Let me type awhile before Rachael and I leave for yoga class."

His concentration broken, Jess looked up. "Okay. Trade you." He took the typewritten papers from Anna and moved toward the couch to lie down and read under the soft glow of lamplight.

Anna took up his warmed seat, sighing contentedly. Her fingers glided over the familiar keyboard.

Something Jess read made him chuckle. "Excellent," he commented, flipping to the next page.

Anna paused, fingers frozen in midair. She responded to his voice with a shiver of pleasure.

"Jess, let's consider how to end the book. Maybe we could use Merry in the final chapter."

"Make a note of it, Annie."

"Here's what I'm thinking" he continued. "You and I were asked to remind people of the Way. So there're specific issues to address. One issue is that people have become so involved in the material aspect of life that they spend less time with the spiritual aspect. We must point out that the material realm is the illusion and the spirit realm is the reality."

"Life is but a dream really fits."

"That it does. Maybe it's no coincidence that tune is always running through my mind. Can we use it, or will it result in a copyright infringement? Add that to your checklist."

The pen in Anna's hand wrote furiously. "So, what's next?"

"Another issue is that so many people go through life believing God doesn't speak to us when *He* actually speaks to us daily through the still small voice within."

"I'm a prime example. Before I met you, I felt like I could *talk* to God, but I didn't know how to listen to His answer. Because of what you've shown me, Jess, I'm more at peace. If folks would use spiritualism along with their religious beliefs, it would open their minds to so much more."

Anna giggled. "Listen to me. I'm repeating *your* philosophy."

Jess's thoughts fleetingly returned to the giant oak with the more unenlightened Anna.

"But it isn't my philosophy, Annie, I merely follow it. It's always existed. Some practice it, some don't."

Anna's expression turned dreamy. "Wouldn't it be great if all churches could be joined through spiritualism and become one united church for God?"

Jess nodded his agreement. "A third issue is to impress upon aggressors that their acts are suppressing their own enlightenment. No deed goes unpaid. Earthbound souls need to right their wrongs while they can. Once transition occurs, it's too late. Karma would come into play—if it hadn't already."

"If only this planet could exist in peace. No more power trips; no more greed; no more war."

"It's a tall order." Jess paused, allowing his mind to process his thoughts. He and Anna were definitely beginning to think alike.

"Tonight, during meditation, we'll make Merry our theme."

Anna looked up from her writing and smiled her approval. "You know, Jess, it won't be long till this book is complete. Then we can sit back and watch its impact."

"Have faith, sweetheart. After all, its purpose is to welcome a new era, one of peace and spiritual growth."

Anna returned to her work. Jess read on.

"I love the lucid dreams. I always look forward to them."

"I agree. They're quite entertaining, *and* the best way to come up with material."

"It's so perfect, so comfortable being here with you."

Anna intuited Jess's smile and was not disappointed. A shared knowing look passed between them.

"Let's get to work on chapter twelve."

Jess settled back and closed his eyes. Anna followed suit. Their clasped hands squeezed in unison. Using the spiritual gift bestowed upon them, the two minds sought to subjugate random thought and seek a joined consciousness.

Beyond space and time, within the spiritual realm, their minds met. Free of their physical bodies, their essence entwined, content to be. Their effluvium joined as one, radiating outward, experiencing the cosmos, achieving that same mind flight with their spiritual guide, Merry, at Birdman's Cave.

The cognizance of their combined essence being mysteriously drawn to an awaiting experience exhilarated the two mind travelers. The sudden impact of rejoining their physical bodies, and that same haunting familiarity of their surroundings slammed them.

Jess whispered hoarsely. "Not *this* place."

Anna spoke soothingly. "Lose your fear, Jess. That's what created your past battle here. Control your thoughts."

"Yes, I remember." Jess used his mind to slow his racing heart. His eyes scanned the immediate area. "Why bring us here again?"

"There must be a lesson. Let's look around." Anna held out a steady hand to her partner.

"Okay, we'll look. But be on guard."

With joined hands, they walked across the white floor. Their footwear sank slightly into its foamy texture. Familiar, soothing multi-hued lights danced across smooth, white walls. The black dais was no longer present.

"I still think this looks like a spaceship." Jess's distracted partner failed to reply.

Their exploration led them down a narrow corridor with a number of doors equally spaced.

Jess stood before a single door with a mounted touchpad. Applying light pressure with his forefinger, the door quietly slid into the wall. He peered inside. "Looks like living quarters."

The two investigators stepped into the compartment. The door closed, triggered by their motion of entry. Absorbed in curiosity, neither Jess nor Anna noticed.

Anna spoke first. "It's small—for a single occupant."

A metallic latch protruded from the smooth wall. Jess pulled it. "Interesting." Braces snapped into place at each end of a fold-out bed forming a ninety degree angle with the wall a few feet above the floor. He witnessed Anna pulling recessed drawers out of the wall. The fine seams were barely visible to the human eye.

"Efficient space."

A raised panel revealed a blank monitor screen. Another touch pad revealed a fully equipped washroom.

Jess sat on the bed.

"Now what?"

"I don't know."

"Do we continue scouting?"

Anna sat next to him. She looked up, unconsciously batting her long, black lashes. Her angelic features caused a stir within Jess. He reached for her, desiring a kiss. Searing bolts shot through their bodies as their lips met. Passionate groans escaped them.

An unexpected knock on the outer door brought the startled couple to their feet.

Wide-eyed, Jess formed the word "who" with his lips.

Adrenalin surged, leaving him dizzy.

Hysterical laughter welled up in Anna. She fought to suppress it. "I don't know. Merry maybe? I'll go see."

Jess whispered vehemently. "*No. Don't——*"

Anna lunged for the touchpad before Jess could voice another protest. She insisted on helping him overcome fear of his evil twin.

It has to be Merry. She's the only one—— Anna activated the touchpad before she could change her mind. The entry silently opened. She shrieked and viciously jabbed at the pad to reverse it.

From his position, Jess couldn't see the visitor. He assumed.

Accomplishing her goal, Anna faced him, pale and trembling. His own skin grew clammy. Beads of cold sweat erupted on his forehead as his body reacted to its chemical rush.

"I'm sorry," Jess whispered, reaching for her hand. "I should've been the one who opened the door. It's me he wants."

"*No. It's——it's not him,*" Anna stuttered. Her fright-filled eyes stared up at Jess.

"Who then?"

Fear seized her tongue.

"All right, e*nough* of this. We have to face our fear."

He closed the short distance in two strides. Physically moving Anna aside, he reactivated the door, fully expecting to come face to face with that he feared most—his dark side once met.

A large, red-skinned man of sinewy build, wearing a radiant smile and little else, casually winked at the pale humans occupying the efficiency room. The red hue, small set of horns, and thick, lengthy tail snaking from behind were his most notable features. A deep, throaty chuckle issued forth from the strikingly handsome, yet seemingly gentle being.

Sensing his audience's fear, he spoke quickly. "I offer my sincerest apology for causing any uneasiness and for having disturbed you unexpectedly. Please, be at ease. I am not one of your old earth lore's devils," he explained in a deep baritone. "Long ago, my ancestors journeyed to your planet from another star system and somehow managed to become tied to your demonic legends. How we came to be labeled after an entity your race views as evil, I cannot say since our race is not prone to violence like your own."

Hinting at amusement, the mysterious caller continued his hurried speech. "The planet I hail from is Hades. Surprised?"

Pausing briefly, the brawny stranger shifted his dense core weight to the opposite muscular leg. His humanlike bodybuilder physique was quite impressive.

The space traveler's heralded introduction abruptly ended with an irresistibly charming wink accompanied by a genuine pearly-white smile. A single brow rose, taking the shape of an inverted V. "Again, please be at your ease." The slight bend of his waist hinted at a polite bow. "May I enter?"

Except for a shiny loincloth made of some mysterious metallic fabric and a pair of human-shaped boots, dispelling the Devil's cloven hooves, the man was naked. His friendly body language convinced Jess to relax. Satisfied no real danger existed, he backed his own six foot-six away from the entrance to allow the equally tall yet stouter alien to enter.

The closeness of the room forced Jess to sit next to Anna. A vague awareness of physical vibration tickled his conscience. Anna's trembling body shook the entire fold-out bed.

The alien politely introduced himself. "You may call me Joule. That's J-O-U-L-E, after the English physicist, James Prescott Joule, the earthling who helped birth of the Law of Conservation of Energy on this planet." The alien paused after his brief history lesson.

"Yes. I'm familiar with such," Jess offered, surprised at the alien's knowledge of Earth's history.

"I believe a handshake is customary," Joule announced.

Still somewhat shaken, Jess rose and moved to accept the alien's friendly gesture. Physical contact caused him to gasp. He jerked his hand back. "Sorry—a little too hot for me."

Simultaneously, Anna and Jess grew aware of the sudden increase in room temperature, Joule being the source.

The alien's threatening appearance having dissipated, Anna's speech returned. "You're burning up."

"My normal body temperature, Madame."

"That must account for the red cast to your skin," Jess reasoned. *And justification for the metal loin cloth.*

Joule chuckled deeply. "Right on the money," he said, borrowing an old English cliché.

Concern that Joule's reply might refer to both his vocalized insight and his private one silenced Jess. *Better curb my thoughts. He could be telepathic.*

"My planet has two suns. It is much hotter and drier than your cool, wet earth."

"Another bit of the legend and lore," Jess reasoned.

"Then you must be freezing."

"I assure you, Madame, I am not freezing."

"Do those horns serve a purpose?"

"Ah, curious, are you? My horns serve as a sexual stimulant for my race. "You see, when the female rubs—"

"I think we get the point." Jess winced at his pun.

Joule smiled mischievously and tossed his head toward Anna. "The lady asked."

Arms and legs crossed, the alien stood leaning into the wall, mimicking Jess's own habitual stance, obviously universal among the male species.

Joule's tapered, arrow-tipped tail slowly crept forward, indicating his control of it. Encircling his lower left leg, the tip occasionally flipped as though affected by his mood. Coal-black eyes continually sparkled with mirth.

The alien sobered and quickly changed the subject, answering Anna's next poised question before she could ask it.

"I come to you as a messenger."

"From another star system?"

One corner of Joule's mouth curled up. "What would I gain by deceiving you?"

Jess exploded. "This *is* a spaceship—*yours*. I *knew* it!"

Joule addressed his male guest. "I am truly sorry about your misadventure with your dark side. The two of you," he nodded toward each of his guests, "had not been prepared to visit this side of the life force. You happened upon a device that requires much skill and thought control for its proper use. The dais is capable of reading and manipulating the genetic code of any living creature. It is mainly used to repair damaged tissue—as you blindly discovered. Once your experience had begun, it became dangerous to interfere. Incidentally, I commend you on your intuitive handling of the separate situations."

The compliment pleased Jess. "So we're . . . on the other side . . . of the life force." His puzzled facial expression drew a response from Joule.

"The plane between. Not all planet inhabits are allowed entry, only those who comprehend that true and precise intent results in true and precise action. Being as there's no envy, greed or war, we are allowed to traverse planes. It is that simple."

Joule sobered. "When we visit Earth, being discreet is necessary. You *know* what happens to aliens on this planet. The inhabitants in their ignorance are obsessed with fear, which erupts into violence. No wonder the higher ups won't allow humans to leave their solar system. I must admit you have a nasty problem on your hands."

Anna broke the heavy silence. "Let us leave?"

"Yes, Madame. This ship is ready for transport, but this planet must first straighten up its act. And so far," Joule's head swung like a pendulum, emphasizing each spoken word, "that ain't happening."

Anna allowed Joule's use of the informal contraction to slide.

Jess addressed their host. "How did *you* get involved?"

"As an astute linguist, I volunteered to show the inhabitants of your world what they may experience when they are ready. New worlds await. There is much to be had in this galaxy alone."

"How come you know so much about Earth's inhabitants?"

"I have been pressed to study your customs, mannerisms and religions." Joule chuckled deeply. "You *do* have some belly shakers—and so *many*."

"I can relate to your humor, Joule."

"Ah, patience, my man. All these specifics are universal. Even—shall we say—the *expressive* religions?"

Joule sobered. "Back to the purpose at hand."

Anna grasped the subject. "Universal religion—Christianity?"

The black V returned above the ship captain's left eye. "Religion, Madame, is universal, but not Christianity. Do you think that your planet has the patent on saviors? All saviors have the same job, my dear, but they may only inhabit one planet at a time." Their host spoke feverishly as if it was his favorite subject. "Each populated world has its own history of living masters. But since we all share the same creator, we all share the same laws—the laws of the One. Makes sense, doesn't it?"

Anna grew uncomfortable and deserted the subject.

"Is Joule your real name?"

Recognizing Anna's discomfort, the Hadean humored her.

Joule's deep chuckle resounded. "Ah, your female companion is delightfully curious. No, Madame. You would not be able to pronounce my name."

"How is it that you speak our language so well?"

"Hadeans are gifted with mimicking tones and vibrations found in all languages. Hence, we make good linguists."

Wishing for any telepathic capabilities to be forthcoming, Anna asked, "Do you know what I'm thinking?"

Jess was pleased with her inquiry.

Joule casually examined an imaginary hangnail. "No, señora," he interpreted in Spanish, rolling his r. In English, he said, "Must I?" and gave Anna a mischievous wink.

This earned a smile from Jess. The actor showed off his own ability to speak the Hispanic language. "¿Hablas en serio?"

"Si, señor Jess."

Anna's exasperation showed. "Well, Joule, I *will* say that you've truly mastered the language of the human *male* species," she commented, cutting her eyes from one humorous expression to the other. "*Can you read our minds?*"

"I read body language and situations. This ability has earned me my present status. No. I do not read minds per se. But I know of races that do."

"Well, Jess. It appears we have a new friend." Anna welcomed Joule with her winning smile, her earlier fright forgotten. The two men returned her grin.

Avoiding further physical contact, Jess bowed. "Welcome, friend." He relied on the alien's ability to read his sincerity.

"Now—about the business at hand." Joule began stating facts. "Your planet is in trouble. A large number of its inhabitants are . . . I believe the term is . . . apathetic? Too much has been forgotten about the Way."

Anna and Jess exchanged knowing looks. Joule continued.

"We have been here countless times, attempting to reestablish the Way. Thus far we have failed, so it has been decided to attempt contact with the commoners of earth. If the government and the military were united throughout the planet, contact with them might have had more positive results. As separate units, they have proven too hostile.

"Alas, something must give. This planet is unnecessarily overcrowded to a serious level. Those souls new to Earth inevitably become contaminated and therefore must remain isolated as well; souls come in, but they do not go out." The host paused to allow his guests to absorb his meaning. He rocked from one foot to the other, his large tail slithering from side to side. "We do not expect perfection. However, there is great room for improvement. Humans need to return to the spiritual path."

"Help! We know all this." Jess looked to Anna for support.

"Exactly why you are now in my presence."

Jess responded, gesturing to Anna and himself. "Give us the details, Joule."

"Where to begin? Not everyone is consumed with apathy. There are some knowledgeable, uncontaminated souls out there. Then again, you will always have your arrogant, your complainers, and your nonbelievers. Some will come around. Some will not. But remember that it is *their* choice—to remain in the dark. Wrong choices led humans into this current mess, and right choices can lead them out. Of course, the best approach to this issue is to have those attuned help reestablish the Way—present company included."

The alien shrugged. "You are now aware of how long the Way has been taught on this planet. Some continue to follow and teach the Way, but their numbers have greatly declined. It is yet to be instilled into the increasing masses."

"How do we reestablish awareness to those who are attuned?" Jess stared at their host, awaiting an answer to a deep question.

"Must I point out the obvious?"

The female guest's puzzled look changed to one of realization. "The book."

Joule recognized Anna's quick response with a confirmed nod. "Right on the money!"

Jess took her hand and smiled proudly.

"You two must concentrate on your original plans."

"Sometimes it's like someone's reading our minds or planting suggestions to aid us in our endeavor," Jess revealed.

"Everything stems from universal thought," Joule explained. "The Way comes through us as thought. Disciplined thought is what makes us one. It's what we all have in common. Merely let go and believe. It's that simple. There is nothing complicated, nothing evil about it—only good."

"Will our book affect many?"

"It will affect some. Other books will be written by other Way followers. Nonbelief will eventually die out—and so on . . . and so on. It is a lengthy process that needs to begin now—yesterday, for your planet."

Joule sadly shook his head. "Time is running out. It is becoming dangerous to breathe the polluted air. What water you have is close to undrinkable. The food supply is slowly being poisoned—in more ways than one. It is apparent that greed outweighs survival. Your global financial system is teetering on the brink of disaster, not to mention that humans continue to threaten one another with annihilation." An expression of contempt marred Joule's handsome alien features. "Will somebody please explain *that?*"

Examining his guests, Joule chuckled at their embarrassed expressions, alleviating the tension in the rather warm, overcapacitated room.

"Do not take me too personally. Ignorance tends to rile me."

Jess shifted uncomfortably, grateful that he wouldn't be forced to explain human insanity.

"We'll finish the book and observe its effect. When it hits the cinema screen, more people will be exposed to the Way."

"That is our wish, Madame. When minds join, mountains can be moved—the equivalent of your, uh, 'Holy Ghost'.

"Awareness is what it is all about. Planet Earth can heal itself. The wounds of all living things eventually heal—another gift from our creator."

"How much time, Joule?"

"Ah, good sir, many years will it take for the healing process. Much damage has been inflicted."

"So when can we *Earthlings* migrate to other planets?"

"Possibly in another ten of your earth years, depending on how quickly the Way is absorbed."

"*Ten years*. I'll be over forty."

"Not an *old* man," Anna soothed.

"Not a young one either. Any chance we could speed up that prospective date?"

"Jess, you'd consider leaving Earth?"

"Well, it looks like I have ten years to think about it."

"Depends," Joule said, shifting his weight. "Let us see how quickly humans progress."

Anna drew up her legs, encircling them with her arms. "Do you have a prediction of the outcome?"

"A prediction it would be, Madame. For now, the best answer has been given."

"And we'll accept it," Jess ended.

Concluding his message, Jule stated, "So, now the two of you understand the, who, what, when, where, why and how, *and* that you are not alone, have I left any unanswered questions?"

"I'm good." Jess responded.

"Me too," Anna concurred.

"Madame, Sir," Joule's cosmic black eyes sparkled mischievously as he addressed his guests, "then how about a ride on my ship?"

The red-skinned man led them from the living quarters as if he were being chased by Satan himself. Breathless, they reentered the aircraft's control room.

"Is this the bridge?" Jess asked, slightly winded.

"Right on the money!"

The captain proceeded to wake up his ship. He revealed the main computer drive where he began plotting their course.

"Care to buzz the nation's capital? Let us add the Empire State Building. And we shall circle the Freedom Lady herself."

Anna seized the thrill of the moment. "I'd like to see Disney World— and the Grand Canyon."

Joule addressed the ship's computer, using a strange guttural language. Respectfully, he dipped his head toward his female guest. "Your requests have been entered, Madame."Turning to Jess he inquired, "And you, Sir?"

Jess joined in. "I have one, if it isn't too much trouble—Yellowstone National Park."

He pointed a forefinger at Jess. "Done—and to make it a bit more interesting, I have added a few selections of my own."

Completing his task, Joule addressed his guests. "Hold on to your hats." Both black brows rose in unison and a devilish grin lit his face. "Better yet, take a seat."

Their host activated a hand-held remote, cuing a small, semicircular structure to rise from the floor. Three seats appeared. A generous space in the upholstery was an obvious design meant to accommodate his lengthy appendage.

"Welcome to the helm."

Joule sat in the middle. Belting himself in, his actions were as quick as his words. "This ship moves as fast as a comet streaking across the night sky. So, time to buckle up."

The two excited passengers copied his moves. Jess sat on his left and Anna on his right.

With the ship's brain now at his fingertips, Joule continued to work his magic. A vertical crack three meters in length grew in the floor beneath them. It opened like a pair of elevator doors. Floodlights exposed the smooth dirt floor of the cave's surface below through transparent media.

"Ready, ready, let's go!" he intoned.

Merry's borrowed phrase drew Anna's attention. Does Joule know Merry? He had related similar topics. She had made mention of more information to come. Was this it? Their spirit guide had spoken of portals. Were the portals actually spaceships? The questions would have to wait.

With the touch of a forefinger, Joule lifted the craft above its temporary nesting ground. It silently hovered while he cued the cockpit cover to open, providing the occupants with a second view. Punching in a series of coded commands brought them about. With precision movement and no room to spare, Joule piloted the ship out of the tunnel, narrow in comparison to the size of the aircraft itself.

Hovering in open air, the gasps from his passengers satisfied the captain that his goal to impress had been achieved.

"This view is *incredible*," Jess remarked.

Inhabited areas soon appeared.

Joule spoke. "We can see them, but they do not see us."

Jess broke his concentration to absorb Joule's information. "That makes it more interesting."

The cloaked alien vessel flew toward the East Coast. The on-board computer slowed the ship so that the human brain could register what the human eye was seeing.

"I imagine you have never considered an alien giving you a tour of your own planet. Our first stop will be the Nation's Capital in Washington, D.C.—District of Columbia, to be exact—not a state, but a district named after the discoverer of your country."

Again, the guests were impressed with their new friend's historical knowledge.

"We're here?" Anna's excitement peaked, triggering her usual habit of fast talk. "Why, it's only been *minutes*. We must be travelin' superfast. I've never been here before."

They observed the reflection of the Washington Monument in the rectangular water pool below as the ship slowly flew over.

"I haven't either," Jess returned, "but I've seen photos."

Their host looked surprised. "So you two have not visited the Capital of your country? How *unpatriotic* of you."

"I'm not really interested in politics," Jess confessed.

"Neither am I. Politics make me feel like a grain of sand on a desert island."

"In your case, I do not blame you." Joule's judgment implied boredom. "Too many choices and no one agrees. In my world, politics are considered interesting indeed. Our politics are—"

"Let me guess," Jess interrupted, "plain and simple."

"Right on the money!"

"As I was saying, our politics are not based on capitalism, communism or socialism. They resemble a collective democracy, but—" Joule caught Jess's curious expression. "—it would take too long to explain. Another time, perhaps."

The ship hovered over the Reflecting Pool near the base of the Lincoln Memorial.

"It is my understanding that humans consume creatures that exist in water-filled pits."

The two constant companions traded amused smiles. "You are correct, Joule. We do. But in this case, the pools of water are created for landscape effect."

It was their new friend's turn to look confused.

"*You* know . . . outdoor scenery . . . to please the eye?" Anna batted her lashes at him.

Joule stared at Anna. A light came on. "Ah, yes." He leaned back in his seat. "I understand. An artistic creation."

"Right on the money," Jess intoned. Joule chuckled deeply.

Visitors and employees below calmly strolled along either side of the Reflecting Pool. A lone woman suddenly hesitated, raising her eyes in their direction. "Look." Anna curiously pointed her finger. "Do you suppose she sees us?"

"It is possible. She could be one of the informed—like yourselves. She may not actually see us, but senses us. Perhaps you and Jess experience similar situations when you are feeling attuned."

"We have."

Joule nodded his acknowledgment. "Let us continue our journey, shall we? En avant et vers le haut." Joule quickly translated his French to English. "Onward and upward."

The remote was again pressed into service. The ship soon crossed over Staten Island. The trio witnessed the Staten Island Ferry approaching its destination. Sixty seconds later, Ellis Island came into view.

Jess glanced at his shipmates. "This area I've visited."

"It's where immigrants first enter the United States. Something we learned in high school civics class," Anna offered.

"I see you two are not entirely ignorant about your country."

Shortly, they were circling Liberty Island in the Upper Bay where Lady Liberty, a gift from France, stood proudly representing the country's independent freedom.

"It is odd to me how living creatures with minds that think can place much emphasis on material objects. This object is not needed to represent freedom—another example of human loss of thought control." Joule moaned. "Ah, to be so undisciplined of mind."

"The use of idols has survived from long-ago days of paganism."

"And yet you have not outgrown it. It is amazing how backward the inhabitants of this planet have become. If left alone, we believe you would annihilate your own species."

Jess again experienced embarrassment for his fellow man. "It's certainly been attempted," he admitted.

After circling the island, the ship turned due west and moved swiftly inland, where Joule skillfully maneuvered the three hundred-and-sixty degrees around the well-known Empire State Building. One revolution seemed to suffice.

"Seen enough? Since we are reasonably within the vicinity of Niagara Falls—one of *my* choices—let us, as you would say, check it out. Are the two of you on board?"

Yes, was the chorused response.

The captain took them in the direction of the famous falls.

"I'm so excited. I've always wanted to see Niagara Falls," Anna confessed, pleased with Joule's selection. When they arrived, she wasn't disappointed. Words couldn't express what they witnessed. The magnificent rainbow spanning the Niagara Falls Gorge with Rainbow Bridge in the background silenced them all. Anna could only stare. Joule sensed her mood and remained in a hovering state until his female guest was able to look away.

"Then it is off to your beloved Disney World. We shall arrive momentarily, Madame." Joule winked at Anna who remained greatly impressed with the alien's command of the English language.

The captain relaxed in his seat and allowed the computer to steer their course. "Flying within your atmosphere is rougher than flying in open space."

"Air turbulence. I experienced a lot of that coming from Springfield on the puddle jumper."

"Is puddle jumper your name for airship?"

Jess smiled. "Only the smaller ones."

He spotted a nearby passenger plane. "How do you avoid collisions, Joule?"

"A force field detects objects in a collision course, so your planet's airships are safe."

"Care for something to eat?" their host suddenly offered.

Anna quickly declined. "No thank you." A bowl of worms or something equally unappetizing loomed in her vivid imagination.

A sudden pleasant aroma permeated the air. Joule magically produced a tray of warm snacks. "Always prepared." He held it out to his male guest. "What you don't know won't hurt you."

Joule's slightly sinister laugh amused Jess. He politely made a selection and allowed his acting skills to belie his doubt. The host waited for him to taste. With a straight face, Jess took a bite. Instant pleasure lit his features. "Mmm, *very* good, Anna. Try some." Jess passed the tray to Joule who in turn passed it to his female passenger. She shot Jess a thanks-a-lot look.

"Oui, Madame, I am pleased that you have changed your mind." Joule's brows lifted in their usual delighted reaction.

"Let us chatter, shall we?"

Joule questioned Jess about his acting career. Jess offered information freely. Anna listened intently, realizing there was much about her partner she didn't know.

He also inquired of Anna's past. She answered between her first bite of the mystery snack.

"There isn't much to tell—never been far from home—till now. Never done much."

"Anna, don't *say* that. You've had thirty years to do."

Joule studied Anna's profile.

"Jess is correct, Madame. All living souls have a unique variety of experiences."

Anna squinted at Joule. She issued an exasperated sigh, failing to hide a childish smile.

"You may as well know, Joule, that Jess is *always* correct—even about this food tasting good."

Anna chewed thoughtfully. "Well, let's see. I spent a lot of growing-up time with my grandma. She taught me to cook, sew, knit, crochet and tend a garden. We harvested and canned all of the fruits and vegetables we grew."

Jess spoke proudly. "She has a green thumb, Joule."

The Hadean looked at Anna's hand. "I see no green thumb."

"It's an expression." The alien still looked confused. "That's a figure of speech."

"Ah, yes, a metaphor."

"Right on the money!" Jess and Anna intoned in unison.

"To say a person has a "green thumb" means that he or she is skilled at growing plants."

"Plants . . . another name for flora?"

"Correct."

"Anna, I don't know anyone who has your skills—except maybe cooking. If it came down to survival, I'd have to put my money on you." Jess's compliment flushed her face.

"My money on you . . . another metaphor?"

"Correct."

"Humans place a lot of emphasis on money."

"No truer words have been spoken," his guest agreed.

Their host shook his head distastefully.

Joule suddenly made the serving tray disappear. "We approach our next destination."

The ship slowed at his prompting and hovered before Epcot Theme Park, the eighteen story geodesic sphere that houses Spaceship Earth. Covered with alucobond tiles, its design engineers included the famous science fiction writer Ray Bradbury.

"From here, it looks like a giant golf ball."

"Golf—a human game of skill."

"How about it, Joule? Is there a being in the universe large enough to tee a ball this size?"

"If there is, Jess, I have not encountered one."

Anna breathlessly absorbed the view below. "I remember a commercial with Mickey Mouse standing on that sphere waving his arm. The zoom-in made me dizzy. Oh, but it's all so *marvelous*."

Their red-skinned host laughed heartily. *"Marvelous,"* he mimicked. "Ah, Jess, your female companion is *such* a delight." His rich laughter rang out. Jess agreed with a smile and a nod, his eyes glued to the lower portal.

The threesome slowly cruised over the vast, sprawling Walt Disney Resort Complex.

"It's so *huge*. Why, it would take *days* to see it all."

"Make a nice honeymoon," Jess offered.

Anna looked up. She shook her head vigorously. "Oh, we *couldn't*. Could we? I mean. . . I wouldn't dare—not without the kids. I couldn't *possibly* keep it a secret."

"So," Jess leaned forward, "who says they can't come along?"

Anna's face registered surprise. "On our honeymoon? I reckon I assumed—"

"You assumed we'd follow tradition. How about skipping tradition? We won't be the first."

"You wouldn't mind?"

Joule interrupted. "Ah, the traditional human marriage ceremony with its endorsed certificate binding two humans together for the span of their earthly life. How very odd."

Anna and Jess ignored him.

"If I minded, I wouldn't suggest it. Don't you know me well enough by now, my wife-to-be? We can bring along a sitting companion— someone they'll have fun with while we're busy with each other." Jess smiled, moving his brows Groucho-Marx style.

Anna laughed. "It's always so wonderful with you." She leaned forward to make eye contact. "How can that be?"

"Lady," Joule addressed Anna, "you must learn to accept your good. Part of receiving is accepting. Believe you are worthy—because you are."

"If we remind her enough, Joule, she's bound to believe it."

The ship left Florida and moved west along the Gulf coast.

"Next stop, Arizona," their starship pilot announced.

They traveled with the sun overhead. The ground below swept by at an exhilarating speed. Anna looked away in an attempt to steady a sudden spell of vertigo. Joule analyzed the situation and closed the lower viewport.

Each guest examined his immediate surroundings.

"I thought spaceships had lots of controls and lots of crew to work them," Anna addressed her host. "This one's nearly bare."

"I'll venture a guess," Jess offered. "A ship is designed according to the knowledge and know-how of the race that builds it."

"Well stated. Ships can be as different as the individuals who fly them. Many types and sizes exist."

The pilot slowed the ship's speed and reopened the lower port. "Recognize this?"

"*Wow.* That thing's *gigantic.*"

"I do. I've been inside. Its size mimics the original pyramids in Egypt. This structure is one of Vegas' many gambling casinos called the Luxor. It's thirty stories tall and has 4,400 rooms. How's that for colossal? There's even an indoor tram ride."

Fascinated, Anna listened to Jess's every word. "What's the outer surface made of?"

"It's a dark bronze glass. When the sun hits it, it reflects like a mirror. See the clouds?"

Anna nodded. "Sounds like we have us a tour guide, Joule."

As the ship moved slowly up the strip, Jess identified some of the massive structures. "There's MGM Grand. And there's Excalibur, where they put on an evening dinner show with horses."

"It's a castle," Anna commented. "I never dreamed that Las Vegas looked so appealing."

"You should see this city in the dark. By day or night, it's a pretty impressive work of art."

They passed a beautiful display of colored water fountains on their left and a smaller version of Lady Liberty on their right.

"That's Treasure Island, and there's Caesar's Palace," Jess pointed out.

"Look, Circus Circus. I bet the kids would like that. Maybe we could bring them out here. They'd love a tour of Hoover Dam."

"*They would?*" Jess kidded.

"Ah, offspring?" Joule queried.

Anna smiled and shook her head. "Ages five and seven—going on eight."

"I have none of my own. Too busy."

"Do I see carnival rides on top of that skyscraper hotel?" Anna turned to Jess with incredulous eyes. "Be sure and keep that to yourself," she warned.

"That would be the Stratosphere, and don't worry, my darling, the roller coaster was removed. Consider yourself safe."

Anna's horrified expression caused Jess to roar with laughter. Joule followed suit.

Sailing past the giant band instrument displayed on top of the Hard Rock Café, Jess entertained them with some air guitar.

"Dude, I'm impressed," their alien host commented, bobbing his head in time to the beat. "I occasionally tune in to FM radio," he explained, showing an appreciation for the musical arts.

It was Jess and Anna's turn to laugh.

"They soon arrived over the downtown strip. "A few years ago," Jess began, "Viva Vision built an overhead canopy spanning the length of Fremont Street. Now the sixty-year-old famous forty-foot Vegas Vic neon cowboy can only be seen from below. And the ninety-foot-high canopy is one gigantic LCD light show. Standing under it and looking up, you can watch it send video images up and down its length. Pretty impressive."

"We must bring the children, Jess. It's all so *marvelous*."

Joule chuckled upon hearing Anna's descriptive adjective again. Jess joined him.

Leaving the city of lights, a sudden view of Lake Mead alerted the trio that Hoover Dam was near. A quick flyover showed contented tourists below, milling about the walkways of the second-tallest Dam in the United States.

Anna deemed a family trip was definitely in order.

A verbal command to the computer in Joule's native tongue caused the starship to dive into the west rim of the Grand Canyon. Jess and Anna clutched their armrests as the g-force pressed their backs into their seats. The proximity of the rust-colored walls enhanced their speed. Anna sucked in her breath. She glanced over to find Jess equally overwhelmed. Their host sensed their discomfort and barked a command that considerably slowed the ship. An accurate calculation of the canyon's center was programmed into the computer. Like a magnet repelling opposing poles, the ship began steering itself directly down the middle.

"Sorry, friends," Joule apologized. "I have erred in human endurance. It will not happen again."

"No harm done," Jess informed, his tone somewhat pinched. "But thanks for noticing."

Jess and Anna eased up on their armrests.

The ship had settled to a comfortable speed. The passengers again began to enjoy the view. The incident was quickly forgotten.

Soon after entering the canyon, the pilot steered left toward an odd-looking structure in an unlikely location. Strategically placed, 4,000 feet above the canyon floor and jutting out of raw rock, was an observation building strictly created for viewing the Grand Canyon. The deck was crawling with spectators.

Once again, Jess provided tell-tale information to present company. "I know this because I recently picked up a magazine and read about it. It's called Skywalk, owned by the Hualopi Indian Tribe. Their land surrounds this part of the canyon."

Joule directed the craft to hover in front of the observation deck. The Grand-Canyon viewers became the viewed. Oblivious to the manned space craft, they stared at objects of interest.

"It's kind of creepy watching them, knowing they can't see us."

"One day, you'll remember," Joule directed at Jess.

Jess allowed the puzzling comment to slide when his host offered nothing further.

Joule's ship continued to maneuver its way through one of the country's most popular wonders, twisting and turning with the canyon's ancient-river course.

"Didn't we take a ride like this at Disney Land?"

"Ah, yes. Your Disney Land is like every day on my planet. However, it does not cost anything."

"How's that?" Jess asked.

"It is all in how the mind is used. Each waking minute can be like a day at Disney Land, once you have control of your thoughts."

"I'd *love* to control my thoughts, but it isn't so easy."

"Madame, one solution is repetitive meditation."

"So much negativism has been impressed upon us since birth that our people swim in it," Jess confessed.

"Yes. Your people persist with their prejudices. They do not understand they are, in actuality, harming themselves. Humans need to understand the law of Cause and Effect. Prejudices and grudges backfire. Humans reap what they sow. It could all end if humans would learn to control their thoughts with correct thinking."

"The Way."

The host nodded.

Conversation ceased. The three comrades remained focused on the scenery below.

The ship climbed out of the Grand Canyon at Desert View, bearing east. The afternoon offered a spectacular view of the Painted Desert as well as the Navajo and Hopi Indian reservations. Dipping starboard, the invisible cruiser first crossed the Third Mesa, the Second Mesa, and finally the First Mesa. Minutes later, the ship's occupants enjoyed a bird's-eye view of Gallup, New Mexico, located amidst the many Native American reservations.

The ship's flight path continued north up the Continental Divide.

"I thought we might enjoy traveling the length of the Rockies." Joule sounded pleased with his choice.

"Joule," Jess stumbled with his question, "how are we achieving this? I mean, Anna and I were in our reading room enjoying a lucid dream.

Can you explain how it's physically possible for us to be here . . . in this spaceship . . . with you?"

"You are in need of material for chapter twelve, are you not? So I am giving you material for chapter twelve."

"He's right, Jess. We *do* need material for chapter twelve."

"And Jess, do you know without a doubt that you are not really here?" Joule again winked mischievously.

Anna and Jess looked at each other. "We don't profess to know anything, Joule," Jess admitted. "We take it steady-as-she-goes," he said, speaking for Anna and himself.

Suddenly finding their situation humorous, both humans burst into lighthearted laughter. The mood was contagious. Joule chimed in with his baritone. Their combined laughter created a merry song.

The ship struck a straight course. At times, the mountain range lay to port, at other times, starboard. Occasionally, the spaceship would dramatically climb to crest the Continental Divide as it meandered haphazardly through the state of Colorado.

"This must be what encouraged John Denver to write his song," Jess said, pointing below. "There's Crested Butte and Aspen is up ahead. I've seen it a few times from the air. Colorado's highest elevation lies to the East. Joule, if you wouldn't mind tipping your ship starboard so we can see to our right—"

Joule complied. The ship rolled on its edge giving a clear view of Mount Elbert, the state's tallest mountain. Admiration was ever apparent in Joule's facial expressions during their scenic flight across planet earth.

"*Absolutely breathtaking,*" Anna remarked, staring at the blue giant with its brilliant snowcapped peak.

"Isn't it?" Jess agreed. "I don't suppose your world has snowcapped mountains, Joule?"

"Like your Hawaiian Islands, our mountains spit red fire, which are equally as beautiful as your white snowcaps."

His guests nodded their agreement.

The ship covered the remainder of the state, crossing the Colorado/

Wyoming border. It stayed with the Continental Divide until reaching Yellowstone National Park. Deviating from its course to cross the crystal-clear waters of Yellowstone Lake, it then resumed its climb up the Divide, carrying them to the park's largest and most famous geyser—Old Faithful. Joule allowed the ship to hover above. "We will not leave until the geyser erupts," he insisted.

"Will you look at all that *steam*—" The eruption of the natural landmark stopped Anna in midsentence. Its highest reaching droplets splashed against the outer surface of the lower viewport. Anna laughed with delight.

Joule joined her. "Your laughter is contagious, my lady."

Leaving Wyoming and entering Idaho, Jess remarked, "Ketchum, Idaho, is fairly close. Can you take us over Sun Valley, Joule? I've skied Bald Mountain."

"Consider it done."

"It's beautiful," Anna commented during their aerial view of Sun Valley, reminding her again of how little she knew of Jess's past. *He's mentioned skiing several times. He must be skilled at it. I've never skied in my life.*

The ship passed over Twin Falls, Idaho. Following Highway 93 south through Nevada until it intersected with the Loneliest Road, the ship now headed due west. After skirting four consecutive mountain ranges, it continued on its beeline course for Yosemite National Park.

A cascading waterfall soon consumed their attention. Jess pointed out a footpath leading up to a railed overlook across from Illilouette Falls. "It's approximately 370 feet of falling water. Close up, the noise is deafening. I say that from experience."

Jess addressed Anna. "I've visited here as well. It was memorable because I was chased by a mother bear protecting her twin cubs."

Joule's laugher had grown quite pleasant. "So many animal species. Please refresh my memory. What is a mother bear?"

Jess's description of the giant brown female included ferocious teeth and fierce claws. "She chased me over a fallen log, through a shallow creek bed, and up an incline leading to the edge of our camp. When I risked looking back, she'd reared up menacingly on her hindquarters. I read her meaning all right. She was informing me that it was in my best interest to stay away."

Jess's audience chuckled at his vivid recollection.

"That event will always remain fresh in my mind," his eyes locked with his true mate's, "like the day we met. Joule, you should've seen her . . . standing on that fountain wall. And then . . . the look on her face when she saw me." He paused, his mind reliving the experience. "My sudden appearance startled her so much that she lost her balance and fell back into the cold water."

The profundity of his memory impacted his thoughts. "You loved me then."

Anna nodded her confession.

"You knew long before I did. *Son*, it must've really been hard."

Anna continued to nod. Sensitive tears brimmed her vivid-blue eyes. She blinked them back.

Jess's eyes remained focused on hers.

"Joule, are you as lucky as I am?"

"I cannot answer affirmatively. Yes, I have loved. But nothing as intense as what you two share. I sense the bond between you. It is said across the galaxy that in order to experience the deeper emotions this planet offers, it is worth enduring the more violent ones." Joule grew silent.

The couple studied their new friend. His words, they found puzzling. With respect for his sudden silence, they waited.

"I do wish to experience true love. Mark my words, someday I will be brave enough."

Joule inhaled deeply and studied each attentive face. "See what I have to look forward to?" He laughed lightly, and the awkward moment passed.

The ship hovered above the national park. "It must be the wrong time of day for your bears. I do not see any."

"True," Jess agreed. "Bears are nocturnal, so they're most likely napping through the afternoon heat. It *is* afternoon, isn't it? It looks like the sun hasn't moved much."

The alien's next announcement surprised his guests.

"I am sorry to say that our journey together comes to an end."

Anna stared out of the lower viewport. "Look, Jess, our house," she announced, pointing to their familiar world below.

Jess confirmed her discovery. "So what's the reason behind this excursion of ours, Joule?"

"Allow me to make a parallel. When I inquired of which particular places you would like to visit, you had your entire world to choose from. Yet you both chose to stay within the realm of your own country.

"Seek first the kingdom at hand. We know that the kingdom is within. Seek first that which is within you while reaching out to help others. It can be done instantly, or it can take a thousand years. The opportunity belongs to all beings. Absorb knowledge and learn from it. Not only the knowledge obtained from books, but also the knowledge from life's experiences—spiritual knowledge from caring, sharing and respecting one another.

"Release yourselves from what your world calls Maya, the Mother of the material universe. Too many covet her."

Joule's eyes sparkled like black diamonds. "Know that you two have done well, else you would not be here."

Anna quickly scrutinized her past. "But there's been nothing special about my life."

Joule looked at Anna and sighed loudly. "Even you, little one, are special. It does not take a Harvard graduate or a worldly traveler to be worthy of being chosen. It is time that you accept the Way. Don't you agree, Jess?"

Knowing looks passed between the two men.

"Take her home, Jess."

Jess appeared lost. "How?"

"The same way you arrived. Join hands and close your eyes."

Anna leaned forward.

"I refuse to leave until you reassure us that we will see you again, Captain Joule."

"Know it in your hearts." Joule's devilish smile impressed a perfect memory of himself upon his new friend's minds.

Anna and Jess reached across the space between them and grasped hands. The esoteric experience rocked the foundation of their being. Neither wanted the sensation to end.

The look of passion that passed between them touched Joule's soul. The thought of sharing such a love sent a quaking shiver through his material form, causing a momentary blank in his conscience. He found the sensation delicious. Joule wondered. *Could that be what it is like—to love so deeply?*

Again, Anna and Jess became as stardust. Their essence entwined, enhancing their ethereal experience. Time sat still.

Another previous life took shape. Together their spirits soared up the steep rocky surface of a blue snowcapped mountain. Perched upon a high outcrop in a nearly inaccessible location was a human-built stonelike structure. Through its threshold, they viewed an old man occupying a chair fashioned of wood and straw. A youth sat at his feet. Jess and Anna watched and listened. The Asian language was comprehensible—a teacher instructing his pupil.

"I'm the pupil," Jess stated through transfer of conscience. "You are the teacher. Don't you get it, Anna? You were once my spiritual instructor. Go deep within and release the pent-up memories of your spiritual awareness. They have always been within you."

Anna opened her mind to the memories. She allowed them to flow unhampered.

With hands yet clasped, Anna and Jess opened their eyes to the familiar surroundings of their writing room. They moved to lie in each other's arms. Neither spoke, allowing the other to absorb and process their newest experience within the realm of the individual private conscience.

13

Love the One You're With

Jess yawned and pounded on Anna's locked bedroom door.

"Anna? You in there?"

"Yes, sweetheart, but you can't see me."

"Why not?"

"*You* know—wedding tradition. This time I'm doing it right."

Jess released an exasperated sigh. "Tonight, Anna. We sleep together *tonight*."

"Tonight, Jess," Anna softly echoed.

"No more waiting, Anna."

"No more waiting, Jess."

After his footsteps faded, she spun around. All of her wedding apparel lay arranged on her bed. Seating herself on the only unoccupied space, she wondered how Jess had slept at all.

With closed eyes, she imagined his firm kiss. Glowing warmth permeated her body. Rocking her head back, she—

A sudden knock interrupted her private dream. Anna jumped.

"*Jess*, I told you *no*. I don't care if it *is* a silly tradition."

"*Mom* . . . it's me and Rachael." Peter sounded impatient. "Can *we* see you?"

"Oh. Yes, of *course,* you can see your mother." Anna opened the door to her children.

Rachael looked up at her mother's face with soft round little-girl eyes. "What's a *tra-di-tion*?"

Anna scooped up her baby girl. Giddy excitement sparkled her voice. She took Rachael's hand in hers and danced around.

"A tradition is a custom that's passed down—like wearing costumes on Halloween." Anna studied Rachael's delicate features. "Understand?"

"Yes, Mommy, I think so. Is it . . . like hangin' our stockings on Christmas Eve?"

"Very good, honey."

Rachael beamed at her mother's praise.

Peter joined in. "How about fireworks on the Fourth of July or carvin' a turkey on Thanksgiving."

Anna laughed at her children's reference to holidays.

"Now, what did you two come to see me about?"

Peter grew solemn. "We want to know if things will be—you know— different when you're married to Jess."

Anna looked at her children with respectful surprise.

"Okay." She briefly hesitated while mentally compiling her answer. "One difference will be that Jess and I will sleep together in the same room—as your father and I did."

"How come?" Rachael asked.

"Well . . . it's what married couples do. It's . . . tradition."

"Oh." Anna's daughter easily accepted her mother's answer.

Peter smiled, but his eyes betrayed a deeper wisdom. Anna winked at her eldest over Rachael's head. He winked back. She wondered how much her son *did* know. *Better plan that talk.*

"Another difference will be that your last name will be Parks, and you'll have to start signing your name that way."

"I've been practicing," Rachael remarked in her little-girl voice.

"Good girl. I need to practice too. Anna Parks," she stated.

"Peter Parks," the oldest copied.

The youngest smiled shyly. "Rachael Parks."

They all broke into giggles.

A firm knock sounded.

Jess called through the door. "Hey. What's the deal? I'm getting lonely out here."

The children giggled harder.

Jess swallowed his laughter.

"Say, kids, come on out here and keep me company, will you? It's a long time till the wedding."

"There's fresh fruit on the table," he intoned.

Rachael and Peter remembered they were hungry and ran to the closed door.

"Wait!" Anna ran into the bathroom. "Okay, you can go now." The door opened and closed. Then silence. Anna came out. A tray of fresh fruit placed on a sitting chair near the door caused her to smile at Jess's thoughtfulness.

Jess hurried to the bottom of the stairs. He turned and looked up. "Ready-ready-lets go!"

Peter descended first. Jess quickly plucked him off of the banister within seconds of Rachael's arrival. "*Whoa*. We need to work on our timing."

"*Rachael*," Peter scolded his sister. "You have to wait longer before you *start*."

Rachael's innocent eyes widened at her accuser.

Jess jumped in to head off the argument.

"*I* know. Next time, we'll count."

"Now, who's hungry?"

The incident was forgotten as the trio raced to the kitchen.

Peter took his seat. "I like eating here better than the dining room. It's more like home."

"Peter, this *is* your home."

"How about we save the dining room for company only."

Both kids nodded their agreement.

"Cherries, anyone? Don't forget to spit out the pits."

Jess placed a Bing cherry into his mouth and seconds later the pit fell onto his china plate making a distinct ping. Rachael and Peter were amused. They each put a cherry into their mouths and spit out the pits onto their plates. Each ping sounded slightly different. They giggled delightedly. Everyone put another cherry into his mouth. Three different pings sounded in a row. They all laughed in unison. A question from Peter sobered them.

"Things aren't gonna to be so different . . . are they, Jess?"

"Well. You can call me Dad—if you like."

"I like." Rachael tried out the new title. "*Dad*." She shyly dipped her head.

"I think I could get used to it," Peter threw in casually. "But I might slip sometimes and call you Jess."

Jess hid his pleased smile behind his spoon.

"And . . . your mom and I will share the same bedroom."

He waited for their reaction.

Rachael spoke unabashedly. "Momma already told us." She wanted an explanation from Jess too. "Why?"

"*Rachael*," Peter scolded. "Mom *told* you why."

Jess soothed the exasperated sibling. "It's okay, Pete." *Wedding jitters.* His future stepson was to be the ring bearer.

The perspective stepfather contemplated his answer. "When you reach a certain age—say, twenties—you want to have a special person of the opposite sex as your partner. Questioning it doesn't help. It's the way life is . . ." he paused, hearing the trill of a bird outdoors, ". . . like birds singing and ants carrying more than their weight in food. We can speculate all we want, but it's much easier to say, it's tradition. Okay, sweetie?"

"Yes." Rachael giggled. "It's *tra-di-tion*. What's spec-a-late?"

"It means guessing, dudn't it Jess?"

It was Jess's turn to be surprised. "Close enough, Pete."*Your IQ never ceases to amaze me. We may have a genius on our hands.* Peter winked. Jess winked back.

"You sure fixed a lot of fruit," the seven-year-noted, rubbing his full tummy.

"I guess I was feeling festive. Besides, I didn't count on your mother,"

Jess rolled his eyes and gestured at the ceiling with his spoon, "staying hidden in her room. Seems a bit silly to me." The three breakfast-table occupants looked at each other and spoke in unison. "*Tradition.*" They all laughed until real tears streamed down their happy faces.

"I must admit it's kind of special having the two of you all to myself," Jess managed.

"Tradition does seem kinda silly sometimes."

"I agree, Pete, but tradition is okay if you know how to have fun with it—like your mom."

Jess glanced from one small face to the other.

Rachael wrinkled her nose. "I don't feel so good."

"Probably wedding jitters—and maybe too much fruit. Have you kids ever been in a wedding?"

They both shook their heads.

Jess beamed at the smaller child. "I'm sure you'll be a bea-uti-ful flower girl, Rachael."

He put on a respectable face for Peter and laid on his best British accent. "Pe-tah, the ring bear-ah, a fine title for a fine lad."

In his normal voice, Jess asked, "Speaking of, shouldn't we prepare your wedding clothes?"

"Mom already has. Can you teach me how to talk like that?"

"Sure, Pete. How about a morning walk in the garden, and we'll work on it. Perhaps we'll see a spider spinning a web, or perhaps your mom left us a weed or two."

"Will there be anything to pick?"

"*No*, Rachael. It'll be another month or more before anything is ready to *pick*."

Jess countered Peter's shortness with his little sister. "Patience, Pete. Patience. Need to work on that."

Peter nodded reluctantly. "*Sorry*."

"Tell your sister."

"*Sorry*, Rachael."

✳ ✳ ✳

Standing in the hall, dressed in an off-white tux with matching hat sitting atop his well-groomed head, Jess called to Anna through the closed door.

"And how are you going to get to the wedding, may I ask?"

Jess had informed Anna that he wasn't wearing any hat during the ceremony. She had reluctantly agreed.

"Francine's taking me. I spoke with her on the phone a few minutes ago."

"Francine . . . yoga class-mate . . . your matron of honor . . ."

"Sweetheart . . . I didn't tell you beforehand because I was afraid you'd say how silly it was."

Jess mentally agreed.

"Anna, dear, it's *okay*. Like I said, it's your wedding too. Have it how you want it. I want you to enjoy it."

"Listen. The kids and I are ready to leave. So you're sure you have a ride?"

"*Yes.* I assure you that I'm not gonna miss my own wedding."

"I don't want to be left standing at the altar because your ride didn't show."

It worked. He was rewarded with the pleasant sound of her laughter. Jess slapped the door. "So, we're off. See you soon."

"See you soon, my darling." Anna's soft reply barely broke the thick, wooden barrier.

Jess spun around and was surprised to find Peter and Rachael standing quietly next to each other . . . patiently waiting.

Rachael wore a cobalt-blue dress heavily trimmed in off-white lace. Peter wore a light-blue suit with an off-white shirt. Their mouths fell open at the sight of their handsome stepfather-to-be.

Jess stared with fatherly pride. Though he'd helped them dress, he again complimented them. "You two look *marvelous*."

Rachael and Peter spoke at once. "So do you." Their unison remark caused them to giggle nervously at each other.

The word "marvelous" invoked a memory of Joule. Jess momentarily closed his eyes and vividly pictured his friend's vibrant red-toned features. *Wish you could be here for our wedding, Joule. I suppose you are—in our hearts. You too, Al. I can hardly wait to see you both.*

Jess thought it odd that he'd known Al for years, yet he felt as close to the alien he'd recently met.

He opened his eyes and looked at his two charges.

"Ready-ready-let's go!"

Anna heard the front door close. "Francine, dear, I'm counting on you. *Please* be prompt."

The excited bride-to-be rushed to the mirror to check her makeup. She looked at her gown—a light-beige silk and lace affair with a short train. Pearl beads dazzled the wedding gown further. Perfect. Her matching rimless hat with a short veil sat atop her raven-colored hair. Perfect. For the first time in her life, Anna truly felt beautiful.

Through her persistence, Jess hadn't yet seen what she'd chosen to wear. She desired that his first vision of his bride be totally new.

With Al gone and no living relatives on either side, she'd settled on Francine's father to give her away. Anna had taken a liking to the Southern gentleman. Upon hearing the request, he'd accepted delightedly. "Having only one daughter, I never dreamed that I would get another opportunity to give a bride away," he'd said.

Anna heard the car pulling into the drive below her window. *Francine. She's here.*

She grabbed her shoes and ran down the stairs, stopping at the front door long enough to slip them on. Wobbling her way to the waiting car, she was reminded of how much she hated stilettos.

Her chauffeur friend responded with laughter. "I can see those shoes aren't your normal style."

❋ ❋ ❋

Rachael dutifully tossed flower petals, decorating the bride's path. She threatened to seize the moment with her innocent beauty. Peter followed.

Stealing glances at the seated guests, the children occasionally meandered from their straight path. Together, the brother and sister mounted the steps and walked the short distance to the podium where they pivoted and faced their audience, signaling their mother.

Anna wasn't disappointed. Her future husband's eyes remained fixed on his bride as she floated down the aisle toward him. The wedding march she did not hear; the onlookers she did not see. Her mind focused on Jess's handsome features, her body reacting to his inevitable touch. How she longed for it.

Francine's father was handing Anna over to Jess. Her lips broke into a radiant smile for him.

The preacher announced that the bride and groom would exchange personal vows.

Anna began, a calm state enveloping her. Her young voice flowed easily.

"You came to me in dreams. My veil lifted, and I instantly recognized your soul. I knew then that I loved you. I now understand the love we share is ageless. No matter how many times we part, my soul will always seek yours, for only in your presence am I complete. I, Anna, take you, Jess, as always . . . forever."

The groom's eyes grew misty. *Don't crack on me now, voice.* Staring into his bride's angelic face, he began his vows.

"I'm so blessed by your companionship. The love I feel for you is totally unexplainable in the human sense. But what is love that it can be explained? God is love, and He loves us through each other. Anna, you are the desire of my flesh, the light in my mind, and the fortune of my soul. Together, we are complete; together, we are one. I, Jess, take you, Anna, as always . . . forever."

Peter recognized his cue and stepped forward bearing the rings on a small pillow that matched Rachael's dress.

The Reverend remained silent while the rings were fitted. He unconsciously cleared his throat and began sharing his thoughts on matrimony. The wedding couple absorbed every word, including the final sentence that would link the two true mates in their current lives, *I now pronounce you man and wife.* The Reverend looked at each face in turn. "Mr. Parks, you may now kiss your bride."

Jess tenderly pulled Anna to him. He lifted her short veil, staring into her azure-blue eyes. Earlier, the two had agreed that the lifting of her veil would symbolize the lifting of their veil of protection. Together they proceeded to present the approving guests with a lengthy wedding kiss.

With the ending of the kiss, Jess displayed the excitement of a man completing his quest. Anna responded. Together they faced their audience.

"Ladies and gentlemen, I present, Mister and Missus Jesse Reed and Anna May Parks."

The couple walked down the aisle amidst enthusiastic cheers. In the foyer, they joined the traditional reception line where the guests singly greeted and congratulated them.

Anna occasioned a glance at her groom. Proper etiquette enhanced her new husband's handsomeness.

A break in the line gave them the opportunity to converse.

"Still nervous?"

Jess shrugged. "Not at all. I'm *utterly blissful.* You?"

The new bride smiled radiantly. "Thanks to you, I'm fine."

The lengthy line of guests finally ended. Jess whispered in Anna's ear. "Stay put. I'll be right back."

Mildly surprised, Anna watched him go. She turned and spoke with her matron of honor while awaiting his return.

He soon appeared, smiling. Anna felt tears of happiness sting her eyes. *Look at him. He sees nothing and no one but me. Father within me, I can't believe this moment is happening.*

Jess spoke handsomely. "Come with me . . . Madame."

He's calling me Madame instead of Ma'am.

"Francine. Will you please hold the fort?"

"But the wedding pictures—" Francine called out to Jess as he hurriedly whisked Anna away.

"Give me five minutes with my bride," Jess replied from a distance, "ten at the most. Then we're all yours."

Francine threw up her hands. "Well . . . it's *your* wedding," she declared, but the departing couple was out of hearing range.

Jess led Anna by the hand through the reception room to a side door, passing a young man of teenage years. Anna saw Jess slip him a bill. "Remember, nobody comes through this door," he demanded in exchange.

The door led to a private alcove neatly partitioned off. A rather large willow, a key specimen of the well-kempt garden, spread its weeping boughs to form a lacy green canopy. Flowering-American- Rose bushes lent their perfume to the fresh air, their blossoms adding brilliant bits of peach and yellow to the occasion. A waist-high brick wall enclosed the alcove from the rest of the world.

Laid out neatly on top of the wall, Anna saw Jess's white silk handkerchief. Jess surprised Anna by grabbing her and pulling her snugly against him. She immediately felt his physical need.

"Anna, my dear wife, either we satisfy my desire for you now, or I fear that it may become known to all our wedding guests for the rest of the afternoon. I've waited for this moment, and I want it to be memorable." He smiled at her keenly. "So drop 'em."

"*What?*" Anna's heart began to race.

"I'm serious. Your underwear, please. Hand 'em over—*now*."

Jess failed to await her consent. He squatted on his heels and reached under her gown to grab hold of her personal undergarment, which he gently lowered.

"Step."

Anna obeyed. After the initial shock, she suddenly felt the thrill of the moment.

Jess handed her the small piece of sewn white silk and lace. Anna gripped it tightly in her sweaty palm.

Her new husband picked her up and gently seated her atop the wall upon his silk kerchief. The back of her gown cascaded down the other side. He pushed the front of her gown up and spread her legs. Jess unzipped his pants, exploding from their confinement. He wedged himself between her legs, easily finding his mark. Anna accommodated him willingly, shivering and swooning in his arms. Jess gently bent her back to kiss her waiting mouth.

Their pent-up desire was quickly quenched. Jess again kissed Anna passionately, experiencing a renewed fire. Anna broke the kiss.

"I know. Our time's up," he whispered, cupping her small face in his large hands. He delicately kissed her once more. With a mischievous grin, he pulled himself away and attended his clothing.

Anna was gracefully lifted off her perch, still clutching her silk and lace undergarment.

"You don't need those—but I do."

Jess folded the material to hide the lace and tucked it into his jacket pocket, replacing his missing handkerchief. They both laughed at his boldness. "No one will be the wiser."

The waist-high wall triggered the memory of their first meeting, a moment he would cherish forever. Happiness made his heart sing.

Jess wiggled his brows. Borrowing Groucho Marx' voice, he said, "Let's go have our pictures made, shall we, doll? Now, we *really* have something to smile about."

Anna giggled. Holding her at arm's length, Jess delicately spun her around, locking his arm in hers. "Mrs. Parks, you're officially mine." Together, the blissfully wedded couple returned to their guests with a newly created memory.

Peter watched in awe as the photographer posed the wedding members into various groups and positions. "That looks fun. Maybe I'll be a photographer."

Rachael overheard. "Maybe I'll be a photo-grapher too." Peter shook his head and rolled his eyes.

Anna and Jess posed for a bride and groom portrait, capturing a pleasant moment in time.

"I will treasure these forever." Anna glowed with happiness.

Jess exhaled contentedly, "More eternal memories, my wife. No matter what happens, I promise I'll never forget this event."

He encircled her tiny waist with one strong arm and squeezed so hard she gasped for air.

"Whacha mean, no matter what happens? I'll *tell* you what happens. We all live happily ever after."

Anna's happiness radiated outwardly. Jess drew her close for another tender kiss. Candid shots preferred, the ecstatic photographer took advantage of the special moment.

The wedding party eventually moved to the reception room with the photographer in pursuit. Their album would hold many photos. Anna could hardly wait.

She whispered into Jess's ear.

"It's *silly*," he replied, to her request.

At her persistence, he agreed to throw her garter. With Anna seated, Jess carefully reached under her dress to remove the 'something blue' and experienced her inevitable shiver. After the garter was thrown, Anna turned her back and tossed her bouquet into the gathered crowd of female guests.

The remainder of the wedding fast-forwarded through time. Jess's keen eyes searched the room for the kids. "I think we can leave soon."

He spotted Peter stepping outside with some friends. Rachael sat alone on a chair, worn down from the day's activities. Her head drooped slightly.

Showing concern, Jess commented, "I don't like how our daughter looks."

Anna followed his steady gaze. Together they approached Rachael.

The bride bent down taking her little girl's face into her own small hands.

"She's feverish." Anna looked up. "We better take her home."

"Okay. Stay put. I'll go round up Pete."

Anna sat next to Rachael. "Mommy, I don't *feel* so good."

"I know, honey. Why didn't you tell Mama?"

"I didn't want to spoil the weddin'. Peter told me not to do *anything* to spoil the weddin'. Can we still go to Disney World, Mama? *Can* we?"

"Of course, darling, but maybe not right away. Now please don't worry your sweet little head about it."

"But Pete's gonna be *so mad*."

"No, he won't, honey. It'll be all right."

Anna picked up her child in her arms. Rachael's fear might not be unfounded. Recently, Peter became more easily incensed.

Jess returned with their son. He took Rachael from her mother.

"Ready to take a ride in the wedding car? Wait till you *see* it. It's a decorated *mess*."

He smiled down at Rachael. The sick child weakly returned it.

Peter quickly interpreted the scene. "What's goin' on? Rachael isn't sick, is she? Are we leaving now?"

Jess spoke casually. "Very intuitive, Pete. Rachael has a fever. We need to take her home to bed."

"I *knew* it was too good to be true. Guess that means we aren't goin' to Disney World."

"Of course it doesn't," his mother soothed. "But can we discuss it later, son?"

Peter perked up. He left to tell his friends goodbye.

News of Rachael's sudden illness spread through the guests like a wildfire. Everyone followed the wedding party outside. Chatter subsided. There was hesitation in tossing the traditional birdseed.

Jess sensed the stalemate and turned to address his friends. "Go ahead and throw it. Rachael's going to be fine. She's come down with a touch of a virus. We'll take her home to rest before our trip."

The guests suddenly relaxed. Laughing, cheerful voices returned.

The departing wedding party received a hardy shower.

Francine shouted over the noise of the crowd. "Want me to call your family doctor?"

"Thanks, Francine, but I think we'll try Jess's home remedy."

Francine drew closer. "What about your flight reservations?"

Jess looked down at the warm bundle in his arms. "I'll have them moved forward. I'm sure Rachael will soon be herself."

"Okay, folks, thanks for your presence at a most wonderful time in our lives. We will remember and cherish it always." Jess raised his hand and gave the wedding crowd one of his winning smiles. His short speech was followed with cheers and well wishes.

The immediate wedding party piled into the overly-decorated family vehicle. Jess honked and drove forward as the crowd followed them on foot down the length of the drive while hands waved farewell.

The driver strained to see through the white graffiti covering the windows. Traditional tin cans tied to the rear bumper had been replaced with equally noisy, empty plastic containers.

Anna studied Rachael in her car seat and commented in general, "Friendly folks, huh?"

After driving a few blocks, Jess pulled over. "Let's lose these plastic bottles, Pete."The strings were cut, and the exaggerated decor was tossed into the back.

Hesitating in the driver's seat, a smile played on the driver's lips, perhaps from a pleasant new memory.

As Jess guided the car back into traffic, he peered into the rearview mirror at his new bride sitting next to their daughter. He then smiled at his shotgun rider.

Peter returned his smile. "You and Mom were supposed to leave the wedding by yourselves. Francine was gonna to take Rachael and me back to the house."

"Things didn't quite turn out exactly like we planned, Peter. Sometimes unexpected responsibilities arise."

After a short period of silence, he continued. "We often find our plans changed. *Our* will is not what we should assume. It is the will of the One that we need to follow and respect."

Jess attempted to read Peter's expression. He didn't want to overdo, but Peter appeared to be listening attentively.

"Remember your spiritual studies. It'll all work out. Besides, a situation like this can draw our family closer together—if we let it."

Anna looked up from Rachael's angelic face showing approval at Jess's wise words.

"*I* know," Peter admitted. "But sometimes it's hard to remember *not* to stress."

"I've been there too, son. Patience is something we learn with time. It saves a lot of unnecessary disappointment." Jess reached over and squeezed Peter's shoulder. "We'll take it one day at a time. Okay, Pete?"

"One day at a time," the boy repeated. "I'm sure we'll enjoy today even if Disney World *does* have to wait till tomorrow."

I can't believe this kid is only seven. "You know it, Pete."

Anna broke her silence. "I'm *so* proud of you, Peter. Look how well you've learned to deal with the unexpected." Anna felt endearing tears sting her eyelids.

"Now, don't go gettin' soggy on us, Mom. It isn't really *that* big a deal. I mean, we *are* still going. Right?"

"Right," Jess and Anna confirmed in unison.

"Now, let's get your little sister home and concentrate on getting her well."

Anna spoke to Jess from the rocking chair next to the sleeping Rachael's bed. "It's ten o'clock. Fever break?"

Jess shook his head.

She carried an exercise mat and placed it on the floor. "I'm going to do some yoga."

"I see. It's late."

"I know, but I'm not sleepy yet."

"Me either. Can I watch?"

Anna hesitated. "You *know* how shy I am."

"Yes, and I'm honored that you're going to allow me to watch."

Anna flashed a smile. "I'm not perfect—but I'm working on it."

He chuckled at his sensitive wife while admiring her physique. His next words bore a double meaning. "Yes, you *are* working on it. And so am I, my dear. So am I."

Jess rose from the rocking chair stretching and yawning, while Anna checked their daughter's progress.

She whispered excitedly. "I think she's beginning to sweat."

"Wonderful. That's what we want," he said, returning to his seat.

Anna approached her mat and began warming up. Jess quietly watched. Neither spoke. She concentrated on balance, stretching her accommodating muscles. The hour passed quickly. For her final pose, Anna sat in full Lotus with eyes closed and hands pressed together in prayer form.

Jess broke the silence with his husky male whisper. "What are you doing now?"

"Transcending."

"Trans-*what-ing*?"

"Trans-*what-ing*, he says." Anna smiled deeply. "Why, I'm transcending my desire for you."

"Ahh." A smile played on Jess's lips.

"Dear husband, don't you know you shouldn't interrupt someone who's meditating?"

"Ahh, yes, so sorry." Jess rose and feigned another body stretch. He silently walked to Anna's mat and sat behind her folding his legs in the same lotus position.

With closed eyes, Anna sensed his movements.

Jess reached forward and lifted his wife's taunt body setting her on his lap with her back against his chest. She giggled, attempting to maintain her pose. A few moments passed.

"It isn't working for me. Is it working for you?"

"*No, it's not working for me.* What do you expect when you touch me like that?"

Anna giggled again as Jess broke his pose and enfolded her with his long limbs. She moved to face him.

"My touch drives you wild, huh?"

"You know it does."

"And yours does me." His husky tone arose from the strong throes of passion. He caressed Anna in more sensitive places.

"We're not in our own room, husband."

"I can fix that. Sit here while I check on Rach."

The small child's forehead felt cool and clammy to his touch. Jess whispered. "Fever's broke. She's sleeping well, Anna. We can check on her again soon."

He approached Anna and scooped her up. "But now . . . I wish to devour my bride on our wedding night."

Jess kissed Anna's waiting mouth.

They first peeked in on Peter. His even breathing fell on welcomed ears.

Carrying Anna to their bed, Jess proceeded to do his best to make their two bodies into one.

Jess brushed away a glistening tear on Anna's temple. Another took its place.

"For years, I've loved you. My tears of joy may fall for a while. I wish we could leave this earth right now, roam the constellations in the night sky, and stay—forever."

Jess smiled at Anna's imaginings. "Be careful what you wish for, my darling wife." He hushed her with another tender kiss.

14

Seeking

The doorbell rang. "I'll get it! I'll get it!" Rachael cried. "It's Francine. I *know* it's her." With a lot of effort, Rachael pulled the large front door open. "*Francine*. I *knew* it was you." The excited little girl pulled Francine in by her arm.

Francine addressed her greeter, barely containing her laughter. "*Slow down*, honey child. You're loud enough to wake the *dead*." Rachael giggled up at Francine's friendly face.

"*My, my*, you're such a happy-go-lucky bunch," she exclaimed, as Anna and Jess approached. "You must let me in on your secret."

Jess laughed. "All in good time, Francine."

Anna took Rachael's hand. "Want to come along to the kitchen? We're working on supper."

Their guest looked up at Jess. "Mmm, mmm. Nothin' like a man in the kitchen, I always say."

The lady of the house led the human train, the youngest in tow.

Francine commented to no one in particular. "Did you hear that, now? Anna called it *supper*. That's Southern talk. Folks 'round here call it *dinner*."

When they reached their destination, Anna and Jess resumed their cooking duties.

"Can I give you a hand?" Francine offered in her pleasant Alabama accent.

"*Absolutely not*. You're our guest. Please have a seat at the bar and keep us company."

Anna smiled to soften her unyielding tone.

Francine sat. "What's that you're fixin'? I know you folks eat in a certain . . . uh . . . manner. What is it, now . . . all natur'al?"

Jess responded. "Oh, just a basic natural-hygiene diet. The rules are simple. Don't mix proteins. Don't mix starches with proteins. Mix starches with other starches—though it's really better to refrain from it. And eat fresh fruit by itself. Never cook it.

"This way of eating keeps the digestive tract in good shape. There are books available on natural-hygiene diets. But the key is maintaining a balanced pH level—around 7.0 or greater is optimal, meaning your alkaline level is greater than your acidic level, which keeps the body from succumbing to illness. Even Rachael stays well these days."

"You know, Francine, a good diet aids a person's physical and mental health. It keeps you well inside *and* out."

The dancing spoon in Anna's hand emphasized her words. "Another essential for well-being that requires discipline, Francine dear, is routine exercise—consistent and persistent exercise. The body needs and wants to be in shape."

"Well, at least I have a handle on that one with my yoga class, but I sure could use some work on my diet, I know. And what about the other—the attitude and all?"

Distracted by the aroma that hung in the air, their guest said, "Mmm, I smell corn bread bakin'."

Jess stood poised in front of the oven, both hands covered with mitts. "You have a good nose, Francine."

"I'm a black woman from the Deep South, Jess. I grew up on that dish." Francine sniffed the air. "And is that black-eyed peas?"

"Crowder peas," Anna corrected.

"Mmm, mmm, crowder peas. My all-time favorite, they are."

"I grew up on these dishes too," the hostess offered.

"That's right, Anna. You're from Arkansas. Just a hop, skip, and a jump over Mississippi to my home state of Alabama. Did you grow up on these dishes, Jess?"

"I've had corn bread, but Anna introduced me to the crowder peas she grows in her garden."

"That's right. You have a garden. I want to see it. Imagine fresh crowder peas *straight* from the garden. *How lucky*. I would *love* to have a garden."

"We'll take a walk after supper."

"There's that *supper* word again," Francine intoned. "Yes, siree, I sure do miss that."

"Well, supper's ready. Jess, if you don't mind to go and call the kids—they've wandered off—Francine and I will carry it into the dining room."

Jess tipped a pretend hat. "Why, I'd be happy to, Madame."

He left the kitchen, whistling.

The two women prepared to carry the steaming hot dishes. "Having an actor for a husband must be some kind of fun."

"I don't think of it that way. Jess is the just man I love."

"You're a lucky lady—so much happiness surrounding you. I can see it in the man's eyes."

On their second trip, Francine hesitated. "Anna, dear, we haven't covered the attitude part. Now, does that include the still-small-voice-within you and Jess refer to?"

"Well, Francine, spiritualism teaches that all individuals are born with the still-small-voice and have it throughout their lifetime. Jess calls it our personal contact with God, separate from the anatomy of the mind. Like thought, no one can explain it. The still-small-voice stems from the subconscious to the conscious. It guides us to conduct our thoughts and activities in such a manner that best benefit us and those around us. It also guides us—if we allow it—in using our individual unique talents to make our way in life."

"Yes. I think I understand." Francine placed her loaded dish on the table. "But isn't that *plain old instinct?*"

"Instinct tends to leave out morals. When my family is hungry, I don't go out and steal food. I go to the store and buy food; I bring it home and cook it."

"I see your point."

"The thing is that the majority of people are unaware of the personal power and success they can achieve by following the still-small-voice within."

"Jess and I are writing our book for this reason. We want to shout to the world that people can have peace, prosperity and happiness by heeding the advice given. We call it the Way."

"The Way," Francine repeated. "Simple."

"Exactly."

The buffet next to the table yielded flatware placed at each setting by the hostess.

"We *are* what we think we are, Francine. We can change our status through our thoughts by creating obtainable goals. But we habitually convince ourselves that we're sick—or unlucky. People don't do it on purpose, but it's a hard habit to break." The women walked back to the kitchen. Anna continued their philosophical discussion.

"We've all heard success stories. It takes confidence and desire to achieve goals. We can't think ourselves wealthy. We need a driving force. Controlling how we think results in controlling how we direct ourselves.

"When Jess and I first met, we had an instant bond. In my mind, there was no way for us to ever be together. I was married, so I had no faith. But *he* did. Now, I realize I was wrong. It took my husband's unexpected passing to bring us together—an event I had no control over. I certainly didn't wish Joel dead. Call it fate; call it destiny. *That* we cannot control in life. But we *can* control how we deal with it."

"You all appear to be coping quite well."

"Rachael's young enough to accept the events going on around her, but Jess has had to concentrate on Peter. He constantly provides him with optimistic perspectives. For example, when the Disney honeymoon trip was postponed due to Rachael's illness, Peter was able to accept that it wasn't Rachael's fault, that life wouldn't be miserable until our trip occurred—unless he made it so. By learning to control his thoughts,

Peter puts less stress upon himself. Jess also helped Peter to accept the two of us uniting."

Anna eyed her friend, contemplating her next words. Joule's face suddenly interrupted her thoughts. *Humans cannot leave this planet until they change their behavior patterns*, he'd implied.

"Bear with me, Francine. I know this may sound strange, but . . . what if God intended for the universe to be our playground? It's hard to accept that He would create the entire universe and not intend to use it.

"Imagine enlightenment in terms of a point system. What if the more positive points we accumulate in life, the more access we're given to the universe? That by itself would be an incentive to gain all the points we can. Loving thoughts, acts of love, compassion, mercy and forgiveness gain points. Greed, resentment, crime, and abuse subtract points. Living positively could buy us access to other worlds, other opportunities, while negativity keeps us isolated. After all, what sane alien would want to get involved with a planet of beings that disrespect one another?"

Her abrupt pause created a silence, allowing Anna to hear her family's voices in the background. After listening intently, she grew satisfied that the conversations were harmonious.

Francine quietly attempted to digest Anna's chatter.

"I'm sorry." Anna batted her long black lashes at her friend. "Where was I? . . . "

Francine laughed. "I believe that you were talkin' about the universe as our playground. Well, child, you certainly send chills through *my* spine talkin' like that. It's never crossed my mind to meet an alien, let alone travel the galaxies." She stared intently at her friend across the plates of warm food. "You're talkin' over my head, girl. But I know your book will be a huge success. My still-small-voice tells me so. You and Jess have worked hard."

A loud request for their presence was directed from the bottom of the staircase. "Come with me, Francine. I'd like you to see this."

"Ready-ready!-let's go!" Jess coached.

Francine giggled at Rachael and Peter taking turns sliding down the banister. "I've seen it on TV, but not in real life."

"Supper's ready," Anna called, herding the group toward the dining room.

Expecting an important call, Jess grabbed the nearest cordless phone and carried it to the table.

"My, my, this food is *delicious*, but my still-small-voice is warning me to put down my fork."

The table occupants chuckled at their guest's remark.

"Now, how about that promised stroll through your garden."

The cordless phone by Jess's plate rang surprisingly loudly. All eyes fell on him. Nervously clearing his throat, he spoke calmly into the handset. "Jess Parks, speaking. Yes, Mr. Moyer, I've been expecting your call."

Jess looked directly at Anna while listening through the receiver. His face remained expressionless. The lengthy silence created suspense in his dinner table audience.

"Yes, sir. The two main characters are required to complete their given task. While doing so, they experience trials and tribulations that aid them in understanding the purpose of their quest while learning about themselves and each other."

Silence reigned as Jess listened.

"I see . . . you need more plot. Okay. Please don't toss it out yet." Jess gave Anna a determined look. "There's something we left out." He ignored her reaction. "It could make all the difference. Tell you what, sir. We'll work on it and get you an edited copy ASAP. So, in all other respects, you do like the book?"

Jess's relieved expression eased the tension around the table.

"Yes, sir. Thank you, E. J. Goodbye."

Jess placed the phone on the table. He raised his hand to silence his wife before she could speak.

"Look. It doesn't really matter. We're passing the book off as fiction. Face it. We need Joule himself, not just what we witnessed while in his presence."

Francine's curiosity peeked. "What *are* you two talkin' about? Who's Joule?"

Anna and Jess both glanced at their invited guest, ignoring her question and continuing their two-sided conversation.

"If you want, we'll attempt to contact him tonight. But he's already given us permission."

Anna remained silent.

"Didn't he say he was providing us with material for the book? Give me a break, Anna. I'm dying here."

A smile spread across Anna's face. "Forgive me, Jess. I know you're right. I'm just feeling a bit overwhelmed."

Jess breathed easier. "You scared me. We must agree on this."

Anna answered abruptly. "No."

"No, what?" He thought she'd disagree after all.

"No, we don't need to speak with Joule. I know you're right. Everything will be fine." Anna's smile confirmed her confidence.

Jess smiled back. The dinner napkin in his hand fell to the table. "Well then," he said, studying each face, ending with their guest, "how about that walk in the garden?"

Francine asked one final question. "Is Joule a character in your book . . . or is he a real person?"

"Both," her hosts chorused.

A stroll through Anna's garden allowed the warm evening sun to erase all remaining tension.

Their contented guest walked slowly through the neatly tilled rows, sometimes bending down to pull an invading blade of grass. Rachael trailed her.

"Such a pleasant evening," she commented in general. A smile played on her lips, and she instinctively reached over to give Anna's arm a gentle squeeze. "It'll all work out. I *know* it."

Anna returned the smile. "Me too." A curious shiver traversed her small form.

Francine admired the variety of flowers decorating the garden.

"Looky at the time. We've done messed around and let the food get hard on the plates. We'd best get at those dirty dishes."

Turning down a second offer for help wasn't an option for Anna. To repeatedly deny opportunities of service would be an injustice.

The two women moved toward the house. The others followed.

Anna looked down at Francine from the upstairs landing.

"You're sure this is what you want?"

"*Absolutely*. There's no reason for me to hurry home to a dark house since my husband's out of town. Besides, I *love* playing children's games, and I don't ever get the chance. Now, you two run along and get some work done. Peter and Rachael and I will have us a *grand* time."

Rachael innocently mocked Francine. "Yes, Mommy, we'll have a *grand* time. Now, run along—get busy," she scolded.

They entered their writing room smiling. Jess dropped onto the couch. "Where do we start?"

Anna sat next to him. "Okay . . . let's begin by writing a chapter about our experience with Joule. Then, we can determine if any other changes are necessary."

"Sounds good."

Jess reached for his wife, and gently pulled her to him. He kissed her soundly.

She unwillingly broke the kiss. "Don't forget why we're here. We've got work to do."

He released her and directed his attention back to the book. He thumbed through a copy of their rough draft. "What if we title the new chapter "The Advocate" . . . because . . . isn't that what Joule truly is? I mean, he's attempting to gain the human race access to other worlds, correct? So, he'll have to plead our case to those I believe he referred to as the 'Higher Ups'."

Anna rose and walked about the room to aid her concentration, "So, how should we describe him?"

Jess propped his legs on the couch where she'd been sitting. "How's this? A brawny, red-skinned man with a set of small horns above his forehead and a lengthy arrow-tipped tail— He stopped and sighed loudly. "I'm describing the Devil of myth."

"The very reason we purposefully left him out. But it's only a physical description, Jess. It isn't who Joule truly is. We have to count on people accepting him."

Jess nodded and continued. "Don't forget his deep, husky laugh."

"The man was practically *naked*," Anna added.

Recalling their experience, Jess impersonated their alien friend. "My friends call me Joule," he quoted, "after James Prescott Joule, the co-founder of the Law of Conservation of Energy. How hot is that?"

They chuckled at Jess's pun.

Anna shook her finger, also mimicking Joule's baritone voice, "I believe a handshake is customary."

"Oh, *you're good*," Jess praised. "And I let him shake my *hand*."

"And *you* said," Anna giggled uncontrollably, "'*sorry*—a bit too hot for me'."

Jess sobered. "I bet he did that on purpose."

"Now that I think about it, the whole thing *was* pretty funny. It was silly to fear him, considering he was *our* lucid dream."

"Yeah, fearing him was silly."

""Right on the money." Where do you think he got that phrase?"

"He tunes into FM radio, remember?" Jess reminded, with an ear-to-ear grin.

"And you *had* to ask him what purpose his horns served."

"And he was about to tell me—"

Jess resumed his laughter."—until I cut him off. I thought you'd be offended."

"I would have been . . ." Anna added, ". . . at the time."

She looked thoughtfully at Jess. "I can't help but wonder if Joule truly exists, or if he's just a figment of our combined imaginations."

Jess shrugged. "I choose to believe he's real."

The twosome thoughtfully returned to their task at hand.

"Any verdict on using the 'Row-Your-Boat' song?"

"We can," Anna informed, "because it was written long before the music copyright became law. The current version is dated around 1881, according to the internet."

"We have the whole weekend to work on this. Let's set a goal to finish the new chapter by tomorrow afternoon. Then we can take a break . . . maybe take the kids to the club for a swim and dinner. Later, you and I can come back here and finish editing. Monday morning, we'll take the revised manuscript over to Moyer."

"E. J.," they both said in unison.

"Sounds like our work's cut out for us." In his best Groucho Marx, Jess said, "Let's get crackin', Sweetheart."

The new script was handed to Moyer.

"Shall I return later, or would you prefer I wait for your call?"

"Nonsense, I'll read it now. How long can it take to read one chapter . . . that is, if you don't mind?"

Mildly surprised at the offer, Jess shook his head.

Settling into his seat, he considered Anna, waiting in the reception area. *Will she ever stop being shy, or is she just one of those people who doesn't mind being alone? That's it. After this book gets published, Anna may lose what little privacy she has. My fault. I chose my profession. Success means taking everything that comes along with it. I wish it didn't have to be.*

To pass the time, Jess concentrated on breathing deeply and clearing his restless mind while Moyer read.

"Mr. Parks? Jess?"

"Yes, sir?" Jess straightened in his chair.

"Taking a nap? You've been working late hours, haven't you?"

"Uh, Anna and I have, sir. Hard work and success go hand in hand as I'm sure you well know."

Moyer nodded.

"Anna's your new wife? Where is she?"

"She's sitting out there, sir." Jess pointed past the office door. "She's . . . a bit shy by nature, Mr. Moyer."

"I thought we'd dispensed with the *mister* and *sir* crap. We must set up a private dinner date some time soon so that I can meet her at her ease."

"So, what do you think?" Jess asked, directing Moyer's attention back to the present.

Moyer looked down at the manuscript in his hands. "I think I'd like to know why you left this addition out to begin with. A little science fiction certainly broadens the plot. You've given this 'Joule' character a lot of life. I can picture him clearly in my mind—very descriptive writing."

"Thanks, E. J. *We* like him. Because of his physical description, we weren't sure the public would take to him."

The casting director peered at Jess over his glasses. "Well, I believe I would, if he truly existed."

Jess smiled knowingly.

"Yes, this new material appears to be the *missing key*. Most story lines for visiting aliens make them the aggressors. In this one, you've turned the table, making humans out to be the *woe* of the universe," Moyer thoughtfully stated.

"So, are we good now?"

Moyer nodded decisively. "We're good. Will you and your wife agree to discuss minor changes with our editor?"

Jess flashed an appreciative smile. "We'll agree to discuss, yes."

"You realize this script will become a movie . . . which is the real reason I'm getting involved. The book-publishing part is out of my hands, but I can get that ball rolling. Are we in agreement?"

The actor rose from his chair and offered his hand across Moyer's desk. "*Yes sir*, E. J.—*sir.*" Jess's more than ample handshake was cut short.

"Well, then," the distinguished director softly chuckled at his client's enthusiasm, "all that remains is to meet the missus. Schedule a dinner date with my receptionist on your way out, and make sure it accommodates the both of you."

Moyer moved to stand. "Glad to be doing business with you." He excused himself for a luncheon, ending their lengthy session.

Before departing, Moyer hesitated and turned.

"Oh say, I think I'll start listening more often to the *little voice* inside my head. I haven't always done that. Now that it's been explained, it makes good sense."

The white-haired gentleman gave a wink and exited through the office door. He approached his secretary and barked an order before noticing the seated Anna. Dipping his head, he grunted a polite greeting. *What a raven-haired beauty. Tiny though.*

Anna smiled in return as he exited the room.

Following closely behind, Jess entered the reception area to find his wife, failing to contain his excitement. "It's all over except the award speech!" He grabbed Anna and spun her about. "*I* know. You said you'd like to visit Hawaii. Let's go right away. We can be back by Friday."

Seated at her desk, the receptionist attempted to ignore their excited conversation.

"*Hawaii*. But, Jess, it's so *crowded*—isn't it?"

Jess spoke confidently. "No problem. I can assure seclusion."

He pulled Anna close.

"What about the kids?"

"They'll come along, of course. This'll be good for them, too. You *know* it will. "Come on, Annie, please *say yes*," Jess intoned.

"*Please*," the receptionist said, making her presence known, "say *yes* to the man."

Anna laughed. "Okay." She gazed into Jess's brown eyes. "I mean, yes."

Jess swept his wife off her feet. Seconds later, he gently set her down and led her to the receptionist's desk to arrange for their future dinner date with Moyer. The date confirmed, he ushered Anna toward the exit.

"Time to get going—there's lots to do."

"Enjoy Hawaii," the receptionist called across the room. "I wish I was going with you."

"Thanks," Anna returned, "I wish you were too," and meant it. While waiting for Jess, she and the receptionist had spoken at length, and Anna had found her to be endearing. *We could use someone like her to help watch the kids*, she reasoned.

"Mommy? What do thoughts look like?"

Anna sighed deeply, her mind attempting to gear down to a child's level of understanding. She became aware of the droning of the plane's engines.

"Well, Rachael, honey, think of our minds as trees. Our thoughts are like the wind that moves our branches, causing them to bend and sway. We can't see the wind, but we know it's there. And like the wind, we can't see our thoughts, but we know they exist. Each thought we have results in a reaction, like the bending and swaying of the branches. Here's an example. Your new dad and I thought this wonderful trip to Hawaii would make us all happy, which is a reaction." Anna gave it a moment to sink in.

"Does that answer your question, sweetie?"

"I think so, Mommy. Daddy Jess had a happy thought, so we're all going on a trip."

Anna smiled down at her daughter. "If we think happy thoughts," she advised, "we'll do happy things. If we think angry thoughts, we'll do bad things, because nothing good ever comes from anger."

Rachael looked up at her mother. "I *want* to think happy thoughts, Mommy, because *I like* doin' happy things."

Anna patted her baby's head. "So do we all, my darling."

"Mommy? Do we have to die to be with God?"

"No, honey. God is with us always. You know it when you hear that tiny voice inside telling you to do whatever is right. That's God's way of helping us to be safe. For example, knowing to put away your toys so no one falls over them."

"Mommy, when we die, will we be together?"

"Yes, sweetie, we'll be together."

"Will we see Daddy again?"

"Yes, honey. We will."

"Mommy?"

"One more question?"

"One more," Anna's child agreed. "Are you afraid to die?"

"No, honey. Only our bodies die. Our spirits live on in God's universe. We're his children, and He loves us."

Her youngest slipped in one more question. "Mommy? Are you and Daddy and Jess God's children?"

Anna smoothed her daughter's hair. "We're all God's children, every one of us."

Rachael nodded her small, blonde head as though she understood. "I'm not afraid to die neither."

Mr. Moyer rang his temporary receptionist. "It's Merry, isn't it? Would you mind coming into my office, Merry?—and bring a pad and pen, please."

He observed her graceful entrance, like a floating thistle seed propelled by the wind. Moyer desired nothing more than to hear her delightful laughter, previously witnessed.

"I'd like to thank you for taking my receptionist's place on such short notice. It was good of Mr. and Mrs. Parks to invite her along on their vacation to Hawaii."

"And it was good of you to give her leave."

"Nonsense, she deserved it—been putting up with the likes of me for years."

Moyer nervously cleared his throat, wishing he hadn't put himself down in front of the charming young woman whose twinkling eyes held him spellbound.

The sudden urgent ringing of the desk phone interrupted their conversation. The older gentleman held the receiver to his face. "Moyer speaking."

"*Mr. Moyer! Mr. Moyer!*" the hysterical caller cried. "*The afternoon flight to Hawaii . . . the one carrying Mr. Parks and his family . . . it went down, sir . . . in the middle of the ocean . . . sir.*"

Moyer sat staring, unmoving. His brain naturally cued all normal response systems in a body triggered by traumatizing news. His pulse rate increased. Perspiration beads popped out on his forehead and upper lip. A low-level tremor invaded his upper extremities.

The air-conditioned room suddenly felt sultry. Moyer managed to pull out his handkerchief and wipe away sweat with shaking hands. His mouth moved to form words, but nothing came out except rapid, shallow breaths.

The caller was forced to speak again. "Are you there, sir?"

Moyer was vaguely aware of his pounding heart. "Any survivors?" he finally managed in spite of his constricted throat.

"No, sir," the caller sadly answered.

"Well, then," was his shocked reply as he placed the receiver back on its cradle without dismissing himself.

His active brain suddenly focused on Merry who sat quietly waiting. His face registered surprise at her expression, a picture of serene countenance, bringing him back to reality. "Well, then," he repeated, his head still reeling from the disastrous news.

"Mr. Moyer," she began, "allow me to comfort you."

"I don't know that I can be comforted, Merry," Moyer returned. "I'm in shock."

The distressed man overlooked Merry's awareness of his one-sided conversation.

"Yes, sir, I know. But allow me to try."

Moyer found his voice. "How could God let this happen to an entire family?"

"Sir."

Deafening silence.

"E. J."

Slowly recovering from his shocked stupor, he said, "Yes. Please. Call me E. J."

"Of course, E. J."

Merry delivered a smile like the *Mona Lisa*. "All mankind must make the transition from life to death," she began. "No one is exempt. What kinder way than to allow all of them to pass together? In this instance, no one had to endure loss."

E. J.'s stressed mind strained to grasp Merry's words. "I realize you have a point," he nodded.

"We will all pass eventually. It is the way of our existence."

"But the *children*—so *young*. They didn't deserve to have their youth snatched away—so . . . *tragically*."

"Perhaps their purpose in life had been served. Perhaps the four of them were intentionally brought together, and their earthly task had been fulfilled."

Another thought disrupted his over-taxed mind. "*My God*, Merry. My receptionist!"

Again, Merry allowed Moyer time to recover.

"E. J., our spirits enter our bodies at birth, occupy our bodies throughout life, and leave our bodies at death. Our spirits are eternal. They do not pass away, but remain—always. Jess and Anna, the children, and your receptionist still exist. They merely followed the light to another place. Their time here—for now— is over. To leave the earth plane when they did was their destiny. Destiny cannot be denied. It is the Way."

"I understand what you're saying, and I'm somewhat comforted, but it's still such a shock."

"Yes, it is, E. J."

Air audibly rushed into Moyer's visibly expanding lungs. "*The book.* They had yet to sign the contract for its release."

"Are you sure about that E. J.? Take it out and look at it, sir."

Moyer stared blankly at the calm, young woman. He numbly opened the desk drawer containing the contract. His trembling hands flipped through the contents to the last page. Scrawled in fresh ink were the personal signatures of Anna and Jess Parks required to make the document legally binding. With neither having living relatives, there would be no dispute. As an added safety, an addendum had been included stating that upon their untimely death, the book and movie were to be published and produced with their share of the proceeds going to charity.

"By God, it *is* signed. But how?"

"Yesterday, while I was learning the office routine, Jess and Anna came in and signed the contract, witnessed by your receptionist and myself."

Her explanation satisfied the grief-stricken man.

"Well, then, Merry. It must be my destiny to ensure that this script is shared with the world—as intended."

"It appears to be so, Mr. Moyer."

"Perhaps the people on this planet will begin to see through different eyes. I know *I* do."

"As do I, E. J. As do I," Merry respectfully voiced, in memory of Jess and Anna's true love.

15

. . . Life is but a dream.

———◆———

The two essences entwined. Their human thoughts joined as one. For the unworldly pair, time did not exist.

A sudden, static pull interrupted their celestial progress. A familiar voice addressed the linked intelligence individually.

"Anna . . . Jess", the voice beckoned.

The combined ethereal essence hesitated, risking separation by the demanded concentration of their seeker.

"You may not yet wander until the two of you meet with us."

Anna's essence responded. "Who are *us*?"

"Your spirit guides and earthly ties," returned the voice. "Your change in form does not mean we have deserted you."

The voice hesitated at such length that the spirits of Anna and Jess began to believe they were again alone.

"Follow my energy," the voice requested.

Though seemingly impossible, they rode the seeker's consciousness like winged birds on a predestined flight. A ferocious, blinding light contrasting the universal darkness awakened their suspended senses.

A great round table much like that described in the legend of King Arthur appeared before them. Seated at this magnificent piece of worked wood was their seeker, Merry, the spirit guide who had aided them in finding each other. She had reminded them who they truly were by lifting their veil of protection provided to each soul coming into an earthly life. Merry's signature laugh—the purest of bells—echoed through the ether.

By her side was their beloved Joule. The Hadean's presence sparked a dual fondness.

The expected guests, miniaturized by the massive furniture, were collectively enveloped in a wondrous, emotional rush of love. A soothing state of peace and harmony settled upon them as if perfection itself had peaked. At this moment, Anna and Jess understood pure God-love.

"Where are my children?" Anna inquired.

Merry answered. "Rachael and Peter are not the children you raised in your previous existence. They too are old souls who follow their own paths of enlightenment. You will meet with them as they have been called to this table."

She continued her role of spiritual guide. "Transitioning from flesh to spirit reestablishes past memories. Your individual stages of enlightenment will return."

"We are all soul seekers," she continued, "searching for our own, preparing to make the transition. Souls nearing completion of enlightenment are discernable, judging their own degree of enlightenment by observing those around them. No longer distracted by material possessions, they step back, allowing others to be first. Having overcome fear and doubt, they walk into any situation, knowing that the outcome will always be satisfactory."

Merry paused, her eyes focusing on each in turn. "For some, it is not necessary to return to the physical world. We all continue to follow the Way back to the Supreme Being at our own pace, carrying with us all of our gathered knowledge. This is how the Omnipotent experiences, through us—bits of self."

Merry's timeless speech was abruptly interrupted. A specter began to take form.

"Mama," Jess cried weakly. Tears flowed. He knelt beside his birth mother's chair and placed his head upon her lap. She stroked his hair and soothed his aching heart with tender words. He looked up to find his father seated beside her. The twinkle in his earth parents' eyes reflected pride. The ethereal contact, more mental than physical, allowed for human emotions to surface. The newest apparition—Jess—was elated.

Emotionally witnessing Jess's vision, Anna's attention was drawn across the table. Her own parents, as she remembered from childhood, were seated before her. Eyes glistening, they sent their earthly daughter delighted smiles. Gibberish spewed from Anna's mouth before she could pronounce intelligible words. "Mama . . . Daddy. I've missed you so," she managed, threatening human tears.

To ease her distraught child, Anna's mother began sharing a treasured memory.

"Sweetheart, do you recall the pink, plastic purse with the gold-chain handle you carried everywhere?"

Anna remembered.

"When your father was in a particularly dark mood, I purposely served something at the supper table that wound up in your purse simply to improve his disposition."

Anna's Mom winked at her earthly husband. Each broke into gentle laughter. Their daughter laughed with them.

The specters suddenly began to fade. Anna grew disoriented. She had briefly forgotten her surroundings. Her eyes searched for Jess, now seated beside her. He too had witnessed Anna's vision.

The moving experience eased his personal pain. "I feel only love," he conveyed to his true mate.

"And I," she returned.

Jess observed Anna's reaction to a new vision. Peter and Rachael, in adult form—though recognizable—now sat directly across. The four remained silent, content to be. Love was enough.

Visions quickly materialized allowing no time to dwell.

Al replaced Peter and Rachael. With smiling eyes, he said, "We too belong to this group. She's coming—my Rosie."

Again Jess was elated.

More activity drew their attention. Anna's first husband materialized. Though the two men had never met, they intuitively recognized one another. The beauty of the young woman seated next to Joel was as startling as her identity—Moyer's receptionist. Her human appearance opposed Anna's; pale locks, taller in stature, brown eyes—rare in blondes.

Joel spoke. "I have surprised you again, Anna. We," he began, nodding at his true mate, "belong to this group."

Jaycee and Joel's eyes met. "My precious love," she whispered, though her fond gaze was proof enough. Their reunion had been equally profound.

Anna studied Joel's remarkably handsome features. The lovely lady in his company complemented him as a true mate.

"I am pleased to see you so radiantly happy, Joel. It certainly becomes you." Anna gave Jaycee a warm smile of acceptance.

Joule joined the discussion. "Greetings, fellow spirits. I applaud the four of you for enduring such a cruel, harsh earth existence. Hades—and other host planets—offers an easier life. Earth is but a pit of snakes in comparison. On this planet alone, emotions run high, the repercussions being mental and physical endurance. However, I cannot imagine any soul purposely choosing to return."

Joule nodded toward Merry.

Jess cut in. "No need for concern, Joule. Anna and I have no intention of returning."

Joel spoke for Jaycee and himself. "Nor do we."

The Hadean continued his interrupted announcement. "My fellow companions, as you know, Merry and I have yet to experience a life on Earth." Joule took Merry's hand. "Being true mates," he offered, pausing to allow comprehension of his revelation, "we have greatly speculated in order to arrive at our final decision. Our desire to know a love as deep as yours, Anna and Jess, and yours, Jaycee and Joel, has greatly attracted us, because once intense love is experienced, you may take it with you. But we must accept the consequence, to endure the harshness of this hostile planet."

Joule and Merry's transfixed gaze moved the hearts of the individual seekers. "We have chosen to experience intense love," he informed his fellow mates.

Silence ruled. Merry gestured for the group to join hands, resulting in a flood of memories.

Each soul seeker recalled the Way—the true path to the source of all that is, and all that will ever be.

Together, the soul seekers continue their quest to advance to the next realm—one realm closer to God.

444

To those who've experienced—and for those who haven't,
it's a matter of opening your mind.